NO LONGER
SEATTLE PU
BROADVIEW LIBRARY

ROBERTO TO THE DARK TOWER CAME

A NOVEL

ALSO BY TOM EPPERSON

The Kind One

Sailor

ROBERTO TO THE DARK TOWER CAME

A NOVEL

TOM EPPERSON

Meerkat Press
Atlanta

ROBERTO TO THE DARK TOWER CAME. Copyright © 2018 by TOM EPPERSON

All rights reserved. No part of this publication may be used, reproduced, distributed, or transmitted in any form or by any means without prior written permission from the publisher, except in the case of brief quotations embodied in critical reviews and certain other noncommercial uses permitted by copyright law. For information, contact Meerkat Press at *info@meerkatpress.com*.

ISBN-13 978-1-946154-08-8 (Hardcover)
ISBN-13 978-1-946154-10-1 (eBook)

Library of Congress Control Number: 2018939238

This is a work of fiction. Names, characters, businesses, places, events and incidents are either the products of the author's imagination or used in a fictitious manner. Any resemblance to actual persons, living or dead, or actual events is purely coincidental.

Author photo © Carlos Gaviria

Cover and book design by Tricia Reeks

Printed in the United States of America

Published in the United States of America by
Meerkat Press, LLC, Atlanta, Georgia
www.meerkatpress.com

To those journalists around the world who have risked or lost their lives in pursuit of their Holy Grail: the truth.

Acknowledgements

I'd like to thank Carlos Gaviria and Mariela Llorente for sharing their country with my wife and me, and Tomás Silva Arirama for guiding Carlos and me through the jungle.

. . . .noise was everywhere! it tolled
　　　Increasing like a bell. Names in my ears
　　　Of all the lost adventurers my peers,—
How such a one was strong, and such was bold,
And such was fortunate, yet each of old
　　　Lost, lost! one moment knelled the woe of years.

There they stood, ranged along the hillsides, met
　　　To view the last of me, a living frame
　　　For one more picture! in a sheet of flame
I saw them and I knew them all. And yet
Dauntless the slug-horn to my lips I set,
　　　And blew. "Childe Roland to the Dark Tower came."

　　　　　—from "Childe Roland to the Dark Tower Came"
　　　　　by Robert Browning

ROBERTO TO THE DARK TOWER CAME

A NOVEL

Ten days until the day
Roberto is to die

"Roberto?"

"Yes?"

Silence.

"Hello?"

"Is this Roberto?"

"I said it was. Who is this?"

"Roberto. Listen."

He listens. He hears outside the soft sound of rain falling. He glances at the clock by his bed. It is 6:03 a.m. The phone is silent and he's about to hang up but then he hears: "You think you have fooled us? You have fooled no one. Only yourself."

The voice is male. Middle-aged perhaps. Impersonal and calm.

"What are you talking about?"

"We know it was you who wrote about them."

"Wrote about who?"

"The poor Indian children who live with the vultures on the garbage heap. Manuel, the crippled soldier. The juggler on the street corner who had his balls cut off."

These are the last three stories Roberto has done for his paper. Because of previous threats, the news editor suggested that he start to write anonymously. The stories all carried the byline "from the staff of *The Hour.*"

Although he's gone along with it, he has never thought for a second this was a secret that could be kept.

"You continue to prove where your sympathies lie," says the voice. "With the Communists and terrorists. Not with the decent people."

"You really think those children—" *Are terrorists?*, Roberto's about to say, but the voice interrupts sharply.

"We've run out of patience. This isn't a game we're playing. It's time for action. On your part or our part."

Roberto lies very still in his bed holding the phone to his ear.

"*Listen*. You must leave."

He wishes the phone hadn't rung. Wishes he was still sleeping.

"In ten days, Roberto. You must leave the country. Or else you will die."

It goes silent on the other end. He puts the phone down on the table by the bed. He sees it is now 6:04.

A lot can happen in a minute.

The gray light of the beginning day seeps in around the edges of the blinds. He listens to the rain and some traffic noise a block away on Avenue Six and then he hears a rapid *clop clop clop clop clop clop clop*, it's getting louder, *clop clop clop clop clop clop clop*, and many things about this city he loves but this is not one of them: the skinny horses pulling the carts carrying junk or produce or construction materials, a hunched, shabby man holding the reins, the horse always moving along at a brisk trot, rain or shine, day or night, when do they ever get to rest, the poor creatures?

* * *

The city is high in the mountains and is surrounded by mountains except to the south. He can see the church on the top of Mount Cabanacande, then it's hidden by a gray tumble of clouds. He takes a sip of his coffee and looks down at the street. It's a pretty street, lined with eucalyptus and acacia trees. A woman walks by beneath him, holding a red umbrella in one hand and in the other hand her dog's leash. It's a long-haired, elegant dog wearing a raincoat.

His apartment is on the top floor of a four-story building. Though it's small, it's not something he could afford on a journalist's salary since it's in the northern part of the city where the people with money live. His father bought it for him. He has plenty of money. He's the preeminent cardiologist in the country. A few years ago he divorced Roberto's mother and married a much younger woman and Roberto's mother in retaliation moved to Madrid and took up with a much younger man. His name is Pedro and he paints.

Since he got up, he's been doing what he normally does: he's made coffee and sat down at his computer in his electric-blue Nike tracksuit and checked his emails and perused the Internet to see what new catastrophes have befallen the world while he slept. Meanwhile, he's been telling himself that the call is nothing to be concerned about, that he's had similar calls and emails and letters in the past and nothing happened, but finally, restlessly, he has stood up and walked to the window because the problem is this: he does not believe himself.

For they kill journalists in this country. Just last week, Susana Cordoba, a young radio reporter in San Felipe, was kidnapped, raped, and strangled to death. And earlier this year, Edgar Leonidas, who worked for a rival newspaper called *The Spectator*, and whom Roberto played soccer with in high school, was shot to death in a coffee shop. And last year a renowned British photojournalist named Frank Giles was traveling through the anarchic northern province of Tulcán when his car was stopped by armed men who took him away. His body minus head and genitals was found three days later, floating in the dark waters of the Aguarico River. Also last year Ricky Cortés, a fat clownish local TV personality who had an enormously popular weekly satirical show on which he made fun of just about everybody, evidently attracted the attention of someone with no sense of humor and was blown to pieces by a bomb in his car. And if Roberto went back through the years he could find more journalists, dozens of them, men and women, the young and the old, the famous and the obscure, the foolhardy and the fearful, who have all, in a variety of more or less terrible ways, died, and Roberto does not want to be among their number.

He brushes his teeth, he showers, he washes his hair. He steps out of the shower and puts back on the wire frame glasses without which the world is a blur. He blow-dries his hair, it's brown and thick and he combs it straight back, and then he trims his dark, fashionably stubbly beard. He gets dressed: a pink, long-sleeved shirt, designer blue jeans, Italian loafers. And then he puts on a black windbreaker and goes out.

He doesn't wait for the elevator but heads down the stairs. His shoes make a rapid rattling noise as he descends, and a casual observer might think him a happy-go-lucky young man eager to meet the morning, rather than someone deep in the contemplation of exile or death. In the lobby, Beto, the doorman/security guard, springs up from behind his desk and hurries to hold the door open for him. Beto's a skinny kid from the country for whom this job is a big step up. Roberto exchanges good mornings with him, and passes outside onto the street.

He's on his way to a little restaurant around the corner where he's in the habit of having breakfast. It's stopped raining and the sun has come out, and thus he walks into an unexpected radiance: all the way down the street he can see bright drops of rain dripping out of the trees.

* * *

The traffic, as always, is atrocious. Hundreds of thousands of little cars and tiny yellow taxis honk and veer and lurch and spew exhaust, vying for space with big blue city buses, motorcycles, bicycles, and the occasional clopping horse and cart. He drives by two soldiers with automatic weapons, hanging out in front of a tall concrete wall topped with barbed wire. They puff on cigarettes as they laugh about something. He sees soldiers everywhere in this part of the city, protecting apartment buildings and businesses and embassies. He passes the American ambassador's residence, as big as a palace. He listens to the news on the radio. The head of the Association of Families of the Detained and Disappeared has disappeared. Rats are being trained to detect land mines. And then he hears the latest vapid pronouncement from President Dávila: "We are committed to transparency. We will do whatever it takes to ensure that honesty shines throughout the government like a bright, rising sun."

The traffic grinds to a halt at a red light. He hears three pings and pulls out his iPhone. He's received a text message. *Good morning my love mama is doing better today daddy is playing golf I am thinking as always of my roberto when are you coming I miss you too much your caroline.* She dazzles him with her coppery skin and light-green eyes and he loves and plans to marry her. Her mother is dying of cancer, and she went four months ago to be with her on the Caribbean island of Saint Lucia. She worries about him and has been imploring him to quit his job and join her on the sunny idyllic island. He texts her back. *I'm trapped in traffic* he's about to write but he only gets as far as *I'm trapped* when he hears a tapping at his window.

A woman with a pink and yellow sty the size of a cherry in her left eye is looking at him through the glass. She's in a wheelchair. He keeps money on the console for such situations as this. He grabs a wrinkled thousand peso note, lowers the window, and passes it out to her.

"You're a good man," she says smiling at him. Her face is rather pretty except for the sty. "May God bless you."

She wheels herself toward the next car. It wouldn't surprise him if this woman was no more crippled than he is, but his grandmother has always told him he should err on the side of generosity and anyway, it must be hard work wheeling through the traffic all day. Other people are moving among the cars, selling gum and lottery tickets and candy and fruit, and here comes another cripple, undoubtedly the real thing this time, a shirtless young man with no right arm and only a stub of a left one, and two people in silver space suits are performing a synchronized robotic dance to the accompaniment of eerie electronic music from a boom box. At every busy intersection in the city he'll see this ragtag army of vendors, beggars, and performers. Recently he wrote a story about them.

As with just about everything, it turned out there was a lot more to their story than met the eye. Not just anybody can wander onto any street corner and go into business. The people who have already staked their claims there are loathe to accept newcomers, and will demand money from them or harass them and drive them away. He interviewed a black man named Uriel, a skillful juggler with a flashing white smile and an endless supply of songs and jokes. He had moved to the cool city from the tropical coast and had enjoyed a prosperous couple of weeks juggling at an intersection downtown when three men dragged him into an alley. Two of the men held him while the third pulled down his pants. As Uriel began to scream and beg, the man took out a knife and cut his testicles off, then he tossed them to Uriel and said, "Here, juggle these." Uriel told Roberto he had seen the men around but they didn't work on the street themselves. Roberto found out who they were: thugs with ties to a neofascist organization called the Committee to Protect the Nation, which is basically a front group for a vicious paramilitary unit called the Black Jaguars. And he discovered the CPN was getting a piece of the action from every major corner in the city. The story has created quite a stir, and an "official investigation" has been launched. Not that he expects anything to come of it. Official investigations in this country have the paradoxical effect of carrying the investigators ever further away from the truth. All becomes a mystery, turns into murk. Hard glittering facts melt away like bits of ice.

The light changes, and traffic begins to struggle forward. The sun has vanished. Rain splatters down again. He turns his wipers on.

He's in the habit of monitoring his surroundings closely. Now he notices the green Renault sedan that was behind him has moved into the lane to his left. There are two guys in the front seat. He doesn't have a clear view of the driver, but the guy in the passenger seat has a moustache and a broad red face. He's looking right at Roberto. Roberto looks away, looks back. The guy is still looking at him.

Hard to tell what's in the look. It's not obviously hostile, or friendly, or curious. Just two eyeballs fixed on him.

Roberto's coming up on a side street to his right, and now he takes a sudden turn on it and plunges down a steep hill, into a neighborhood he ordinarily avoids. It's not unusual in this city that even areas of affluence contain pockets of poverty and crime, and on these few blocks a policeman is hardly ever seen and drivers like Roberto taking short cuts are routinely robbed. He drives fast past dilapidated apartment buildings and cheap shops and restaurants and people on the sidewalks beginning their day. The pavement is crumbling and his right front tire bangs into a pothole and he feels lucky it didn't blow. He turns left and then right again, his tires squealing a bit. He honks at a guy crossing the street who has to scurry out of the way. Roberto looks in his rearview mirror. The guy is bending down and picking up a loose chunk of asphalt and now he throws it at Roberto. But he misses and Roberto reaches the bottom of the hill and turns left. He's out of the neighborhood, on course again for downtown.

He checks his mirror. He doesn't see the green sedan. He has no idea whether it was chasing him down the hill or not. Was the guy in the passenger seat the same person that called him at dawn, or at least connected to him? Was this just an act of intimidation, or was he on the verge of pulling a gun out and scattering Roberto's brains across the front seat of his car? Or was he staring at Roberto because he looked familiar but he couldn't quite place him? Or maybe he was gay and thought Roberto was cute. He knows one thing for sure: he's unlikely to get chunks of the road thrown at him while driving in Saint Lucia.

* * *

The sky is really pouring by the time he reaches *The Hour*'s offices. Dark clouds are curling over the tops of the mountains as if the mountains were a dam barely holding back some vast, unimaginably powerful storm. The gutters gush with filthy water. He's about to turn into the parking lot under the building, but he has to wait for a guy who looks like he's out of a zombie movie to walk by. His long stringy hair is dripping with rain and he's talking to himself and slapping his face. Probably he's high on *basuco.*

Roberto opens his trunk so a security guard can poke around in it while another security guard circles his car with an aging, plodding, bomb-sniffing dog. Nobody, not even the publisher or editor, is allowed to enter uninspected since it's reasoned that a bomb could have been planted in their car without their knowledge, or their family could have been taken hostage and will all be killed unless they bring a bomb into the building. This is not mere paranoia. Aside from the fact this is a crazy country where anything can happen, five years ago a car bomb ripped the building wide-open, killing three and injuring eighteen.

He missed the explosion by about a minute. He had been at his desk when he got a phone call. He was working on a story about a massacre in a town called Contamana, where the killers had worn masks and their identities were unclear. The caller claimed to have inside knowledge of the massacre, and was willing to meet with him and tell him what he knew in one hour. He wouldn't give his name and Roberto was suspicious of him, but he finally agreed to meet in a public place where his murder was unlikely: at the statue of Simón Bolívar, in Bolívar Park. He wasn't surprised when the guy was a no-show. He hung out with the Liberator and hundreds of pigeons for half an hour, and then headed back to the office. He was a few blocks away when he heard the boom and saw the smoke.

He knew immediately it was his newspaper. When he got there he saw coworkers stumbling out of the building and he will never forget how white and red they were: covered with dust and streaked with blood. He saw a woman's bare leg sticking out of the rubble, a stylish black high heel still on the foot. He ran over and started clawing away the bricks and plaster but discovered there was no woman attached to the leg. His grandmother suggested that it was divine intervention that saved him from the blast, that perhaps the caller wasn't a person at all but a spirit, his guardian angel. He told her he didn't believe in guardian angels and she said that was okay, angels didn't hold it against you when you didn't believe in them.

He takes the elevator up to the fifth floor and enters the newsroom. It's a huge space that used to be filled with people and energy but now seems more like a warehouse where row on row of empty desks are stored. *The Hour* is an elderly paper in very poor health kept alive only by infusions of money from its founders and owners, the Langenberg family. He sits down at his desk and opens his computer. An email from his stepmother has just come in. *Roberto, your father and I are having a few people over for dinner on Saturday. Please come. It would make your father so happy. We never see you anymore. Sometimes I think you don't even like me. Clara.* He emails back his disturbingly attractive stepmother that he will be there, then Gloria Varela, who seems incapable of doing anything other than dramatically, strides dramatically past his desk.

"Good morning, Roberto!" she says, not looking at him, with a breezy wave of her hand. She is tall and wears a long skirt, knee-high leather boots, and a black cape blotched with rain. Her most striking feature would be her hair, which is long, wild, and a blaze of red, except for the fact she has a piratical black patch covering her left eye. Which was put out by a bomb. Not the one five years ago but one twenty-two years ago that was meant just for her.

"Gloria," he says, "can I ask you something?"

She stops, looks back at him, and smiles. "Of course."

But he doesn't ask anything, doesn't say anything, he just sits there with his mouth shut. Seeing he's at a loss, she walks back. She sits down on the edge of his desk and crosses her boots (she always wears boots; it's rumored she has an entire closet filled with nothing but boots). She takes cigarettes out of her purse. You aren't supposed to smoke in the newsroom, but Gloria is not the type of person to whom the rules apply.

"How do you do it?" he finally says.

She flicks her lighter into flame. "Do what, darling?"

"Be a journalist in this fucking country. For so many years."

"That's not nice, Roberto, you're making me feel so old."

"Tell me."

She blows a cloud of smoke over his head. "Okay, here's my secret. Have them make some stupid movie about you so you'll be too famous to kill!"

When Gloria was just starting out as a journalist, she made a fateful trip to the southern jungles. It was to an area controlled by the Popular Revolutionary Movement, a Marxist guerrilla group that had been battling the government for decades. She was seeking an interview with one of the PRM leaders, Luis Valesquez, who had earned the nickname Commander Romeo because of his dashing good looks that set the hearts of even right-wing women aflutter. A go-between put Gloria in contact with the guerrillas, and she was conducted to their headquarters. She had been led to believe that Valesquez was eager to be interviewed, but the PRM prided itself on being tricky and devious, and Gloria was promptly taken prisoner and held for ransom. After a little over a year, her release was negotiated, and it created a sensation all over the country when the movie-star-gorgeous redheaded reporter emerged from the jungle with her belly big with child. She was mum about the father, but promised to write a book in which she'd reveal everything.

Gloria wanted to call the book *One Year, One Month, Eight Days: My Life as a Captive of the PRM*. Instead, her publisher called it *Commander Romeo and Me*. In it she told of being chained for months like some hapless animal to a tree in the jungle, and of occasional visits from Valesquez during which a mutual respect and curiosity began to develop, until finally whole nights would pass with him and her talking and talking about the war, their pasts, their fears and dreams and their inmost selves as the equatorial stars blazed down through the gaps in the rain forest canopy, and then came the night when Commander Romeo unlocked the chain. "I felt a swelling sense of relief and joy as I realized I was free," wrote Gloria. "But neither my body nor my soul remained at liberty for long, for they both became captives in Luis's strong arms."

Reaction to the book was passionate and divided, with many readers enthralled by Gloria's soaringly romantic adventure, and others seeing her as at best a dupe of the Communists, if not their outright ally, who had concocted the story of her kidnapping as a way to get money for the PRM. A few weeks after the book came out, Gloria was walking up the stairs to her apartment with her and Valesquez's year-and-a-half-old child in her arms when a bomb went off. She lost consciousness briefly, then opened her remaining eye and saw her son Martín lying at the bottom of the stairs—still alive, waving his arms around, but with a jagged piece of wood sticking out of his head. Two days later, in a hospital recovering from her injuries, she saw on TV a photograph of grinning government soldiers posing with the bloody corpse of Luis Valesquez as if he were a big-game trophy. Instantly the story started that Commander Romeo had been killed while on a desperate journey to the capital city to see Gloria and their injured son, but the truth was more prosaic: he'd cut his foot while swimming in a river, the cut had become infected, and he was on his way to see a doctor when he and some of his men had blundered into a government ambush. The movie rights to the book were acquired by a famous Spanish director who cast two Spanish movie stars in the lead roles. *Commander Romeo and Me* (with of course the tear-jerking Romeo-trying-to-reunite-with-Juliet ending) became a worldwide success, and Gloria was on hand in Hollywood when it was awarded the Oscar for Best Foreign Film.

"But they kill famous people," Roberto says to Gloria. "Look at Ricky Cortés."

"Yes, poor Ricky," Gloria says. "But he wasn't one tenth as famous as me." The hand holding her cigarette is delicately cocked at the wrist, and her eye is gazing thoughtfully at nothing. "The truth is, I'm certain I *would* have been killed. If I hadn't left."

She moved to Paris after the movie came out. She became known for her eye patch and her flamboyant ways. She had a famous fling with the French president. She conducted a series of notorious interviews with world political leaders whom she somehow charmed into putting up with her often rude and outrageous questions. She returned to her own country after eleven years.

"Why did you come back when you did?" he asks her. "Why did you think it was safe?"

"Well, one never feels completely safe, you know, but—time passes, people get older, some of your enemies die, others begin to forget or just lose interest. And it helps that I'm not the writer I used to be."

"Oh, that's not true," he murmurs, but he knows that it is. She's no longer the fiery radical figure of her youth. For the last several years she's been writing a gossipy political column that seldom takes any discernible side. She studies the glowing tip of her cigarette as if it's some odd phenomenon she's never noticed before.

"It changes you," she says. "Being blown up along with your baby. How could it not?"

He feels sad for her. For her and Martín. He is a permanent patient in a Catholic hospital called the Home for the Relief of Suffering. Physically a young man but still trapped mentally in the time he was being carried up that staircase.

Now Gloria smiles. "So what's with all the questions, my handsome one?" She reaches over and ruffles Roberto's hair. Her demeanor toward him has always been a mixture of the motherly and flirty. "What's up with you?"

"I'm thinking about leaving," he says.

"The country?"

"Yes. I think maybe it's becoming too dangerous for me here."

"And where would you go?"

"Saint Lucia, at least for now. My girlfriend and her parents are there."

"And what would you do in Saint Lucia?"

"The same as here. Only I wouldn't be looking over my shoulder every three seconds."

Gloria seems unsurprised by any of this. She's quiet for a moment, looking at him speculatively—and then says, "I would miss you, Roberto. But maybe it isn't such a bad idea that you go. I'm a little surprised they haven't killed you already."

* * *

He makes some phone calls, types up some notes. He's begun work on a story about so-called "death bars." Supposedly there are bars in the seedier parts of the city where young men go, not simply to drink and carouse, but expressly to seek fighting and maybe killing and maybe death. They fight with knives, and it's said spectators cheer and lay down bets as if they're watching cockfights. He's made contact with a man who claims to be somehow involved in the scene, and he's agreed to act as Virgil to Roberto's Dante and conduct him on a tour of the death bar underworld. He's doing it for a price, but it wouldn't be the first time Roberto has paid sources; as the saying goes, truth is a whore and you must pay for her. But now, as he sits at his desk and looks at the man's number, he decides not to call, at least for now. A story like this would take weeks of work, and in ten days, he might be gone.

* * *

He drives south, the neighborhoods disintegrating as he goes, poorer people on the street, more jolting potholes and skinny dogs, crummier cars spurting smoke. To the east and west, where the most impoverished live, dismal slums crawl up the sides of the mountains. This is a world that people in the north of the city can live out lengthy lives and never once visit.

It's quit raining again, though the sun hasn't come back out. There are two seasons in this country, rainy and dry; this is the middle of the rainy season, though there hasn't been much rain yet. In other parts of the country, the rainy season has never come. Rivers are drying up and jungles are catching on fire. The drought is entering its third year, and scientists say they have never seen anything like it.

He's on a wide commercial avenue. He stops at an intersection and a vendor approaches, selling cigarettes and sweets. He buys a Jet. It was the favorite candy bar of his youth. He was a little bit chubby when he was a kid, and candy bars seemed important then. But today, the Jet is not for him.

He reaches a neighborhood called Caballito. He turns onto a narrow side street lined with ramshackle houses, shacks, huts, whatever. He drives a couple of minutes and turns again and then parks in front of Manuel's house. In case he actually does go to Saint Lucia, he wants to see Manuel one more time. He didn't bother to call first. He knows he's here. He's always here.

He gets out of his car. It's a blue Kia Sorento. Four-wheel drive. Six years old. He could afford a nicer car but he wants one that blends in. A vacant-eyed teenage boy approaches. In this city when you park your car someone is always approaching.

"Hey, Nemecio. What's happening?"

"Nothing's happening, man," says Nemecio. "Life stinks."

"Sorry to hear that."

He gives him a two thousand peso bill. The money is so he will "watch" his car. "Protect" it. Protecting it primarily from himself.

He skirts a wide puddle of water. Different kinds of music drift out of different houses and mingle discordantly in the street. Above the roofs, beads of rain hang from tangles of black electric lines. A little girl stands in the doorway of Manuel's house, looking at Roberto with black bashful eyes.

He sticks his hands in the pockets of his windbreaker.

"Which pocket?" he says.

She ponders him, biting her lip, then points to his left pocket. He pulls out of it the Jet candy bar and hands it to her.

"It's amazing, Nydia! You always know. What are you, some kind of witch?"

He's being serious. It is amazing, Nydia does always know, she is like some kind of little witch. She giggles and tears the wrapper off and bites into the bar of solid chocolate. She's eight. She's related to Manuel and his mother but Roberto's not sure exactly how. She's a recent refugee from the fighting in the countryside. A bit of inconsequential flotsam cast up on the shore of the enormous city. He knows she can talk because he's heard her talking to others, but she has never said one word to him.

He moves past her, calling "Hello?" into the dimness of the house.

He sees Manuel's mother, sitting in her usual chair, a wooden bowl filled with peas she is shelling resting on her arthritic knees. She's watching a cooking show on TV called *Fernanda!* She's surrounded by religious bric-a-brac. His eye is caught as always by a porcelain figurine of Christ. It's a particularly macabre representation of the crucifixion, blood spilling down Jesus's face from his crown of thorns, his eyes bugging out and his mouth agape in horror, as if to say, "Hey, I don't care if I am the son of God, it's no fucking joke to be crucified!"

"How are you?" he asks. "How are your knees?"

She keeps her eyes on Fernanda, a hyperactive blonde whose big tits seem to be threatening to fall out of her low-cut top and land with a plop in the food she's preparing.

"As good as God wants them to be. He's in the back." Meaning presumably her son and not God.

He goes out the back door into a tiny fenced-in yard. Mateo, Manuel's dog, a low-slung burly brute with a muddy belly, greets him with some growls and hearty barks.

"Hello, Mateo!" he says.

"Mateo, shut up!" says Manuel. "It's okay, it's Roberto!"

Manuel is sitting on a low bench in an open-fronted shed built of flattened soda and beer cans and scraps of wood. Around him are dumbbells and a barbell and stacks of iron weights, and a radio is playing a peppy salsa tune. He's a good-looking guy in his early twenties. He's wearing white workout clothes that have somehow remained clean despite the griminess of his surroundings, and his upper body is bulging with muscles. His face is turned toward Roberto but he does not really see him except for his general shape. His left leg is missing at the hip. He was a soldier who stepped into a booby-trapped hut in the rebellious province of Tulcán.

"How are you, Manuel?"

He gives Roberto a big smile, showing his even white teeth.

"I'm doing great, Roberto. Something wonderful has happened!"

"What?"

"Some people from the Army came by yesterday. They said I'd been accepted into the Center for the Courageous. I'll be going there next week."

The Center for the Courageous is a treatment facility for soldiers who have suffered grievous injuries. Now Roberto grins as widely as Manuel.

"Hey man. I'm really happy for you."

Manuel extends his fist and Roberto bumps knuckles with him.

"It's because of you, Roberto. I have you to thank."

He wrote an article about the many Manuels who have been casualties in his country's unending warfare with guerrillas and subversives and are living on meager pensions in grubby little shitholes minus eyesight or limbs or reproductive organs or feeling below the waist or any combination of these and most of all minus a future. The Center for the Courageous has an excellent reputation but also a very long waiting list. Roberto quoted a retired Army general who called the country's treatment of its wounded warriors "a stain on our national honor" and radio and TV talk shows went into a self-righteous tizzy and panicky officials promised reforms and launched investigations. Most of what Roberto does seems without consequence, usually a story he writes is like a stone dropped into a well so deep he never hears it hit the bottom, so it makes him feel good that he seems to have had an effect on at least one person's life.

"I'll miss Mateo," says Manuel, scratching his dog's head. "But they said he could come visit me any time I want."

A white rabbit with gray spots hops slowly around a corner of the outhouse. Manuel's mother got it with the idea of fattening it up and cooking it in a coconut milk stew, but Manuel has become attached to it and has made it his pet. Matéo, though, is giving the rabbit a murderous look, leaving no doubt that if it were up to him, its protected-pet status would be immediately revoked.

"What do you want them to do for you?" asks Roberto.

"Give me a new leg and teach me to walk on it. Teach me to read with my fingers. Help me find a job. My brother is a plasterer, I planned to go into business with him when I got out of the Army, but I don't guess you can be a blind plasterer. But I'm very strong, I'm full of energy, I know I can do good work at something. And then I'll take care of my mother instead of her taking care of me."

Manuel had a girlfriend that ditched him after what was left of him came back from Tulcán. He has hinted to Roberto that his injuries have left him incapable of having children, and he has told him how sad he is that he will probably never have a wife. Roberto's happy about his good news and yet he feels bad that Manuel now wants so little out of life but will have to struggle mightily to achieve even that.

Manuel reaches for the radio and turns the music down. It's like a cloud or a shadow has passed across his face.

"What's wrong?" Roberto asks.

"I need to see a priest."

"Why?"

"To confess my sins. I did bad things . . . we all did . . . in Tulcán."

Since the days of the conquistadors, outsiders have not been welcome in Tulcán. The war there has nothing to do with the PRM. The mostly Indian population is resisting the encroachment of the modern world. It does not wish to be globalized. Miners have been massacred and loggers have been captured and then dismembered with their own chainsaws. The conflict there has been exceptionally savage, even by the extreme standards of Roberto's blood-soaked country. He's never talked to Manuel about his service in Tulcán, but he's unsurprised to hear him admit he did bad things. It's hard to imagine this gentle man sitting in front of him who loves dogs and rabbits committing terrible acts, and yet he's used to the realities of this country outstripping the capacity of his imagination to deal with them.

"I can take you to a priest now," he says.

But Manuel acts as if he hasn't heard him.

"This will be a new beginning for me. So I want to make a clean breast of it. Start over."

"I understand. So you want to go find a priest? I'll be glad to take you."

Manuel puts the heels of his hands into his scarred eyes and rubs them, as if trying to remove the darkness in them.

"The thing I want to tell a priest . . . it's very difficult . . . because we killed a priest."

Roberto sits. He waits. The rabbit comes cautiously hopping over to him and sniffs his shoe. Its name is Humberto.

"It was a bad place . . . Tulcán. I know sometimes we did bad things to the people there but they did bad things to us too. I saw many of my friends die. But it wasn't only the people, it was the trees, the animals, the birds—it was like they all hated us, they wanted to kill us. The day before we killed the priest, my best friend, Gonzalo, he was bitten by a *mapaná* snake and died. And then that night when we made camp, we could hear an animal walking around. Something big. We heard it growling and breathing and twigs snapping under its feet. We shined our flashlights and couldn't see anything but we kept hearing it. Someone said it must be a jaguar, but someone else said maybe it's the Mapinguari."

"What's the Mapinguari?"

"The Indians say it's a ferocious animal that protects the forest and can't be killed. We'd heard stories about it and we laughed about it, but that night we wondered if maybe the stories were true. The next morning we went into a little village, it was called Las Animas." The Spirits. "We were looking for a priest who had been causing a lot of trouble."

"What kind of trouble?"

"They told us he was a Communist. But I sit back here all day and think, all I do is think, Roberto, and I think maybe anybody that tries to help the people they call a Communist. He didn't try to run away or hide, he walked out of his church and met us. His name was Father Benecio. He didn't look old enough to be a priest, he didn't look very much older than me. He said, 'This is a peaceful village, you are all welcome here, how can we help you?' Our captain told him he could help us by taking off all his pretty priest clothes. He looked surprised, he asked the captain if he was joking. The captain just laughed, and then he ordered me and another man to take off his clothes for him. We stripped off all his clothes, Father Benecio didn't resist, it felt wrong to do this to a priest but orders are orders. He was standing naked in the street. He had blue eyes and fair skin, the sun was shining on him and his body looked so white, Roberto, he reminded me of a little baby bird without feathers that had fallen out of its nest.

"The captain ordered us to round up all the people of the village. The priest began praying. The people looked at him and many of them were praying too and weeping and making the sign of the cross, because they knew something terrible was about to happen. The captain ordered the people to run and get sticks, hoes, rakes, shovels, and they just stood there and looked at each other and then we began to shoot our weapons in the air and hit them and kick them and they ran and came back with hoes and sticks. The captain ordered them to form two lines facing each other. They lined up, all the people of Las Animas: men and women, old people and children. The captain told them it was their privilege today to do a good deed; they were going to send Father Benecio to heaven. He told the priest to start walking between the two lines, and he told the people to strike him. The priest began to walk slowly. He was whispering to himself and crossing himself, but nobody struck him, they loved the priest, and the captain walked up behind a young girl and shot her in the head. He yelled at them to strike, and then a man hit the priest on the back with a shovel, and the captain screamed 'Not hard enough!' and shot the man in the head. And then all the people began to hit the priest with their sticks and rakes, and he stumbled forward and blood was running down his white skin, and I heard him yell, 'Strike hard, my children! Please! End it, for the love of Christ!'"

Manuel breaks off. He turns his face toward Roberto, his usually dim eyes bright with tears.

"Roberto, how can I tell a priest about this? How can God forgive me?"

Roberto doubts there is a God but he says, "They say that God forgives everything."

He leaves Manuel with his dog. He finds his mother in the kitchen, preparing a meal. He gives her some money. She slips the bills into her pocket without looking at them or him and mumbles her thanks. He goes out of the house and walks toward the street past Nydia, who is squatting on the ground and playing like a little boy with a toy truck.

"Good-bye, Nydia," he says, not expecting a response, but he's surprised to hear behind him a shy "Good-bye."

* * *

She is there in front of him. Her blonde hair falling about her shoulders. Her green eyes looking at him. Her mother is English, that's where she got the eyes and hair. The golden skin she got from her father. Caroline's mother had a secretarial job at the British embassy. She went to a disco one night, where Caroline's father asked her to dance. She was nearly a head taller than him, but he was a tremendous dancer and they fell in love fast. He was a young executive at the local Coca-Cola branch. By the time he retired to paradisal Saint Lucia, he was the chief operating officer for Coca Cola in all of South America. Roberto's father is well off, but his future father-in-law is out-and-out wealthy. Not a bad guy either.

The first time Roberto saw her, as he and his friend Andrés were crossing the lobby of a theater during the intermission of a terrible play, he was so taken aback by her beauty he came to a stop and with his mouth hanging slightly and stupidly open just stared at her. She was standing with some guy, and she happened to glance over at Roberto, and when she looked at him again a few moments later, this time with a certain amount of curiosity, he finally had the presence of mind to close his mouth. He couldn't even do it the first time he tried to sleep with her, he was so in awe of her. But the second time it was the opposite, the two of them were in a frenzy all night as if trying to set some sort of record for climaxes and positions.

It's night. He's sitting in front of his computer. He has called her on Skype. She's telling him about something she saw on the news: a polar bear and her cub swimming in the Arctic for nine days because the pack ice had all melted.

"The mother bear made it to safety," she says, "but her cub drowned. It's all because of stupid global warming and nobody is doing anything about it. It made me cry for ten minutes!"

"I don't like to think of you crying," says Roberto.

"Too bad you weren't here to comfort me."

"That was too bad."

"So what's new with my Roberto?"

"Well, let's see. I'm having dinner with my father and Clara on Saturday."

"Just you and them?"

"Some other people are coming. I don't know who."

"Oh, one of Clara's fancy dinner parties?"

"I guess so."

"Well, give your father a big kiss for me."

"What about Clara?" he says, teasing her. She's crazy about his father but can't stand Clara. "Should I give her a big kiss for you too?"

"No," she says firmly. "No kissing Clara."

"Why don't you like her? She's so sweet."

"Sweet! Roberto, have you lost your mind? You know she married your father for his money."

"Who knows why people do things?"

"Everything about her is phony. Including her teeth and her tits."

"Her teeth, maybe. But I think her tits are real. They certainly seem real."

"Oh, and so you've spent a lot of time studying them?"

"No, not a lot. Only when I'm with her."

Caroline has three big fat cats, one of which is stretched out on her desk. Now she picks it up under its front legs and addresses it. "Roberto is so awful, Hombre. Why do I love him so much?"

"It's simple," Roberto says. "It's because I'm so handsome."

"It's true, Hombre," she sighs, and puts the cat down.

Roberto takes his glasses off, and cleans them with a tissue.

"What are you thinking?" she says.

"Hm?"

"You're always thinking something when you clean your glasses."

He smiles a little and puts his glasses back on.

"Something else is new."

"What?"

"I got a phone call this morning. Very early."

"From who?"

"I don't know. But it wasn't a pleasant call."

"Not pleasant in what way?"

"It was a death threat."

"Oh Roberto."

She looks at him with both dismay and reproach, as if he's at fault somehow. He shrugs.

"You should change your number," she says.

"What good would that do? And besides, how can I do my job if no one can get in touch with me?"

"What did they say exactly?"

"They made reference to some of the stories I've written. I don't think they liked them very much. And they said if I didn't leave the country in ten days, I'd be killed."

"Then leave. Come, Roberto!" she says, holding her arms out to him. "Come to me!"

He doesn't say anything. Her arms disconsolately drop.

"You're so stubborn. All you think about is your next story. I need you here. It's hard for me, with Mother so sick, and Daddy so sad and lost, and—"

"All right."

"All right what?"

"All right. I'm coming."

"You're coming here? To Saint Lucia?"

He nods.

"When?"

"Now. I mean, in a few days. I've got a lot to do first. I have to quit my job, and do something about the apartment, and my car, and—"

"Roberto," she says, suddenly leaning forward as Hombre leaps out of the way, her face filling the computer screen as if she's about to jump right through it, "you're really coming? I can't believe it."

He can hardly believe it either, he feels as exhilarated as she. It's such a relief to have the decision made. It's like he has just emerged from a dark tangled forest, and he sees now openness and sunlight and the pleasant path he will soon be walking on.

* * *

He falls asleep quickly when he goes to bed, and he has a dream. He's making love to Caroline, but then she becomes Ana María, the woman whose leg he found in the rubble of the newspaper office after the bombing. She worked in the advertising department, she hadn't been there long, he never really got to know her but she always had a nice smile and a hello for him whenever he encountered her in the hallways or the elevator. And now as in his dream he makes love to her, she begins to weep.

"Ana María," he says. "What's wrong? Don't you like it? Am I hurting you?"

"I do like it, Roberto," says Ana María. "You're not hurting me."

"Then why are you crying?"

"Because I'm afraid."

"What are you afraid of?"

"Of being alone."

"But you're not alone. I'm here."

"Don't leave me, Roberto."

"I won't."

"Promise me!"

"I promise," he says, but he is saying it to nobody. Ana María has faded away. All that is left of her is the sound of her weeping.

Nine days until the day
Roberto is to die

It rained during the night but it's not raining now. The TV is on to the city's most popular morning show, *Good Morning, Everyone!* They're doing a story about a bakery that is making pastries in the shape of iPhones. The reporter's name is Cristina Ocampo. She's a knockout, like all the girls that work on local TV; they all seem to have the same big eyes and heart-shaped faces. They all laugh a lot and are always cheerful and seem to inhabit a different city than the one that Roberto reports on. Probably the only kind of death threat Cristina Ocampo might receive is a guy threatening to kill himself if she won't have dinner with him.

He walks slowly around his apartment in his blue tracksuit, sipping coffee and looking things over. He'll be sad to leave. He's been happy here. It wasn't much till Caroline moved in. She basically got rid of all his stuff and started afresh and he was fine with that since her taste is so much better than his. The style she imposed was clean and modern, crisp and white. There were two tiny bedrooms but not for long as she zestfully knocked down walls and made the apartment one open space with just a half wall separating the bedroom and the living room. She laid down organic moso bamboo flooring, refurbished the cabinets, added a capacious closet for her clothes, painted all the walls white, brought in simple wood furniture, and installed track lighting that artfully illuminated her unfolding creation. In the bathroom, she put in white porcelain subway tile and a glass mosaic backsplash behind the stone sink. He's all thumbs when it comes to practical things but Caroline did much of the work herself and was never sexier than when she was dressed in old clothes and was a little dusty and sweaty and disheveled and was hammering or sawing or polishing something.

Since she would not look out of place working on *Good Morning, Everyone!*, he was initially surprised to learn she had a bookish, scholarly side. She recently finished work on her master's degree in art history and is thinking about getting her PhD, but he's encouraging her to go into interior design or something similar, since that seems to be what she enjoys the most.

He finds himself in the bedroom, staring at the bed. He remembers having sex with her a year or so ago, she was on her period and he had entered her from behind and a rubious drop of menstrual blood plopped down on the white sheet. He remembers gazing at the blood as he thrust into her and how vividly red it was against the white.

The phone by the bed rings. He walks over to it. It says "private caller" in the ID window. He lets the answering machine take the call.

"Roberto?" says the voice from yesterday. "We know you're there. Afraid to pick up the phone? Look out the window."

He hesitates—then goes to the window and looks out the blinds. The green Renault from yesterday is parked across the street. Behind the wheel is the guy with the moustache and the broad, red face, looking up at him, like yesterday, with a careful lack of expression. He's smoking a cigarette, and he takes a puff then throws the cigarette out on the pavement. Now he starts the car, and it moves away unhurriedly. Roberto tries to get the license plate number, but it's blocked by the foliage of the trees. The cigarette sends up a thin wavering line of smoke till a passing car crushes it out.

* * *

When Roberto first started working at *The Hour*, an old-timer reporter named Alvaro took a fatherly shine to him. He was a haggard alcoholic and heavy smoker who would die of lung cancer within a few years. Alvaro simply hated editors. He said to Roberto more than once: "Always remember, Roberto, the editor is your enemy. He answers to the owners and the advertisers. His job is to obstruct you in your search for the truth in every way possible." But Roberto happens to like his present editor, Rubén. Rubén's given him a lot of freedom to pursue the stories that interest him, and doesn't usually screw around with them much once he's turned them in. He's a small man with a pixyish sense of humor. As Roberto sits across his desk from him and tells him about the death threat, he smiles and nods, as if Roberto's launched into a rather long-winded joke and he's waiting patiently for the punch line.

"So I've decided to leave the country," Roberto concludes. "I'm going to Saint Lucia to be with my fiancée. It wasn't an easy decision, Rubén. You know how much I love working here."

"Oh yes," he murmurs. "Yes."

"I'm sorry I can't give you more notice. I hope it doesn't cause any problems for you."

"Oh no, no, no, no."

The smile modulates a bit but doesn't quite disappear. His hands are clasped on his paunchy belly. His thumbs go up and down in an alternating way as he looks pensively into space, and then he looks back at Roberto.

"So you have ten days?" he says. "Until they say they're going to, um . . . ?" His voice trails off delicately.

"Well, nine days now. But I'm not going to wait till the very last day. I don't want to push my luck."

"No. Of course not. Luck. Yes."

His thumbs keep going and he nods slowly, as if pondering the profound mystery of luck. And then he says, "Have you ever thought about wearing a bulletproof vest?"

"No. Not really."

"*I* wear one."

"Yes. I know."

Rubén looks surprised. "How do you know?"

"Everyone knows. I mean, you can see it under your shirt. The shape of it."

"Hm," he says, frowning down at his shirt.

"Anyway, I don't think they do much good. They usually shoot you in the head."

"Yes, you're probably right. They really don't do much good," but then he brightens. "Of course, we've all received death threats. The best one I ever got was an engraved invitation to my own funeral. I was very impressed. They put a lot of time and thought into that one."

"I know what you're saying, Rubén. But it feels like something has changed in the last few months. It's like the air has gotten colder. The country feels more dangerous to me. Do you know what I mean?"

Rubén unclasps his hands from his stomach, reclasps them behind his head, and thinks about it.

"I guess I'm just sad, Roberto. I'm losing all my best reporters. They're either leaving the country, or they're going into other professions like public relations or advertising, or they're going to work for shitty papers that pay them more and only expect them to write shit. What happens to a country when there are no real reporters left?"

Since he's not expecting a response, Roberto gives none. Rubén looks at him with a musing smile.

"So you're going off to live the good life, hm? In Saint Lucia?"

"Yes, I suppose."

"You don't sound very enthusiastic about it."

"I'm sad too. I feel like I'm deserting the ship."

"Oh don't be silly, Roberto, you have to do what's right for you," and then he sighs. "Now I have to tell Diana. She'll be upset. You've always been her favorite."

Diana is Diana Langenberg. She's the member of the Langenberg family who has taken it as her task to be the paper's publisher.

"Really? I'm her favorite?"

"Don't tell me you didn't know," Rubén says, and then adds slyly: "Why else do you think you've been allowed to be a little prima donna who does whatever he wants?"

Now he picks up his phone.

"I'll call Irma in accounting, and have her issue you a check."

* * *

A big blue city bus cuts in front of him, and he honks and hits his brakes. It doesn't matter where the bus stops are, the buses will bully their way toward the curb any time they see like now a prospective passenger waving at them, sometimes two buses will even compete for the same passenger and fistfights have broken out between drivers because they're not paid by the hour or the week but according to how many passengers they pick up. This all began a decade ago when the bus system was privatized, with the promise that the entrepreneurial spirit of the individual bus drivers would be unleashed resulting in better and cheaper service for all. Everyone realizes now that was an extremely stupid idea that has turned the city's once reliable buses into blue blundering traffic-disrupting menaces. Every politician running for office in the city pledges a return to the old sane system but year after year nothing changes because the bus company is making a lot of money and nothing that hurts the people but enriches the rich in this country ever changes.

Another reason he hates the buses is a huge construction project that was undertaken a year and a half ago: certain thoroughfares are being widened so an extra lane dedicated to the buses can be created. The idea is that the buses with their entrepreneurial drivers will be able to zip around the city unimpeded by the traffic; however the whole thing has turned into a nightmarish boondoggle, running far behind schedule and over budget. Drivers, redirected from the torn-up streets, find themselves wandering through hellish mazes that seem to have no end. The mayor of the city was charged last week with taking kickbacks from contractors he had hired for the project, and since he was deemed a flight risk he was tossed into La Picota prison. One might think it a cause for optimism that a high-ranking official is being held accountable for corruption, but in truth this is a story that has been repeated so often it has taken on the form of ceremony: a sacrificial victim is thrown into the volcano to distract and appease the public, while the serious business of plundering the country continues unabated.

His cellphone rings. It's Iván, calling him back.

"What's up, Roberto?"

"You still looking for an apartment?"

"Yeah, you know of one?"

"How about mine?"

"Roberto, you're kidding. I love your apartment. You mean you're selling it?"

"I'm renting it. Furnished. I want to keep everything as it is."

"That would be perfect. But where are you going to live? Are you getting a new place?"

Roberto doesn't want to go into this on the phone. He arranges to meet Iván at his apartment at three this afternoon.

* * *

Iván is lean and wiry, with a shaved head and an emerald in one ear. He was a colleague of Roberto's at *The Hour*, where he covered movies and television. He was one of those reporters Rubén was talking about who changed professions; in his case, he was seduced in a somewhat literal way by the TV industry, taking a job with a local station as a producer and quickly embarking on an affair with a cute young production assistant named Peppi. His wife found out about it and reacted in an unexpectedly dire manner: throwing him out of their apartment, filing for divorce, getting a boyfriend who in no time at all was living in the apartment with her. Iván moved back in with his parents, and is sleeping in the bedroom he had as a child. He has a dazed, incredulous air about him, like one who has barely survived a natural calamity that has swept his life away. But when Roberto opens the door for him, he's wearing a big smile. He looks around the apartment, shaking his head a little.

"I can't believe my luck, Roberto. What a great place."

"Thanks."

Iván rubs his hand along the gleaming blond wood of the dining room table, then walks over to a lamp.

"I've always loved this lamp."

Black metal silhouettes of naked men and women go around the lamp shade.

"Caroline designed it herself, right?"

"Yes."

Iván is doing nothing wrong, but Roberto doesn't like the feeling he's getting as he watches him walking around like he already lives here.

"Can I get you some coffee or something?"

"No thanks, I can't stay long. The TV business is really crazy."

"I'll bet."

Now Iván turns and looks at Roberto.

"So what's going on? Why are you moving out?"

Roberto tells him. Iván shakes his head.

"Man, Roberto, I'm really sorry."

Roberto shrugs. "I always knew this might happen. I just wasn't expecting it to happen now."

"My therapist says any big changes in your life are an opportunity for growth. This could be the best thing that ever happened to you. You look skeptical. Listen. Your articles are wonderful, but they're also very long. I read them, but I'm not sure how many others do."

"Well, somebody does. That's why they want to kill me."

"Do you want to know the future, Roberto? The future is 140 characters. Twitter is the future. Just think of it as a new journalistic form. Like a haiku."

"Iván, if you're trying to cheer me up, you're having the opposite effect."

Iván laughs. "Sorry, man. You know me, I was just running my mouth off. So how much will this cost me?"

Caroline, who is a lot more canny about such things than Roberto, has already told him what to ask.

"I was thinking 2,250,000."

"Hm. I don't know, Roberto. It's a nice place but my wife left me with a lot of debts. No one could shop like that woman. It was a sickness with her."

"Okay. How about 2,000,000?"

Iván grins and holds his hand out and Roberto shakes it.

"You have a deal."

Now, with his hands on his hips, he surveys the apartment like a triumphant climber who has just attained a mountaintop.

"My therapist told me I should do this."

"Move into my apartment?"

"Into any apartment. She said as long as I was staying with my parents, I was holding out hope that I would go back to Margot and our lives would be like they were before. She said getting my own place would be my first big step into my new life."

Roberto knows that Iván, despite his indiscretion with Peppi, was crazy-mad in love with his wife.

"So how are you doing, Iván? Is it getting any easier?"

"I don't know. Maybe. I'm maybe only thinking about her most of the time instead of all the time. You remember that old song? 'Love Hurts'? *Love is just a lie told to make us sad.* That song is so true, Roberto. So true."

* * *

Roberto's lying on his bed at dusk. About five minutes ago, he came into the bedroom to lie down because he was hit by a sudden crushing fatigue. He didn't sleep well last night but that's not the cause of it. Maybe he's about to fall victim to a virus, or maybe it's that so much was done today or rather undone. His life in this city is drawing to a close. Iván will usurp his place in the apartment, and his job at the paper will probably simply disappear. All because of a couple of phone calls, of a guy staring at him out of a car window. Maybe it's all a bluff and no one has any intention of killing him. But he'll never know, he's made his choice, he will be with Caroline on her island and will not be shot or blown up or dumped into a river without his head and his dick and his balls.

The blinds are up, and the traffic sounds from Avenue Six drift in. It's only a block away, but it seems much further, and it doesn't seem to have anything to do with him. It's as if he's no longer a resident of this city but is already a citizen of Saint Lucia. Through the window he can see the outside but with his glasses off, it's like an abstract color pattern with three different sections: twenty percent brown buildings, twenty percent green mountains, sixty percent faintly glowing sky.

Drowsiness begins to tug at his eyelids. He can't hear the traffic at all anymore. Fleeting half-formed thoughts blow through his head like wisps of clouds. Once he covered a political rally where the protesters made no noise but in lieu of cheering, waved white handkerchiefs. Their silence had an eerie power. And now he sees the white handkerchiefs, a silent shaking sea of them, extending to the horizon where they fade away . . .

* * *

The phone wakes him up. The window is filled with night. He puts on his glasses and checks the caller ID. It's Andrés. Roberto says hello.

"Roberto, where are you? We're all waiting."

He looks at the clock. It's a little after nine. He completely forgot that he was supposed to meet Andrés and two more of his friends for a drink at eight.

"Shit, I'm sorry."

"You're usually so punctual. What's going on?"

Andrés is talking loud so he can be heard over the sounds of music and laughter.

"Nothing, I just fell asleep. You're at Sparks, right?"

"Yes," says Andrés and then somebody else grabs the phone.

"Hurry, Roberto!" says Franz. "The women are unbelievable tonight."

"Okay, I'll be there soon."

He goes in the bathroom, splashes water on his face, brushes his teeth. He's not really in the mood to go out, but this is as good a time as any to tell his three best friends that he's leaving.

* * *

He's known Andrés the longest. Since they were kids. He's a history professor at the National University. He's married to a former girlfriend of Roberto's, Teresa. He's prematurely losing his hair. He's gentle and sweet and wears glasses.

Franz's grandfather was from Switzerland. He was a maker of chocolate. Now the company he founded exports fine chocolates all over the world. Franz is heir to a large fortune, and works in the family business. He's blond and blue-eyed with square-jawed regular features. Once he was the judge of a beauty contest, Roberto forgets the name, something like Miss Mango or Miss Pineapple; he picked a girl named Blanca as the winner then married her a month later. She's one of the least likeable people Roberto has ever met. They have three young children.

Roberto worked with Daniel at *The Hour*. He was a photographer. He left journalism two years ago, and now takes pictures of jewelry and cars and food and furniture that appear in ads in newspapers and glossy magazines. He's tall and a little overweight and has an unruly mass of reddish brown hair. He pays no attention to how he dresses, wearing rumpled clothes that always seem to be a little too big or too small. But despite his unimpressive appearance, he has amazing success with women.

Roberto and Andrés met Daniel and Franz during their first year at the National University, and immediately the four became fast friends. Roberto, Franz, and Andrés were all very left wing and active in campus politics, but Daniel couldn't have cared less about any of that. He was into drinking and chasing girls and Spanish and English literature. His favorite poet was Algernon Swinburne, and when he got drunk he would recite from memory in English whole pages of his poems, howling them out in a horrendous accent. One night he drove Roberto, Andrés, and Franz so crazy that after failing to get him to stop they jumped on him and bore him to the floor, and as he thrashed and fought and continued to shout out Swinburne Roberto forced a wet towel into his mouth—and even then he continued making grunting, poetry-like noises. And thus it was very ironic that the only one of the four of them ever arrested as a subversive was Daniel.

He became enamored of a Communist girl named Monica. He went around with her to various meetings and rallies, figuring it was the price he had to pay for getting laid. At one such rally, the protesters were attacked by the police with tear gas and clubs. The protesters began to flee, but many were chased down and handcuffed and thrown into the backs of vans. Monica got away but Daniel didn't.

They kept him for three weeks before he was finally able to convince them that he wasn't a Communist but was just some poor horny guy who had fallen for the wrong girl. No doubt Daniel was tortured because they tortured everybody, but after his release he refused to talk about what had happened to him. All he ever had to say about it was: "Captivity is terrible."

Sparks isn't too far from Roberto's apartment, so rather than fight the traffic he walks there. It's a Friday night, and Sparks is packed. It's been open about a year, and is one of the hotter clubs in the Pink Zone, an area of a few square blocks where the young and the hip hang out. He looks around. Beautiful girls abound, as Franz said. On a floor painted in rainbow colors, couples dance to recorded techno *cumbia* music. They're bathed in scintillating colored lights that have been known to induce seizures in the epileptic. Now he sees his friends, sitting at a corner table near the bar. They're smiling at him and waving him over. He feels a pang as he walks toward them because they have been such good friends to him and this is probably the last time for at the very least a long time he will be getting together with them like this.

"Guess who was just in here," says Andrés as Roberto sits down. "The Puppy."

The Puppy is Pío Landazábal, the youngest son of the country's previous president. He's earned his nickname because of his small stature, his soft brown eyes, and his stunning lack of maturity.

"Oh really?" says Roberto. "I haven't seen him around lately."

"He's been in Europe, I think," says Franz. "I remember seeing an absurd picture of him on a yacht at the Cannes Film Festival."

"Why was it absurd?"

"Any picture of the Puppy is inherently absurd."

"He came in with two women and four bodyguards," says Andrés. "And he danced with both of the women at the same time."

"Everyone was laughing at him," says Franz. "So he got mad and left."

"Women are disgusting," says Daniel. "They'll go with anybody with money."

A waitress appears and Roberto gets a beer. Andrés and Daniel both drink a lot and will get drunk tonight, but Franz drinks very little. He's a health nut. He runs many kilometers daily and works out on elaborate exercise machines and strikes torturous yoga poses and eats only plants. He takes a tiny sip of his glass of wine and says to Roberto, "Did you see Landazábal's latest tweet?" Speaking of the Puppy's father.

"No, what did he say?"

"Well, you know how Dávila is always saying it's his job as president to inspire the country and so forth. And Landazábal tweeted that Dávila couldn't inspire a flea to jump."

Roberto laughs. "That's funny. And it's also true."

Basilio Landazábal was a retired Army general who ran for president on the promise of restoring honor, honesty, and manly strength to the moral life of the nation. He served two terms and was very popular but since the new president Carlos Dávila took office a year and a half ago Landazábal's reputation has been taking a lot of hits. So far nothing has been proven against the old general himself, but it's clear many of his cronies grew ridiculously rich during his presidency. His agriculture minister was recently jailed for sending subsidies meant to help small farmers who were being weaned away from growing coca into secret bank accounts in his own name in Panama, and his cousin, who was head of the country's top spy agency, the Department of Domestic Security, is awaiting trial for allegedly funding paramilitary death squads. Landazábal, ensconced in his walled estate in the province of Alta Verapaz, seems to be spending all his time seething at the ill treatment he's getting from his ungrateful country. Somewhat amusingly for such a resolutely old-fashioned man, he's discovered Twitter, and several times a day like Jove hurling thunderbolts he fires off tweets attacking his enemies. His main target is President Dávila. In the last election, Dávila, a self-styled "centrist," easily defeated Landazábal's handpicked candidate, a dull and pompous man whose only apparent virtue was being loyal as a dog to Landazábal. Dávila is young and good-looking and has a beautiful wife who wears the latest styles from Paris and New York and two adorable daughters and went to school in America where he got

a master's degree in economics from Harvard University. He supposedly sleeps only four hours a night so he can have more time to grapple
with the country's impossible problems.

"I don't think Dávila's been so bad," says Andrés.

"People think because Landazábal hates him he must be okay," says
Roberto. "But Landazábal hates anybody who's not an out-and-out lunatic like himself. It's all words with Dávila. Nothing's going to change,
you'll see."

"I think Roberto's right," says Franz. "If he was a real reformer he'd
be dead already."

Daniel, smoking a cigarette and gazing into space, doesn't seem to be
listening.

"So Daniel, what's up?" says Roberto. "Is everything all right?"

He blows out some smoke and shakes his head. "I'm worried about
something."

"What?"

"My penis. I've been worried about it since I was twelve or thirteen."

"What's the matter with it?"

"I'm afraid it's too long."

Everyone laughs.

"Actually," says Daniel, "I was thinking about some good news I got
today. You know that cooking show? *Fernanda!*?"

"Sure, the crazy blonde with the big tits," says Andrés.

"I saw some of her show just this morning," says Roberto.

"So what about her?" says Franz. "You and she have become engaged?"

"She's written a cookbook, and I've been hired to do the photos for it.
It's pretty good money."

"Great," says Roberto, "let's drink to your cookbook!"

They all bump glasses with one another. But Daniel is looking a bit
sheepish.

"I know this is a stupid way to make a living. But work has been slow
lately, so it's come at a good time."

"Teresa loves *Fernanda!*," says Andrés. "She never misses it."

With a sour look on his face, Daniel takes a gulp of his drink.

"Anyway," he says, "so much for my good news."

"I have news too," says Roberto.

"And it's also good?" says Franz.

"No. Not really. I quit my job today. Because they're threatening to kill me. I'm leaving the country. I'm going to Saint Lucia."

His friends just stare at him.

"Shit," says Franz.

"When are you leaving?" asks Andrés.

"Soon. Within ten days. That's how long they gave me."

"Any idea who 'they' are?" asks Franz.

Roberto shrugs. "The usual anonymous motherfuckers."

Andrés sighs. "You've pissed off so many people, Roberto. There's lots of suspects."

"They can't bribe you because you have plenty of money," says Daniel. "So those they can't bribe, they kill."

It gets quiet at the table. It's not the style of the four of them when they're together to take anything too seriously, so sincere emotion tends to remain unexpressed.

"I'll bet Caroline is happy," says Franz.

"Yes. Extremely."

"So things aren't so bad," says Andrés. "When you have a girl like Caroline to go to."

"You're right, Andrés. Things aren't so bad."

He takes his glasses off. Cleans them with a bar napkin.

"But—you know—one moment I'm sure that going is the right thing to do. And then I think that I've been threatened before and nothing happened so why should this be any different? Maybe I'm just panicking."

"No, Roberto," says Daniel, "you should go. Why take a chance?"

"Daniel's right, for once," says Franz. "We'll miss you, but we can come visit you in Saint Lucia."

"Yes," says Daniel, "better than coming to visit your grave."

Roberto looks at Andrés. "What do you think?"

"I think it would be very unpleasant for the three of us if they killed you, Roberto. So for selfish reasons, I want you to go."

Roberto puts his glasses back on as the waitress passes by. She's young and cute and she smiles at the handsome Franz because waitresses always smile at him.

"Does anyone need anything?"

"More drinks for everyone," says Daniel. "We're all going to get shit-faced."

"Just some water for me please," says Franz.

Andrés eyes the waitress and her tight black pants as she walks away. "What a beautiful ass. It's a work of art."

"You know the girls with the most beautiful asses?" says Daniel. "The ones who live in the slums on the hills. Because of all the exercise they get walking up and down."

"There's one thing I don't understand," Roberto says.

"About girls' asses?"

"About the political situation. Most countries in South America move to the left at least sometimes, but we stay stuck in the right. Why is that?"

"Electing Dávila," says Andrés. "That was a move to the left."

"Yes," says Franz, "but in a way, things are worse than ever. Look at what's happening with Roberto."

"Historically that's the way it's always been," says Andrés.

"Fuck history," says Daniel. "How can you still believe in that bullshit?"

"When the right wing is in power," Andrés continues, ignoring Daniel, "they don't kill people like us. They do their massacres and so forth out in the countryside, but they leave people like us alone because they don't want to stir up any trouble. It's when they're out of power, like now, that they become dangerous."

Roberto nods. "Landazábal has become this mad old man plotting revenge. Like a character in a novel."

"I remember he tweeted something about you a few months ago," says Franz, "what was it?"

"It was after I wrote the story about the psychiatrist who got kidnapped." The psychiatrist was taken from her office then raped and tortured by unidentified men who wanted her to tell them all the secrets, the more salacious and embarrassing the better, of one of her patients, a liberal senator who happened to be a long-time nemesis of Landazábal. Not surprisingly, Landazábal denied any connection to the kidnapping, and even suggested that it had never occurred but was the invention of a hysterical woman who ought to be under psychiatric care herself. "He said I was like a little scorpion hiding in a shoe. It was kind of weird to read that. To know he knew I existed and he was sitting around in his big house in the country thinking about me."

"I try never to attract anyone's attention," says Andrés. "You can be reasonably safe as long as you don't do that."

"Do you think Landazábal is behind it?" says Franz. "The threats against you?"

"Who knows?" Roberto says, as he gazes out on the dancers in the phantasmagoric light; they seem to be made out of light too, with no substance, like holograms. "Who ever knows anything in this fucking country?"

* * *

The four of them emerge from Sparks about three hours later. Roberto and Andrés somewhat drunk, Franz completely sober, Daniel extremely drunk.

"Flower o' the quince," yowls Daniel in English, *"I let Lisa go, and what good in life since?"*

"Oh no," says Franz. "He's reciting poetry. I'm going home."

"But you can't!" says Daniel, looking stricken, clutching Franz's shoulder. "It's so early! We're just getting started!"

"Blanca texted me, Abril isn't feeling well, she has a stomachache. She wants to see her daddy."

"What kind of man are you? Putting your family in front of your friends?"

"So I'll see you again, won't I?" Franz says to Roberto. "Why don't you come to dinner? You need to say good-bye to Blanca and the kids."

"Yes, I'll do that."

"Rico!" he says, motioning to someone. "Let's go!"

Rico is standing on the sidewalk a few meters away. He's a big man in a sports coat who is Franz's driver/bodyguard. One might not always immediately notice him, but whenever Franz is out in public Rico is somewhere nearby. Franz has a great and not unfounded fear of being kidnapped. People are kidnapped left and right in this country by all manner of kidnappers—guerrillas, narcos, paramilitaries, cops, soldiers, common criminals, covert operatives from this or that government agency. There is even something called "self-kidnapping," where you arrange to have yourself kidnapped and then you and your kidnapper split the ransom. A dozen years ago Franz's elderly Swiss grandfather was kidnapped by the PRM. He was held in the jungle for many months while a ransom was painstakingly negotiated. His wife began to receive messages from him asking her to send him various pieces of her very valuable jewelry. Assuming the guerrillas were forcing him to make these requests, she complied without question. Only much later after her husband had been released did she find out that he had fallen in love with a pretty young guerrilla named Lupita and was giving the jewelry to her. He assured her it was just a passing infatuation but she didn't believe him and even today she thinks he's secretly pining away for his lost guerrilla girl; she accuses him of murmuring "Lupita" in his sleep, and if for a moment he's quiet and pensive she'll sharply say, "You're thinking about *her* again, aren't you?"

Franz and Rico walk off down the crowded street. Daniel lights a cigarette.

"Poor guy," he says. "Imagine being married to a bitch like Blanca."

"I should probably go too," says Andrés.

"But why?" says Roberto. Disappointed. The alcohol making him feel convivial like Daniel.

"I should get home to Teresa."

"But she won't mind."

"No, but I know her. She's lying in bed awake waiting for me. When I'm out at night, she can never fall asleep till I come home."

The neon sign for Sparks is reflected in each lens of Andrés's glasses. Golden sparks go fountaining up then come floating down. He smiles at Roberto. His smile is gentle and sad, like always.

"You're coming by to see her, aren't you? Before you go?"

"Of course."

"Let's see, where is my car?" Andrés habitually forgets where he parked his car. "Oh, I think it's down this way," and he hugs Roberto and Daniel. "Don't drink too much, guys. Stay out of trouble."

Andrés goes one way and Roberto and Daniel stroll off another.

"I don't understand how you can even consider getting married," Daniel says, "when you have the horrible examples of Franz and Andrés in front of you. Don't you see that it's the end of freedom?"

"Oh, someday you'll probably walk the plank like the rest of us."

"I'd rather pull the pin out of a hand grenade and hold it to the side of my head."

Roberto tends to believe him. He seldom has relationships that last beyond a month or two. "I get tired of a girl after a few weeks," he once told Roberto. "It's like eating the same thing for dinner every night. Pretty soon you want a change."

Roberto wanders through the Pink Zone with Daniel. The cobblestone streets are clean and gleaming. Employees stand out in front of the clubs and bars and discos and restaurants and smile warmly and beckon to them to enter. The sidewalks are thronged with people who all seem young, well-dressed, happy. Even the policemen and the soldiers with their automatic weapons seem happy and young and their uniforms unusually spiffy as they hang out on corners and ogle the girls. The hedonistic Pink Zone is ironically the creation of the moralistic Landazábal administration. This neighborhood used to be quite dirty and dangerous, but Landazábal worked with the now imprisoned mayor of the city to clean it up. What some call the disposable people—beggars, addicts, whores, orphans—were removed, along with hundreds of stray dogs. It's known the dogs were taken to the pound where they were electrocuted, but it's not so clear what became of the people. The politicians insisted they were treated respectfully, the orphans put into orphanages, the addicts into rehab facilities and so forth. Most people think they were simply taken to distant slums and dumped. Darker stories circulate. The disposable people never actually left but are living in the sewer system underneath the Pink Zone. The disposable people were transported out of the city and put to work as slave laborers in foreign-owned factories. The disposable people suffered the same fate as the dogs.

"I'm mad at you, you motherfucker," says Daniel.

"Why?"

"You get yourself in hot water, and now you're going to take off and leave me here. All by myself."

"Andrés and Franz will be here."

"I hardly ever see them anymore. Because of their fucking wives."

"I'm sorry, Daniel. I don't know what else to do."

"So we'll go no more a roving," he declaims in slurred English, *"by the light of the moon!"*

* * *

Roberto and Daniel go to three more places and seem to have gotten exponentially drunker as they leave each one.

"Time to go home," Roberto mumbles. "Really truly time. Don't try to talk me out of it."

"Just one more drink."

"No."

"Okay, you pussy. Where are you parked?"

"I walked."

"I'll give you a ride."

"You're in no shape to drive."

"You're in no shape to walk."

The crowds have thinned out, and there's a chilly dampness in the air. Roberto follows Daniel down a narrow ill-lit alley to where his car is parked. A yellow Renault Twingo. An old man with a skinny orange cat in his lap is sitting on a wooden box. Now the cat jumps off as the old man rises.

"Hey Esteban, are you having a good night?" Daniel says to the old man; just about anywhere you go in the city Daniel will know people by name.

"Not too bad a night, sir," Esteban says as he shuffles toward Daniel, and then he smiles as Daniel shoves some money into his hand. "Many thanks."

Daniel bends down and scratches the cat under its chin. "Hey kitty, what's happening? Been catching any mice?"

Roberto and Daniel get in the Twingo. As they move past Esteban, he waves a clawlike hand. This little stretch of alley is probably his whole life. Old man, skinny cat, narrow alley.

The radio is playing and Daniel is talking but Roberto isn't listening to him. This is the drunkest he's been in quite some time. He closes his eyes, wondering if he can stay awake till he reaches his apartment.

The horn erupts with three sharp honks. "Jesus," says Roberto, opening his eyes and looking around. "What's going on?"

"Nothing," says Daniel, "it's the car alarm. Something's wrong with it. It goes off whenever it wants to."

Roberto closes his eyes again. The horn honks three times again.

"You should get that fixed," he murmurs.

The song on the radio becomes faint and ghostly. He can feel the motion of the car but he's being captured by a different motion, it's as if he's slowly drifting around the circumference of a dark, indolent whirlpool, and then he wakes up. He's not at his apartment building but is entering the underground parking at Daniel's apartment building.

"Daniel, what are we doing here? You were supposed to take me to my place."

"Shit, I forgot." Daniel pulls into his parking space. "We'll have a quick drink. Smoke a little weed. Then I'll take you home."

Roberto doesn't want a drink or to smoke weed but knows there's no point in arguing with Daniel when he's like this. Roberto rides up in the elevator with him. It's a high-rise building, and his apartment's near the top.

Big windows give out on views of the city and the mountains. The building is near the bullring, and if one stands on the balcony on the days they're having bullfights one can look down into the arena and witness the bloody spectacle if one is so inclined. Daniel moved here after he quit the paper and became a commercial photographer. It's a big step up from the dumps he used to live in.

Roberto sinks down onto the soft maroon sofa. "What do you want to drink, Roberto?" Daniel calls from the kitchen, and Roberto calls back, "A beer!" Daniel comes in with two beers and sits down next to Roberto. He takes the lid off a wooden box on the coffee table and busies himself rolling a joint. Roberto gazes at him fondly.

"I'm going to miss you, Daniel."

"Let's don't even talk about it."

"You say I ought to go, but you're mad at me because I'm going."

Daniel doesn't reply. He finishes up the joint, lights it, inhales, and then hands it to Roberto. He breathes in some smoke then quickly coughs it out.

"Shit," he says.

"Good, huh? It's called creepy. It's this new genetically modified Frankenstein kind of weed."

Roberto hands the creepy back to Daniel. He takes a drink of his beer. He looks at Daniel's aquarium, at the luminous bubbles trickling up and the bright tropical fish. Daniel would like to have a warm-blooded pet but since he travels a lot feels that it's not practical. But he loves his fish. Particularly when he's stoned, he will sit in front of the tank and watch them like television. He recognizes them all individually and thinks they recognize him. He ascribes human thoughts and emotions to them. He will say things like: "The little blue angelfish is in a good mood today. See, she's zipping all around the tank. I think she's happy the tiger barb died. It was always nipping at her."

Daniel offers the joint to Roberto again, and he takes another hit.

"Have you ever done *ayahuasca*?" says Daniel.

"No, have you?"

"Yeah, a few weeks ago. A friend took me to see this shaman."

"In the jungle?"

"No, the shaman lives here."

"What happened?"

"I met this giant anaconda that glowed in the dark. It said it was glad I'd come because it had been waiting on me for thousands of years. Then this giant green parrot flew at me, it was very pissed off, it was pecking at me and beating me with its wings."

"What happened then?"

"I don't know. The next thing I remember is vomiting into a bucket."

Roberto looks around the room. He can't quite get used to the idea that sloppy, disorderly Daniel is living in such a cool place. He had a girl-friend named Petra who was like Caroline in that she fixed up the apart-ment for him though compared to Caroline she was very short-lived as a girlfriend. Daniel has always loved the Beatles, especially John Lennon, and hanging on the wall is a large framed black and white photograph of a very young John Lennon, wearing a black leather jacket with the col-lar turned up, and gazing somberly into the camera. Other photographs are on the walls, all taken by Daniel. They show victims, mostly. Of war, crime, poverty, earthquakes. Roberto was there when most of the pic-tures were taken. He wrote a story about a bomb going off in an assassi-nation attempt on a government official but the only casualty was the dog of a homeless man. Daniel took an award-winning picture of the weeping man holding the body of his dog. For the thousandth time, Roberto looks at it. It really is extraordinary.

"Why did you stop, Daniel?"

"Stop what?"

"Taking pictures. You were so good."

"I didn't stop taking pictures."

"You know what I mean."

"I decided I didn't want to be poor all my life. You have money,

Roberto, it's easier for you. And I got sick of all the suffering. It's not like when you take pictures of the suffering it goes away, it's still there, so what's the point? Now I live in a nice apartment and I take pictures of Fernanda's tits. And no one can accuse me of being a sell-out because I'm not like you or Franz or Andrés, I never believed in any of that revolutionary let's-all-save-the-world bullshit to begin with."

Roberto's very close to Andrés and Franz, but his connection to Daniel goes deeper. It can't be summed up in words, it can be present in a fleeting glance that passes between them, it is akin to the bond between soldiers on a battlefield. Roberto and Daniel's battlefield has been the country. They've covered stories all over its mountains and jungles and swamps and plains, and its big cities and tiny villages. They've been thirsty and hungry and hot together and wet and cold and happy and drunk and have fucked girls in the same hotel room together and stared at the smoking engines of cars that have broken down on desolate roads with the night coming on and they've seen death in its myriad forms and more times than Roberto can count they've been scared shitless together. It's a part of Daniel's personality that under difficult circumstances he will whine and complain and claim to be a coward and yet when it has been necessary to advance to complete an assignment Roberto has never seen him take a backward step and when Roberto has looked around because he was in need of help Daniel has always been right there.

And thus it seems paradoxical that despite his closeness to Daniel he feels as if he knows and understands Andrés and Franz much better. There is a part of Daniel that he keeps hidden. Roberto thinks it has to do with the three weeks he was a prisoner of the police. He came back changed. There was a darkness and bitterness in him that hadn't been there before, and a loathing not only for the world he lived in but for himself.

"Tell me just one thing," Roberto says.

"About what?"

"About when you were arrested. About what the police did."

Daniel laughs. "Who the fuck cares? It was a long time ago, Roberto. Forget about it. I have."

"I don't think you've forgotten. And I don't think it's good to keep things bottled up."

"What are you, a psychiatrist now? You should stick to being a reporter."

"Don't you trust me? Just tell me one thing."

"And then that's it? You won't bother me again?"

"Yes. That's it."

Daniels sucks on his weed, and thinks about it.

"First of all, I was only with the police for a couple of days. Then they turned me over to the Army."

"Okay."

"I'll tell you about what was the worst moment for me. I guess it was about two weeks after I was arrested. I don't know for sure, because they never wanted you to know what day it was or what time it was. They never let you see the outside, and they kept you places where the lights were on all the time or it was dark all the time. And you never knew when the door was going to open and they would drag you out to another interrogation session. It was terrible, the waiting. Well, one day, they came and put me in handcuffs and put a blindfold on me. And then they led me to a car, and then we were driving. I could hear the sounds of traffic. Nobody in the car said anything. I was wondering what could this all mean, were they moving me to a new place, were they taking me somewhere to be killed, were they about to let me go, what, what? And then the car stopped, and they took off the blindfold. I saw I was sitting in the back seat of an SUV with tinted windows. And then I looked out the window and saw we were parked across the street from my mother's house.

"There were three other men in the car. The man in the back seat with me said, 'Cooperation, Daniel. You have a lot to learn about it.' And then one of the other men got out of the car and walked across the street and knocked on my mother's door. I felt in a panic, what were they going to do, kill my mother right in front of my eyes? My mother opened the door. I could see the man talking to her, and my mother replying, it looked like a friendly conversation. And the man next to me said, 'See, Daniel? We can take your mother any time we want, we will do to her what we've done to you.' And I felt at that moment as if I were about to lose my mind. Thinking about my mother in their hands. And me helpless to stop them. Helpless." His voice trails off.

"And then what happened?"

"The man came back and got in the car. And then they put the blindfold on me and drove me back to where we'd been."

Roberto mulls his story over.

"But you were already cooperating with them, right? Because you had nothing to hide. So what else could you tell them?"

"Roberto, come on. You said there wouldn't be any more questions."

Roberto nods. Then he yawns.

"I think your creepy just about did me in. Will you give me a ride home?"

"Sure."

"I want to take a leak first."

He goes in the bathroom. He stands at the toilet peeing for a long time. Then he goes to the sink and washes his hands then takes his glasses off and splashes water on his face. Then he towels his face and hands dry and puts his glasses back on and looks at himself in the mirror. Wondering where he'll be exactly one year from now. On Saint Lucia with Caroline? Will they still be happy together? She wants to have children with him, will she already be pregnant? Will he remember this moment, or will it have slipped into oblivion like practically all moments?

He returns to the living room. Daniel's head is lolling back on the sofa. His eyes are closed, his mouth is open, he's breathing noisily.

Roberto takes his cellphone out and calls for a taxi.

Eight days until the day
Roberto is to die

"It's distressing," says Caroline.

She's talking about seaweed. It's been washing up in great brown tangled heaps onto the pristine beaches of Saint Lucia. It smells bad and attracts bugs. Caroline is sure it has something to do with pollution or climate change.

"Don't be distressed," says Roberto. "It's only seaweed."

"But I want everything to be perfect for my Roberto when he comes."

It's nearly noon. He slept late, and then awoke with a temple-pounding headache. He had just enough time to take some aspirin and make coffee when Caroline Skyped him.

"So when *are* you coming?" she says. "You don't want to wait till the last minute."

"I'm not waiting till the last minute. I still have eight days."

"Why do you trust these people? They might be out on the street right now waiting for you. They might kill you as soon as you step outside."

"It doesn't make sense for them to give me an ultimatum to leave in ten days and then to kill me before that. It's easier for them if I just leave. Then they don't have to go to the trouble of planning an operation, it could always go wrong and there might be witnesses. And I'm a fairly well-known journalist and there would be an investigation and so forth. They'd just rather not deal with that. I'm not worried."

"Well, as long as you're there and not here, I'm going to be worried."

Caroline loves to sleep late and she just got out of bed too. Her beauty's a little blurred around the edges. She is makeupless and her hair is in disarray. She's wearing a torn yellow soccer jersey she's had forever and likes to sleep in. Looking at her, Roberto wishes he was there so he could take her right back to bed.

"You look like hell," she says. "How much did you and Daniel drink?"

"Too much."

"You always drink too much when you go out with him."

Caroline is fond of Franz. Adores Andrés. Disapproves of Daniel.

"There's nothing wrong with a few drinks sometimes," Roberto says. "And who knows when I'm going to see him again?"

"Maybe it's not such a bad thing that you don't see him. I know you love him, Roberto, but—he's such a mess. So self-destructive. And he wants to drag everybody else down with him."

"That's a little harsh." But, he thinks, only a little.

Señor, Caroline's fat gray tabby cat, jumps up on her desk. She starts to stroke him.

"You didn't answer my question," she says.

"What question?"

"When are you coming?"

"In a few days. I still have a lot to do."

"Like what?"

"I have a lot of stuff to pack up. My books and clothes, plus you left a lot of your clothes and things here."

"Oh, you can throw them all out the window for all I care, I just want *you*."

"Okay, I'll do that. And I have to do something with my car. I have to draw up some kind of rental agreement for Iván to sign. And there are some people I want to say good-bye to."

"Old girlfriends?"

He takes a sip of his coffee, and nods. "Yes, there's quite a few of them. They'd all be heartbroken if I didn't say good-bye to each one personally."

Caroline addresses her cat. "Did you hear that, Señor? Roberto is so wicked. The devil is coming to Saint Lucia!" And then she turns back to him. "Wednesday is a few days. Why don't you make plans to come Wednesday?"

He thinks about it. "Okay. That should work."

Her face lights up. "Really?"

"Yes."

She smiles. Radiantly. "Wednesday!"

* * *

He takes a shower and feels a bit better, and he refills his coffee cup and returns to his computer. There's an email from Clara reminding him about dinner at his father's tonight. *We'll have a fascinating mix of people. Pombo will be there, have you ever met Pombo?* He has. He's the most famous painter in the country. He's always referred to just by his last name, like Picasso. The one thing about his paintings that everyone knows is that the people in them are all enormously fat. *I know you're not crazy about this sort of thing, Roberto, but don't back out! I'm sure we're all going to have a wonderful time.* Maybe not so wonderful, he thinks, after he tells his father he's leaving the country under the threat of death. *As usual, I can't decide what to wear. I've been moving in and out of my closets at a feverish pace, dressing and undressing, dressing and undressing.* And so Clara, who never does anything by accident, ends her email with the image of herself undressing.

He takes a look at the news. A hospital in the coastal city of Puerto Alegra has had to be closed down because of an invasion of fruit flies. A labor leader trying to organize workers at an oil palm plantation in the province of Trujillo was gunned down by men in police uniforms. The local police deny involvement and say the killers weren't really police but were just dressed up as police. Raising the question, was the labor leader killed by killers dressed up as policemen or by policemen pretending to be killers pretending to be policemen? In Tulcán, an Army patrol was ambushed and seventeen soldiers were killed. President Dávila has issued a stern warning to the insurgents: "Violence is not the way. Demobilize, because as we have said many times, otherwise, you will end up in jail or in a grave."

He googles himself, checking activity over the last twenty-four hours. An article on the website of a right-wing group called the Journalistic Alliance for the Preservation of Patriotic Ideals comes up. "We are a democratic multi-party country that allows people to express their views in accordance with the related laws," writes the anonymous author. "But we do not need chaos that harms public security and abuses democracy."

Then Roberto is criticized by name for "semi-clandestine, subversive activities aimed at discrediting the organs of power."

All right. There it is. Right there in front of him. His death sentence being pronounced publicly in a semi-official way.

He wishes there was a number he could call to let them know that they don't need to try to frighten and harass him anymore. That he has got their message. That they have won.

He goes on the website he always uses to book flights and sees what they have to Saint Lucia on Wednesday.

* * *

He takes a walk up Avenue Six. He goes in a bakery and buys two pastries filled with guava jelly and a cup of lulo juice; when he has a hangover, his body always craves sweets. He resumes his walk, eating his pastries and drinking the juice. He gazes up at Mount Cabanacande and he thinks: My last Saturday in the city.

It is windy and the sun is shining. The shadows of clouds move over the face of the mountains and across the valley where seven million people live. There is a sameness to living here in terms of the weather and the daily ebb and flow of light. The city is near the equator so the days all year round are split about equally between day and night. And even though it's near the equator, because it's high in the mountains the weather isn't hot. Nor is it cold. All year round it is temperate and pleasant except for when it rains and even the rich don't have heat or air conditioning in their homes since it's simply not needed. To put such a fucked-up city here almost seems like a waste of good weather.

He reaches Flower Park. It's small, green, lovely, and filled with flowers. A guy and a girl are lying in the grass in the sun sleeping. The girl's head on the guy's leg. The girl holding a leash, at the end of which a dog, also asleep, is lying half in the sun and half in the shade of a tree. So peaceful, man, woman, and dog. This is the way things should be, he thinks. No need for all the violence and horror.

His cellphone rings.

"Hello?"

"Roberto?"

"Yes?"

"It's Diana Langenberg." The publisher of *The Hour*.

"Hello, Mrs. Langenberg," he says, a bit taken aback. She's always been a benign but distant boss, and he's not used to getting phone calls from her. "How are you?"

"A little unhappy, actually. Rubén told me that you're leaving."

"Yes, that's right."

"Is your mind made up?"

"Yes."

He hears her sigh. "What a shame. But I understand." And then she says, "Could you do me a favor?"

"Of course."

"Could you come by my house today? Say, around three? I won't keep you long. I have something I want to give you."

"I'll see you at three."

"Good-bye, Roberto."

"Good-bye."

He puts the phone away, wondering what Diana Langenberg could possibly want to give him. The dog lying in the grass suddenly lifts its head and looks at him, as if he's called to it. Then it flops its head back down and goes back to sleep.

* * *

He follows a winding road up into green hills and the neighborhood of Rosales. Once, it was where all the elite of the city lived, but now most of the rich have moved on to new neighborhoods to the north and west. Magnificent old homes are being pulled down everywhere you look and being replaced with high-rise condominiums. But a few of the old families remain, like the Langenbergs.

In 1898, Simon Langenberg, an adventurous young immigrant from Sweden, happened to acquire a tattered letter written by a priest named Ignacio. In it Father Ignacio wrote that "the mines of Pangoa are situated on the point of a ridge from which the Guapi and Matarca Rivers can be seen." When the Spanish conquered the country, they found the Indians in the region of Pangoa in possession of a great quantity of high-quality emeralds. The location of the emerald mines was a secret the Indians couldn't keep after the conquistadors began to torture and murder them. The Spaniards were beside themselves with joy when they reached the mines and saw emeralds everywhere just waiting to be plucked out of the earth as easily as apples out of a tree, but then the Indians counterattacked and slew them nearly to a man. Only three Spaniards escaped, including Father Ignacio. They managed to take with them just one emerald apiece.

In the ensuing centuries, uncounted questers journeyed into the remote cloud forests of the Central Cordillera in search of the lost mines. The only thing they found was failure; they were bitten by poisonous snakes or killed by Indians or they died of diseases or tumbled shrieking into deep ravines. The mines of Pangoa began to be regarded as legendary, nonexistent, a fairy tale luring fools to destruction. But then Simon Langenberg bought two mules, one to ride on and one to carry supplies, and late one afternoon, in the mountains and the mist, reached that point on the ridge described in the letter where the two rivers could be seen. A blue and yellow parrot squawked overhead at the precise moment he became one of the wealthiest men in the country as he bent down and picked up a shiny green stone. Shortly thereafter, Simon fell in love with and married a young woman named Emilia, who was reputed to be the most beautiful socialist in South America. Though Simon had little interest in anything beyond making money, Emilia persuaded him to start a progressive newspaper called *The Hour*. And they seem to have passed down socialist and capitalist genes in equal measure to their progeny all the way to the present.

The Langenberg house is surrounded by high stone walls. Roberto drives up to the gate and identifies himself to a security guard with a pistol on his hip. The gate swings open and Roberto passes through.

He's been here twice before, during his first two years at *The Hour*, at an annual Christmas party for the employees of the paper that has since been discontinued. The house was built by Simon and Emilia a few years after their marriage. It was inspired by houses they saw on a trip to France. It's a three-story stone mansion with a massive arched entryway. Its walls rise up as sheer and forbidding as cliffs. It seems much older than it actually is. Roberto can't imagine why Simon and Emilia would have spent so much time and money in constructing such a gloomy monument to their love.

As he gets out of his car a smiling young black man comes out of the house to greet him. He's sharply dressed in black pants and a shimmering purple silk shirt. It is Hermés, Diana Langenberg's assistant. He takes Roberto inside, brightly chitchatting all the way. "Did you see *The*

Singer this week?" he wants to know. That's a televised singing contest based on a British show that has taken the country by storm. His favorite is Sarita, a petite teenage pop singer, what a big voice for such a little girl but he doesn't think she's going to win because she's black and the judges are prejudiced against her. Hermés seems surprised when Roberto tells him he's never seen the show. He leads Roberto under slanting timbered ceilings, over old oak flooring, and past ponderous antique furniture into a book-lined study.

"She'll be with you very soon," says Hermés. "Can I get you anything before I go? Coffee? Tea?"

"No thank you."

"Anyway, please watch *The Singer*. You'll love it. And then vote for Sarita!"

"I will."

Hermés smiles, inclines his head, and leaves.

Roberto looks around. Floor-to-ceiling windows give out on a lush shady garden. The only furniture is a big cherry-wood desk with a high-backed leather chair behind it and across from it another chair that, somewhat incongruously, has a ukulele sitting in it. On the wall behind the desk is a large oil painting of a middle-aged man in a blue business suit. Fleshy lips and thinning brown hair. Smiling slightly, an amused look in his eyes. Roberto recognizes him as Axel Langenberg, Diana's grandfather, and the most famous Langenberg except for Simon. He left the emerald business and entered politics and almost became president. It was in the middle of the last century, during a period of civil war known as the Killing Time (the fact it is called that indicating the enormity of the violence, since all times in this country's history have been killing times). Although he was favored to win, his family and friends tried to persuade him to drop out of the race because they were concerned that the malignant mad energy loose in the land would destroy him before he could ever take office. He assured them that he was being tightly guarded and was taking every precaution and he would be fine. He was wrong and they were right. Axel was assassinated at a campaign event in a little town on the Santa Catalina River by a young gunman who quickly followed his victim into death when he was shot down by Axel's incompetent guards.

Roberto hears the door opening, and Diana Langenberg comes in. She seems even paler and less substantial than the last time he saw her.

She's wearing a long white dress that hangs limply off her bony shoulders and a single strand of pearls around her neck. She looks older than she is, like the house. She advances slowly into the room as Roberto quickly walks to meet her.

"Roberto," she says with a smile. "So glad you could come on such short notice."

"Good to see you, Mrs. Langenberg."

She extends her hand. Its fingers and knuckles are as gnarly as old roots. Roberto doesn't actually shake it but gives it the gentlest squeeze possible.

She goes behind her desk.

"Please sit down," she says.

"Whose is this?" Roberto asks, as he picks the ukulele up out of the chair.

She laughs. "Oh, that's Hermés's. His latest enthusiasm." She carefully lowers herself into the leather chair. "He saw some old movie where someone was playing the ukulele and immediately fell in love with it. He practices every day and has become quite good at it. He posts videos of himself on YouTube playing it and singing songs he's made up. He's actually developed a bit of a following. I expect him to put it down soon and then never pick it up again. That's Hermés."

"What's his story?" says Roberto. Habitually inquisitive.

"Two years ago I was in my car. We were stopped at a traffic light, and a ragged young man came up to the car selling oranges. My driver tried to shoo him away but he was very persistent. He had such a nice warm smile I told the driver to buy some oranges. He lowered his window, and the boy peered into the back seat at me and smiled and said, 'Hello, beautiful lady!' And then he insisted on giving me the oranges for free. There are millions of ragged boys like him in this country but for some reason something about him in particular touched me. I couldn't bear to drive away and leave him on the street, where so many lives are snuffed out so casually, for no reason at all. So I've tried to help him. Do you think I'm a fool?"

"No, of course not," and then he smiles. "He wants me to vote for Sarita."

She rolls her eyes. "Oh, he's so crazy about Sarita. Not in a romantic way. He's gay, if you haven't guessed. But I think he sees himself in her.

It gives him hope." She pulls open a drawer in her desk. "I think perhaps that's what I like in your stories. Despite the terrible things you write about, there's always a little bit of hope in them. An odd optimism. Like some bright bubble arising out of the dark water."

Diana takes something from the drawer, then holds it out to him across the desk in her crippled hand: a gold medal on a silver chain.

"A going-away gift."

He takes it from her. On it is the image of a robed, bearded man with what seem to be flames around his head.

"St. Jude Thaddeus," Diana says. "The patron saint of desperate cases. Of the last resort."

"Thank you, Mrs. Langenberg."

"It's supposed to have protective properties."

"Great, I could use that." He fastens the chain around his neck. "I can't tell you how much it's meant for me to work for *The Hour* for the last six years. It's been a privilege."

She smiles sadly at him. "My life, Roberto, as you know, has been somewhat . . . restricted . . . so I've tended to live vicariously through my reporters. And now you're all going away." She puts her hands on the desk top and pushes herself up. "Let's go for a walk."

He goes out into the garden with Mrs. Langenberg. A handsome black Alsatian is waiting by the door. He looks Roberto over suspiciously, and Roberto hears a barely audible growling.

"It's all right, Fredy," Diana says, rubbing his neck. "It's Roberto. He's a friend."

Roberto and Diana and Fredy move slowly through the spacious grounds. There are waterfalls and fishponds and tall trees. Roberto can't hear the sounds of the city, just the songs of birds. It is a world unto itself. Diana seldom leaves it. Her appearances at the offices of *The Hour* have become increasingly infrequent as her health has gotten worse. Last year a blood infection nearly killed her, and she spent weeks in a hospital recovering.

She was struck by a savage form of arthritis in her early twenties. When she was twenty-seven she met a tall attractive young man from an old and prominent family. She was taken aback but happy when he began paying a great deal of attention to her. They became a couple and went everywhere together. People told her to look out for him because he had the reputation of being a charming ne'er-do-well who had gambled away his legacy, but Diana ignored them, and when he proposed marriage she said yes. The story goes that after being married less than a year she found out that her father had paid the young man a small fortune to marry his invalid daughter. She had become pregnant, and she divorced her husband as soon as their son was born. His name was Carlo. She loved him more than everything else in life put together. Four years ago, when Carlo was eighteen, he hopped on his motorcycle with his girlfriend and rode up into the mountains where on a tight curve they met a lumber truck and were obliterated.

"What does your family think of your leaving?" Diana asks.

"I haven't told them yet. I'm seeing my father tonight. I think he'll have mixed feelings. He'll be sorry to see me go, but glad that I'll be safe."

Fredy looks up at him with seeming interest as he talks. He has the most human-looking eyes Roberto's ever seen in a dog. As if he were some prince who had run afoul of a witch and was the victim of enchantment.

"I just hope you don't leave journalism," Diana says. "The fact that someone wants to kill you for doing your job should make you realize how important that job is."

"I know I'll always write, but my fiancée, Caroline . . . she wants me to write about different things. Not wars and crimes and massacres. She wants to have children and a settled kind of a life, and she doesn't want me to have a job where I'm always going away."

"How do you feel about that?"

He laughs a little. "I guess it seems kind of boring. But . . . I don't know . . . maybe you only have a certain amount of luck, and then it runs out. I know I've had a lot of close calls."

Diana smiles. "But that's why I gave you the St. Jude's medal."

The sunlight finds the silver in her blonde hair, and then they pass into the shaggy shade of a cypress tree.

"Do you really believe a piece of metal can protect you?" says Roberto.

"I'm not sure what I believe. I would say the evidence for some sort of spiritual or supernatural dimension to life is . . . ambiguous. When I was a little girl I had a brown and white dwarf rabbit named Poco. One night I woke up screaming and crying because I had dreamed Poco was eaten by a wolf. The very next day one of our dogs killed Poco. Certainly not proof of anything, but I would call it interesting. But the night before my son

Carlo died, did I have any warning in my dreams? No, not a thing. So was I warned about my rabbit and not my son?"

"To me the answer is easy. No, you weren't warned about the rabbit. It was just a coincidence."

"Yes," she sighs, "I suppose you're right. But one so wants to believe in something . . . something beyond *this* . . . this brutal, heartless world."

"I think the world is brutal but it's not heartless. There are plenty of people with huge hearts. You're an example of that."

"Thank you, Roberto."

She looks tired. Though it's not hot, there's a film of sweat across her forehead.

"Would you like to sit down?" says Roberto.

"Perhaps I'd better."

He sits down with her on a stone bench by a fishpond. Fredy sits down on his haunches beside her. The three of them eye the fat goldfish in the crystalline water.

"Have you ever wondered what it would be like to be a fish?" Diana says. "It seems like such a simple, serene existence."

Roberto feels sorry for Mrs. Langenberg. Born into a life of wealth and privilege, and yet she wants to be a fish. Her two closest companions apparently her paid assistant and her dog.

Roberto hears off in the distance a ukulele being strummed, and he and Diana glance at each other and smile.

"Ukuleles are very cheerful, don't you think?" she says.

"Maybe Hermés will be on *The Singer* someday."

"Oh, he would love that."

As suddenly as the ukulele began, it falls silent. A wind stirs the trees. Roberto notices the Alsatian is pondering him with his dark, deep eyes, as if struggling to remember what it was like to walk on two legs, to be a man.

* * *

Reluctantly Roberto puts on a coat and tie because Clara likes for people to dress up, and then he drives over to his father's apartment. The sidewalks are thronged with people, there is such drunkenness and revelry that a visitor to the city might think he had arrived on the date of some wild holiday but Saturday nights are always like this. Despite the country's problems, it's the opposite of a dark and depressed place. Its people seem determined to be happy to the extent that that is possible, although sometimes their laughter sounds awfully close to screaming.

He took a long nap after he got back from Diana Langenberg's and is recovered from his hangover, but he does not feel a part of the festive night. He keeps seeing that red face staring at him out of the green sedan, keeps hearing that calm voice on the phone threatening him with death. He has in a sense up to now won every battle, just by virtue of still being here, still reporting. So it feels bad to leave. As much as he's looking forward to being with Caroline, the dry and dusty taste of defeat is in his mouth.

* * *

Pombo is holding forth.

"People come up to me and say, 'Pombo, what's up with you? When are you going to start painting pictures of the world the way it really is? You paint fat people flying kites and playing badminton, but there are hardly any fat people in this country, if you want to paint fat people go to the United States. Here the people are skinny and most of them are poor, and yet you paint pictures of fat people riding on little ponies, what is the matter with you, Pombo?' And you know what I say to those people in reply?"

Pombo looks around at the little group he's standing in, which includes Roberto. None of them know the answer.

"I say nothing!" Pombo says. "I stand mute. Dumbstruck! For they're right. The world is falling down around our ears, and the skinny people are dying in droves and running over cliffs like the lemmings while I paint pictures of fat people dancing the ballet and so forth. It's a compulsion for me to do so, that's all I can say. I either paint fat people doing frivolous things or I die, it's one or the other."

"I love the one of the family flying kites," says a tall thin woman with fat lips filled with collagen. "I think it's a masterpiece."

Pombo nods in agreement. "Yes, I like that one too. You know, they say we have no seasons but next month is the windy month, it's kite-flying season. Kites will be all over the city, there's something inspiring about seeing them floating over the slums. I'd say it seemed like a symbol of something if I believed in symbols."

"Why don't you believe in symbols, Pombo?" the fat-lipped woman says.

Pombo shrugs. "I'm a very literal man. Unfortunately, my imagination doesn't seem to work, except where fat people are concerned."

He's a small man with the round innocent face you see in all the people in his paintings. Standing next to him is his third or fourth wife, a young woman with a horsey face but a hot body. She's quite a bit taller than he is. "Oh Pombo, poor thing, no imagination," she says, pulling his head against her shoulder and kissing his bald spot. He sighs blissfully and bats his eyes as everyone laughs.

He is a clown. Roberto knows the whole self-important artist thing isn't real and is just a way for him to have fun. He grew up in the south part of the city in a cramped apartment in the back of the grocery store owned by his family. His first drawings were done on the coarse paper used to wrap cheap cuts of meat. Even when he was a kid, he's told Roberto, he liked to draw fat people. Maybe because of all the skinny people he saw coming into the store with barely enough money to buy food. He thinks it a kind of supreme joke that his whimsical paintings have made him famous and wealthy.

A waiter comes over bearing a silver platter of fried plantains stuffed with cheese. Roberto takes one and chews on it and looks across the living room of his father's penthouse apartment. His father and Clara are standing in front of the window that looks out on the roof garden and are talking to an American named Willie Rivera, who works at the American embassy.

"Your stepmother looks stunning tonight, Roberto," Pombo says.

"Yes," says Roberto, "she does."

"Oh Pombo," says his wife. "You're always ogling the girls."

Pombo is eating a stuffed plantain too; now he licks his fingers. "If I weren't always ogling the girls, I never would have noticed you to begin with, would I, my love?"

"That's true. But now that you have, I think the ogling should stop."

Pombo shakes his head. "Women, Roberto. Our blessing and our curse."

Roberto laughs.

"What are you working on now, Roberto?" says a voice at his side. "Anything interesting?"

He looks into the sad, drunken eyes of Ricardo Cárdenas. He's a prominent academic and activist, heartily hated by Landazábal and his crowd. Roberto hasn't had a chance yet to tell his father about his plans, so he gives Ricardo a vague reply, and then he says, "So I hear you resigned from the Human Rights Commission."

Ricardo nods. "There are four of us in the office. Last week when we arrived for work we found four dead cats with their throats cut lying in front of the door. I've seen a lot worse, but for some reason that was it for me. I've simply had enough. I'm weary, Roberto. I use the same old words that everyone uses and I don't get any better results than anyone else does. I believe that such a thing as a Human Rights Commission is ridiculous in this country. It is like the cows and the pigs in a slaughter-house getting together to form the Animal Rights Commission. From now on I'm going to be on the We Are Fucked Forever Commission and not worry about anything."

"Of course you don't mean that."

"But of course I do."

Ricardo takes a gloomy gulp of Roberto's father's fine scotch whiskey.

"I've been thinking about the San José de Ariporo massacre," he says.

Roberto's very familiar with it. He and Daniel went to San José de Ariporo the day after it happened. Daniel got a great picture of an old woman and her little granddaughter on their knees scrubbing the blood off the floor of a beauty shop.

"I spent several days there interviewing witnesses," Ricardo says. "I'm an aficionado of old colonial churches, and they have a small but very charming one there. One afternoon I went to the church and was taking pictures when the priest came up. He suggested I might want to go up in the bell tower. He said the bell was five centuries old and had been brought over from Spain. He said the church had been destroyed four times, twice by fire and twice by earthquake, but the bell had survived and would probably survive another five centuries. So I climbed up in the tower to take a look at the bell. It was a big bronze brute of a bell, it seemed too big for the little church, it was scorched and scuffed and gashed. Inside it was an engraving in Latin: *Vivos voco. Mortuos plango.* I call the living. I mourn the dead.

"I squatted by the bell and looked out over the town. It seemed very peaceful. I suppose most towns seem peaceful after half their population has been suddenly subtracted by death. And I remember wishing that I could just stay up here with the bell as it called the living and mourned the dead, century after century after century. I'm beginning to believe in God a little again, Roberto. Because I can no longer believe in man. I believe we are powerless to save ourselves from ourselves."

Some woman Roberto has never met comes over and starts talking in tedious detail about her vacation in Greece. He leaves her with Ricardo and drifts over to the bar to get another drink.

He seems to smell her and feel her heat before he actually hears or sees her.

"I'd like a drink, Roberto."

"Sure, what do you want?"

"What you have looks intriguing."

Roberto asks the bartender, a red-haired man lost in the contemplation of Clara's cleavage, to prepare another Gray Goose tonic.

Dressing and undressing, dressing and undressing, he remembers. She's wearing a clingy black dress with a low-cut top and a slit up the left leg. High black heels. An antique diamond and ruby necklace.

"Are you having a terrible time?" she asks. "Are you already bored to tears with all of us?"

"No, only with that woman talking to Ricardo."

Clara glances over at them. "I doubt that Ricardo finds her boring. He's having an affair with her."

"How do you always know who's sleeping with whom?"

"Just a sixth sense, I guess."

The bartender presents her with her drink. She lifts her glass. "What shall we drink to?"

"Your book."

She beams. "My book!"

He clinks glasses with Clara. Her book is called *Goodbye, Stork!* It's a kind of humorous handbook for young girls about the facts of life. It's her first book, and it's selling so well her publisher has given her a contract for another.

"Thanks for all you did," she says. "I won't forget it."

She asked him to read the first draft. He was expecting the worst but was relieved to find the writing bright and fresh and funny. He saw ways to improve it though, and gave her a lengthy list of suggestions; she assiduously followed every one of them.

"I didn't do much," he says, "but I was glad to help. So what's the next one going to be about?"

"Oh, I don't know. Probably something along the same lines. They say you should always repeat yourself if you want to be successful."

Clara, in her own dark brown-eyed way, is just about as beautiful as Caroline. She's only a little older than Roberto. She was a receptionist in his father's office. He surmises the affair began not long after she started working there, though a couple of years passed before his father asked his mother for a divorce. His mother was shocked (as was Roberto) because it was not the first affair his father had had and previously their marriage had weathered them all, but this time it was different; his father said he was in love with his receptionist and intended to be with her no matter what, so his mother took a sizeable chunk of his father's money and decamped for Spain. Initially Roberto saw Clara the way Caroline still does, as a wily seductress, a greedy beguiler, but four years into their marriage his view has changed. His father has always been a naturally happy man, but Roberto likes the way that Clara has clearly made him even happier. Roberto likes in fact just about everything about Clara. The one thing about her he doesn't like is how whenever he talks to her he begins to feel an (under the circumstances) inappropriate tingling in his dick.

"Come, Roberto," she says, suddenly grabbing his hand and pulling him away from the bar.

"Where are we going?"

"I want to show you something."

They move across the room. His father is still talking to Willie Rivera. He looks their way curiously.

"Clara," he calls, "where are you dragging Roberto off to?"

"I'm going to show him my anniversary present to you."

His father laughs, showing his shining even teeth (veneers, he's just spent a small fortune on them). "Oh, it's splendid, Roberto! Just splendid!"

Clara continues to hold on to Roberto's hand as if he's some small child that needs to be led around. They walk down a hallway till they reach his father's office. She opens the door and they go through.

"What do you think?" she says.

He looks around, a bit blankly. Clara's amused.

"Men are so oblivious. A bomb could go off and destroy a room and you still wouldn't notice anything different. Your father's desk and chair, Roberto! I totally redid them!"

"Oh, I see."

He looks at the semicircular desk and the swivel chair. They had been custom-made for his father's father, a very successful manufacturer of household appliances. When Roberto's grandfather died he left them to his son, who adored his father and had always cherished them.

"They were falling apart but of course your father never did anything about it," Clara says. "I re-veneered the desk in macassar ebony, don't worry, it's not one of your endangered rain forest trees. And the chair was just an accident waiting to happen! I gave it new springs, new wheels, a new turning mechanism." She walks around behind the desk. "And I replaced the old cracked leather with this velvet mohair fabric, come feel it, Roberto, it's soft as a dream!"

She bends down and rubs her hand over the seat of the chair. He goes behind the desk and does the same. Not that he much cares about things like velvet mohair fabric.

His face is close to Clara's. He glances up into her eyes. She is smiling. Flirting with him. As she always does.

"It's great," he says, as he straightens up and moves away. "The perfect gift."

Clara comes out from behind the desk too.

"He's actually very easy to get things for," she says. "He likes whatever anyone gives him."

"That's true, he's like that."

She leans back against the desk, crossing her legs at the ankles, which causes one Pilates-toned leg to emerge from the slit in her dress.

"So how is Caroline?"

"She's okay. She's sad, because of her mother. She doesn't think she'll live out the year."

"And she's close to her mother?"

"Yes, very."

"I envy that. My mother is such a bitch. I'd be happy to never see her again."

He's doing his best not to look at her leg.

"I guess we should be getting back," he says.

But Clara doesn't move.

"You haven't said one word about what I'm wearing." She puts on a petulant look. "It's always so hard to get a compliment out of you, it's like pulling teeth."

"You look amazing."

She smiles sweetly. "Why, thank you, Roberto."

"Clara—can I ask you a question?"

"Anything at all."

"Do you love him?"

"Yes, of course."

"Do you *really* love him? You know what I mean."

"I do love him. Yes."

She thinks about it.

"I know what people thought about me when we got married. And maybe they weren't entirely wrong. You see, I come from a different world than you. My father was a drunk who repaired shoes when he did anything at all. I was a girl who knew nothing and didn't have anything going for her except she maybe had the kind of legs men like to look twice at. So to attract the attention of a powerful, accomplished man like your father, it was overwhelming to me. Maybe I didn't really know who he was at the time, but maybe he didn't really know who I was either. But now we do know each other. I think I've been good for him, and as for me, I'm a totally different person now because of him. You know how your father is, he's like some invincible battleship, steaming through the ocean, nothing ever seems to bother him. And I used to never know where I was going, it was like a feather could knock me off my stride. Clemente has taught me to be calm and disciplined. Do you think the old Clara could have written a book and gotten it published? People from my neighborhood just didn't do things like that."

Roberto hears someone in the hallway, and then his father appears at the door.

"Magdalena wants you, darling," he says to Clara. "There's some kind of emergency in the kitchen."

"What now?" Clara sighs, and hurries out.

He walks into the room smiling at Roberto, he's nearly always smiling, invincible as a battleship, Clara is right about him, she really does have a way with words. He sinks down into his chair with an exaggerated sigh of contentment, swivels back and forth.

"She really outdid herself this time, Roberto."

Roberto touches the gleaming new surface of the desk. "One of my first memories is about this desk. You took me to Grandfather's factory, and I got scared because all the machinery was so big and loud, and I ran in Grandfather's office and hid under his desk. You had to give me candy to get me to come out."

His father has been nodding along and grinning and now he says delightedly, "I remember that too!"

He's a little shorter than Roberto, with broader shoulders but the same thick head of hair. Doesn't have Roberto's weak eyes. Dresses in elegant suits bought at the same store on a yearly trip to London.

Now is the time to tell him. It matters to Roberto what he thinks because there are just two people in the world whom he completely trusts: his grandmother and his father (he trusts his three best friends only up to a point, for there is something weak in Andrés, something selfish in Franz, something dark and unstable in Daniel. He trusts Caroline in all important things except his heart. He does not trust her never to break his heart).

"I have something to tell you," he says. "It's not good news, but maybe it's not so bad, either."

The smile fades from his father's face, and he becomes still and looks at Roberto.

"All right, Roberto."

"I'm leaving the country. In a few days. I'm going to Saint Lucia to be with Caroline. I don't know when I'll be coming back. It might be years."

"Why?"

"I think my life is in danger."

"There have been threats?"

"Yes."

"Be specific."

"I received a phone call on Thursday morning. I was told I'd be killed in ten days if I didn't leave the country. And then today there was an article on the website of this right-wing journalism group, and I was called a subversive. Do you remember Edgar Leonidas? I went to school with him."

"Yes, of course. I know his parents. The poor boy."

"A few days before he was killed, he was denounced on the same website. So I think the smart thing for me to do is go."

For a few moments his father engages himself in removing an invisible bit of lint from his trousers; when he looks back up at Roberto, he's surprised to see his father's eyes are filled with tears, for he cannot remember ever having seen him cry.

"It makes me so angry . . . the thought of these men harming you. A father is supposed to protect his child. But I can't do anything."

"You don't have to worry, they're not going to harm me. And the good thing about leaving is I'll be finding new things to write about. I keep reporting the same stories over and over, this country never changes, it's like a cat chasing its tail."

His father takes the carefully folded silk handkerchief out of his coat pocket, wipes his eyes, and dabs at his nose.

"Do you think I'm doing the right thing?" Roberto asks.

"I trust your instincts, Roberto. If you think it's time, it's time."

He stands up, and comes walking around the desk. The usual bounce in his step is absent.

"I don't suppose you've told your grandmother yet."

Roberto shakes his head. "I'm going to see her tomorrow."

"It will be hard on her. Her health is really too poor for her to travel anymore and . . ." He leaves the thought unsaid: that it is unlikely Roberto will ever see her again.

He's in front of Roberto now and he can't stand the crushed look in his father's eyes and he hates the men who have caused it. His father manages a smile and puts his hand on Roberto's shoulder.

"Let's both cheer up. Life goes on, right? Now let's go into dinner. Clara has worked all day on it, I'm sure it's going to be fantastic."

* * *

"It's delicious, Clara," says Tomás Valdivieso; he's a designer of women's clothing whose name is nearly as well known in the country as Pombo's. "Clemente says you made it yourself, according to some secret family recipe."

"Oh no, Magdalena did most of the work," Clara declares magnanimously. "I only helped out a little. And the only secret family recipe I know is for bootleg rum. My uncle used to put rusty nails in it to give it a nice reddish color."

Everyone laughs, Roberto's father loudest of all. Magdalena is the dour old cook who's been with the family since his father was a boy. And the dish under discussion is *ajiaco*, a chicken and potato soup with chunks of corn on the cob in it, served in black bowls nestled in straw baskets, with sides of rice, capers, avocado, and heavy cream.

The long table is covered with a Swiss linen tablecloth. The flames of tall white candles are reflected in innumerable wine and water glasses. A pair of small brown maids in prim uniforms move around and serve the twelve at table. Roberto's father and Clara sit at either end, while Roberto is in between Rolando, Valdivieso's companion, a handsome young telenovela star whose many female fans would be devastated if they knew he was gay, and the woman with the fat lips who liked Pombo's kite painting. Roberto knows there's a reason even if he doesn't know what it is that he's sitting here, because Clara works out everything about their dinner parties down to the smallest detail. They're held monthly, and he knows she has the ambition of creating a sort of salon where the most prominent and interesting people in the city come together to eat and drink and say witty provocative things to one another; she seems to be having a certain amount of success at it, judging by how coveted invitations to these dinners have become.

"Rolando," says Pombo's wife, "are you ever going to sleep with Eva?"

She's talking about *My Cousin Eva*, the telenovela Rolando's on.

"But it would be wrong to sleep with her," Rolando says coyly. "She's my cousin."

"You didn't answer my question."

"Give it up, Beatriz," Valdivieso says. "He won't even tell *me* what's going to happen next. He's sworn to secrecy. He'll be executed at sunrise or something if he talks about it."

"I haven't had the pleasure of seeing the show," Pombo says, "so I need to ask two questions. Is your character sympathetic?"

"Oh yes," Rolando says. "Very."

"And is Eva sympathetic?"

Rolando shrugs. "More or less."

"Then I would say it is absolutely inevitable that Rolando will sleep with Eva. It's what the audience wants. You cannot disappoint the audience."

"I agree," Clara says, who usually speaks only enough to keep the conversational ball rolling. "But how do we know that's what the audience wants? Is there some principle involved?"

"The principle," says Pombo, "is that we as a culture feel compelled to make up stories and then live vicariously in them. When Rolando fucks Eva, we will all be fucking Eva."

"Speak for yourself," says Valdivieso grumpily.

"Pombo," says his wife, "you better not fuck Eva vicariously or you'll find yourself sleeping on the couch!"

Everybody laughs. Clara looks pleased.

"I had a tremendous crush on my cousin when I was a boy," says the American, Willie Rivera. "Her name was Mary Beth. She was a year older than me. She lived in Dallas, and I lived in this dusty little town in south Texas. I thought she was the most gorgeous, sophisticated girl in the world."

"And how did Mary Beth feel about you?" asks Roberto's father.

"Oh, I was just her dumb little cousin with the big ears. It's been thirty years since I've seen her, but I still think about her from time to time."

"Ah, first loves," says Valdivieso. "They haunt us like ghosts."

"Tell me, Mr. Rivera," says Ricardo Cárdenas, "what do you Americans think of our new president?"

"Please call me Willie. He's been getting very good marks. I even heard the secretary of state say that he seemed like one of us."

"And he meant that as a compliment?"

Willie Rivera grins. "Oh yes. The highest."

The talk turns to politics but Roberto does not take part. He's always been more of a listener than a talker, a trait that has stood him in good stead as a reporter. But tonight he's not even listening much. He eats his soup and drinks his wine. One of the silent little maids fills up his empty glass. He glances over at his father and finds him looking somberly at him; now his father smiles and looks away.

The woman with the fat lips says something to Roberto that he doesn't quite hear.

"Pardon me?"

"Do you hear someone singing opera? I know it must seem like an odd question."

He listens for a moment. Hears nothing.

"No," he says. "Do you?"

"Yes. Very faintly." Her head is cocked to one side, she is staring off into space. "This has never happened before. I'm a bit concerned."

He's puzzled. "What exactly is it you're concerned about?"

"I know who it is that's singing."

"Who?"

"It's a spirit. He lives in my house. I usually hear him in the kitchen, when I'm cooking. But *this* has never happened. I've never heard him *outside* the house."

He looks at her. She doesn't seem drunk, on drugs, insane.

"Do you think he followed you here?"

"So it would seem."

"And you've never seen him? Just heard him?"

"Yes, that's right." She assumes a listening look again. "There . . . now . . . it stopped."

"I'm sorry, I never caught your name."

"Patricia."

"I'm Roberto."

"Yes, I know."

"How long have you been hearing this opera singer?"

"Since within a week of moving into the house. That was a year and a half ago. I told my doctor about it, he said tumors or epilepsy in the frontal lobe can cause auditory hallucinations, so I had my brain checked out, but it was fine. Maybe you can write a story about me and my ghost. It's a very old house, so there's no telling who used to live there. I've done some research, but I haven't run across any opera singers yet."

She slurps up some soup then dabs at her big lips with her napkin.

"I can tell you don't believe me, but don't feel bad. Nobody does."

"In this country, you govern with the military or not at all," Valdivieso is saying. From the front Valdivieso looks okay, but in profile he becomes remarkably ugly, with a long pointy nose and a sharp pointy chin. Now Roberto notices Clara observing him and Patricia with a slight frown. He realizes he's transgressed, because he knows that Clara likes to have one big general conversation at the table and not separate little ones. But now she smiles and forgives him.

* * *

After dinner he wanders out onto the roof garden. He moves past vine-covered trellises and a gushing fountain and flowers in small pots and small trees in big pots till he reaches the railing. It's eleven stories up. He's in the exclusive San Andrés neighborhood, which is on the lower slopes of Mount Cabanacande. Up at the top he sees the lights of the church, but in between it's mostly darkness; no construction is allowed in the area since it's been set aside as a nature preserve. The sky is dark too, covered up with clouds. Even on clear nights, the lights of the city make it impossible to see more than a few dim stars.

It's peaceful up here on the roof garden. He can hear a murmur of traffic but not much else. He reflects that the people in the north part of the city live in a lovely bubble. The troubles of the country seem abstract when discussed between bites of delectable food and sips of expensive wine. In the mellow candlelight, you can know intellectually but not feel the fact that you live in one of the most violent places on the planet.

Ten or so kilometers to the east, the blinking lights of a passenger plane descend toward the airport. Roberto will be there in a few days, going the other way.

Willie Rivera joins him at the railing.

"Oh man, I ate too much," he groans, patting his stomach. "And I've drunk too much too. How am I ever going to lose twenty pounds if I keep acting like this?"

"It's Saturday night, don't worry about it," says Roberto, and then he asks, "Where's Helen?" His wife.

"Home, with a cold. Sneezing her head off."

"Give her my regards."

"I will. She'll be sorry she missed you."

Roberto likes Willie Rivera. He's in his mid-forties, balding, paunchy. Nothing flashy about him except his watch: a black Concord, glittering with diamonds. He's been working out of the American embassy for the last five or six years. His boss is the assistant secretary of state for international narcotics and law enforcement affairs, but Roberto's not sure exactly what it is that Willie does. He knows he travels around the country a lot. He's been a secret source for Roberto on several stories. He's the guy he goes to when he needs to get past the bland blather of politicians and find out what the Americans really think. Obviously, he doesn't tell

Roberto everything he knows, but everything he has ever told him has turned out to be true.

He met Willie through his father, and his father met him through his practice. Willie's wife developed a heart condition that required emergency surgery; his father performed it, and Willie credits him with saving her life. When Helen had to go back to America for further treatment, she was terrified that something would happen to her heart during the flight, that she'd be stuck up there at the top of the sky with no one to help her. So his father sat beside her on the plane to Houston, literally holding her hand the whole way, and since then, Willie has not been able to do enough for him. And Roberto knows Willie helping Roberto falls under the category of Willie helping his father.

Willie takes a drink of his scotch on the rocks as they ponder the lights of the sprawling city.

"I'm glad you were here tonight," he says. "There was something I wanted to talk to you about. Not the kind of thing you can talk about on the phone."

Roberto looks at him. Knowing he's about to get something good.

"Okay, Willie. What's up?"

"I was up in Tulcán last week. I wanted to see how the NTS was going."

The NTS is the Northern Transversal Strip, which is a road being built through the jungle that will connect Tulcán to the coast and open it up for "development." It's a massive undertaking being backed by loans from the World Bank. It's a very popular project among the political and business elites of the country. Not so popular in Tulcán.

"And how is it going?" says Roberto.

"It's way behind schedule. Some of the locals are making a nuisance of themselves: planting bombs, assassinating workers, and so on. In the long run, it's not going to matter. The NTS is a done deal. But I ran across something while I was up there."

He falls silent as if he's finished, absently shaking the ice in his glass and making it rattle. Roberto hears a high-pitched giggle and sees Valdivieso standing near the fountain with Rolando. They're both smoking cigarettes. Rolando is talking and gesturing and now Valdivieso giggles again.

"Have you ever heard of the Sri Lanka option?" Willie says finally.

Roberto knows Sri Lanka is the island nation in south Asia that was formerly called Ceylon. He knows there was an insurgent group called the Tamil Tigers that recruited pretty young women as suicide bombers but eventually, the Tigers were crushed by the government. And that is all he knows.

He shakes his head. "What is it?"

"Go home. Google it. And if it piques your interest, we'll talk some more. But let me tell you this, there's a big story up there in Tulcán. It's ripe as an apple, and it's just waiting for some enterprising young journalist to go up there and grab it."

"Thanks for the tip, Willie. But I don't think I'm your guy."

"Why not?"

He listens quietly as Roberto tells him. Drains the rest of his drink.

"That sucks," he says, in English, after Roberto's finished. "Does your father know?"

"Yes, I told him right before dinner."

"I guess that's why he looked like he was about to throw up," and then he sighs. "Poor Clemente. You should hear the way he talks about you. I've never seen a man so proud of his son."

"Yes, I know, I feel terrible—"

He hears a brisk clicking and turns and sees Clara walking toward him over the roof on her high heels, her leg flashing in the slit in her dress.

"Roberto, your father just told me, is it true? Are you really leaving?"

She has tears in her eyes, she seems more angry than sad. Before he can say anything more than "Yes," she reaches out and grabs his forearm.

"But this isn't fair, we need you here."

"I know, but—"

"Why didn't you tell me?"

"I was going to tell you, I just haven't had the chance—"

"Clara," says Willie, "give Roberto a break. This can't be easy for him."

"This is unacceptable, we're just not going to let you go," she says. Still grasping Roberto's arm hard as if she means exactly what she says and she is going to keep him here on the roof for as long as necessary.

* * *

When he returns to his apartment a little after one, he finds a black funeral wreath on his door. He pulls out of a small white envelope a note card on which is written neatly: *You have seven days, Roberto.*

Seven days until the day Roberto is to die

I'm counting the days, Caroline says in her email. *Seeing you on Skype is nice but the thought of hugging and kissing the real flesh and blood you again makes me dizzy with happiness. You know the little guest bedroom on the second floor? Well I will be working furiously between now and Wednesday to turn it into your office, I want you to walk in and have your breath taken away because it's so beautiful and perfect, I know just the desk I want, a Victorian walnut desk from the mid-nineteenth century, it's in a store on the island, I've been eying it for a while, it will sit in front of the window and what will you see when you look out? Ocean and sky my love and sky and ocean going on and on, so your thoughts can go on and on with nothing to limit them as you sit at your desk and write.* Moving without transition from the romantic to the practical, Caroline says she has prepared and attached a lease agreement for Roberto's apartment and all it needs is Iván's signature.

It's Sunday morning, and he hears a church bell off in the distance. Calling the living. The view from his window is gray, drizzly, melancholy. The tops of the mountains are obscured by clouds. He sits at his computer in his blue tracksuit and he thinks: *What next?* He's got plenty to do to get ready to go. Pack his clothes and all of Caroline's stuff, box up his books and papers, throw things away. But he just sits there, gazing out on the sad gray day.

His mind drifts back to last night. To Willie Rivera on the roof garden, talking about Tulcán. Should he go ahead and google the Sri Lanka option? No point really. He wouldn't have the time to do anything with it before he left. And if it's really as big a story as Willie thinks it is, it will just make him feel bad that he's missing out on it.

He takes a drink of his coffee—and then he types "sri lanka option" into the Google search box.

Sri Lanka was riven for a quarter of a century by a savage civil war between the majority Buddhist Sinhalese, who controlled the government, and the Hindu Tamils, who sought to establish their own state in the northern and eastern parts of the country. The Tamil Tigers, as the rebel army was known, waged ruthless guerrilla warfare and sent suicide bombers to the Sinhalese. The Sinhalese launched an offensive in 2006, aimed at ending the insurgency once and for all. The Sri Lankan army rampaged through the Tamils' lands, murdering and raping, burning and torturing. They made no distinction between the rebels and civilians, who died by the tens of thousands. Humanitarian workers and journalists were expelled by the army, who wanted no witnesses. When word of the atrocities leaked out, the army simply denied it, saying that any atrocities had been committed by the Tigers, and all they were doing was trying to save the country from Tamil terrorists. The war came to an apocalyptic conclusion in 2009 when the surviving Tigers along with three hundred thousand civilians were trapped between the army and the sea on a narrow strip of beach on the north coast of the island. The army pummeled them for days with artillery and air strikes, the beach was an inferno of smoke and explosions and mangled corpses littered the beach and the heads and limbs of children flew through the air. The people desperately dug holes in the sand and tried to hide and then the army moved in and threw grenades in the holes. The bodies of forty thousand civilians were buried in graves scooped out by bulldozers or burned in bonfires, while the dazed survivors were rounded up and put into detention camps. The Tamil leaders who hadn't already died were killed along with their families when they tried to surrender. The United Nations made disapproving clucking noises about what had transpired, but the government blithely ignored them and got away completely with their ghastly acts.

Militaries around the world have become intrigued with what has come to be known as the Sri Lanka option. That means solving the problems of insurgency not politically but militarily, isolating the insurgents and the civilian population so you can do to them what you will with no pesky reporters or human rights workers around to object, and basically telling the international community that if it doesn't like what's going on it can go fuck itself.

Roberto lifts his eyes from the computer screen to the wet Sunday morning outside the window, and he thinks about it. It's clear to him what Willie's big story must be: the Army is preparing, if it hasn't already begun, to implement the Sri Lanka option in Tulcán.

* * *

He's driving to his grandmother's. She lives in Montería, the old colonial district north of downtown. He's having to take a somewhat circuitous route since on Sundays many of the main thoroughfares are closed to cars and open only to bicycles—this in an effort to cut down on the insane traffic and the choking pollution. He feels as if he's being watched and followed but this is nothing new and he sees no sign of any followers or watchers.

On the radio he hears that the superintendent of industry and commerce has ordered the company that makes the beauty product Revertrex to remove the claim that it's "the secret and source of eternal youth" from its advertising. "They're suggesting their customers will live forever," says the superintendent, "which is clearly untrue." Supermodel Alexa Cediel, the spokeswoman for the product, indignantly defends herself, saying "I never said it will make you live forever, just that it has helped me to look young. And I can assure you that yes, it has helped me."

Tulcán. He knew something was cooking there. In recent weeks in the press there have been numerous pronouncements from high government and military officials about the rising terrorist threat in Tulcán. They've been selling a message in the same relentless way that Alexa Cediel has been selling Revertrex. General Horacio Oropeza, the commanding general of the armed forces, went to Tulcán last week to "assess" the situation. Oropeza, who grew up very poor in the countryside, is fond of homely metaphors involving animals, and he's been issuing rather menacing statements like "Kill the dog, you kill the rabies" and "A cat with gloves on doesn't catch any rats." But in case anyone is concerned that the Army will be overly zealous in pursuing the insurgents, Oropeza had this to say: "We are training our soldiers to be strict observers of international humanitarian law. We will never use more force than the circumstances dictate. The size of the stone you throw depends on the size of the toad."

Roberto's wondering what he should do with the information Willie has given him. It's about the future of many people, it's about massacres and mass graves and he cannot simply sit on it. Maybe Willie would be willing to supply him with more details and when he gets to Saint Lucia, he can write up something and put it on some left-leaning website. Though he realizes a story without any first-hand reporting to back it up will probably have as little effect on what happens as shooting a water pistol at a house that's on fire. But he does have a certain reputation for accuracy, and maybe some other reporter will be encouraged to undertake the perilous journey into Tulcán.

He's stopped at a traffic light. A gusty wind has come up, and a newspaper is rolling over and over across the intersection. A beggar is approaching—a woman limping along on a crutch with a foot sticking out exactly sideways. A light rain speckles the windshield, is removed by the wipers, speckles the windshield, is removed by the wipers . . .

* * *

He finds a parking spot on a crooked side street and walks through the rain toward his grandmother's apartment. Mount Cabanacande looms above him in the clouds and mist; Montería is built on its foothills. Steep cobblestone streets descend in a rolling way till the topography flattens out at Liberty Plaza and the tall buildings of downtown arise.

The capital city was born in this neighborhood 450 years ago, when a band of vicious Spanish adventurers arrived and burned down the Indian village they found here and killed all of its inhabitants that they could lay their hands on and pursued the survivors up the face of Mount Cabanacande, tracking them with large hunting dogs, until they were all killed too. For three centuries this is where the elite of the city lived and most of the houses they built still remain, painted brightly in yellow and orange and green and blue with ochre and turquoise balconies and terracotta roofs. Montería has become a favorite of artists and writers and other bohemian types. There are galleries and museums on every block, including the very popular Pombo Museum, which Roberto is now walking past. Pombo bought the building and donated it to the city along with many of his best-known paintings, as well as works from his private collection by Monet, Matisse, Picasso, and Dali. As if drawn there by some mysterious affinity, a cluster of fat gringo tourists stand in front of the museum, consulting a guidebook.

Roberto hears the raucous cries of birds above him, looks up and sees some large birds with greenish plumage hopping along a rooftop. He doesn't know what kind of birds they are, he's not very good about knowing the names of his country's flora and fauna. They're moving along at the same speed he's walking, and it's as though they're intentionally keeping pace with him. A chilling memory is called up. He and Daniel had traveled to a miserable little town by a brown, sluggish river. A wealthy landowner in the area had begun to grow japtropha, a plant used for biofuel, and Roberto was there to investigate reports that workers on his plantation were being brutalized and kept virtually as prisoners. It was a Sunday, like today. It was hot and humid. Daniel has always been a big sweater, and sweat was pouring off him, and he cursed as it trickled into his eye. They were walking down a street. The town seemed eerily empty. Something was wrong, they both felt it. Even the sunlight seemed sinister. A skeletal dog hobbled out of their way, rolling his brown bulging eyes at them in fear. And then Daniel nudged him with his elbow and said softly, "Look."

Daniel was looking up, and Roberto's gaze followed his. Armed men in black masks were on the rooftops watching them . . . hopping from roof to roof as they followed them . . .

"Roberto?"

An elderly man with a neatly trimmed white beard is peering at him from under an umbrella. It's Professor Gaviria, one of his favorite teachers at the university. He hasn't seen him in years. Roberto smiles and stops and talks to him in the rain. As above him he hears the birds . . .

* * *

"Ismenia! Ismenia! Bring Roberto some *aguardiente!*"

"I don't really want any, Grandma."

"It's Sunday, and it's raining, and my grandson is going away," his grandmother says firmly. "We are going to drink aguardiente."

As it turned out, he didn't have to break the news to her. His father came by this morning and did it for him. Ismenia comes in from the kitchen with two cups of the clear liquor, made from sugarcane and flavored with anise. Roberto can't stand the stuff, but he's always getting stuck drinking it when he goes to his grandmother's.

He's sitting with her on an overstuffed purple sofa; Ismenia sets the cups down on the coffee table in front of them. She is a cheerful young black woman with a gold ring in her left nostril.

"When are you going to get rid of that hideous ring?" his grandmother says. "Why would you purposely mar such a pretty face?"

Ismenia giggles. "But it's the style, the boys like it."

"Oh, that's a good reason, the boys like it," grumbles his grandmother, and then she picks up her cup. "Let's drink to your safe journey, Roberto."

"And to your health, Grandma."

He clinks cups with her and then takes the smallest sip possible.

She's living on the second floor of a two-hundred-year-old house that's been divided into apartments. When his grandfather died seven years ago, she sold their house and moved here. She had lived in the Montería district when she was young, and she says this is where she wants to finish out her life.

She is thin and frail. She has sparse white hair cut in a boyish way. She's wearing a light-blue blouse and white pants and shoes covered with flowers and butterflies. But despite the shoes, she is not at all sentimental, and is one of the strongest people he's ever met. Still faintly visible in the wrinkles of her face is a long scar running diagonally across her forehead. It's a souvenir of the massacre that took place on the steps of the National Cathedral during the Killing Time. She and dozens of other students were chanting socialist slogans and shaking their fists in the air when the Army opened fire. Students were screaming and falling and many were crawling across the steps trying to find cover behind the stone columns of the cathedral as bullets hit around them and chips from the marble steps flew through the air, but his grandmother ran. She ran as fast as she could and leapt over the bodies of her friends and she felt bullets plucking at her clothes but somehow none touched her. She ran off the steps and ducked down behind a food vendor's cart; she could smell the meat cooking on the grill, but the vendor himself had wisely taken off. She stayed crouched there and listened to the gunfire and the moans of the wounded, and then she saw the green pants of a soldier tucked into his shiny black boots. She looked up. He was looking down at her. Young. Surprised-looking. And then he pointed his rifle at her head. She had time only to suck her breath in sharply then he pulled the trigger. But nothing happened, either he was out of ammunition or the rifle had jammed. But her reprieve was brief as he turned the gun around and cracked her in the forehead with the butt.

All became silent . . . she was drifting down an endless river in an eternal dusk . . . the water was warm and she couldn't feel her body . . . she was staring at a single star low in the sky . . . and then she woke up. To pain in her head, to a rumbling, rolling motion, to the smells of piss and shit and blood, to a smothering and a crushing, and to a blackness she thought was blindness. She struggled upward for air, pushing her way through what were unmistakably human beings. And then she could breathe again. And then she clawed at her eyes and she could see again; the soldier's rifle butt had split her forehead open and her eyes had been covered with blood.

She was in the back of a van moving down a street. By mistake she had been put in with the dead. The corpses were both male and female. In the tangle of bloody limbs it was hard to tell how many there were. Maybe twelve or fourteen. Her friend Nora was lying facedown, but she recognized her by her dress—white with big black polka dots, which everyone had been teasing her about a few hours before. Nora had never had any sense of fashion. She saw her friend Rafael in a corner of the van. His upper body and his head were propped up by other bodies. One eye was open and appeared to be looking at her; the other was a gruesome empty hole. He was not a handsome guy, he had a scrawny body and a narrow, beakish face, but that didn't stop the girls from liking him. He was always joking and he would make them laugh until they slept with him. Not her though. She had not yet slept with anybody. She was a budding revolutionary, but she was also still a good Catholic girl.

Wondering if it was all just a nightmare, she began to scream. She screamed until she screamed the van to a stop. She heard the door at the end of the van opening and then she saw the civilian driver and a soldier peering in. They were clearly spooked by the sight of a live girl covered with blood and screaming her head off in the middle of all the dead bodies.

His grandmother was lucky. She did not disappear into the twisting dark bowels of the state's security apparatus never to be heard from again. Her father's brother, it so happened, was a prominent member of the government, the deputy minister of finance. He interceded for his wayward niece, and after a few days, and the payment of an enormous bribe to the head of the Army, the notorious General Hurtado, she was released—on condition that she leave the country.

She went to New York. She enrolled at Columbia University and began working on a graduate degree in sociology. She never intended not to return. She also never intended to give up trying to make her country a better place for its people. But how could she do both? At least without winding up once more in a pile of corpses?

The Killing Time ended and was replaced with just another killing time. She got her PhD and then came home. She looked around for something to do. Not something that would shake the world but that would just make it slightly better. She befriended a twelve-year-old girl and her eight-year-old brother she found living on the street near her apartment. The girl was prostituting herself to take care of her brother. She would take men to what was called Carton City, which was a weedy vacant lot where prostitutes had sex with their clients on flattened cardboard boxes. His grandmother got them off the streets and into a Catholic orphanage, but now that she was aware of them she started seeing homeless children everywhere and what could be done about *them*?

She realized she needed to create her own institution for homeless children and set about looking for a location for it. Every place she saw was too small, too costly, too this or that, but then a friend told her about an abandoned military base not too far outside the city that might be suitable. She drove out to take a look. It had once been the headquarters for the Army's cavalry unit, but there wasn't much use in modern warfare for men armed with swords who would jump on their horses and charge the enemy. There were office buildings and stables and barracks, set amid many hectares of beautiful countryside. A sparkling steam ran through it all and his grandmother looked at it and imagined children swimming in it and knew she had to have this place.

She found out the Army still owned it. Rather than try to navigate the labyrinth of military bureaucracy in an attempt to find someone who could say yes or no, she thought it best to start at the top.

For her meeting with General Hurtado, she put on her sleekest skirt, her sheerest nylons; she had heard Hurtado had an eye for the ladies. It was unpleasant to make herself alluring to the man whose men had murdered her friends, but she had decided that nothing mattered except the ultimate goal. If Nora and Rafael could give up their lives, she could certainly give up such a petty thing as her pride.

His grandmother had brought her connections to bear in getting the meeting, and the general, perhaps resenting that, received her coolly. He was a small man with oily dark hair; his eyes never left her face as he listened in stony silence to her enthusiastically outlining her plans. She told him she knew he had a big family and asked him how he would feel if one of his little grandsons somehow wound up on the street, would he not move heaven and earth to help him? And discreetly leaving unmentioned all the atrocities the Army had been accused of committing during the Killing Time, she said what better way to get good publicity than to turn some dilapidated old Army buildings into a bright little paradise filled with laughing innocent kids?

When she was done, General Hurtado maintained his silence; then she saw his gaze shift just a little, from her eyes to her forehead, and the scar that ran across it. He asked her if she was still a Marxist.

She said no, and she didn't think she ever had been really, she had just been naïve and confused, it was a long time ago. A few years could seem like a long time only to someone very young, the general replied. She told him to think back to when he was very young, a man such as himself must have been filled with a nearly uncontrollable vigor and energy that occasionally got him into a lot of trouble. This caused the general to smile a little, and then she noticed him glance at her legs and she knew she had him.

So she had secured her location, but she still needed to raise a great deal of money to bring her plans to fruition. She began to make the rounds of the city's rich, and this is what led indirectly to Roberto's own existence. She showed up for a meeting with a wealthy manufacturer, but he was very busy that morning and passed her along to his son, who had just recently begun to work in the business. He was a nice-looking but rather shy young man with a bit of a stutter. He and Roberto's grandmother swiftly fell in love, and in the course of time, he became Roberto's grandfather.

His grandmother ran the Carlota Home for Needy Children (as it was called—named after General Hurtado's late beloved mother) for over forty years, until she retired. It helped thousands of children and is still the foremost institution of its kind in the country.

His grandmother complains she is cold, and Ismenia comes swooping in with a black mantilla that she drapes over her shoulders. His grandmother looks critically at her nose ring, as if it's the first time she's ever seen it.

"Why don't you get rid of that thing?" she says. "You look like an Indian in the jungle!"

Ismenia laughs and looks at Roberto. "She tells me to get rid of it twenty times a day!"

"Grandma, leave Ismenia alone."

"But do *you* think it looks good?" his grandmother says.

"Yes, I do, but that's not the point. It's what Ismenia thinks that counts."

His grandmother snorts and shakes her head, dismissing the matter for the moment.

Last year, she had ovarian cancer. She was operated on and received chemotherapy. She responded well to the treatments, but Roberto's father has told him that the prognosis is not good, that he expects the cancer to come back and kill her. Roberto will be very sad when that happens. She's the person whose approval means the most to him. More so even than his father's, because from the time he was a child, she has seemed to understand in some uncanny way everything about him. She's told him she knows he won't believe her but she's convinced there's some deep soul-to-soul connection between them, a connection that probably predates the birth of either of them. She's right, he doesn't believe her, but he has come here today hoping to hear she approves of his leaving the country. After all, when she was young, she did the same thing and for the same reason.

She drinks some more aguardiente, then clutches the mantilla more closely around her.

"Are you still cold, Grandma?"

"No. Are you?"

"I wasn't cold to begin with."

She looks vaguely out the window at a rooftop glistening with rain.

"The country was so much colder when I was young. All the snow is melting off the high mountains."

Ismenia brings in a plate of bread and hard cheese to go with the odious aguardiente.

"It was just on the TV," she says excitedly in her high-pitched childish voice, "Mario Garro is running for mayor!"

There will be a special election soon to replace the city's recently disgraced and jailed mayor. Mario Garro is the star anchorman of the country's number one TV station. He's long been hinting he has political ambitions; Gloria Varela recently wrote a column about it. He has a deep voice that is sweet to the ear and a big, handsome head that has never had an original thought in it.

"Are you going to vote for him?" asks Roberto.

Ismenia giggles and says, "Why not?"

"What about you, Grandma? Are you going to vote for Mario Garro?"

She looks blank.

"You know, the guy on TV? He's running for mayor."

She frowns and shakes her head. "Voting. It's always like choosing between the plague and cholera."

He laughs. Before she leaves Ismenia bends down and whispers in his ear, "Get her to eat something, she won't eat."

He eats some cheese and bread.

"Mm, this is delicious. You should have some, Grandma."

"No thank you, darling, I'm not hungry."

"I'm going to miss you."

"Why? Am I going someplace?"

"No, Grandma, I am. I'm going to Saint Lucia. We just talked about it."

"Oh, yes. To see that girl. What's her name?"

"Caroline. But I'm not going just to see her. I have to leave the country. Because they've threatened to kill me. Remember?"

"Of course I remember," she says peevishly, "I'm not stupid."

He takes his glasses off, and begins to clean them with a napkin. He's noticed she's been having problems with her memory ever since the operation, but it's never been this bad before.

"Whose hands are those?"

He looks up. She's staring at his hands as he cleans his glasses.

"They're my hands, Grandma. Who else's would they be?"

"But they don't look like Clemente's hands."

"I'm not Clemente. I'm Roberto. Your grandson."

She looks at him thoughtfully, and nods, as if they've been having a serious discussion and he's just made an excellent point. And then she sighs.

"Poor Ismenia," she says.

"Why poor Ismenia?"

"She's losing her mind. She doesn't know where she is, or what to do."

* * *

The rain has stopped. He leaves his car where it's parked and walks down San Francisco Street to Liberty Plaza.

It's only two blocks from the offices of *The Hour*. He would often come here to sit on a bench and eat lunch, or just to watch the people and the pigeons and think about things. Four large imposing buildings face in on the plaza: the Capitol Building, where Congress meets to run the country for the benefit of the rich and ruthless, the Ministry of Justice, which is the seat of the Supreme Court and where a generation ago most of the justices died fiery terrible deaths during a guerrilla attack, the Municipal Building, which houses the mayor's office (temporarily minus its mayor), and the National Cathedral, where his grandmother was almost murdered. In the middle of the plaza is a large bronze statue of a cavalryman on his horse. The cavalryman is holding a flapping flag, and the horse is frozen in mid-leap. This is Colonel Cordoba, the country's national hero. Every schoolboy can tell you how, in 1883, Colonel Cordoba rode himself and his horse off a cliff to their deaths to keep the country's flag from falling into the hands of an invading army. It's a thrilling statue. Cordoba is bent low over his horse's back, his eyes fixed on the valiant void in front of him, while the horse seems just as eager for self-sacrifice and glory as its rider. Colonel Cordoba seems to be the perfect hero for Roberto's doomed, crazy country.

He walks slowly across the plaza, thinking about his grandmother. The world is slipping from her grasp, just as she is slipping from the grasp of those around her. How can you say a proper good-bye to someone who can't remember for more than a minute or two that you're going? He hopes if he ever gets to such a point, someone will take pity on him and put a bullet in his head.

Puddles of rain on the plaza reflect the gray, uneasy sky. He remembers as a child looking down into puddles and imagining jumping in and falling into the sky forever.

A group of soldiers stroll by, casually carrying Israeli assault rifles. One sees soldiers everywhere, it's like living in an occupied country, but people don't even notice them, they're part of the scenery.

A middle-aged couple sit on a bench. The woman is feeding popcorn to the pigeons. The man is reading a tabloid called *The Pulse*. On the front page is a picture of a TV star whose breasts are barely contained in a tight top under the headline: "VALENTINA: 'I DON'T REGRET MY BOOB JOB!'" Further down the page is a picture of a worker killed in a grotesque accident at a building site, a piece of rebar sticking out of his neck. The man as he reads is digging vigorously into his right ear with his little finger.

A twelve- or thirteen-year-old boy walks up to Roberto with a squirming tiny puppy in his arms. He says that both he and the puppy are hungry and he asks Roberto for money so he can buy food. The puppy's probably a prop, to be discarded as soon as it's served its purpose, but he gives the kid some money anyway. He looks like he could use a good meal. He's wearing a grimy T-shirt that says, "THERE WILL BE A FUTURE!" Roberto recognizes it as the rather wistful campaign slogan for one of the major parties a couple of elections ago. T-shirts by the truckload are typically distributed by the various parties and candidates in the run-up to elections, and the mostly poor people of the country are happy to have them. They don't throw them away if they get stained or torn, they keep wearing them and wearing them and thus you see on the streets the faded ripped reminders of long-ago campaigns, with their vacuous slogans and grinning candidates who promised the people the world but delivered only more misery unless they were one of the honest few who were probably assassinated before anyone ever had a chance to vote for them.

He's walking back up San Francisco Street when his phone rings. The number looks familiar but he can't connect a name to it.

"Hello?"

"Roberto?"

"Yes?"

"This is Manuel."

The soldier who lost his leg and his eyesight in Tulcán.

"Hi, Manuel. How are you?"

"Not good. Something has happened."

"What's wrong?"

"Maybe it's best not to talk about it on the phone. Can you come to my house?"

* * *

His blue Kia bounces through potholes and splashes across puddles. He's worried about Manuel, his voice sounded terrible. Maybe something has gone wrong with his planned admission to the Center for the Courageous, maybe he's lost his spot. Or maybe something has happened to his mother and he's alone at the house with no one to help him. But why would he not want to talk about that on the phone?

Traffic gets jammed up and people start honking. Roberto's car is creeping along, and then he sees what the trouble is. One of those horse carts that he hates has been involved in an accident with one of those buses that he hates. The cart is lying on its side with its load of fresh fruits spilled brightly across the drab pavement. Its driver, who is wearing a cowboy hat and has a soggy olive-green blanket wrapped around him, is arguing with the bus driver, who is angrily pointing this way and that way; they seem to be on the verge of a physical fight. No one's paying any attention to the horse, which is lying on the street, badly injured. It keeps trying to lift its head, but it keeps flopping down, as it lives out the final moments of its life in a hell of gasoline fumes and honking horns and men screaming.

Roberto drives south into the slums for about thirty minutes and then he reaches Caballito and Manuel's house. As soon as he steps out of the car, the neighborhood feels different. Hardly anyone is on the street. No one approaches him to "watch" his car. He can hear music in some of the houses, but it's not as loud as usual. It's like everyone has turned down the volume because they're listening for something. It's almost as if they're listening for him.

In the crummy little yard he sees the toy truck Nydia, the little girl, was playing with on Friday. It's lying on its side, like the horse cart. The front door is open a crack. He can hear the TV. He knocks and calls out "Hello?"

No answer. He pushes the door open.

The only light in the dim room comes from the TV. A Mexican telenovela is on. A beautiful girl with dangling diamond earrings is staring at herself in a mirror; it must be a pretty dramatic moment judging from the swelling music. Manuel's mother sits in her usual chair, her eyes closed and her chin on her chest. She now bears a resemblance to the porcelain figurine of the gory Christ on the cross sitting on the shelf behind her because she's covered with blood, it's like a crimson shawl has been draped over her head and shoulders.

He glances around the room and into the kitchen. For all he knows, the killer or killers might still be in the house.

"Manuel?" he calls out. Not expecting an answer.

He walks down the narrow hallway that leads to the back. His heart's thudding. He hears Manuel's radio, it's playing salsa music. The back door is wide open, and the first thing he sees is Manuel's dog, muddy and bloody, lying on his side. And then he sees Manuel.

He's in his shed lying facedown by his workout bench. Shot in the head like his mother. As Roberto gets closer he sees a note has been pinned on his shirt. He steps over some dumbbells and bends down and takes a look.

Roberto why are you still here? Their blood is on your hands.

He straightens back up. Stands there and tries to absorb it all.

When Manuel called him he doubtless had a gun to his head. He had been told that if he didn't get Roberto to come not only he but his mother (and Nydia? Where is she?) would be killed. But of course all along it was part of the plan for them to be killed anyway.

He looks again at the dog. Mateo. His mouth is open, his sharp yellowish teeth are showing, it's like he was killed in mid-snarl. He bets Mateo put up a fight protecting his master. He hopes he bit the fuck out of somebody.

The song on the radio rollicks on.

*Their blood . . .*was that meant to include Nydia's? Maybe she's not here. She could have gone to the corner grocery to buy some candy, or maybe she's somewhere playing with a friend. Or she hid in a closet, or under a bed . . .

He walks over to the outhouse. The door is closed. At its bottom he sees what appears to be the leading edge of a puddle of blood. He pulls the door open.

She's slumped against one wall, her legs hanging off the seat. She too has been shot in the head, but that's not all. Her pants and underpants have been removed, and she's been mutilated between her legs. One could hardly imagine that that much blood could come from a little girl.

Roberto steps back and closes the door. Very softly, as though he's intruded onto a scene that should have remained private. He takes his cellphone out to call the police. He knows they will take their time getting here. Till they arrive, it will be up to him to keep the dead company, but he's done it before. He has found the dead to be a strange lot. So silent, still, and indifferent . . .

* * *

Lieutenant Matallana, a police homicide investigator, scrutinizes Roberto's identification card.

"You're the journalist, yes?"

He affirms that he is.

"I've read some of your stories," he says. Leaving it carefully up in the air what he thinks about them. Now he hands his ID back to him.

"Tell me your connection to these people."

Roberto tells him. They're standing in front of the house. Other investigative personnel are taking pictures, dusting for fingerprints, talking to neighbors—the kind of things they ought to be doing when investigating a gruesome triple murder. The most likely outcome, of course, is that it will all lead to nothing. The next most likely outcome is that an innocent man will be arrested. The outcome so unlikely as to seem barely within the realm of possibility is that the actual perpetrators will be brought to justice.

Lieutenant Matallana nods and writes in a notebook as Roberto talks. He's dressed rather well for a policeman in an Italian sports jacket and sharply creased pants. He wears glasses like Roberto. Looks, Roberto suddenly realizes, a little like Roberto. He would not like to have a job such as his in a city such as this. Death all day long. For breakfast, lunch, and dinner. And for a midnight snack? More death.

"Was he involved in anything illicit?" Matallana asks. "Drugs, or—?"

"No. He was blind and had one leg. He never left this house. He lifted weights and listened to the radio."

Matallana nods, writes.

"Okay. Can you tell me about the note?"

The note. Roberto seriously considered destroying the note just so he wouldn't have to answer questions like this. Like most citizens of his city, he's never thought there was any point in letting the police know anything at all about his business. Nothing good can come of it. But destroying evidence is a crime, and while it seemed unlikely he would be caught, he couldn't be sure. Who knows what the police already know or will learn about what happened here today? In fact, it's not unheard of for the police to investigate crimes that they themselves have committed.

"I've been receiving death threats. Because of my work. I've been given ten days to leave the country."

"Ten days. Hm," says Matallana, as he writes in his notebook; usually it's Roberto scribbling while somebody else is talking. "And how many of these ten days have already passed?"

"Three."

"And what are you going to do?"

"Leave. On Wednesday."

"And where are you going?"

"Saint Lucia."

Matallana smiles. "Saint Lucia. I hear it's beautiful there. I wish I could be exiled to Saint Lucia."

"The thing is, I'd already decided to leave. So all this was . . ."

"Unnecessary?"

"Yes."

"Any idea who's behind it?"

"I don't have any particular names, no. There was this guy that was following me, in a green Renault, but I didn't get the license plate number."

"Could you identify him if you saw him again?"

"Yes."

Lieutenant Matallana reaches up to his face, adjusts his glasses; they have gold wire frames, like Roberto's. He's looking at Roberto with seeming sympathy.

"I'll miss your stories. I thought they were very good. I'll never forget the one about the old general who had a brain tumor and it made him think he was a great violinist. So funny and yet so sad."

"Thank you. Could I ask you a question?"

"Sure."

"The little girl. Do you think she was already dead when they . . . they did that to her?"

"There was a lot of blood," the lieutenant says matter-of-factly. "That would suggest that her heart was still beating." He sees the look on Roberto's face. "Unbelievable, isn't it? What people do to one another."

"Can I go?"

"Not just yet. There's something I'd like you to do."

"What?"

"I want you to walk me through your exact movements from the time you arrived till the time you called us. Where you stepped. What you touched. What you saw."

"Okay." They start to walk into the house. "Am I a suspect?"

Matallana laughs. "They say when a pickpocket looks at a man, all he sees are his pockets. Well when a homicide detective looks at a man, all he sees is a suspect."

Roberto has to behold again the blood-shrouded figure of Manuel's mother. And then down the narrow hallway into the back yard. The dog. Manuel. His radio still playing. Matallana observing Roberto closely. He's friendly and claims to be a fan and looks like Roberto and wears the same kind of glasses but Roberto cannot afford to let his guard down. Who knows what his game is?

The door to the outhouse is open and a police photographer is taking pictures of Nydia like some depraved pornographer. Another policeman laughs and says, "Hey, we have a survivor!"

Roberto looks toward where he's pointing. Humberto, Manuel's white rabbit with the gray spots, is hopping around near the outhouse, his nose nervously sniffing the air.

* * *

The sun is sinking toward the western mountains as he drives north along Avenue Three. He peers into the cardboard box that's sitting in the passenger seat. Humberto is crouched tensely in a corner, a smudge of blood on his white fur. It was the right thing to take the rabbit with him, Manuel would have wanted that, but now what in the hell is he going to do with him?

His cellphone pings, announcing a text message. From Caroline. *I bought the desk it's in your office in front of your window waiting for you hurry roberto hurry!*

He's not going to say a word about what happened today to Caroline. She would go crazy, insist he catch the next plane out.

It's not surprising to him—nothing in this country is surprising to him—that they have killed someone he knows in an effort to frighten him into leaving. But why Manuel? Why not a friend or a family member? Maybe the military was behind it, because the article he wrote about Manuel and the other wounded vets embarrassed them. Well, good luck to Lieutenant Matallana in going up against the military. Though it's doubtful he has the slightest inclination to do so. More likely he is spinning some elaborate web around Roberto. Let's see, what could be his motive for killing Manuel, his mother, and Nydia? Oh it's obvious. He's a pedophile. He was caught molesting the little girl and to cover up his crime he killed everyone in the house. And that would explain the sexual nature of the mutilation inflicted on the girl. They're probably rounding up witnesses right now that will testify Roberto's molested children before. What an entertaining circus it would be if the crusading investigative journalist were exposed as a pervert and tried for murder. Maybe catching the next plane out isn't such a bad idea.

He hears Humberto stirring around in the box. He tries to think of someone he knows who could give him some guidance.

Gloria. Gloria Varela. She loves animals. He calls her.

"Gloria, it's Roberto. I need your help."

"Roberto, what's wrong?"

"I've come into possession of a rabbit, and I don't know what to do with it."

Gloria laughs. "Oh Roberto, you scared me. The way your voice sounded, I thought something bad had happened."

* * *

She lives behind tall adobe walls in a pretty cottage painted sky blue. She puts Humberto in the kitchen with some food and water and closes the door so he won't be bothered by the cottage's other occupants: a big dignified Doberman and two standoffish cats; she also has a parakeet in a cage and two turtles in a terrarium. She brings a bottle of wine and two glasses into the living room and sits down and lights a cigarette and listens as Roberto talks about what he found at Manuel's house.

"So it's in the hands of the police now," he says. "Who of course will do nothing."

"I'm sorry, Roberto," Gloria murmurs.

He gulps down the rest of his wine. Impatient to feel the warm tingle of it hitting his brain, infiltrating the misery there. Gloria leans forward and refills his glass.

"I know exactly how you feel," she says. "I've written about people, and then they've turned up dead, and I knew that my story probably had something to do with it, but you can't blame yourself. The evil bastards that did it, they're to blame."

He nods. Looks around the room. Sees lots of reminders of Gloria's old successes, of her glory days. Framed journalism awards and photographs of her and her wild hair and black eye patch with some of the most famous people in the world: Yasser Arafat, Vladimir Putin, Mick Jagger, Pope John Paul II. All men, he notices. She has always loved men.

He looks at a picture of her engaged in earnest conversation with a baby-faced American president in his office at the White House.

"What was Clinton like?" he asks. "Did he make a pass at you?"

"He was very smart and charming and no, he didn't make a pass."

His gaze falls on a photo of her lost love, Commander Romeo. Black-bearded, in a beret, jauntily smiling, much handsomer than the movie star who played him in the film.

"Do you think about him much? Luis Valasquez?"

"Oh yes." She looks at the photo, smiles musingly. "Odd. How he's stayed the same age, and I've gotten so old. I could be his mother now." She takes a drag on her cigarette, then lets out a languid stream of smoke. "At night, sometimes, when I sleep, Luis comes to me, and we talk under the stars again. I always ask what it's like to be dead, and he always says, 'I can't tell you that, my love. That's the one thing I'm not allowed to talk about.'"

A brown and black cat jumps in her lap.

"What's happening, Chocolate?" she coos.

"Caroline has three cats."

"Do you like cats?"

"Not particularly. But I'm trying to learn to like them."

"What's not to like, hm, Chocolate?"

"Do you think he was afraid to die?"

"Luis?"

"Yes."

She is quiet for a moment, petting the cat.

"I think on the day it happened to him, it must have come as a surprise. He was very confident and resourceful. He'd been in plenty of dangerous situations and had always gotten through them, and I think he expected that to continue. But clearly he had thought about his own death. I remember something he said to me once: 'Here's the thing, Gloria. You have to decide ahead of time that even if the worst happens, if your side loses and you're caught by criminal lunatics and you're tortured and killed . . . it was worth it anyway.' And then he repeated it, like it had already happened: 'It was worth it anyway.' So hopefully, at the very end, there was some kind of peace for him."

The parakeet begins to chirp loudly; it's like bright little chips of sound are flying out of its cage. The Doberman pads over to the open front door and stares out—into a dusk now teetering on the knife's edge of night.

"What's out there, Hugo?" Gloria says.

The dog looks over his shoulder at her, then back out the door.

Gloria is wearing faded blue jeans and a soft tan alpaca sweater but not her trademark boots. Her bare feet seem a little big and unfeminine-looking. Roberto has never seen her bare legs; he knows there are scars there from the bombing that she wants to conceal.

"Is it true what they say about you, Gloria?"

She smiles and leans over and taps some ash from her cigarette into an orange ashtray shaped like a fish.

"Probably. What are you referring to?"

"Supposedly you have a closet just for your boots. Dozens and dozens of pairs of boots."

"That's absolutely true. It's such a sight I usually charge admission, but I'll let you see it for free."

"Some other time. I should go."

"Why don't you stay awhile? We can both get drunk and I'll fix you dinner."

"No thanks. I'm not hungry."

He finishes off his wine and stands up.

"Thanks for taking the rabbit."

"I'm happy to, Roberto. Don't worry, I'll find him a good home."

* * *

Although he did not get a speck of it on him he feels somehow as if he's covered with blood, and when he gets home he takes a shower and lingers in it for a long time. As he washes himself he feels the St. Jude Thaddeus medal that Mrs. Langenberg gave him around his neck; he doesn't believe in its alleged protective power but still he finds something comforting in the presence of it on his person. He knows one thing: he cannot wait to get out of this nightmare of a country.

He towels himself dry and puts on his Nike tracksuit and pours himself a glass of wine. He was supposed to Skype Caroline tonight but he emails her that he's been busy packing all day and he's worn out and is going to bed early. He gets a prompt reply wishing him the best of nights and the sweetest of dreams, and it hardly seems possible he will soon be holding her in his arms, inhaling her scent and losing himself in her luminous eyes.

He turns the TV on to watch the news. The National Police, in a joint operation with the U.S. Navy, have captured two and a half tons of cocaine from a boat in the Caribbean Sea off San Felipe. Pop diva Shanterelle is expecting a baby with her boyfriend, Spanish soccer star Jaime Escalante. Police report a troubling increase in so-called "strangle muggings," which involve tourists being victimized by muggers who strangle them till they pass out then take off with their stuff. No mention by the handsome and beautiful newspeople of what happened at Manuel's house; it's not news to Roberto that the violent death of the poor in this city is not news.

He goes to bed. He closes his eyes and tries to think of nothing but is instead sucked again and again into a vile vortex of butchery and blood, of terror and screaming, of the crucifixion of the innocent. And then finally he falls asleep.

He finds himself in a death bar. Also there is Edgar Leonidas, his friend from school. He and Edgar are stripped to the waist and armed with knives. They're fighting each other. They both are bleeding and sweat is pouring off them as onlookers yell and make bets. And then he wakes up.

He's sweating, as in the dream; it seemed so real it's almost a wonder he's not bleeding too. He casts the bedclothes off, lies on his back naked in the dark.

It is disconcerting how he keeps dreaming about the dead.

Six days until the day
Roberto is to die

What he remembers most about what he was told about the massacre in Contamana is the silence. All the inhabitants of the town except a handful who managed to hide or run away were herded into the central plaza. Contamana is to the northeast, where it's hot and steamy, and palm trees surrounded the plaza; survivors remembered how unusually still the air was and how the fronds of the palms didn't move at all, as if they were frozen in fear, just like the people were.

The intruders were wearing green uniforms and green ski masks. They had a list of names on a notebook computer; the first name to be called out belonged to the mayor. The mayor had a little dog that went with him everywhere, and it trotted out with him as he walked toward the silent staring men in the green uniforms, and the mayor commanded his dog to run away but it didn't so it was shot along with the mayor. Over the next quarter of an hour or so thirty-two people one by one were made to kneel and then shot in the back of the head. None of the victims either begged for their life or shouted out defiantly "Long live Contamana!" but they all went to their deaths without a word, and one might think that the people watching would be moaning and crying and whimpering in grief and terror but all of the survivors said there was absolute silence on the plaza, even the birds didn't chirp and the insects didn't buzz.

The killers did not explain themselves nor did they wear any identifying insignia on their uniforms so who they were was in dispute. But since most of the dead seemed to fall into categories deemed to be socially undesirable by the extreme right wing, like liberal politicians, school-teachers with "modern" ideas, labor leaders, drunks, thieves, prostitutes, the physically or mentally handicapped (they shot one poor wretch of a teenage boy with cerebral palsy), it seemed reasonable to assume they were with the Army or the paramilitaries—unless of course they were a bunch of tricky insurgents who wanted the right wing to get the blame so the people would be driven into their Marxist arms.

When Roberto wrote about the massacre in *The Hour* five years ago, he still didn't know who the men in the green uniforms were, but he's made several trips to Contamana since then and has figured it all out, at least to his own satisfaction: the murders were committed by members of a paramilitary organization called An Eye for an Eye, hired by local landowners to teach the leftist town a lesson. He's had the idea of writing a book, he even has a title: *A Town Called Contamana.* He's sitting now on the floor of his apartment looking through three cardboard boxes filled with material he's collected about the unfortunate town. He hasn't begun the book for a couple of reasons: he's never written a book and doesn't really know if he can and since he's already acquired more than enough enemies, he hasn't been eager to antagonize An Eye for an Eye, a group that has a reputation for extreme ruthlessness, as the name they have chosen for themselves suggests. But he realizes this would be a perfect project for Saint Lucia. Everything he needs to write the book is in these boxes. He can see himself sitting in his office at his Victorian walnut desk, pouring over photographs and notebooks and transcripts and reports, in front of the wide window filled with ocean and sky . . . one of Caroline's fat cats wandering in every now and then to bother him . . . Caroline herself coming in with a fresh cup of coffee for him and a kiss on his cheek and a *How is it going, Roberto, I can't wait to read the new pages—*

The phone rings. It's Beto from the lobby, announcing a visitor.

Roberto's surprised. He tells Beto to send her up.

* * *

Clara enters in a swirl of perfume, and the air in the room seems instantly to get a degree or two warmer.

"I hope I'm not bothering you," she says.

"No, of course not."

"I was in the neighborhood, running an errand, and, you know, everything seemed so rushed and sudden Saturday night, I didn't feel we had the chance to say a proper good-bye. How's the packing going?" she asks, looking at the boxes and books and piles of clothes cluttering the floor.

"Okay. I'm trying to throw away as much as I can, but I seem to find a reason to keep just about everything."

She's dressed stylishly, as always. A tight beige jersey top with a plunging V neck. A thin wool beige wrap skirt. Matching high heels. Slung insouciantly over her shoulder, a light jacket in the same material as the skirt. Roberto moves with her into the room.

"It's such a charming place," she says. "I know you'll miss it."

"Can I get you anything? A cup of coffee?"

"No, I'm fine, thanks."

"Sit down."

She sits down on the couch. He sits in an armchair. She crosses her legs so the wrap skirt separates and her legs are displayed in a splendid fashion.

"You look tired," she says.

"I didn't sleep well last night."

"Why not?"

"Oh, you know . . . everything."

She regards him in silence. She wears her short dark hair in such a way that a wave of it is always threatening to fall across her right eye, and now she pushes it back with her fingers, continuing to look at him.

"What?" Roberto says.

"I was just thinking . . . how selfish I am."

"Why do you say that?"

"I realize I've been thinking of this as something that's happening to *me*. You're going away, so I'm losing such a good friend and the only one who understands me and so forth, but it's not happening to me, it's happening to *you*."

"It's happening to all of us. How's my father?"

"He's upset, Roberto. Even though he's pretending to be the battle-ship. He says you're having lunch with him tomorrow."

"Yes."

"That's good. You need some time . . . just the two of you."

"So I don't think I ever really thanked you for dinner Saturday night. The food, the wine, the conversation . . . everything was wonderful."

Clara's face lights up. "Yes, it was fun, wasn't it? So let's gossip, Roberto, what did you think of everyone?"

"Well, I still liked Pombo. I still disliked Valdivieso."

"And what about his boyfriend, Mr. My Cousin Eva?"

"I think he and Valdivieso make a good couple."

"Yes, he seemed very full of himself, didn't he, considering he's such a bad actor. And I don't think he's even attractive, he's far too pretty for a man."

"You haven't been hearing a disembodied voice singing opera by any chance, have you?"

Clara laughs. "No, why?"

"The woman sitting next to me, Patricia . . . she said her house is haunted by a ghost that sings opera and that it followed her to your apartment. But I guess the ghost must have gone back home with her."

Clara's smile fades. "Poor Patricia. She's one of my oldest friends. She suffered a terrible tragedy two years ago. Her husband and their daughter took a trip to the Amazon, she was supposed to go with them but something came up at work. They were in a small private plane that went down in a thunderstorm while it was flying over the jungle. They didn't find the bodies for weeks. I don't think she's ever really accepted it. She never talks about it, I've never seen her cry. But ever since it happened, she's been having strange experiences. One week she'll see a gigantic flying saucer floating over the city and then disappearing over Mount Cabanacande. And then the next week she'll look into a mirror and see not her own face but the face of an ancient Egyptian princess who she somehow knows was herself in a previous life. And so on."

"I'm sorry, Clara. I didn't intend to make fun of her."

"Oh, I know. Does that offer of a cup of coffee still stand?"

He goes in the kitchen, pours cups of coffee for himself and her. Ever since she walked through the door, his dick has been tingling. He wonders why she's here. His first thought when he heard she was in the lobby was that she had come to seduce him, but was that just his imagination running wild? She's an inveterate flirt but that doesn't mean she wants to sleep with her own stepson.

He goes back to Clara, a cup of coffee in each hand. Finds her sitting on the floor next to a box of old photographs. She holds one up.

"Roberto, is that you?"

He looks at a chubby little boy in blue shorts and a red shirt on a tricycle.

"Yes."

"Oh, you were adorable. Look at those fat little cheeks!"

He hands the coffee down to her.

"Thank you," she says, smiling up at him, then returning her attention to the pictures in the box.

His gaze moves over her long, elegantly folded legs. Dives down into the V neck of her jersey top. Lingers on a faint freckle on the upper slope of her right breast.

"Who's this stern gentleman?" Clara asks, holding up another photo.

It seems awkward to keep standing, so he sits down on the floor cross-legged. He takes a drink of his coffee as he looks at the picture. It shows an unsmiling, gaunt-faced man with a pointy beard sitting on a stone bench. He's wearing a light-colored suit with a flower in the lapel and is resting both hands on the top of a cane. Near him, in a splash of sunlight, sits a cat, caught in the act of licking its paw.

"That's my great uncle Adrián. He was my mother's mother's brother. He's sitting in front of the hotel he owned in Puerto Alegria. It's not there anymore, it was destroyed in a hurricane."

"Do you remember him?"

"No, he died long before I was born. When my mother was a little girl. She said he never smiled but he had a very dry sense of humor and he was always making people laugh," and then he adds, "I think that's the famous cat."

"Why 'famous'?"

"During the Killing Time, Puerto Alegria was strategically important because it was located where the Mavaca River emptied into the sea. It was a liberal town, and it was taken over by a unit of conservative militia. Uncle Adrián and all the other important men of the town were imprisoned in the hotel. Have you ever heard of the parrot's perch?"

Clara shakes her head.

"It's a torture method. The victim's stripped naked and his hands and his feet are tied together and then he's suspended from a horizontal pole. He's left hanging for hours or days without any food or water. Well, that's what was done to Uncle Adrián and the other men. They eventually would have ended up in front of a firing squad, but then they had a great stroke of luck.

"Hurricanes of course are very rare in this country, but it just so happened a hurricane chose that time to hit the coast. The hotel was right on the beach. The conservative militia came from the interior of the country, and most of them had never even seen the sea. When the wind started blowing over trees, and they saw big waves crashing against the beach, they were terrified, and they jumped in their trucks and fled Puerto Alegria. They left my uncle and the others still dangling naked from poles in the hotel. The windows were blowing out, and the lobby was beginning to flood. But some townspeople came and rescued them just in time. They all made it to higher ground and were safe. And everyone praised God for having sent the hurricane to save them, as if God takes sides in a civil war."

"Okay," says Clara. "But why was the cat famous?"

"After Uncle Adrián escaped the hotel, he remembered that he'd forgotten his beloved cat, so he went back for it. Unfortunately, my uncle was drowned. They found his body in what was left of the hotel the next day."

"Oh," says Clara—clearly not expecting the story to end in this way. She sips her coffee, and takes another look at the photograph. "So what happened to the cat?"

"It was fine. It turned up a day or two later. It must have climbed up a tree or something." He looks back at the box. "Mother gave me these pictures. Right before she left for Spain. She said I spent too much time in the present, and I should start paying attention to the past, because the past is the country all of us come from. But this is the first time I've looked at them."

Clara picks up some more photographs, as Roberto examines the one of Uncle Adrián. He's struck by how fiercely and directly he's gazing at the camera, as if he's trying to look through the years right at Roberto. It's like he's saying, *Yes, I was here, on this day, sitting on this bench, and I was just as alive as you are, oh you wouldn't believe how alive I was!*

"Here's one of you and Clemente," Clara says. "What happened to your arm?"

Roberto's nine. He's standing with his father on the veranda of the house he grew up in. Behind him on the wall is the many-colored peacock sculpture that he remembers always being there. He wonders what happened to it. Is it still hanging on a wall somewhere, or did it end up broken to bits in some rubbish heap? His father's hand is on Roberto's shoulder. He's looking down at him and smiling, Roberto's smiling at the camera. His left arm is in a cast.

"I was at Andrés's house. He had a eucalyptus tree in his back yard. We were climbing around in it and I fell out and broke my arm. It actually didn't heal very well. This arm's a little shorter and you can still feel a bump on the bone."

"Where?" says Clara.

"Right here," he says, touching a spot on his forearm.

Clara touches the same spot. "Oh yes, I can feel it."

But her hand stays on his arm. Rubbing it a little. He looks up into her eyes, and she glances at his lips.

He knows that she is his for the taking, that he can be inside her in seconds if he wishes, fucking her on Caroline's organic moso bamboo floor.

"Clara," he says. "This is not a good idea."

"Why not?"

"Obvious reasons. My father . . . Caroline . . ."

They both are talking very softly, as if his father and Caroline might be in the hallway just outside the door.

"They'll never know," says Clara.

"But we will."

"So?"

"I thought you said you loved him."

"I do. This has nothing to do with him. Or Caroline. It has to do with you and me. You've always wanted me, don't lie to me, and I've always wanted you."

"But it wouldn't be right—"

"Oh Roberto," Clara sighs, reaching out and touching his hair. "Life is so full of pain and trouble, and if we have a chance to be happy for an hour or two why not take it? We wouldn't be hurting anybody. And this might be our last chance, who knows if we'll ever even see each other again?"

"Why would you say that? We'll see each other again."

"Kiss me."

"Clara—"

"Stop talking."

She moves toward him and he knows if they kiss they'll be utterly lost in each other's ecstatic flesh and however much he wants exactly that he makes himself stand up.

"I'm sorry, Clara."

Clara looks up at Roberto. Not happily. Pushing that bewitching wave of hair away from her right eye. Now she starts to stand up too; he offers her his hand but she ignores it.

"You're a fool," she says. "All men are fools about sex. In one way or another."

The phone rings. He goes over to his desk and looks at the number. It's the city police department.

"I have to take this," he says to Clara and then he picks up. "Hello?"

"Roberto?"

"Yes?"

"It's Lieutenant Matallana. We need to talk."

Roberto glances at Clara. She's walking back to the couch and picking up her jacket. "Can I call you back in a few minutes?"

"We need to talk in person. It's very important."

"All right. Do you want me to come to your office?"

"No. Can you meet me at the London Billiard Club? It's downtown, on Ninth Street, near Avenue Two."

"Yes, I know it. What time?"

"In one hour?"

He looks at his watch. "Okay, I'll be there."

"Thank you, Roberto. I'll see you soon."

He hangs up. Clara is looking at him.

"I should go," she says. "You've obviously very busy."

"Yes, there's a lot to do."

He walks her to the door. Trying unsuccessfully to think of something to say.

"Well, I suppose you think I'm a terrible person now," she says. "Like everyone else does."

"You know better than that, Clara. You know I think the world of you."

She smiles. "Travel safely. Don't forget me."

"I won't."

He opens the door. She turns and looks at him.

"And Roberto?"

"Yes?"

"You're not stopping me from kissing you good-bye," and she throws her arms around his neck and kisses him. He kisses her back. Her lips and her tongue and her soft warm body pressing against him make him nearly dizzy with desire. Now she steps back, to observe the effect she's had on him. She brushes the bulge in his jeans with the tips of her fingers, and is gone.

* * *

Roberto eyes a guy on a motorcycle in his rearview mirror. He's been behind him for several blocks. His features are hidden by his helmet and visor; the sun gleams on their hard surfaces, giving him an insect-like, implacable look. Like all motorcycle riders, he's wearing an orange vest bearing the license plate number of his bike; a law was passed requiring this because so many people were being killed by assassins on motorcycles.

The guy suddenly whips into the lane on Roberto's left. As he comes up alongside him, Roberto's hoping he's not some dead-eyed killer with a phony number on his vest, but he doesn't look at Roberto and keeps going and roars away.

Roberto wonders what Lieutenant Matallana wants. He can understand him not wanting to talk about it on the phone but he cannot understand why he would want to meet him at some pool hall instead of the police station. He's concerned it's a set-up and Matallana won't be there but somebody else will. So many have died in just this way: a phone call, meet so-and-so at such-and-such a place. Sometimes the killer is a stranger, sometimes it's your best friend.

The traffic slows, then stops. The air is bad today and stinks of gasoline and burns his eyes. Up ahead at the intersection, a black man is standing on the shoulders of a partner. He has two batons that are on fire. He twirls them and throws them in the air and catches them then throws them up again in the most amazingly skillful way and never for an instant doesn't smile.

* * *

Roberto walks through the shadows of aging plasterwork buildings down a sidewalk crowded with poor people. In front of him, in the newer part of downtown, great glass and metal skyscrapers shoot up into the sunlight. They're only a few blocks away, but they seem celestial and out of reach, not part of the same city.

An Indian woman is sitting on the sidewalk on a colorful blanket with three small children climbing all over her. She's wearing a straw hat, and her shiny black hair is in a long braid. She is tiny. She's probably only in her twenties but her face is disconcertingly old, it's like the head of a forty-five-year-old woman has been put on the body of a little girl. The city is filled with people like her; violent men have come to visit their villages and they have fled. Roberto has seen tall, well-dressed, light-complexioned residents of this city curse and spit on and one time even kick people like her, calling them filthy vermin and urging them to go elsewhere.

A plastic soda cup sits on the blanket with a few coins and bills in its bottom. He drops some money in and she mumbles thank you without looking at him. He asks where she's from. She probably doesn't speak much Spanish and she says, "What?" He repeats the question, and she says, "Tulcán."

He turns into a wide doorway and climbs a curving flight of bright-red stairs and enters the London Billiard Club. It's been here since the 1930s, when an Englishman on vacation fell in love with a local girl and decided to stay and open up his own business. It was a popular place at first, customers flocking to play billiards and drink beer and eat exotic English dishes like shepherd's pie and bangers and mash and every night at midnight boisterously sing in English "God Save the King" as they stood at attention and faced an oil portrait of King George V but it all ended wretchedly for the Englishman. He had a drinking problem, which caused his wife to leave him and take their two young children with her, so the Englishman swallowed poison and crawled underneath one of his billiard tables and died.

The first thing Roberto sees as he reaches the top of the stairs is the smoke-dimmed portrait of King George V, looking impossibly self-important in a black uniform and red and white robes, right hand cocked on his hip, left hand resting on the hilt of a sword; he reminds Roberto a little with his beard and his solemn gaze of his great uncle, Adrián. The floor is cracked linoleum in a pattern of red and white squares. Bronze lamps hang over the green tables, all empty except for one, where two tattooed young toughs are playing a listless game of eight ball. Now he sees Lieutenant Matallana. He's sitting at a table near the bar, head bent, absorbed in his iPhone.

He smiles and stands up when he sees Roberto coming. "Hello, Roberto. Glad you could make it on such short notice."

"Hello, lieutenant."

Roberto shakes hands with him and sits down.

"I've already eaten," he says, "but please order something if you're hungry. The food here's not half bad."

"Your juice looks good, I think I'll just have that."

"Lupe," the lieutenant calls out to the guy behind the bar, "another tangerine juice please!"

He's dressed more casually than yesterday: a light jacket, khaki pants, a navy-blue polo shirt. Roberto still thinks he resembles Roberto, and wonders if he thinks the same. But it would be an odd question to ask. *Do you think you look like me?*

"How's the rabbit?" asks Matallana.

"It's fine. I left it with a friend, she'll take good care of it."

Lupe brings over the tangerine juice. It's warm today and Roberto's very thirsty and he takes a big gulp of it.

"You've been here before?" asks Matallana.

"A few times, over the years." Including one particularly noteworthy night with Daniel. It's not easy getting thrown out of a seedy joint like the London Billiards Club for being excessively drunk and obnoxious but Daniel managed it. Then he tripped going down the stairs and took a horrific tumble all the way to the bottom. Roberto screamed out his name, certain he must have killed himself or at the very least be paralyzed, and clattered down the stairs after him, but by the time he reached him Daniel was already rising to his feet, swaying, giggling, bleeding profusely from a cut on the bridge of his nose, and then, loudly singing in English "Strawberry Fields Forever," he staggered out into the night.

"I grew up around here," says Matallana," and this was my hangout. See those guys?" Roberto looks at the two guys playing pool. "I was one of them."

"That's hard to picture. How'd you wind up a cop?"

The lieutenant laughs. "Well, it's like this. The cops were always hassling us, but I wasn't like my friends, they hated the cops, but I was always fascinated with them. Their uniforms and their guns and the way they talked, they seemed so tough and confidant, not like us, we were just pretending. So I started hanging around them, pestering them with questions about police work. A couple of them took an interest in me. They saved me from the streets, really," and he laughs again. "So here I am." He's quiet for a moment, looking at Roberto. "Still leaving on Wednesday?"

"Yes. What did you want to talk to me about?"

"I have good news, Roberto. I think I know who killed your friends."

Roberto is cautious. He wants to hear what Matallana has to say before he gets too excited. "Yes?"

"In fact, I'm quite sure of it. It's just a matter of proving it."

"Okay. Who?"

"Before we go any further," and then he stops as two men come in. Roberto and Matallana look them over as they sit down at a nearby table. They're wearing baseball caps and clothes spattered with dried paint. They light cigarettes and order beers. They're paying no attention to Roberto and Matallana. Now Matallana continues, but in a softer voice. "Before we go any further . . . you have to promise me something."

"What?"

"If this case goes to trial, you have to promise me you'll return to the country and testify. The case will fall apart without you."

"Yes, absolutely. I'll come back."

"It will be dangerous. They won't want you to testify."

"Lieutenant, don't worry, I'll come back, I promise. Now tell me who did it."

Matallana takes a photograph out of a manila envelope. Slides it over the table to Roberto.

"Recognize him?"

It's a mug shot of a red-faced man with a black moustache and cold, inert eyes.

"It's the guy that was following me. In the green Renault. He did it?"

"He was at Manuel's house yesterday, along with two other men. His name's Toño González. He's been a killer-for-hire since he was fourteen. A guy that lives across the street peeked out his window and recognized him. Neighbors usually clam up, but this guy has a grudge against Toño, he killed somebody close to him. He was arrested for it, but then the charges were dropped. You know how it goes. So the question is, who is Toño working for?"

"I've been thinking it was the military. Because they're pissed off about the article I wrote about Manuel."

"Good guess. But wrong." Matallana is smiling, pleased with himself. "I found out this morning Toño's been doing a lot of work recently for the CPN." The Committee to Protect the Nation. "That story you wrote about the jugglers and the beggars is causing them a lot of trouble. The district attorney's investigating, Congress is investigating, it looks like they're extorting the street people in other cities as well. There's a whole string of murders and assaults they might be connected to, they're going to have to pay off people like crazy to stay out of prison. On top of everything else, they've been embarrassed. They talk about honor and virtue, but they've been revealed as thugs. It's a bad idea to embarrass certain people if you want to have a long life and die in your bed."

"So you're confidant the CPN's behind this."

"Two and two still make four, Roberto. Even in this country."

"Are you going to arrest Toño?"

"Not yet. The neighbor's scared to death, he was willing to finger Toño to me but that's all he'll do. We haven't found any physical evidence connecting Toño to the crime scene. And so I've got a lot of work to do. And the goal of course isn't just to get Toño and the other two guys but the guys that gave the orders. Which probably means the top leadership of the CPN."

Roberto drinks some tangerine juice, and looks across the table at Matallana. It's as if he's reading Roberto's mind.

"We're not all on the take."

"Why are we meeting here, lieutenant? And not at the police station."

Matallana plucks a paper napkin from a metal dispenser, takes his glasses off, and begins to clean them. "Let me put it this way. I need to be discreet in how I carry out my investigation if I don't want to be interfered with."

He puts his glasses back on, then waves away some cigarette smoke that's drifting over from the guys in the baseball caps.

"Let's get out of here. This is bad for my asthma."

* * *

"I've known a lot of cops," says Roberto, "and you don't particularly seem like one."

Matallana laughs. "Is that good or bad?"

"Neither. Just an observation."

"Well, you seem exactly like a journalist to me."

They're walking along Ninth Street. The sun's shining down and it's very warm, and Matallana pulls his jacket off.

"How long have you had asthma?" asks Roberto.

"Since I was a kid."

"I had it when I was a kid too, but I outgrew it."

"I wish I'd outgrow it. The worst thing for me is horses. If I even think about a horse, I start to wheeze."

"Do you have a good doctor?"

"He's okay, I guess. Nothing special."

They make their way through the throngs of people. Vendors are selling food, drinks, jewelry, sunglasses, wristwatches. A blind woman is hawking pirated DVDs of recent American movies. A guy is waving his cellphone in the air, selling time on it, 200 pesos a minute. A shrunken, hobbling man with a face like a rodent grabs Roberto's arm.

"You're looking lucky today, my friend, how about buying a lottery ticket?"

Roberto jerks his arm away.

"Beat it," says Matallana, in a firm but calm cop voice.

But the man keeps limping after them.

"You too," he says to Matallana. "You got that lucky look!"

"I'm not telling you again."

"Okay, boss, relax," and then as he drops back he yells, "My tickets are the luckiest in town, ask anybody! They're blessed by a priest!"

"They're like pigeons in a park," Matallana says, "fighting over some birdseed. Whenever I feel down, I come here and walk around and I think: well at least I don't live here with the pigeons anymore."

"I was lucky," says Roberto. "My father's a doctor. My life was easy when I was growing up."

"Did you always want to be a journalist?"

"No, it never even occurred to me till I got out of college. My grandmother said to me one day, 'Roberto, there are two worlds, the real world and the world of dreams. It's time you stopped living in the world of dreams.' So I started thinking seriously about what I wanted to do with my life. One of my best friends was a photographer, and he was working for a small weekly newspaper. He got me an interview with the editor. He turned out to be a real asshole. He said there weren't any job openings, and it was unlikely there would ever be any job openings, and I should just forget it. I wasn't even sure I wanted a job with his crummy paper until he told me I couldn't have one. I said what if I could get an interview with Memo Soto, would he give me a job then?"

Matallana smiles. "The Chess Master."

Memo Soto was a drug trafficker who a dozen years ago retaliated against efforts to extradite him to America by terrorizing the country with assassinations and bombings. He was called the Chess Master because of his tactical brilliance in planning the attacks and his uncanny ability to outwit the forces trying to capture or kill him.

"Soto had never given an interview because he hated the press," says Roberto. "He felt they always told lies about him. So the editor just laughed and said, 'Son, if you get an interview with Memo Soto, I'll resign and make *you* the editor.' What he didn't know was that I was good friends with Soto's daughter, Lucero."

A dog with a bad case of mange trots by, carrying a dead rat in his jaws. He looks very pleased with himself.

"She was at the National University at the same time I was. I remember she was always surrounded by bodyguards, and she seemed very lonely. We had a couple of classes together, and we hit it off."

"Was she pretty?" asks Matallana.

"Yes, very."

"Did you have a romantic relationship?" and then the lieutenant smiles apologetically. "Sorry to ask so many questions, it's what I do all day."

"Yeah, me too. No, we were just friends. For one thing, I already had a girlfriend. Also, you have to be careful about getting involved with someone like Lucero. She told me that when she was fifteen, she was staying at their cattle ranch in Espinar. She got a crush on an older boy who worked with the horses. They were in the barn one day making out, when Memo Soto walked in. He saw the boy's hand on Lucero's boob, and he just went nuts. He grabbed the boy and hauled him over to a wooden block where the cook chopped the heads off chickens. He forced the boy's arm down on the block. Lucero was screaming at him to stop, but the hand that had been touching his daughter's boob? He chopped it right off."

Matallana winces, and laughs. "I guess he was lucky he wasn't *kissing* her boob, or he would have got his head chopped off."

"Memo Soto was a bad guy, no doubt about it, but he did really love Lucero. He would have done anything for her. So I told her what I wanted. I said it was an opportunity for her father to tell his side of the story to the public, I promised I wouldn't change a word. And she got in touch with him and told him I could be trusted and he agreed. I was blindfolded and taken to one of his hideaways in the mountains."

Matallana shakes his head. "Man, Roberto, that must've been scary."

"Actually it wasn't. I felt like I was the safest man in South America, because Memo Soto would never allow any harm to come to his daughter's friend."

"As long as his daughter's friend didn't touch her boob."

Roberto laughs. "Right."

"What was he like? Soto?"

"Funny, warm, smart, intense. He asked me a lot of questions about myself and seemed interested in my replies. He said he was just a businessman who had made a lot of money but he was using it to help the common people. He said it was his dream to be the president of the country someday. He just seemed like the greatest guy ever."

"A charismatic sociopath. I know the type."

"We talked all through the night. For fourteen hours straight. And I remember the next day when I was being driven out of the mountains, I was glad I was wearing a blindfold, because it meant no one could see I was crying."

"Why were you crying?"

"Because I was so happy. Because I knew I'd gotten what I came for."

"So did the editor quit and hire you to be the editor?"

"No, I never gave him the chance. I took my story to a bigger paper, and they hired me."

"You know, I remember that interview now. It was a big deal at the time."

"It's still the biggest story I've ever done. I guess I've been trying to top it ever since."

They've reached a narrow parking lot jammed in between two crumbling brick buildings.

"I'm parked here," says Roberto.

He turns to Matallana. They consider each other for a moment.

"Have a good trip to Saint Lucia," he says.

"Thanks. Good luck with your investigation. And if I can help in any way, just let me know."

"I will."

"Well—good-bye, lieutenant."

Roberto shakes hands with him.

"Good-bye, Roberto."

Roberto walks into the parking lot. The attendant is a bent old man with a yellowish cataract in one eye; his other eye is watching Roberto keenly, as if he looks to him like a man up to no good.

"Roberto?"

Roberto turns around. Lieutenant Matallana is standing at the edge of the parking lot. He's smiling, and the sun's glinting off his glasses.

"I think we're going to get these bastards! I really do!"

* * *

Roberto gets lost getting out of downtown. It happens in one of those torn-up areas where a street is being widened to add a lane to accommodate the big stupid blue buses. Dump trucks rumble past and hard-hatted workers wield yammering jackhammers. Signs with arrows redirect traffic onto a rough dirt road defined by flimsy sheets of plywood and orange traffic cones. Roberto's Kia and some other cars slowly bump along for a bit, but then it begins to get confusing. Some of the cones and plywood sheets have fallen or been knocked over. Now he sees other cones straggling off in a different direction, along with a single sign with an arrow on it, and so he goes that way.

It's not long before the road, or what he took to be the road, peters out into a wasteland of weeds and bushes. He comes to a stop. He doesn't see any other cars around. A warm wind is whipping up dust. A pair of vultures rip at the carcass of a dog. And then Roberto sees shambling shapes approaching, five or six of them, from different directions, and he realizes he's about to be robbed.

They're ragged, wild-eyed, high on basuco. They're carrying crude weapons. A rusty machete. A tire iron. A board with nails sticking out the end of it. The one closest to Roberto is lugging a heavy rock in both hands. His lips are flecked with foam. If it were merely a matter of being robbed Roberto would just hand over his money but there is too much madness in all their eyes, he fears he's about to be beaten or even killed. The guy raises the rock over his head with the intention of smashing Roberto's windshield. He jams the gas pedal and the car lunges forward as the rock bangs off his roof. The guy with the tire iron has to jump out of his way. He shifts gears and blasts through a bush. He starts to circle back toward the road but doesn't see the shallow ditch filled with rubbish till he's right on top of it. He hits his brakes and skids into it. The guy with the machete brandishes it and runs toward Roberto as his tires spin in the dirt and he sees a brief image of himself dead in the ditch amid tin cans and old condoms and crumpled paper and rotting rats and then the tires gain traction. His car lurches up and out, and he heads back the way he came.

He looks in his rearview mirror. The disappointed *basuqueros* are watching him go. They stand motionless and wraith-like in the blowing dust.

* * *

"Gilberto Barco," says Roberto's father. "He's the top pulmonologist in the country, he wrote a whole book about asthma. I know him quite well, we play tennis together. If I can keep the ball away from his forehand, I have a chance. His forehand is like lightning. I'll put in a call to him so your friend won't have to wait for an appointment."

"That would be great, Dad. I'll find out when a good time would be and then I'll get back to you. Thanks for the help."

"Anytime, Roberto. What time is our lunch tomorrow?"

"One thirty at Osaka?"

"I'll see you at one thirty."

Roberto calls Lieutenant Matallana and gets his voice mail. He leaves a message saying it's nothing urgent but would he please call when he has a moment.

He puts the phone down. Glances around the room. Still a lot of packing to do and a great resistance on his part to doing it. He looks at the box of photos on the floor, where he sat with his father's wife. He hasn't really had a chance to mull over what happened and didn't happen this morning.

Maybe Clara was right and he was a fool not to have fucked her. It's not every day that a beautiful girl like that throws herself at him. And him ridiculously fighting her off like some virtuous old virgin. It would have been a perfect time for something like that to happen, with him leaving the country, for years perhaps. No awkward meetings with her with his father or Caroline there, no temptation to keep it going. Just an hour or two of fun and pleasure, as Clara said, and then it would be the secret of the two of them forever. What other people don't know, as Clara said, isn't going to hurt them.

She looked so good this morning. Smelled so good. She had prepared herself for him. Clara never goes into any situation unprepared. He imagines clutching her breast through the thin jersey top. Plunging his hand under her skirt and up and in between those incredible legs. Finding flimsy panties—

His computer emits the electronic burbling noise that means someone's trying to contact him on Skype.

It's Caroline. The computer screen blossoms with her blonde and coppery beauty.

"So what are you doing?" she says. She's smiling, but he has the uncomfortable feeling she knows exactly what he was just thinking about.

"Packing. It's so boring, and I'm so bad at it."

"You need me there, I'm a great packer."

"I know, I wish you were here."

"You look tired."

"I am. There's so much to do."

"Poor Roberto. I know how you hate to do anything practical."

He laughs. "I'm not like that."

"But you are. Have you sold your car yet?"

"Not yet. I really like that car. I hate to give it up."

"It doesn't make sense to put it in storage. It's an unnecessary expense, and it will just deteriorate."

For the daughter of a rich man, she's surprisingly thrifty.

"You're right, I'll take care of it."

"And how is it going with the old girlfriends? Notifying them that you're leaving?"

"One or two are contemplating suicide. But the rest are holding up fairly well."

"I'm glad."

He hears an off-screen hacking noise.

"Uh-oh, Gabriela's throwing up," says Caroline. She disappears from the screen, then returns a few moments later. "Hair ball."

"How's your mother?"

"She's been a little better the last couple of days." Caroline looks sad. "But is that a good thing, really? All these little rallies do is just prolong things. Probably it would be better if she just took a drastic turn for the worse, and then it was over. As it is, her torture just continues. So does my father's."

"And it can't be easy on you either."

"As long as I know that you're in my life, I'm okay. I can handle it."

Roberto feels a sudden pang of guilt about having been mentally unfaithful to her with Clara.

"I'll be in your life as long as you want me."

"That means always."

"I don't deserve you."

"You're crazy."

"I love you."

"Oh I love you too. I want to see you. It seems like it's been years since I've seen you. Wednesday can't come soon enough."

"It's just two days. It will pass in no time," and then he says, "Caroline? Take off your shirt."

She gives him an odd, crooked little smile, then pulls her T-shirt over her head. She's not wearing a bra. Her breasts aren't large, but are perfectly shaped. He's always loved her compact little nipples.

"Stand up," he says. She stands, and "Now the rest," he says.

She strips off pants and panties, revealing the dark gold of her pubic hair. She sits back down and says, "Your turn."

He takes off his clothes. He's already hard. He starts to stroke himself.

"Touch your nipples," he says, and she does, and then he says, "Touch yourself down there."

She does. She closes her eyes, and sighs.

"You're inside me, Roberto. Do you feel it? I feel it. You feel so good inside me. I've never felt anything like this. It's you, Roberto. It's you, it's you, it's you, it's you—"

* * *

Blanca, head to toe: teased bleached blonde hair, green metallic eye shadow, bright-orange lipstick, an elaborate emerald necklace, a green chiffon bustier with a spray of glittering green beads extending over the right boob, fingernail polish that matches the lipstick, skin-tight orange satin stretch pants, and orange stiletto heels. She has a vivid, fruity quality about her, as befits a former Miss Mango or Miss Tangerine.

She's a centimeter or two taller than Franz. She has a tremendous figure that looks as though it ought to appear in the tabloids. If with Clara it's a matter of conjecture whether she's ever had cosmetic surgery, Blanca has never tried to hide the fact she's had many procedures, nose, eyes, lips, breasts, especially breasts. She's paid a visit to the "tit factory," as Franz calls it, four different times, most recently because she felt she had overshot the mark the third time and wanted them scaled back a bit.

At the moment, she's berating the nanny for allowing the youngest of the three children, Abril, to drop some food on the floor.

"I'm tired of the children making messes, Josefina."

"I'm sorry, ma'am," Josefina says, starting to rise from her chair. "I'll clean it up."

"Stay where you are," says Blanca, "that's the maid's job," and on cue one of the maids comes scurrying over to clean up the not very messy mess. "The maids clean things up. You control the children. Do you understand?"

"Yes ma'am," Josefina says meekly.

Blanca is hard on nannies, and goes through several a year. They all look more or less the same: Blanca has liked them to be as dark and little and ugly as possible, ever since she caught Franz having sex with a cute nanny from France. Now Blanca flashes her big white teeth at Roberto in an apologetic smile.

"How do you like the chicken?" she asks.

"It's delicious, Blanca."

Everybody is having chicken and rice except for the vegan Franz, who is having grilled tofu and vegetables.

"Papa says you're leaving," says Siegfried. At eight, he's the oldest child. He's looking at Roberto solemnly. He seems much older than eight.

"Yes, on Wednesday."

"But Papa didn't tell us why. It seems to be a big secret."

Roberto glances at Franz. He nods slightly.

"There are some people in this country who don't like the stories I write. Some of them are dangerous. So I thought it would be a good idea to leave for a while. But I'll be back."

"When?" says Britney. Named after an American pop singer who is a favorite of Blanca's.

"It won't be too long, I hope."

"Will you be back by Christmas?" asks Britney.

"Probably not."

"That means you'll be gone a long time," Abril says. "Christmas is a long time."

He'll miss Franz's kids. Despite having Blanca as their mother, they have turned out well. They're all calm and good-natured like Franz. They also have his blond blue-eyed good looks.

"We'll visit Roberto in Saint Lucia," says Franz. "You've never been there before. They have beautiful beaches. We can swim in the ocean. It will be fun."

"Do they have volcanoes there?" asks Siegfried. "I've always wanted to visit a volcano."

"They actually do have one," says Roberto. "It's dormant though."

"It doesn't have lava in it? I want to see lava."

"A little steam, but no lava. Sorry."

"They have volcanos with lava in Hawaii," says Blanca. "We should go there."

"Can we, Papa?" asks Siegfried.

"Okay."

"But what about me, Siegfried?" Roberto teases. "Don't you want to visit me in Saint Lucia?"

"Yes, Roberto, very much. Even more than I want to see a volcano with lava."

He says this with such earnestness that all the adults laugh.

"What's the shopping like in Saint Lucia?" says Blanca.

"I don't know. I'll ask Caroline."

Blanca loves above all things to travel and shop. Her closets are filled with the clothes and the house is cluttered with the curios and artifacts and artwork she has bought on their frequent trips. She has no job, no cause she supports, no charitable work she does. All her days are the same. She's entirely a creature of the moment, like a bird or an insect. She laughs often, but seldom at anything actually funny. Roberto still finds it hard to believe Franz ever married her.

She was the daughter of the chief of police in the little subtropical town of San Tomé, about a hundred kilometers from the city. Franz bought a farm near the town as a vacation retreat not long after he graduated from college. He took an interest in the affairs of the town and donated a large sum of money so a new school could be built. The mayor of San Tomé asked him if he would do the town the honor of judging its yearly beauty contest, Miss Pineapple or Miss Guava, and Franz, who loves women, was happy to oblige. And so he met and married Blanca.

Franz is very reticent about his personal life, even with his closest friends, so his relationship with his wife is something of a mystery to Roberto. They seem spectacularly ill-matched, and yet they've stayed together for nine years. Probably if the kids hadn't come along so quickly, the marriage would have been over a long time ago. There doesn't seem to be much if any passion still simmering between them. Roberto knows Franz doesn't like change, so perhaps over time he has simply grown accustomed to a life with Blanca. Roberto's guess is they have an arrangement, even if it's never been put into words: she's free to do whatever she wants, and he can see other women, as long as it's not like the French nanny and doesn't happen physically in front of her face. Franz always seems to have a girlfriend or two; occasionally he will vaguely allude to one, although Roberto has never met any of them or even learned their names.

"Caroline's so sweet," Blanca says, "I like her so much."

"She's very fond of you too, Blanca," Roberto lies.

"So when are you getting married? Have you set the date?"

"Not yet."

"Is it going to be a big wedding?"

"I don't know, we haven't talked about it. I hope not."

"Oh, every girl wants a big wedding. I know I certainly did," and she looks at Franz. "Remember how big ours was?"

Franz nods grimly.

"I love to plan weddings," Blanca continues, "it's really my field of expertise. My mother's the same way, they call her the Wedding Queen of San Tomé. Please tell Caroline I'd be more than happy to help her when the time comes. I'll fly to Saint Lucia at a moment's notice!"

"That's very generous of you, Blanca," says Roberto. "Yes, I will tell Caroline that."

* * *

"There is an ancient Arabic saying," Franz says, toying with the glass of wine from which he will barely drink. "'There are as many paths to God as there are children of Adam.'"

"But to me that's simply nonsense," Roberto says.

"But Roberto, don't you see? That's the particular path you're on. The path of denial. You can't escape being on a path, no matter how hard you try."

"So is a killer on a path to God?"

"Yes. Because who's to say the journey's supposed to take just one lifetime? Maybe it takes a nearly infinite series of lives to get to God."

"Define God. Just so we'll know exactly what we're talking about."

"God is that which cannot be defined."

"How convenient."

"The truth is what it is, Roberto. Whether or not you or I find it convenient."

"Okay, here's some truth for you. I saw a little girl yesterday. Sitting in an outhouse. Covered with blood. She'd been shot in the head, but before she was killed her sexual organs had been mutilated."

Franz looks surprised. "My god, Roberto. What happened?"

Roberto tells him about the three murders, and then about Lieutenant Matallana.

"I talked to him today. He thinks he knows who the killers are. And I don't believe they're on a path to God."

"I understand."

"Anyway. I've had enough of this country, at least for a while. I'm more than happy to leave."

"I don't blame you."

Roberto's in Franz's study, sitting on a low couch with plenty of pillows. The floor is polished stone. Water flows down over glistening rocks into a pool with goldfish in it, producing a soothing trickling noise. In front of a golden and mysteriously smiling statue of the Buddha is a mat on which Franz does his yoga. Franz likes candles, and there are several burning around the room. Beyond the room is the rest of the house, far too large for a family of five, and reflective of Blanca's eclectic taste. Beyond the house are surveillance cameras and high, ivy-covered walls, and beyond the walls is a gated community patrolled by security guards with shotguns. And beyond the gated community are the chaotic city and the crazed country and the perishing planet, and so it is always pleasant to sit with Franz and sip his excellent wine in the enclave of simplicity and serenity he has established here.

The room is silent now, except for the trickling water. Roberto's aware that Franz, after hearing his story about what he found in the outhouse, doesn't know what else to say. Franz is very generous in a general way, he gives away a lot of money to people in need and his various causes, but Roberto knows he has an aversion to being burdened with other people's problems. He is not generous with his heart. Roberto takes him off the hook and changes the subject.

"How are your farmers doing?"

Franz's face brightens. "They're doing wonderfully. They love the new methods. They're beginning to understand that if you're kind to the soil that doesn't mean you won't make money. It's quite the contrary."

Franz is conducting a sort of experiment on his farm in San Tomé. He's divided it into plots of land he's turned over to local farmers, on condition they use the latest organic techniques he's gleaned from endless hours spent searching through technical journals and the Internet. He monitors their work closely, requiring monthly reports. At the end of ten years each farmer will receive title to his plot of land, provided Franz is satisfied with what he's done. Daniel calls the farmers Franz's "lab rats."

"I wish you had time to come to San Tomé before you left," says Franz. "It's changed so much since the last time you were there. I have to admit, things are going so well it's making me a little nervous."

"You're afraid it's going to be destroyed because it works?"

"Yes, exactly."

There's a timid knock at the door.

"Come in," calls Franz.

The door opens. Abril peers in. She stands there speechless.

"What do you want, Abril?"

"Siegfried wants to know if he can show Roberto his new video game."

"What game is that?"

"The one with shooting and monsters."

"Why didn't Siegfried come and ask Roberto himself?"

"I don't know."

"Tell Siegfried Roberto and I are talking, and Roberto can see it later."

"Okay."

Abril keeps standing in the doorway, looking around at Franz's study. She doesn't see it very often. No one—wife, kids, employees—is allowed in here without Franz's permission. Roberto can tell it's a place of wonder for her, like a mysterious cave where a wizard lives. Suddenly she smiles brightly, showing a missing front tooth.

"Bye, Papa!"

"Bye, Abril."

She closes the door softly.

"Where were we?" says Franz.

"We were talking about the farmers . . . their future."

Franz shakes his head. Touches the glass of wine to his lips and drinks a drop or two. "Anything new in this country is considered 'dangerous' and 'subversive.' Murder the farmers and burn the fields, that's our answer to the new. How can progress even be possible here?"

"Maybe it's not possible. Maybe the future will be like the past."

"I've been rereading *Resurrection* by Tolstoy, have you ever read it?"

Roberto shakes his head.

"It's fascinating. It's a total top-to-bottom indictment of Russian society in the 1890s: the government, the church, the military, the rich, the poor. It's about the greed, the corruption, the phoniness, the hypocrisy. It's astonishing how much that time in that country is like this country right now. It makes you wonder why human beings can't ever seem to get it right."

Roberto gazes at the goldfish, only half listening as Franz continues to go on about Tolstoy. He got a degree in philosophy at the university, and Roberto thinks he probably would have been happier as a college professor like Andrés than working in the family business. He disapproves of the products they make and would never allow one of their delicious chocolates to pass between his own fastidious lips.

The goldfish make Roberto think of Diana Langenberg. He wonders what she's doing now. Petting her dog with the yearning human eyes? Listening to her assistant Hermés play the ukulele? Through his shirt, he touches the St. Jude's medal she gave him. He may not believe it protects him but he likes feeling it there. Occasionally when you get a gift, it's not as if you're receiving something new but it's as if something lost has been restored to you and you know you will keep it to the end of your days.

And then something odd happens. It's like a gust of cold wind blows right through his bones. He looks around to see if a door or window has been opened but none have. The flames of all the candles remain upright, unwavering. And then it is like the wind dies away.

He looks at Franz. He doesn't seem to have noticed anything. He's still talking, talking, though not any more about Tolstoy evidently, he can go on for hours when he's like this.

"'O monks,' said the Buddha," says Franz, "'know that all things are on fire.' Every atom of each one of us is on fire, Roberto, with passion, anger, and delusion. How can we possibly save ourselves?"

* * *

Roberto waves at two guards with shotguns, who wave back and open the gates. He heads toward home. He feels an agreeable buzz from Franz's wine. He listens to music, and thinks about what's left to do.

Lunch tomorrow with his father. And at some point he needs to stop off at Andrés's apartment and say good-bye to him and his wife. He's called and emailed and texted Daniel but hasn't got a response. No surprise. Typical of Daniel. He'll doubtless resurface before Roberto leaves. He thought Daniel could drive him to the airport. He needs to hook up with Iván tomorrow, have him sign the lease and give him a check and Roberto will give him the keys. The packing's practically finished. He still has to do something with the car. And then Wednesday the airport, and soaring away on silver wings.

He checks his voice mail. Lieutenant Matallana left a message about two hours ago. He sounds excited. "I'm returning your call, Roberto, but I also have something to tell *you*. It could be a real break for us. Please call me on my cellphone as soon as you get this."

As Roberto calls him, he feels a tingle of anticipation. What luck it is for Roberto that he is the one handling the case. Not one cop in a thousand in this city would be pursuing it like him.

"Hello," says a voice. It doesn't sound like Matallana.

"May I speak to Lieutenant Matallana?"

"Who is this?"

"Who is *this*?"

"Sergeant Salcedo, police department. Your name please."

The voice is cold and abrupt; Roberto doesn't like the voice.

"José Rodriguez," he says.

"What is the purpose of your call?"

"It's a personal matter. Now will you please put him on?"

"That would be impossible."

"Why?"

"He's dead."

"What?"

"The lieutenant is dead. I'm standing by his body."

"How?"

"He's been shot. Now tell me. Why did you want to talk to him?"

But Roberto can't speak. He can hardly breathe.

"Rodriguez?" says Salcedo.

He slows down. He pulls his car over to the side of the road.

"Rodriguez? Rodriguez? Rodriguez!"

Five days until the day
Roberto is to die

Beto is sitting behind his desk in the lobby, tapping at his smartphone with his thumbs. He jumps up and smiles when he sees Roberto and wishes him good morning.

"Good morning, Beto. Let me ask you a question."

"Yes sir."

"Do you need a car?"

"A car?"

"You don't have one, do you? Don't you ride the bus?"

"Yes sir. Back and forth from La Vega." A neighborhood to the south.

"I'm leaving tomorrow, and I won't be needing my car anymore. I thought that maybe you'd like to have it."

Beto stares at Roberto, wondering if he's heard him right.

"Your car? The Kia?"

"Yes."

He swallows nervously, which causes the Adam's apple in his skinny neck to bob.

"And you want to . . . to give it to me?"

Roberto nods. "I'll be needing it today, but tomorrow I'll give you the keys and the title."

"But why give it to *me*?"

"Why not you? I've put a lot of kilometers on it, but it's in pretty good shape. Except for the roof."

"What's wrong with the roof?"

"Some idiot hit it with a rock yesterday."

Now Beto smiles. As wide a smile as Robert's seen in quite some time. "It's not a problem. I'll have it fixed!"

Roberto goes back upstairs to his apartment. Fourteen cardboard boxes and three suitcases sit near the front door, all bearing the Saint Lucia address of Caroline's parents. A shipping company is supposed to arrive within the hour and pick them up.

He calls Andrés and asks him when he should come by.

"My last class is at two," says Andrés. "I should be home no later than four. Any time after that."

"Five?"

"That's fine.

"How's Teresa?"

"Well, honestly, Roberto, I'm hoping you'll be able to cheer her up. Ever since I told her you were leaving, she's barely had a word to say. You know her, you never know where her mind is going."

"Teresa is tougher than you think. I think maybe she's tougher than any of us."

He hears Andrés sigh. "Okay, Roberto. I'll see you later."

Roberto checks his emails. He has one from Gloria Varela, under the subject line: **Humberto has found a home!** *With two retired lesbians (to be clear, they're retired from their careers, not from being lesbians). Their cat died recently, and they're delighted to have Humberto. They live just down the street, so I'll be able to look in on our long-eared friend from time to time and give you a report. So bon voyage, Roberto! It is time for you to leave our happy, sad, wonderful, terrible country. Forget about all the dark things, and enjoy life on your enchanted island.*

He googles: "tulcán."

He looks for news stories in the last week.

Five workers have been killed in a terrorist attack on the Northern Transversal Strip.

President Dávila announced Monday a "humanitarian mission" to Tulcán to protect civilians from the terrorists. "The security situation is deteriorating rapidly," Dávila said, "which is why I am immediately ordering twenty-eight thousand of our best-trained troops into the province. Our ultimate aims are peace and stability, but make no mistake: the war against terror will continue until terror is uprooted and terminated, regardless of the sacrifices."

The minister of mines and energy was in Tulcán last week touring a gold mine. "In uncertain economic times such as these, smart investors go to gold," said the minister. "That's why the discovery of these new gold fields will prove to be a great boon to all the people of Tulcán."

He sees the broad brown peasant features of General Horacio Oropeza in a video of an interview conducted by an obsequious TV reporter. "It's time for Tulcán to finally choose between good and evil, violence and peace, civilization and the law of the jungle," Oropeza says, looking straight into the camera with his heavy-lidded, indifferent eyes. When the reporter asks him about an offer from the Tulcán Independence Movement, the main opposition group, to negotiate directly with the general to head off what they call an "impending bloodbath," the suggestion of a smile pulls at the corners of the general's lips. "The leaders of the TIM are very impressive men. They dress in expensive suits, they are pleasant, and they smile a lot. They speak well, using many big words that I don't even know the meaning of. So why am I so suspicious? Maybe because of something I learned as a boy growing up on a farm deep in the jungle: though the monkey dresses in silk, it's still a monkey."

He checks in on the Twitter feed of former president Landazábal, and sees that just a few minutes ago he issued this pithy tweet: *The terrorists in Tulcán are mosquitoes requiring insecticide.*

Okay, Roberto thinks. It's happening now. The Sri Lanka option in Tulcán.

The Black Jaguars, the paramilitary arm of the Committee for the Defense of the Nation, have a history of working closely with the Army; in fact, their peppy slogan is: "We do things the Army can't!" They're led by a shadowy figure with the nom de guerre of Hernán 40, known for his extraordinary cruelty. The situation in Tulcán, where there's a need for innocent civilians to be brutalized and murdered, seems tailor-made for them. He googles: "tulcán black jaguars." But nothing turns up.

His cellphone pings three times. He takes a look at the text message that has just come in: *see you at usual place 11 w.*

* * *

Dreamlike, over the green trees, he floats up the slopes of Mount

Cabanacande. He shares the orange cable car with about twenty other people, including a cheerful cluster of teenage Asian girls, probably students on a trip, who are chirping away at one another like birds. The view of the city as he gets higher and higher really is amazing and is why so many tourists flock here, though most of the people who actually live in the shadow of Mount Cabanacande tend to take it for granted and seldom make the trip to its top.

When he steps out of the cable car it's chilly and windy, and he's glad he's wearing his windbreaker. The air is very clear today and the sun is shining and white clouds drift over the broad valley.

He walks up the winding stone path toward the white church. It gleams so brightly in the sun it nearly hurts his eyes. It was built two centuries ago after the original church that had been built two centuries before that was leveled in an earthquake. He walks up the steps of the church and goes inside.

A scattering of people are sitting quietly in the pews and a few tourists are wandering around taking pictures but he doesn't see Willie. He's a little early. He sits down in an empty pew.

The city is full of old churches and this one is pretty but nothing exceptional. Behind the altar is a statue of the Fallen Christ. It's four hundred years old, and was the only thing in the original church spared by the earthquake. Its survival was immediately labeled miraculous; since then, thousands of sick or desperate people have come to the top of the mountain to pray to the statue, and many purported miracles have occurred. The Fallen Christ is lying on his side, propped up on one arm; he's fallen while carrying the cross up the hill to his crucifixion. The statue is made of bronze but long, stringy, apparently real hair hangs from his head and a purple and gold cloth is wrapped around his middle. He's bloody and scourged and has an appalled look on his face like the Christ in Manuel's mother's house and Roberto thinks how strange it is that a religion would take as its symbol the image of a man being hideously tortured, though it seems to have a kind of appropriateness in a country such as this.

Willie Rivera sits down beside him. He's a little winded from the walk up from the cable car.

"I've got to lose twenty pounds," he says.

"Thanks for coming."

He nods. He's wearing sunglasses. He looks around the church.

"I love coming here. It's so peaceful. I could sit here forever."

But he doesn't come close to sitting there forever, he sits for just another second or two before he sighs and stands up. Roberto walks with him out of the church.

It's not just the church that's up here, there's a whole little world. Beautiful gardens. A fancy French restaurant, and a couple of cheaper places. A brick street lined with shops selling handicrafts and religious junk and snacks and soda. And a colony of polydactyl cats. They've been here as long as anybody can remember. There's a tradition that cats with extra digits on their feet bring good luck, and so they're pampered and spoiled like Caroline's cats.

Roberto and Willie stroll along, in the gusty wind, on top of the mountain, under the huge sky.

"How's Helen's cold?" asks Roberto.

"Better. So I assume this is about Tulcán."

"Yes."

"You're going there?"

Roberto nods.

"What changed your mind?"

Roberto tells him. About Manuel and his mother and Nydia, and Lieutenant Matallana, and the lieutenant's murder.

"He was shot down on the street in front of his apartment building. As he got out of his car. No witnesses, of course. He had a wife. Three daughters."

"Yeah," says Willie, "I heard something about it on the news. So I wonder what he wanted to tell you."

"He must have gotten some hard evidence against Toño González or the CPN."

"Too bad. Sounds like he was one of the good guys."

He doesn't sound too sad about it. People die all the time, the good and the bad, in Willie's world.

They're walking up the brick street lined with shops. Willie stops at one, and buys a pink apple-flavored soft drink.

"I'm addicted to this shit," he says. "Helen's been trying to get me to stop, but it's no use. I just can't help myself." He takes a long drink then says, "So what's the connection?"

"Between what?"

"Between these four murders, and you going to Tulcán."

Roberto thinks about it.

"I guess I just can't let them win. At least not completely. I'm still leaving the country, but I'm going to do something before I do."

"What's the plan?"

"I've booked a flight for tomorrow to Saint Lucia. When I go to the airport, I assume they'll be following me. Make sure that I leave. Except I won't be going to Saint Lucia, I'll fly to Robledo. I'll get a car there and drive to Tulcán. I'll spend three days in Tulcán. I know that's not much, but it's the best I can do. Then I'll go back to Robledo and fly to Saint Lucia on Sunday."

"Have you told Caroline?"

Roberto gives a tight smile. "No. Not yet."

"What are you going to tell her? Wait, I know. You're going to lie like a son of a bitch."

Roberto laughs.

"Okay, Willie. Now tell me what I need to know about Tulcán."

"Homero del Basto. The minister of mines and energy. He's the key guy."

"I saw he was in Tulcán last week. At a gold mine."

"He's still in Tulcán, and gold has nothing to do with it. Do you know what coltan is?"

"Some kind of metal they mine in the Congo. They use it in cellphones, right?"

"Cellphones, laptops, video games, all kinds of electronics. And you're right, most of it comes from the Congo. But there's a problem with coltan mining: it makes a hell of a mess. They're cutting down the jungle and polluting the rivers and when the workers get hungry, they shoot a gorilla, which makes the Save the Gorillas people mad. They've also got a war going on that's killed six million people, and the security situation's terrible. And so there's a worldwide hunt on for more sources of coltan."

"And they've found it in Tulcán."

"A massive fucking shitload of it," he says in English. "In the southeast, along the Otavalo River. It's been selling for as much as $200 a kilo. That's why greedy bastards like del Basto are there."

"But is Tulcán really any better than the Congo? In terms of security?"

"No, and that's the point. The military's been looking for an excuse to go into Tulcán for years, and now it has it. The Sri Lanka option is being imposed to make Tulcán safe for coltan mining. Keep an eye on your president. He's going to be making an announcement in the next few weeks about the discovery of coltan, and he's going to declare the southeast part of the province a 'national security reserve.' Which means it will be under the permanent control of the military. He's going to say his reasons are to prevent illegal mining operations and to protect the environment and the local people, but of course by that time most of the local people will be either dead or refugees. Rights will be auctioned off to transnational mining companies, and the Otavalo Valley will become their private little playground."

They're still walking along the brick street. Willie pauses at a shop selling jewelry. One of the polydactyl cats is stretched out on the top of a glass display case, drowsing blissfully and soaking up the sun. Willie peers in at the jewelry.

"It's Helen's birthday Thursday, and I still haven't gotten her anything. She loves birthdays and birthday presents. The pressure's building. I'm starting to panic."

Now they walk on. Roberto looks at Willie thoughtfully.

"Why are you telling me this, Willie?"

"You want the cynical answer, or the more or less true answer?"

"Both."

"The cynical answer is your country's our best friend in South America, but you drive us crazy sometimes. For instance, one American president after another has tried to push a free trade agreement between you and us through Congress but it's been blocked by the liberals because you guys have the nasty habit of killing your labor leaders. Though the situation seems to have improved under Dávila."

"That's because there are so few labor leaders left to kill."

"Maybe. But right now we're very close to an agreement. But we can kiss it good-bye," he says in English, "if the shit hits the fan in Tulcán."

"And the more or less true answer?"

"Some of us in the government don't like mass murder. Even if it's being done by our friends."

"I'm going to need a guide. Someone who knows the Otavalo Valley."

"Let me work on it. I'll call you later."

"Okay."

Willie checks his Concord watch.

"I better head back."

They walk back down the sloping street.

"I've always wondered about your watch," says Roberto.

Willie laughs, and looks at it. Big and black. Covered with diamonds.

"It's some watch, huh?"

"It's never really seemed to fit you."

"Why not?"

Roberto shrugs. "Memo Soto was wearing a watch like that when I interviewed him. It seemed to fit him."

"Yeah, I suppose it's a little extravagant. But I've always had a thing for watches. When I was only four years old, I pestered the shit out of my parents till they bought me a Mickey Mouse watch." He's quiet for a moment. "You know, I remember Memo Soto's watch."

"You met him?"

"Yeah. Except he was dead already. He'd been shot about fifty times."

"I thought that happened before you came here."

"I've been here twice. The guy had balls, I'll say that for him. Said he wouldn't be taken alive and he wasn't."

"And you were in on it?"

He nods. "I was on one of the Black Hawks. Zooming in over the mountains. It was exciting as hell, I'll tell you that."

"Is it true you used his cellphone to track him down?"

"No, that was just a cover story. One of his own guys gave him up. They'd known each other since they were kids. He started feeling the heat, so he cut a deal with us. Last I heard, he was living the good life in Miami Beach. A beer in one hand and a tit in the other." Willie laughs. He throws his empty soft drink bottle in a trash can. "Guys like Soto. Their biggest threats are their friends, not their enemies."

They're on the stone path that leads down to the cable car station. Roberto's not quite ready to go.

"I think I'll catch the next one, Willie."

"Okay, sure."

They stand there in the windy sunlight and look at each other.

"I feel kind of guilty," Willie says.

"About what?"

"If I'd kept my mouth shut, you'd be flying out of here tomorrow. Instead of heading into that shithole."

"I'll be fine," Roberto says, and they shake hands. "Thanks for everything. And please keep an eye on my father."

"Don't worry, Roberto, I will. I'll be calling you about the guide."

"Okay."

Willie walks off down the path. He calls back over his shoulder in English, "Downhill's better than uphill, that's for damn sure!"

Roberto laughs and waves. Now he moves over to the stone wall that flanks the path. He leans his elbows on it and gazes out upon the valley. He doesn't believe in anything of a spiritual or transcendent nature most of the time but occasionally, like right now, he does. Because what he is looking at is so unspeakably beautiful. Luminous clouds extend to the horizon; they are shot through with great shafts of light. A ragged line of white birds floats past, shining in the light, bound from one unknown to another unknown. And the city, the city of his birth, of every one of his thirty-three years, he can see it all, this city of seven million, in a single sweeping look. Lying there as though resting in the giant hand of God.

He feels something brush past his legs. He looks down, and sees one of the polydactyl cats. A gray and white one, begging for attention. Roberto reaches down and pets it and scratches it behind the ears. For luck.

* * *

He calls Daniel, and leaves another message.

"Daniel, I really need to talk to you, it's important. Quit fucking around and call me."

He's driving back to his apartment. He's supposed to meet Iván there but Roberto's running late. He talked to Iván earlier this morning. He sounded excited. He can't wait to get out of his parents' place and plans to move in as soon as Roberto's left. It seems strange to think another person will be living in his apartment tomorrow, cooking in his kitchen and showering in his shower and maybe if he gets lucky, making love to a girl in his bed.

A National Police helicopter buzzes overhead, crossing the street he's on at an angle. He's been driving through an upper-class neighborhood that with no transition has given way to an Army base on both sides of the street. He's always thought it an unusual location for an Army base but everyone in the city seems to accept it. Through a chain-link fence he sees soldiers climbing into trucks. He wonders if they're going where he's going.

As usual he's constantly checking his mirrors and keeping an eye on any car or motorcycle that gets close to him. He doesn't think anyone's been following him this morning but he can't be sure. He operates under the assumption that all phone calls are being listened in on, all emails and text messages intercepted, all movements monitored when he leaves his apartment. For all Roberto knows, yesterday people were grinning and giggling as they watched his and Caroline's passionate interaction on Skype. But no matter how careful he is, he can never be certain he hasn't screwed up in some disastrous way. Unless he curls up in a corner of his apartment twenty-four hours a day and sucks on his thumb.

His cell rings and he's hoping it's Daniel but it's only eager Iván, impatiently waiting for him in the lobby.

"Ten minutes, Iván. I'll be there in ten minutes."

* * *

Osaka is the best Japanese restaurant in the city, and Roberto and his father have been eating here for years. They're sitting at a table next to the front window. Sunlight angles in and lights up the colorful food: white and orange and green and yellow rolls of various kinds, pink ginger, green wasabi, dark-green seaweed, golden glasses of tamarind juice.

"Try the salmon roll, Roberto, it's excellent," his father says. He's eating hungrily and smiling; he seems to have recovered his customary sunny equanimity.

"It is good," Roberto says of the salmon roll.

"What time does your plane leave tomorrow?"

"Ten fifteen."

"You fly through Caracas?"

"Yes."

"You know, something you said Saturday night has stuck with me. You said you're always doing the same stories over and over, like a cat chasing its tail. I think there's no other way to look at this move except as a good thing. You can spread your wings, see world. I've always thought this country was too small a stage for someone with your talent."

Roberto doubts he's ever had such a thought but all he says is "Thanks, Dad. I'm thinking about it the same way you are."

He takes a drink of his tamarind juice; one thing he's going to miss about his country, it has the most marvelous juices.

"I'm concerned about Grandmother," he says. "When I saw her on Sunday, it was like she was in a fog. At one point she seemed to think I was you."

His father sighs. "I'm afraid she's slowly descending into dementia. She seems to be heading for exactly the kind of ending that I know she fears the most. But what am I supposed to do? Tell her I'm giving her a vitamin shot and instead give her a lethal injection? If an animal gets sick, you can put it out of its misery. But not a human being."

Yoshio Fujita, the owner and chef of Osaka, comes to the table. He's a slight man with a somber face and kind eyes.

"How is everything, doctor?" he asks.

"Splendid, Yoshio, as usual."

A waiter following Yoshio places another plate of food down on the table.

"Please, with my compliments," says Yoshio. "Very special whitefish."

Roberto and his father thank him. His father is one of Yoshio's favorite customers, and he's always giving him things.

Horns are blowing out front, there's a terrible traffic jam. Yoshio looks out at it, shaking his head.

"People should calm down," he says. "Not be in such a big hurry."

His father joins Yoshio in frowning at the street.

"I agree, Yoshio. What's life for if not to enjoy it?"

"Japanese people," Yoshio says. "Earthquake and tsunami was warning to them from God not to be so materialistic. I have a T-shirt twenty-nine-years old, why do I need new one?"

His father nods along. Wearing the perfectly cut gray suit he got three months ago in London.

"Businessmen come to me, they say, 'Yoshio, why not open up Osaka restaurants in other cities? I'll give you the money, we'll all become rich, hundreds of Osakas all over world!' But I have plenty of problems with only one Osaka, hundreds of Osakas will drive me crazy."

His father laughs. "Just promise me you'll keep this Osaka going, Yoshio, no matter the problems."

Yoshio smiles. "I promise, doctor. Enjoy whitefish." Now he bows a little and withdraws.

"Clara said she stopped by your apartment yesterday," his father says.

Roberto is glad his mouth is full of food, so he doesn't have to immediately respond. He wonders why she told him that. Probably to cover her tracks on the off chance she'd been observed by some nosy someone going to his apartment. She's very smart that way.

"Yes," he says, "it was good to see her. I'm going to miss her."

"She'll miss you too, Roberto, believe me. I think you have no idea how grateful she is to you. For your help with her book, and also for the way you treated her in the beginning. When everyone else was taking your mother's side. But you gave her a chance. Which is all Clara ever needs."

He is still starry-eyed in love with her. Roberto's almost positive he's been faithful to her, which is not necessarily in his nature. Thank god, Roberto thinks, that he didn't sleep with her. This lunch would have been unbearable otherwise.

"I showed her some of the old photographs Mother gave me." He feels the need to sketch in a few details about what he and Clara did in his apartment. "She seemed fascinated with them."

"Yes, she mentioned that. Your uncle Adrián and his cat—she loved that story. You and I are lucky, Roberto, we're members of a real family, we know where we came from, we have uncles and aunts and cousins and grandparents whose lives we can look back on with pride and sadness and amusement and love. Clara has none of that. She came from a place where they didn't love their children and treat them like treasures, they abused and terrorized them. It's a wonder Clara was able to escape from all that. I know she envies what you and I and . . . and your mother . . . have had." He pensively fingers his glass of juice. "She wants us to have a child. What do you think of that?"

Roberto's taken aback. Although having a child is an obvious possible consequence of marriage, for some reason it's never occurred to him it might happen with his father and Clara.

"Do you want a child?"

"I don't know. Maybe. But maybe I'm too old. I'm worried I'd be more like a grandfather than a father."

"Dad, you're not too old. You should do it if that's what you want."

"You wouldn't mind having a little brother or sister?"

"No, I think it would be cool."

His father is quiet for a moment as he thinks it over—and it is on the tip of Roberto's tongue to say something like this: "Any child would be unbelievably lucky to have you as his father. Just like I've been unbelievably lucky. Your love and approval have never been absent from my life for a second, I've always known your strength was never far away. Once when I was a shy little kid afraid of his own shadow, you told me I should walk like I belonged on the earth, not like an uninvited guest. I've never forgotten that, there are so many things you've taught me I have never forgotten."

But Roberto is silent, and the moment passes.

"Have you called your mother?" his father asks. "Does she know your plans?"

"No, I thought I'd wait till I got to Saint Lucia. She'd just freak out if I told her now. She'd be calling me every hour to see if I was all right. You know how she is."

"Oh yes." He laughs. "I know quite well how she is."

Roberto's cellphone rings.

"I'm sorry, I need to answer this." His father nods, and Roberto says, "Hello."

"You know a club called Blonde? In the Pink Zone?"

It's Willie.

"Yes."

"Can you meet someone there in an hour?"

"Yes."

"Good-bye, Roberto. Good luck."

"Thanks."

*　*　*

He walks into Blonde. It's the middle of the afternoon, and it's nearly empty. A young couple are sitting at a table, cozily talking over cocktails. A guy about Roberto's age is sitting at the bar drinking a beer. Thinking the guy may be his contact, Roberto sits down on a stool near him. But he's busy with his smartphone and doesn't act like he's waiting for anyone.

Behind the bar are larger than life pictures of tall blonde gringo girls wearing bikinis. An American rap song is pounding out of the sound system: *Nasty girl, I want to do you all night long!* Roberto came here with Caroline about a year ago because it was the hot new place and Caroline likes to check out such things. It was wall-to-wall people that night. They lasted barely twenty minutes before fighting their way to the exit and escaping.

The bartender, looking as though he could not be more bored, comes over and asks what Roberto wants.

"Get my friend a beer! A Brava!"

The guy next to Roberto is leaning toward him and grinning with his hand stuck out.

"Hello, Roberto," he says, "I'm Javier."

Roberto shakes hands with him.

"Good to meet you, Javier."

"Hey man, it's my pleasure. I'm a big fan of your work."

"Thank you."

Javier speaks the somewhat Italian-sounding Spanish of Argentina. Now he looks around the room with apparent admiration. "This is quite a place, huh?"

"Yeah. Have you been here before?"

"No, this is the first time. I'm meeting a friend here later, he suggested it." He looks up at the frieze of blondes. "I'm in love with every one of those girls."

The bartender sets Roberto's beer down. Javier insists on paying for it.

"Thanks," says Roberto. "Let's grab a table."

They walk through the dim light and the loud music. Javier's wearing a red flannel shirt, green pants that are too short for him, and hiking boots that look as if they've gone thousands of miles. He's tall and lean, with fair skin, thinning hair, and an unkempt beard. He has big lips and buck teeth, and his face manages to be both ugly and appealing.

They sit down at a table.

"Willie says you want to go to Tulcán," he says.

Roberto nods. "To the Otavalo Valley in particular. Willie says there's a lot going on there."

"Willie's right. I've been living there for the last three years. I just got out two days ago."

"Got out?"

"The Army was looking for me. I was on some list or other."

"How come?"

"I'm an anthropologist. I've been studying the Indians in that area. Particularly the O'wa. The O'wa are seen as an obstacle to 'progress.' Which they are. They want to keep the forest just the way it is. I support them in that." Javier takes a swig of his beer. "Shit, I don't blame the Army. If I were them, I'd want to kill me too."

"How do you know Willie?"

"Willie makes it his business to know people like me. He knows more about this fucking country than most people who have lived here their whole lives."

"You're Argentinian, right?"

"I am. But don't hold that against me."

"I like Argentinians."

"Really? Most people can't stand us. They think we're obnoxious and egotistical. Which I don't understand at all, because we're actually the most wonderful people in the world."

Roberto laughs. "You're from Buenos Aires?"

"Yes. My father's a shopping mall developer there, he thinks developing shopping malls is the highest form of human endeavor. Me, I wanted to get as far away from shopping malls as I could, so I went into the jungle. I love it there. I can't wait to go back."

"So you'll be my guide? In Tulcán?"

"Jesus Christ no. Are you kidding me? I barely got out of there alive, they almost caught me three different times. I had to leave everything. All my books, all my fieldwork." He plucks at his flannel shirt. "The friend I'm staying with gave me this. All I got out with was the clothes on my back. But I think I can set you up with someone. What is it you want to accomplish?"

"Did you know that coltan has been discovered in the Otavalo Valley?"

Javier smiles. "How do you think that Willie found out?"

"I want to report the story of how the Army is terrorizing the people into leaving the valley in order to pave the way for the mining companies. But the problem is, I only have a short time to do this. I have to leave the country by Sunday."

"Why?"

"For the same reason you had to leave Tulcán."

"That's too bad."

"So you can see I'm not going to have time to fuck around once I get there."

Javier nods. "You need a definite destination."

"Let me ask you a question. Have you heard of the Black Jaguars?"

"Yes. They're there."

"In Tulcán?"

"In the Otavalo Valley. As of a few days ago, they were operating in the vicinity of a village called Santa Rosa del Opón. They committed an atrocity there."

"What happened?"

"Not far from the village is a ranch called El Encanto." The Enchantment. "It was owned by a very wealthy man named Juan Carlos Mejía. He raised dairy cattle and farmed sugarcane."

"How come he called his ranch El Encanto?"

"Because it really is a place of enchantment. The house looks like this little fairy tale castle set down in the middle of the jungle. There's fountains and flowers and peacocks and a hedge maze. You feel like you're in a different time and place. Which you are, in a way. Juan Carlos hated the modern world, and so he made El Encanto. It was his refuge."

"Was he married? Did he have children?"

"No. He'd gotten married at a young age, but his wife died of yellow fever. Everyone thought he never remarried because he was still in love with her, but that wasn't it. He was gay, that was his big secret."

"But you knew it."

"Yeah, we were pretty good friends. Sometimes I needed a break from the jungle, and I'd go to El Encanto. I'd have a hot bath and a good meal. Juan Carlos would always make me play chess with him, even though I'm terrible at it. He had an antique Italian chess set, the pieces were made of gold and silver. We'd stay up half the night, drinking and smoking weed. He had names for all the individual chess pieces, even the pawns—it was like Sir This and Lady That and Bishop So-and-So. While we played, he'd be making up stories about them. They were really funny and entertaining. I'd tell him he should write them down, put them in a book, but he would always shake his head and laugh me off."

Javier has been smiling as he remembers Juan Carlos . . . but now he's quiet for a moment, and the smile goes away.

"A few days ago," he says, "the Black Jaguars arrived at El Encanto. They rounded up the workers and their families. The lucky ones were shot. Others were killed in other ways. They made Juan Carlos watch all this. Then they took him in the kitchen and stripped off all his clothes and threw him on a table and skinned him alive with a cheese grater."

"Jesus."

"When they were finished with him, they started eating his food and drinking his liquor and watching his satellite TV. And they let him walk around the house. He wasn't going anywhere with no skin. And then, pretty soon, he went outside and curled up under a bush and died."

"How do you know all this?"

"There were four survivors. Fercho, the cook's helper, he was hiding in the pantry, and a young boy climbed up in a tree when he saw the Black Jaguars coming, and a woman and her daughter hid in the jungle."

"Was Juan Carlos a political kind of person?"

"No, not at all."

"Why do you think they killed him?"

"Well, they had to kill somebody. That's what they do. To inspire fear."

"But why him? And not some other wealthy landowner?"

Javier scratches his scraggly beard as he considers the question.

"It was probably because . . . he was harmless. Because he was sweet, and silly, and gentle. Because he let the children of his workers play in his maze. It probably came from the same sort of impulse that causes a certain kind of man to step on a butterfly."

Despite the horror of Javier's story, Roberto feels something inside him that is not unpleasurable. It is like a bright vibration . . . a radiant welling up of possibility. El Encanto, Juan Carlos, the Black Jaguars, the massacre . . . it's all perfect for his purpose.

"Who can take me to El Encanto?"

"I might have just the guy for you. His name is Chano. He's an O'wa Indian, half an Indian anyway. He's a member of the TARV. The Tulcán Armed Revolutionary Vanguard. They're crazy, those guys. They think negotiating is for women and homosexuals, all they believe in is killing the enemy. Chano's one of those indestructible types. He's got scars all over him, and he loves to tell you the story of how he got each one. Last year he got captured by an Army patrol. They were taking him back to their base to be interrogated, but somehow Chano got hold of a knife and cut his guard's throat and escaped. You'd be in good hands with him."

"He sounds great. You think he'd do it?"

"I think so. If I can track him down. You're leaving tomorrow?"

"Yes."

"I'll do my best to make it happen."

"Thanks, Javier. I really appreciate this."

"Hey man, glad to be of help." Javier lifts his bottle of Brava beer. "Good luck in your journey, Roberto. And may you nail those cowardly bastards to the wall."

"I'll try," says Roberto, as he bumps his bottle of beer against Javier's. Now Javier shows his big buck teeth in a grin as he looks around the room.

"At the moment, this ridiculous place is exactly my idea of heaven."

Roberto laughs. "Why?"

"Because I got out of Tulcán. To be in a tight spot and get out of it, there's no feeling like it—it makes you feel like you're on the top of the fucking world. But you know what I'm talking about."

He's right, Roberto does. He expects to be feeling just that way on Sunday on his flight to Saint Lucia.

The young couple that were sitting at the table are now on the dance floor. They hold each other as they move to the throbbing music. His hand wanders down her back and rubs a buttock. Javier watches approvingly.

"He'll be fucking her before sundown."

* * *

It's been dry for two days but raindrops begin to stipple Roberto's windshield. He turns on his wipers to fight them. He's not usually sentimental about inanimate things, but he feels a bit of a pang now as he thinks about parting from his car. It's been almost like a second home to him. He's looked at so much of this country through its windshield and windows and seen menace reflected in its mirrors and he's slept in it and had sex in it and once a bullet turned the rear window into crumbling glass and thudded into the back of his seat as Daniel screamed at him to go faster, go faster. He's been to every province in the country in this car except the southern jungly ones that are accessible only by boat or plane, plus one other: he has never had occasion to go to Tulcán.

His cellphone rings. It's Daniel. Finally.

"Daniel, where the hell have you been?"

"Well, right now I'm at the Corral. Eating a gaucho burger. Why don't you join me?"

"I can't. I'm on my way to Andrés's. Can we talk later?"

"Sure, give me a call."

"No, I mean in person."

"Okay. Why don't you just come by my place?"

"Around seven?"

"Sure." Roberto hears chewing and swallowing noises. "Hey Roberto, when are you leaving?"

"Tomorrow."

"Tomorrow. Shit. Why didn't you tell me?"

"Because you haven't been calling me back, you bastard!"

"Sorry. I'm an asshole. I'll see you at seven."

* * *

Andrés answers the door.

"Sorry I'm late," says Roberto.

"Hey, no problem. Come in."

Andrés and Teresa live on the fourteenth floor of an apartment building, one below the top. Their apartment has always seemed rather charmless to Roberto, the rooms small and boxy, the furnishings merely functional. It also has a musty smell since they seldom open the windows.

"Want something to drink?" says Andrés.

"No thanks."

"Sit down."

Roberto sits down in his usual chair and Andrés sits down in his. He blinks at Roberto benignly through his glasses.

"Been busy?" he says.

"Yeah, I've been running around like crazy. But I've nearly got everything done."

"Do you need a ride to the airport?"

"No thanks, I'm taking a taxi."

Andrés smiles his sad smile. "I'm going to miss you, Roberto."

"I'm going to miss you too, Andrés."

The sound of a police siren drifts faintly up from the street.

"How were your classes today?" asks Roberto.

"All right, I suppose. Like usual."

He plucks at a frayed thread in the arm of his slightly shabby chair.

"What's the matter?"

"Year after year I say the same boring things to my students. How any of them stay awake till the end of the class, I don't know. Who am I to teach anyone anything anyway?"

"Oh come on, Andrés, you're a wonderful teacher. Hey, I forgot to tell you, I read that article you sent me. About the night President Lovera's mistress stole the horse and rode over the mountains to warn him about the assassination plot and saved his life. I thought it was great."

Andrés smiles. "You did?"

"Yeah, it was so exciting, I felt like I was riding over the mountains with her. You really have a way of making historical characters seem like flesh-and-blood people. You should think about writing a novel."

"Oh, I could never do that," he says, but Roberto can tell he's intrigued.

"You know so much about the nineteenth century, there's so many stories you could tell. And I think there's a real market for books like that. You should think about it."

Now he sees a rare spark of hope in Andrés's eyes.

"Okay," he says, "I will."

Andrés likes to write about the safely distant past. He would never write about what's happening in his country now for fear of what it might bring down on his head.

"I guess you're excited about seeing Caroline tomorrow," he says.

Roberto doesn't answer. He's been undecided about whether to tell Andrés his plans. Andrés is his oldest friend and he's always shared things with him, but at the same time he's the type of person who always expects the worst and why worry him about something that will be resolved in a few days?

"Roberto," he says, "what's wrong? Is Caroline all right?"

"Caroline's fine," says Roberto, and then he decides to take the plunge. "But I won't be seeing her until Sunday."

Andrés sighs twice and shakes his head three times as Roberto tells him what has happened since the last time he saw him.

"I don't know, Roberto," he says when Roberto's done. "I don't like this. You're going into the jungle with some lunatic named Chano that you've never even met? And for what? You can write the best story in the world but it won't change what's going to happen there. I can write the story for you in one sentence: The people in Tulcán are fucked. There. So now you don't have to go."

Roberto shrugs. "Look, Andrés. I'm a journalist, it's my occupation. I need to be where the news is." And then he says, "Don't tell Teresa about any of this."

A look passes between them.

"Of course I won't," says Andrés.

"Can I see her now?"

Andrés nods. They stand up. They walk in silence to Teresa's door. As Andrés pushes it open he says, "Teresa, Roberto's here."

She turns her head a little towards Roberto and smiles. "Roberto."

"How are you?"

"I'm fine."

He walks to her bed and bends down and kisses her on the cheek.

"I lied," she says. "I'm not fine. I'm sad. And you know why."

"Roberto has to leave," says Andrés. "He doesn't have any other choice."

She looks up at Roberto gravely. Once she was a very pretty girl, but not much of that remains. Her face is pale and puffy, her hair dry and dull. But her large brown eyes are bright. They've always been her best feature.

"Is that true?" Teresa says. "Does he not have any other choice?"

She often refers to Roberto in the third person when talking to him.

"I guess you've always got choices," he says. "But I think I'm doing the right thing. I'm just looking forward to what comes next."

"Yes," Teresa says, "Roberto was never much for looking back, was he?"

"That's true about you," says Andrés. "You never seem to get stuck in the past. Like so many of us."

What they are saying is so fraught with meaning that Roberto doesn't know how to respond.

On the other side of the bed, a middle-aged Indian woman is sitting in a chair, leafing through a fashion magazine; "Stripes Are Back!" it says on the cover. Beyond the woman is a window looking out on the western mountains. A nature show about wildlife in Africa is playing on the muted flat-screen television affixed to the wall in front of the bed. On the bedside table amid a clutter of medications a transparent green frog is spurting water from its mouth into a basin. There's a hospitalish disinfectant smell in the air, along with a whiff of weed; Teresa's been smoking a lot of it since her accident.

"Do you want to hear a joke?" she says slyly.

"I'd love to," says Roberto.

"Why are dogs and men so similar?"

Roberto and Andrés look at each other and shrug.

"Because when you speak to them, they seem to understand."

Andrés and Roberto laugh.

"That's very good," says Andrés. "Where did you hear that?"

"Not telling."

Teresa has always been very funny; that's probably what attracted Roberto to her as much as anything. He met her in an elevator in an office building downtown. He was there to interview someone for a story; she worked there at an advertising agency as a graphic designer. She spoke to him first, he no longer remembers exactly what it was she said, she liked his shirt or his shoes or something. Funny how fate works. If he hadn't stepped into that elevator that day, she wouldn't be lying in this bed now.

She was his girlfriend for a little over a year, but he was never really in love with her and moved on. He was aware that he was breaking her heart and felt bad about it, but what was he supposed to do?

In the meantime, Andrés had fallen in love with her. He'd never had much luck with women. He was a naturally shy person, and at times was afflicted with such a crippling self-consciousness that he could barely walk across a room if he thought he was being observed, he would move in a kind of controlled stumble as if he had a neurological disease or were a robot whose inventor still hadn't worked out all the kinks. He'd had only a couple of serious girlfriends in his life and had been devastatingly dumped by both. He was forever getting a crush on some new girl, some sensitive graduate student or buxom waitress who never had any real interest in him. He was around a lot when Roberto and Teresa were together. She liked Andrés enormously, thought he was cute and amusing. Roberto could tell Andrés was falling for her, but he didn't consider it to be a problem; Teresa, he thought, was just the latest girl-Andrés-would-never-get, and pretty soon he would go on to someone else.

Not long after Roberto and Teresa broke up, he met Caroline, and not long after that, Andrés and Teresa became a couple. Roberto was surprised. He didn't think Teresa had ever regarded Andrés in a romantic way. Eventually he realized he was right; not only was Teresa not in love with Andrés, she was still in love with Roberto, and being with Andrés was a way for her to remain in Roberto's world. And without it ever being talked about among the three of them, Roberto understood that Andrés knew the truth too, and that Teresa knew that both of them knew. But it was obvious Andrés was happy to have her under any circumstances. When he walked into a room with her his face would be aglow with pride and pleasure because he knew he had hit the jackpot, won the lottery of love.

They got married and Roberto was the best man. A year and a half later, Andrés and Teresa went to the coast and vacationed at Playa Linda. Pretty Beach. On the third day they left their hotel and went out to the beach to swim. The weather was calm and sunny but beyond the horizon there was a storm and unusually large waves were breaking against the beach. Teresa was a timid swimmer and was reluctant to enter the water, but swimming was the only physical activity Andrés was actually good at, and he took her by the hand and half led and half pulled her in. They'd both been drinking mango juice and vodka, and they were intoxicated with the sea and the sky, the sparkling waves, the wheeling white birds, the fact of being alive and young.

Andrés started to body surf. He wanted Teresa to give it a try. She said no, I can't. He said don't worry, it's easy, it's all in the timing, just launch yourself like this, and he demonstrated, gliding along as sleek as a seal and it looked like fun and she said okay. They waited for a wave. This looks like a good one, Andrés said, and get ready, Teresa, Andrés said, and *now*, Andrés said, and she tried to do what he had done, plunging forward with the wave with her arms held out in front of her, arching her back a little, and the wave tumbled her and sent her feet over her head and her head slammed down into the hard-packed sandy bottom and she broke her neck.

Andrés is looking at the TV. A lion is attacking a water buffalo. Andrés, who literally can't bear to hurt a fly, winces.

"How can you stand to watch these shows, Teresa?"

"Oh don't worry, Andrés," Teresa says, "I've seen it before. The water buffalo gets the better of it. See, the lion is running away!"

He blames himself for what happened, for dragging her drunk into the sea. "There is just no pain like guilt," he once told Roberto. "When you feel you're responsible for someone else's suffering. It feels better to stick your hand in a pot of boiling water." Sex means a lot to Andrés but he says he will always remain faithful to her; even in his masturbatory fantasies, he makes love only to her. He says it is as if he died that day at Playa Linda and what exists now is just a pale copy of himself, a posthumous Andrés whose only purpose is to take care of her.

"I have something I need to tell Roberto," Teresa says.

Andrés takes it in stride. "Okay. Rosario?" he says to the Indian woman. "Why don't you take a break?"

Rosario smiles and stands up and puts her magazine down on the chair. She and Andrés leave.

Roberto looks down at Teresa and waits.

"When I was eight?" she says.

"Yes?"

"I had very long hair."

"When I first met you, your hair was pretty long."

"But when I was eight, it was much, much, much, much longer."

"Down to your ankles?"

She laughs. "No, not *that* long. But it fell all the way down my back and then when I went outside and ran it streamed out straight behind me, that's how I remember it anyway. But then I asked my mother to cut if off."

"Why?"

"Because I liked this actress on a TV show and I wanted my hair to look like hers. It was an American TV show; she was a policewoman and that's what I wanted to be. But I hated my hair and it was never so long again and I never became a policewoman. And so ends," she says, with comic solemnity, "the saddest story ever told."

"That is a sad story. Is that what you wanted to tell me?"

"No."

It's quiet for a moment. He listens to the trickling noise the water makes as it spurts from the mouth of the green frog.

"Roberto?" says Teresa. "In the drawer?"

"Yes, I know."

He pulls open the drawer in the night table. He takes out an ashtray with a joint in it and a cigarette lighter. He puts the joint to his lips and lights it and then puts it to Teresa's lips. She takes a shallow drag, coughs softly.

Her eyes drift toward the window. The rain has stopped and the clouds have cleared out enough to disclose the sun. It is poised to set behind the mountains, and it is flooding the valley with golden light, and the light comes into the room.

"'Blessed are those who mourn,'" Teresa murmurs, "'for they will be comforted.'"

She was an unbeliever when Roberto met her, but since her accident, she's taken a turn toward religion.

"Are you mourning someone?"

She doesn't answer. Her gaze moves from the window back to him. "You don't have to stand there hovering above me. Like an overly attentive waiter. Sit down."

He pulls a chair closer to the bed and sits. She smiles a rueful little smile.

"Poor Roberto. We used to talk about a thousand things. And now he never knows what to say to me."

"Is that what you think?"

"It's true."

It is true. He's never been able to get past the enormity of what happened to her enough to have an ordinary conversation. He wonders what it must be like to suddenly feel your body below your neck disappear and know your old life has been irretrievably lost and you will never be able to do again ninety-nine percent of what you have always thought of as making you human and in the stillness and darkness of three a.m., what do you think about? It's possible Teresa would be glad to talk about such things but he never asks the questions, maybe because he doesn't really want to know the answers. Maybe there's a little bit of Franz in him, a reluctance to get that close to the white-hot furnace of human suffering.

"Listen," Teresa says. "Here's what I wanted to tell you."

"Yes?"

"Good-bye."

"But . . . we'll see each other again."

"I don't think so."

"I definitely plan to come back."

"I wasn't thinking about you. I was thinking about me. People like me usually don't live very long."

Her arms are lying on top of the bedclothes; Roberto reaches out and squeezes one of her soft, inert hands.

"I'll see you again, Teresa. I really believe that."

She looks at his hand on hers, then into his eyes.

"Do you know what I pretend sometimes?"

"What?"

"No, never mind. It's silly. Give me another hit."

He fires up the joint again, puts it to her lips. She breathes out some smoke. The sun turns it golden. She seems transfigured in the light.

"Tell me, Teresa. What were you going to say?"

"All right. I pretend that I'm a princess. Held prisoner in an enchanted tower. And Roberto is a knight who's coming to rescue me. But he must have many adventures first. Fight dragons, wander in dark forests. But every day brings him a little closer to me."

"Teresa? I'm sorry."

"For what?"

"For what happened to you."

"It wasn't your fault. It wasn't anybody's. No use regretting it."

"You've always been so calm about it. I've never understood that."

"Oh, Roberto's crying. Do you know what I'm pretending to do right now?"

"No, what?"

"I'm pretending I'm wiping away his tears."

* * *

Andrés walks him to the elevator. Andrés looks dejected.

"It's not going to be the same without you, Roberto."

"It's not for forever. It's just temporary."

Roberto pushes the down button for the elevator.

"Call me," Andrés says. "As soon as you get out of Tulcán."

"I will."

"Is Daniel going with you?"

"I don't know. I haven't asked him yet."

"He'll go. He won't want to. But he will."

* * *

Daniel breathes in some smoke, then passes the joint to Roberto. He examines it dubiously.

"Is this that creepy shit?"

"Yeah. Go ahead, man, it's the best."

Roberto inhales a small amount of smoke. He and Daniel are sitting on the couch in Daniel's apartment. Daniel's wearing a shirt with broad blue and white stripes. It's too small for him, and from time to time he tugs it down to cover his soft hairy belly. There's a brownish stain on the shirt. Probably sauce from his gaucho burger.

"Stripes are back," says Roberto, pointing at the shirt.

"I didn't know they went away."

"Me neither."

Daniel frowns at his aquarium.

"I'm concerned about the clown triggerfish. He wasn't interested in his food at all today. It's not like him."

"You think he's sick?"

"Maybe."

"Which one is he?"

"You can't see him, he's hiding. Because you're here. He doesn't like people. Except for me."

"Those are lucky fish. Nobody takes care of their fish like you."

Daniel sucks on the joint again, then sighs out the smoke.

"I can't believe you're leaving tomorrow. I thought if I didn't think about it, that would mean it wasn't happening. But I guess it is."

"There's been a change in plans."

"You're not leaving tomorrow?"

"I'm still leaving. But I'm not going straight to Saint Lucia. I'm making a little side trip first. For a couple of days."

"A side trip where?"

"Tulcán."

Daniel looks surprised. "Why are you going there?"

"The Army's invading Tulcán. It's already started. They're going to wipe out the independence movement. They're kicking out journalists and NGOs so there won't be any witnesses. It's going to be a mass slaughter."

"So there's going to be one more mass slaughter in this pestilential hellhole of a country. So what?"

"It's a big story, and somebody needs to cover it."

"Well, that somebody doesn't need to be you. Just get on the plane to Saint Lucia tomorrow. That's the smart move."

"Look, it's all planned out. I'm meeting up with this guy named Chano, he's with the rebels, he's half Indian, he knows the jungle like the back of his hand. He's going to take me to this ranch called El Encanto, there was a massacre there last week. I'll talk to some survivors, you'll take a few pictures, and then by the next day, I'll be out of the country."

Daniel is staring at Roberto. "What did you say?"

"I said the next day I'll—"

"No. Before that."

"I want you to come with me."

"You're fucking nuts."

"I knew you'd probably react this way, but—"

"Forget it, Roberto."

"I'm flying to Robledo tomorrow. You can drive there in your car and meet me—"

"I'm not meeting you in Robledo. I'm not going to a crappy, evil place like Tulcán and get my fucking head cut off."

"You won't get your head cut off, Daniel. It'll be like the old days."

"The old days were terrible. How either of us ever survived them, I don't know."

"I need you. I don't know if I can do it without you."

"You've been doing just fine without me. There's a lot of good photographers out there."

"But I don't trust any of them like I trust you."

"God damn it, Roberto! This just isn't fair!"

Daniel scrunches his eyes shut, runs his fingers through his reddish disheveled hair. He stands up, walks over to the window. Roberto joins him. They look out on the lights of the city. The darkened bullring.

"Why do you think it isn't fair?" Roberto says.

"If you were in some kind of trouble, you know I'd try to help you. Right?"

Roberto nods.

"But that's not what's going on. What you're going to do is really stupid. You need to leave the country or they're going to kill you, have you forgotten?"

"But they said I have ten days, the tenth day isn't till Sunday. I have plenty of time."

"What if they get impatient? What if they decide to kill you on the eighth or the ninth day?"

"Tomorrow it's going to look like I'm flying to Saint Lucia. They won't know I'm going to Tulcán."

"How do you know they won't know? You're assuming everything's going to go according to plan, but things always get fucked up, Roberto, you know that."

"Then I'll come up with a new plan. We've done that plenty of times. And it's always worked out all right, hasn't it?"

"It's the law of averages, you can't flip a coin and have it come up heads fifty times in a row. It's time for us to lose."

"I don't agree."

"The law of averages doesn't give a shit if you don't agree! I just know that I'm not going to get myself killed just so you can win a Bolívar Prize!"

"You think that's what this is about?"

"I'm not sure what it's about with you. I just know you enjoy this kind of shit and I hate it but I always just get dragged along. But not this time. I finally have a halfway decent life and I'm not going to fuck it up!"

Daniel's face is turning red and spit flies out of his mouth as he yells at Roberto.

"Calm down, Daniel. It's okay. I understand."

"Do you?"

"Yes. And don't worry about it, I'll be fine."

"Now you're trying to make me feel guilty."

"No I'm not."

"Are you going to get another photographer?"

"There's no time for that. I'm not a bad photographer, I'll just take the pictures myself."

"But you're not a *good* photographer."

"I'm good enough."

"I don't trust this Chano. How do you know he's not going to rob you and kill you at the first opportunity?"

"I guess that's possible, but it's not very likely."

Daniel lights a cigarette. His hands are shaking.

"I should go," says Roberto. "I still have some things to do."

"But you can't go, you just got here. Let's have a few drinks."

A part of Roberto would like nothing better than to stay here with Daniel, to enter with him into a blissful oblivion of alcohol and drugs.

"I have to get up early," Roberto says, and he begins to move toward the door. Daniel walks with him.

Roberto glances at the picture of the young John Lennon in his black leather jacket. He seems to be watching Daniel and him.

"Do you think I'm so crazy?" Daniel says. "That I'd rather stay here and take pictures of Fernanda's tits than go in the jungle and take pictures of a bunch of rotting corpses?"

"I don't think you're crazy at all."

* * *

He's just walked in his apartment when his cellphone rings. He's expecting it to be Daniel, letting him know he's changed his mind. But it's Javier.

"I've talked to my friend," he says, "and he's looking forward to meeting you."

"Great. When? Where?"

"The town of Tarapacá. A bar called Juanito's. Eight o'clock tomorrow night."

"Is there a number I can reach him at?"

"No, sorry."

"But what if something happens? What if he doesn't show up?"

"He has your number—if something happens he'll call you. But don't worry, he'll be there. He's looking forward to it."

Roberto hears music and talking in the background of the call. "Are you still at Blonde?"

"Oh yes."

"How's it going?"

"Do you know what Boolean logic is?"

"I've heard of it. But I don't know exactly what it is."

"I'm in the same boat. But I've met a computer programmer with abnormally large breasts who's been trying to explain it to me. I've learned her apartment's just around the corner, and I'm hoping to continue the conversation there."

Roberto laughs. "Well, good luck."

"Good luck to you, my friend."

Roberto's heard of Tarapacá, but he doesn't know anything about it. He goes to his computer and googles it. It's a town of twenty-seven thousand in Chimoyo province on the Gualala River, not far from Tulcán. He feels in his chest his heart pick up its pace, for it's suddenly becoming very real to him. This time tomorrow night he will be in Tarapacá, at a bar called Juanito's, sitting at a table with a stranger named Chano, and then he will cross with Chano into Tulcán.

He takes his glasses off and cleans the lenses. He's been dreading this moment all day.

Caroline is at her computer waiting for Roberto. Her smile, he sees with a sinking feeling, could not be any happier.

"I'm so excited, Roberto. I probably won't sleep at all tonight."

He forces a smile of his own. "Yeah, me neither."

"Did you get everything done?"

"Yes, everything."

"What about your car?"

"I sold it."

"Who to?"

"A dealer."

"How much did you get?"

"Twenty-two million."

"That's a very good price for that car."

"Well, that's not what he offered at first, of course. I had to bargain with him."

Caroline gives a surprised laugh. "But Roberto, you hate to bargain."

"It's the new me. A Roberto who drives a hard bargain."

"I liked the old you just fine."

"The new one is even better. You'll see."

"I can't wait. My parents are really excited too. Mother made me take her to the hairdresser today, she wants to look nice for you. Do you know how long it's been since she left the house? And Daddy's determined to teach you to play golf. So get ready!"

"Okay, I will."

Caroline peers at him through the computer screen.

"Roberto? Is everything all right?"

"Everything's fine. But there's been a slight change in plans."

"Are you taking a later flight? I hope not, I've been literally counting the hours till you arrive."

"You're not going to like this, Caroline. I'm not coming tomorrow. I won't be coming till Sunday."

She looks stunned. "Sunday! But why?"

"I have to go to Contamana. You know I've been gathering material for a book about the massacre. I've realized I need to make another trip there. Because if I don't do it now it might be years before I'll be able to. And then I won't be able to write my book."

"Roberto, you need to leave, they're going to kill you!"

"I still have plenty of time, it's just for four extra days. And Contamana's not dangerous anymore, I've never had any problems there."

"The whole country is dangerous for you, Roberto, that's why you're leaving!"

"What I'm going to do isn't dangerous," he blatantly lies. "If it was I wouldn't do it. You have to trust me."

"I can trust you to always put your job ahead of me! If there's ever a conflict, I always come in second."

"That's not true."

"It is true."

"Look, Caroline. I can't come to Saint Lucia and do nothing. That email you sent me, about the walnut desk in the office you've made for me—I've been thinking about it a lot. It sounds wonderful. I can't wait to get there and write my book. There won't be any reason for me to leave."

He can tell Caroline is listening.

"Not ever?" she says.

"Well at least not for a long time."

"And you won't go to any more dangerous places?"

"No."

"You promise?"

"Yes. And something else I've been thinking. Why don't we get married?"

"You mean now?"

He nods. "As soon as we can get the license and all that."

"Are you sure?"

"I'm sure. What are we waiting for?"

Caroline smiles. "We've been waiting for you to say exactly what you're saying now. This will mean so much to my parents. Especially my mother. I know how much she wants to be at our wedding."

"Great, make the plans."

"They'll want us to be married in the church."

"That's fine with me."

Caroline is silent.

"What is it?" says Roberto.

"Don't think I don't know what you're doing. You're telling me something that will make me happy because you've told me something that made me unhappy. You're a brute, Roberto. You trample over my emotions because you know you can get away with it. Because I love you so much."

"I'm sorry I'm a brute. But I'm a brute that's crazy about you."

"I won't have a peaceful second until Sunday. I'll be worrying about you all the time. Promise to be careful."

"I'm always careful. But don't worry if you don't hear from me, cell-phone service is awful in that part of the country."

Caroline is looking at Roberto wistfully.

"It's almost as if you're not even real anymore. It's like you're just an image on my computer screen."

"When I get there on Sunday, I'll show you how real I am."

* * *

He has to get up early, and so he goes to bed early but he cannot sleep. He heaves and twists under the covers, assailed by visions of what might happen to him in Tulcán. He sees himself running and hiding and captured and tortured and killed. How will his little gesture of going there to write a story help Manuel and his mother and Nydia and Lieutenant Matallana? They have gone into the darkness and will not return. If Daniel is right it's not about them anyway, it's not some noble quest he's on to expose injustice, but rather he's chasing personal glory and the Bolívar Prize. And what would the effect be on his father and mother and grandmother, on Caroline, on his friends, if he went into Tulcán and disappeared?

If he doesn't go, what are the consequences? Willie will be disappointed, but also relieved; he won't feel responsible if something bad befalls the son of a close friend. He'll no doubt get in touch with another journalist, if he hasn't already. Daniel will be happy, Andrés will be happy.

And Caroline will be ecstatic when he calls her in the morning and tells her he'll be arriving in Saint Lucia at 7:35 p.m. after all.

A vast relief washes over Roberto as he makes the decision to not go to Tulcán. It's as if he's awakened from a bad dream or emerged from the delirium of a high fever. This time tomorrow night, he will not be with some scarred killer in a malodorous bar in a woebegone town on a muddy river but in the arms of his beloved. And suddenly he's sleepy. Overwhelmingly so. But he doesn't want to fall asleep just yet, these are the first moments of pleasantness and peace he's experienced since he was awakened by that phone call on Thursday morning, and he doesn't want to let them go . . . he doesn't want to let them go . . . he doesn't . . . want . . .

* * *

The ringing phone startles him awake. He looks at the bedside clock. It's a little after midnight. He gropes for the phone and says, "Hello?"

"You motherfucker," he hears. "You son of a bitch."

"Daniel?"

"What a pathetic excuse for a person you are," Daniel says. "I'll get even with you, you asshole."

"What are you talking about?"

"I'm coming with you, all right? I'll probably get killed, and it will be your fault."

Roberto doesn't say anything.

"Roberto? Are you there?"

"Yeah, I'm here."

"Are you okay?"

"I was asleep. I'm just kind of groggy."

"You haven't changed your mind, have you?" Daniel asks hopefully.

"No. No, of course not. I'll meet you in Robledo."

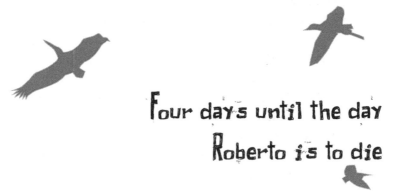

Four days until the day Roberto is to die

Beto takes Roberto's bags out to the taxi. He can't stop talking about Roberto's car.

"I keep going down to the garage and looking at it. I'm afraid it's going to be gone, but it's always there. What a beauty it is! The dent in the roof isn't bad at all. When it's fixed, it will be perfect. I can't wait to drive it."

"Where are you going to go?" asks Roberto. "On your first drive."

"I'm just going to drive through the city. I'll go wherever I want to go, I'll stop wherever I want to stop!"

It's a gray, drizzly morning. The driver gets the bags stowed in the trunk and slams down the lid.

Roberto and Beto shake hands.

"Good luck, Beto. I've enjoyed knowing you."

Beto is smiling, but he has tears in his eyes.

"Thank you again. I'll take care of your car like it's made out of gold! May God protect you on your journey."

A horse pulling a cart clops by quickly. Roberto squeezes into the back of the tiny taxi. The driver grunts and sighs as he slides into his seat. He's a large, weary man. He seems to take up the whole front of the taxi. He glances at Roberto in the rearview mirror.

"The airport," Roberto says.

* * *

The drizzle becomes a downpour. Roberto gets wet getting his suitcase and backpack out of the taxi at the airport. He goes inside and wheels his suitcase past two soldiers with assault rifles and heads toward the ticket counter. He's walking faster than normal, irrationally fast since he has plenty of time to catch his plane, and he makes himself slow down; he realizes he's nervous because, despite what he told Caroline, he's not entirely confidant that the people upset with him haven't changed their mind about letting him leave the country. Several assassinations have taken place at the airport, including a very famous one in 1997 when a presidential candidate was murdered right in the middle of a mob of journalists and admirers. But Roberto doesn't see anybody heading grimly toward him with his hand thrust suspiciously in a coat pocket. He gets his boarding pass, checks his suitcase, and carries his backpack through security.

Feeling more relaxed, he walks toward his terminal. He stops at a shop selling snacks and drinks. In a display case are row on row of little plastic packets containing guava-filled cheese. He never sees them anywhere in the city except in the airport; he's loved them since he was a kid. He buys ten, along with a bottle of water for the plane.

He climbs a flight of stairs to a coffee shop that overlooks his terminal, and orders a coffee with milk. As he waits for it he looks around. There are three other customers: a guy sitting by himself hungrily digging into a big tamal wrapped in a banana leaf, and a diminutive old lady drinking hot chocolate with what appears to be her daughter. He takes his coffee and sits down at a table where he can look down at the terminal. The packets of cheese have a picture on them of a happy cow beneath which it says: "Ex . . . quisite!" He tears one open and the cheese and guava really are exquisite and he quickly eats two more.

He sips his coffee, gazing at the waiting passengers below. Most of them seem mesmerized by their various electronic devices. Roberto's come to this terminal many times over the course of his life, it's old and high-ceilinged and drafty but has a certain charm but it's slated for destruction. The airport is being privatized, they'd privatize the air you breathe and the blood pumping in your veins if they could, and it's now basically owned by Landazábel's best friend. The old airport was fine but it's all being gradually demolished and rebuilt, they can make more money that way.

The old lady and her daughter are descending the stairs, the old lady laughing at something as the daughter holds her arm. Roberto glances at the guy who was eating the tamal and finds him talking on his cellphone and looking right at him.

Roberto reaches for his coffee, takes a drink, and looks back at the guy. He's wearing a denim jacket and a red shirt. He notices Roberto looking at him and looks away.

Below Roberto, the passengers have begun to line up for boarding. He stands up, grabs his backpack, and goes downstairs.

He joins the line. He looks out of the terminal's tall windows. It's still raining. Beyond the big tails of the waiting planes are the gray runways and, off in the distance, the cloud-shrouded mountains.

He looks up at the coffee shop, and is glad to see the guy in the red shirt isn't standing there watching him. Roberto probably just happened to be in his line of sight as he talked on the phone and the guy wasn't even aware of him. It would not be good if the guy knew who he was. If Roberto was leaving the country, it would make no sense that he'd be getting on a plane to Robledo.

* * *

It's a prop plane seating about forty. As chance would have it sitting next to Roberto is the old lady, as small as a child. She gives him a warm smile and starts talking to him the moment he sits down.

"What a nice beard you have," she says. "My son has a beard exactly like that. He's a doctor. A pediatrician."

"Oh really?" says Roberto a bit coolly, not wanting to encourage her lest he doom himself to an hour and a half of hearing about her son. He takes his cellphone out and checks messages. He has two texts. From Caroline: *Have a safe and productive trip my love in 105 hours roberto will rejoin his caroline.* And from Daniel: *Sitting in my car scratching my balls and picking my nose. A bad traffic accident, fatalities, blood. You'll beat me to Robledo. If you feel you can't wait and need to start your insane adventure without me I'll understand.* He replies to Caroline that Sunday will be here before she knows it and to Daniel to not worry, he'll be glad to wait, then a flight attendant tells him to put away his phone. The plane shudders down the runway and lifts into the rain, rips up through the clouds, and finds the sun.

He feels like he hasn't slept in days. He's never had trouble sleeping on a plane and he soon nods off. He dreams about Clara. He's on a sailboat with her on a glittering sea and then a bright silver fish jumps into the boat. It flops around in the bottom, Clara is agitated, she tells him to catch the fish and throw it back in the water before it dies, but it's slippery and keeps squirting out of his grasp. He's awakened by the captain announcing the plane's beginning its descent into Robledo. The old lady is looking kindly at Roberto.

"Did you have a nice sleep?" she says.

"Yes, I did. Thanks."

She's so nice he feels a little guilty he hasn't been more friendly to her.

"Do you live in Robledo?" he says.

"Yes, my husband and I moved there several years ago. Such a beautiful town. What about you, do you live there?"

"No. I'm just meeting a friend."

* * *

Roberto's flown from mountains to more mountains. The mountains here are different though, brownish, mostly bare, with oak trees scattered across them. The climate is very dry. When the Spaniards arrived, armor clanking, nearly half a millennium ago, they looked around the broad valley and were reminded of southern Spain. The town they established has been officially frozen in time; by law, no structures can be higher than two stories and no modern construction is allowed, which means all the buildings have whitewashed walls and red-tiled roofs, green doors and window frames, and enticing balconies with overflowing flowerpots. It's beautiful, as the old lady said. Perhaps the most beautiful town in the country.

He's been to Robledo before, once as a child with his parents, and just over a year ago with Caroline. He doesn't remember much about the first trip except he spent a lot of time walking around looking at things and being bored, but the handful of days he was here with Caroline were among the best he's ever had. The food, the wine, the sun-soaked walks, the immense sky and the white clouds, the lovemaking in the hotel room in the indolent afternoons. Soon they were talking about living here, about buying a house. For centuries Robledo had existed in a Shangri-la-ish solitude, but a highway had been built some thirty years ago connecting it to the capital city, and an airport followed and then lots of people with money like Caroline and Roberto were buying houses in Robledo. It was such a peaceful place, one saw no soldiers, the guerrillas and the drug cartels seemed far away. But then Caroline's mother got cancer and Caroline went off to her Shangri-la in the sea.

Roberto gets a taxi at the little airport then reaches the town in just a few minutes. The streets are all stone, tough on tires, tough on feet. The taxi slowly bumps along to the hotel where he's supposed to meet Daniel. It's where Roberto and Caroline stayed. It's 300 years old. It used to be the hacienda of the Saldamandos, the town's most prominent family. Portraits of several Saldamandos hang in the lobby, the men handsome and haughty, the women pretty, with bold eyes. The hotel has kept an eighteenth century décor. The lobby has a high ceiling with exposed beams. Just inside the front entrance stands a suit of armor, supposedly worn by the first Saldamando, fresh off the ship from Spain, when he was fighting the Indians who used to infest the area. There's a picture of Caroline kissing the visor of the helmet, and one of Roberto standing beside the suit of armor, unsmiling, staring into the camera; people were supposedly much shorter in the olden days, but not evidently the first Saldamando because the suit of armor's exactly Roberto's height.

He recognizes the desk clerk, a studious-looking young man wearing glasses with heavy black frames; Roberto and Caroline became quite chummy with him, and now he remembers his name.

"Rodolfo? I'm Roberto, I was here about a year ago. With my girlfriend, Caroline."

Rodolfo laughs; he remembers Roberto, probably remembers Caroline even better, and he and Roberto shake hands. Rodolfo seems disappointed when he finds out she's not with Roberto.

"But you'll be staying with us for a while?" he asks.

Roberto explains he would love to but he'll be taking a trip by car and he's meeting someone here first, and asks him if he could leave his bags here while he takes a walk around the town. Rodolfo replies he's happy to help him in any way. Roberto tries to tip him but Rodolfo refuses to take it.

He walks through the breeze-tossed shadows of oak trees in a park then reaches the central plaza. It's a huge cobblestone expanse with a fountain in the middle. It's supposed to be the biggest plaza in the country; it's certainly outlandishly large for a town the size of Robledo, as if its founders imagined one day it would become a great city. Shops and restaurants surround the plaza, with a church at one end. A cluster of nuns walk toward the church. Lots of people are strolling around. A tourist is taking a picture of two dour Indians in ponchos. Dogs are sleeping or just hanging out, looking well fed and happy. A little boy runs at breakneck speed diagonally across the plaza—Roberto tries to remember if he ever had energy like that. He walks past a restaurant where he and Caroline sat at a table outside drinking wine and watching the sun go down and the lights beginning to glow in the buildings around the plaza and then a wisp of a moon appearing.

They've begun to grow grapes in the hills around Robledo and the wine they were drinking was locally made and not half bad. A band was playing blues and rock, she pulled him out of his chair and made him dance with her, they were both drunk, he stumbled a little on the stones but Caroline who is a great dancer didn't miss a step. Everyone was watching them and laughing and clapping and ordinarily he hated being the center of attention but for once he didn't mind because he realized he was with a superb girl in a unique town in a mystic deepening dusk and he felt joy mixed with sadness, sadness knowing this was all temporary, it was going to end. As Roberto stands and gazes on this sunny morning at the empty table where he sat with Caroline, it seems savagely ironic that he finds himself in Robledo. The only reason he's here is he looked at a map and saw Robledo had the closest commercial airport to Tulcán, but more than if he were in any other place, being here makes him not want to go to Tulcán.

His cellphone rings.

"Roberto," says Daniel, "get your ass back to the hotel, I'm tired of waiting for you."

Roberto sees the yellow Twingo parked crookedly in front of the hotel. He walks in the lobby. "Your friend's in the restaurant," Rodolfo says.

He finds Daniel sitting at a table, engaged with his cellphone. He barely glances at Roberto as he sits down.

"I ordered breakfast, do you want something?"

Roberto shakes his head. "I'm not hungry."

"You should eat. Probably our last chance to have decent food for a while. Maybe ever."

"Did you really see a fatal accident?"

"Yeah, two German tourists were killed by a truck. I'll bet they didn't think their vacation would end like that."

"What happened?"

"The truck ran right into them. The police had arrested the driver, he was crying, he said he'd fallen asleep because he had to drive all night or the trucking company would fire him, but he looked drunk to me."

Now Daniel puts away his phone. He's wearing an orange T-shirt and brown pants and a tan vest with many pockets. He's bleary-eyed and puffy-faced.

"Thanks for coming," says Roberto.

"I came because I haven't given up trying to talk you out of this."

"It's too late."

"My mother always tells me it's never too late to come to your senses."

The waitress arrives with Daniel's breakfast: eggs scrambled with tomatoes and onions, and bright slices of papaya and mango. It looks delicious. She asks what Roberto would like.

"Just some coffee," he says, then he looks again at Daniel's plate. "And exactly what he has."

The waitress walks away. "And two glasses of whiskey!" Daniel calls after her.

"Daniel, this is no time to get drunk."

"But it's my understanding that if you're drunk, it hurts less when they kill you."

"Nobody's going to kill us."

Daniel picks up a piece of mango and bites into it.

"Either you have a drink with me or I'm going to go home. Fuck Tulcán."

Roberto sighs. He looks out the window into the old courtyard, where generations of Saldamandos walked, and still walk as ghosts, according to Rodolfo. It's filled with greenery and flowers, brimming with the beauty of the morning.

The waitress comes back with Roberto's coffee and the two whiskeys. Daniel grabs his glass.

"Let's drink to the trip, Roberto. May it be successful, and may we be safe."

Roberto smiles. "To the trip."

He touches glasses with Daniel, then downs the whiskey in two gulps.

* * *

They leave Robledo on a two-lane blacktop highway that winds over the dry mountains. Not far from the town, they pass half a dozen guys in single file on bicycles, all lean and ascetic-looking, with tremendous thighs. One of the things Roberto's country is a world leader in, along with extrajudicial killings and internal refugees, is great bicycle racers, and most of them come from here in Espinar province.

"Look at those guys," says Roberto. "That'd be a great life, being an athlete. It's so pure and simple. If you're the fastest guy you win. Hard work pays off."

"Are you kidding me?" says Daniel. "Do you realize how corrupt the world of professional cycling is? There's a new doping scandal every week!"

"Okay, you don't want to be a bicycle racer. So what would you do if you weren't a photographer?"

"I don't know. Be a poet, I guess. Except there's not any money in it. And I'm a lousy writer," and then he says loudly, in his "poetry" voice, *"Our lives are rivers, gliding free to that unfathomed, boundless sea!"*

"Jorge Manrique. I studied him in high school."

"I'd give my left nut if I could write like that."

"Photography's an art form too."

"Yeah, I'm sure someday they'll be hanging my pictures of Fernanda's tits on the wall right next to the Mona Lisa."

As Robledo recedes behind them, Roberto feels a lifting of his spirits. He's forgetting and he needs to forget about Robledo, as well as Caroline and Clara and his father and his friends and the job he's lost and the home he's left and the grandmother he will never see again and the terrors of last night. All that matters now is the road beneath him and the friend beside him and the destination they both are moving toward. He's going into the unknown in search of another story, and there's a deep and familiar joy in this.

The road begins to descend, and with the change in altitude comes a change in landscape. There are green fields and clumps of trees and cattle everywhere. This is dairy country. Gleaming metal tanker trucks roll past, looking like they contain gasoline or oil but actually filled with milk.

Cows are grazing not only in fenced-in pastures but are tied up in shallow ditches right next to the road to take advantage of the free grass, and then, when Daniel comes round a curve at his usual high speed he has to hit the brakes because the road ahead is blocked by twenty or so cows trotting along, being herded not too skillfully by two young women with sticks. The cows are spilling over onto the other side of the road, stopping traffic in both directions. Daniel curses and honks his horn. Finally the women get the cows to a little dirt road and open a gate. As the cows crowd through it Daniel swings his Twingo around a couple of stragglers and grumbles, "When is this country going to enter the fucking twenty-first century?"

Once, there was a great lake here, sacred to the Indians. But the dairy farmers have taken the lake bit by bit and turned it into pasture for their cows and now there isn't much left of it. Roberto can see its pitiful remnants, glittering off in the distance. The three-year drought has just made things worse. He wonders what will happen to the green valley when the last of the lake is gone.

Daniel pulls off the road and parks at a restaurant, saying he needs to pee. All the whiskey and coffee of the morning have given Roberto a full bladder too and he follows Daniel into the bathroom. Then they take a table and get more coffee and Daniel orders a dessert: a curd cheese called *cuajada* drenched in sugarcane syrup. Daniel takes a bite then closes his eyes as he chews.

"Roberto, you better hurry because this is too good to be true."

Roberto has one bite and allows Daniel to gobble up the rest. Then Daniel takes a pill bottle out of one of his vest pockets and shakes out an orange tablet into his hand and washes it down with some water.

"What's that?" says Roberto.

"Malarone. I don't want to get malaria again. I've never been so sick."

"That's not the medicine that made you go crazy in Orito, is it?"

Roberto was awakened in the middle of the night in his cheap hotel room in Orito by a commotion outside his door. Daniel was running up and down the hallway in his underwear, while a harried hotel employee was trying to get him under control. He seemed to be avoiding invisible objects on the floor, and it turned out he was hallucinating he was lost in a twisting maze filled with slithering crocodiles.

"No, that was mefloquine," Daniel says. "I think this shit's okay. Want one?"

"No thanks. I'll just put on plenty of mosquito repellent. I never seem to get bitten."

"Mosquitoes love me," Daniel says, "like I love cuajada."

They pass out of dairy country and move into a different kind of mountains. They're heavily forested, with clearings here and there where small farms nestle. With each turning of the road a new prospect is revealed of deep-green mountains, they seem to be not mere mountains but rapturous dreams of mountains, white clouds drifting among them, and for a little while it is like Roberto has left the car and is drifting among the mountains with the clouds.

"Just think," Daniel says, breaking the spell, "that moron Mario Garro might be the next mayor. Did I ever tell you about the time I met him at a party?"

Roberto only half listens as Daniel tells his Mario Garro story; he's looking at the mountains and the old joke comes to mind. When God created this country it was so beautiful the angels wanted to leave heaven and live there, so to make it less attractive God was forced to populate it with the most vile and evil race of men on earth.

* * *

They turn off on another road and begin to twist down slowly out of the mountains. The climate changes. Roberto sees banana trees and then coffee plants as the air gets warmer and more humid and they lower their windows and Roberto takes his jacket off. This road is older and narrower and full of cracks and crumbling at the edges. They pass little shrines with crosses and flowers where people have died in wrecks. And then a big purple truck is bearing down on them as they round a blind curve, it's passing another truck and Roberto thinks the last thing he will see in his life is purple. He grabs the dashboard to brace himself as Daniel shouts "Fuck!" and hits the brakes and swerves half off the road. They seem to be just centimeters from plunging over a steep slope and then the purple truck cuts in ahead of the other truck and misses the car by a whisker.

As they have so many times in the past, Daniel and Roberto exchange a look of relief at the close call.

"Crazy drivers in this fucking country," mutters Daniel, a pretty crazy driver himself.

They've gone only another kilometer or two when Daniel slows down and pulls off the pavement. Roberto sees a heavily eroded dirt road that goes up the side of a hill.

"You'll never guess who lives up there," Daniel says.

"Who?"

"Ramiro Navia."

"You're kidding."

"No, he bought a house here two or three years ago."

"That's right, he's from around here."

"His family owns a big coffee plantation. We drove right by it."

"Wasn't his father kidnapped by the guerrillas?"

"Yeah, they had to pay a huge fucking ransom."

"Man, I haven't seen Ramiro in years. So you guys are still friends?"

"Yeah, we still see each other pretty often."

Ramiro Navia was in their circle of friends in college. He was like Daniel in that he was apolitical and fun-loving, but unlike Daniel, he was also an excellent student. He got a degree in architecture then joined one of the top firms in the city.

Daniel just sits behind the wheel, gazing through the windshield at the rutty road. Roberto can guess what's on his mind.

"It would be nice to see Ramiro," he says, "but we don't have time."

"He's not there anyway. He and his wife and kids are on a trip to Europe."

"Okay."

"But he said I could come stay there any time I want. It's really beautiful and peaceful. There's this young couple that are the caretakers, she's a great cook. There's a swimming pool. Plenty of booze."

"Daniel, come on. We don't have time, all right?"

Now Daniel looks at Roberto. "Or else we've got plenty of time. We drive up that road, eat, drink, bullshit, swim in the pool. Go to bed late, get up late, get you back to Robledo in plenty of time to catch your plane. And then tomorrow night you'll be with Caroline. Bet that'd make her really happy, huh?"

"I thought you didn't like Caroline. You said if I married her it would be a disaster."

"I think being married to Caroline would definitely be better than getting your head cut off in the jungle."

"I'll tell her you said that, she'll be so pleased. Now let's get going."

Daniel pulls the Twingo back out on the road. He looks so glum Roberto feels a little sorry for him.

"On our way back," says Roberto, "if we have time, we'll stop off here and have a drink and take a swim in the pool."

"Don't talk to me like I'm twelve years old."

They complete the descent from the mountains into equatorial heat. They're now in the province of Chimoyo. It's mid-afternoon. They're around 150 kilometers from Tarapacá. They ought to get there in plenty of time for Roberto to meet Chano in the bar at eight.

On both sides of the road, fields are planted in sugarcane. The plants can grow over three meters high, Roberto's seen fields stretching end-lessly and blowing in the wind in an emerald rippling, but these plants look stunted and tattered because of the drought. They pass the shacks of the sugarcane workers, see their scrawny children and flea-bitten dogs, and then Daniels says, "Jesus, look at that."

A bony cow is grazing in a brownish patch of pasture. Lying beneath it on her back is a little girl, who's grasping one of its teats and sucking on it.

Daniel pulls off the road. He reaches in the back seat for his camera bag, which contains two Nikon D4 cameras, filters, lenses, lens-cleaning cloths, memory cards, and batteries. He gets out of the car with one of the cameras. Now Roberto notices two men standing by a fence in the shade of a small tree. They're both holding machetes, and are glaring at Daniel as he walks toward the pasture.

"Daniel!" calls Roberto.

Daniel looks back at him and he nods at the men. Daniel looks at them, then returns to the car. He gets back in, points the camera at the cow and the girl and adjusts the long zoom lens and snaps a couple of pictures and then takes off.

Pretty soon, they run into a line of cars and trucks held up by road construction. Even out here in the countryside, beggars and vendors have gathered. An obese black man with massive arms and short withered legs is spinning around and around on the road in a wheelchair. A guy is walking around with a basket of bootlegged DVDs and a small monkey on his shoulder; if you want a DVD, you hand the money to the monkey. A young guy with a bashful smile leans down to Daniel's window and says he lost his job at a sawmill and is trying to get enough money for a bus ticket so he can return to his home in Macallacta; Roberto's never heard of Macallacta, but he says it like it's an instantly recognizable name like Paris or London. He lives in Macallacta with his two younger brothers, one of whom dove off a bridge into a river and injured his brain and now crawls around on the floor like a baby. He says he's worried about his brothers and wants to get back to them as soon as he can. He has such an earnest and likeable way about him Roberto and Daniel both half-believe him and give him what ought to be enough money for a ticket to Macallacta even if it's on the other side of the country, and the guy is so choked up he can hardly thank them as he vigorously shakes their hands.

In a few minutes the traffic starts to move. They drive by the young guy, who's smoking a cigarette and talking to the guy with the monkey. He sees them and smiles and waves and they wave back.

"Does it look to you like he's in a hurry to get to Macallacta?" asks Daniel.

"Not really."

They look at each other and laugh.

In ten minutes they're stopped again. Roberto thinks it's more construction, but then he sees young men with guns wearing green camouflage fatigues and black boots. It's an Army checkpoint. Roberto's encountered over the years many checkpoints and roadblocks, manned by various types of men with guns: soldiers, police, paramilitaries, guerrillas. Since bad things can befall you at a checkpoint, you don't ever want to seem suspicious, so even if you're shaking in your shoes, you try to act relaxed, and if you plan to lie or dissemble, you need to think it through ahead of time.

"We're going to Tarapacá," says Roberto.

"Okay," says Daniel. "What are we going to do there?"

"See a couple of girls?"

"Great. Are they good-looking?"

"They're amazing. Especially mine."

"But mine is better in bed."

"How would you know that?"

"Believe me, I know."

Roberto laughs, but he's nervous. He wonders if the checkpoint has anything to do with what's going on in Tulcán. There are eight or ten vehicles ahead of the Twingo. As it moves slowly forward, Roberto and

Daniel see off to the side of the road a guy in handcuffs standing among some soldiers. The guy is wearing red shorts and flip-flops and a white T-shirt with blood on it. The soldiers are practicing martial arts moves on him, striking and kicking him with high-pitched Bruce Lee-ish mews and screams. He staggers and bleeds but is empty-eyed and silent.

Daniel gives Roberto a glance, but neither says anything. Only one car is ahead of them now. A sergeant wearing sunglasses is taking a look at the driver's identification card when suddenly the horn of Daniel's car begins to blast. *HONK HONK HONK!*

The sergeant gives the car a startled look.

HONK HONK HONK! HONK HONK HONK!

A panicky-looking private is pointing his assault rifle at the car.

"Daniel, stop it," yells Roberto, "they're going to shoot us!"

"I can't stop it, it's the fucking car alarm!"

Roberto looks around and sees half a dozen rifles pointed at them. They hold their hands up. Daniels sticks his head out the window and shouts to the sergeant: "I'm sorry, it's the car alarm, I don't know how to fix it!"

Abruptly the horn falls silent. The sergeant has unholstered his side-arm and is approaching the car.

"I'm really sorry about that," Daniel says. "It's the fucking car alarm, it just goes off like that sometimes. I've been meaning to have it fixed."

The sergeant leans down and peers through the window at Roberto and Daniel. Roberto's relieved when he sees him reholster his gun.

"IDs?" he says.

They quickly get their ID cards out of their billfolds and hand them to the sergeant. He looks them over.

"You're a long way from home."

"We're on our way to Tarapacá," says Roberto.

"Why are you going there?"

"To see some friends."

"What are their names?"

"Vera and Dolly." Two sisters that lived down the street when Roberto was a kid.

"We met them last week," says Daniel. "At a bar. They were on vacation. They're nurses."

"We bought them dinner," says Roberto, "and they invited us to visit."

The sergeant looks at them impassively through his sunglasses—and then he smiles, and hands them back their IDs.

"You should be in for a good time. Nurses are very wild, in my experience. They've seen everything, they know all about the human body, and they have absolutely no inhibitions."

"I hope you're right," says Roberto.

The sergeant laughs. "About women, I'm always right," and Roberto and Daniel laugh along with him. Now he gives the top of the car a slap and steps back from it.

"Get that alarm fixed. My men are very jumpy, they've been seeing a lot of action against the terrorists. It wouldn't have been their fault if something bad had happened."

"I'll get it fixed in the next town," says Daniel.

"Thanks a lot, sergeant," says Roberto.

"Have fun with the nurses," says the sergeant. "And be careful in Tarapacá. It's crawling with criminals."

Soon they come to San Lorenzo, a dismal little sugarcane town built along the toxic trickle of a nearly dried-up river. They pass by smoke arising from a pit of burning trash, kids kicking around a soccer ball made out of plastic and string, a begrimed white statue of the Virgin Mary in front of a decrepit church. On the banks of the river is a low brick building with ten or twelve vultures and about the same number of very poor-looking people waiting around outside. Roberto wonders what kind of place this is then sees a man leading a big pink pig on a rope toward the building and realizes this is the local slaughterhouse. The pig's tail is wagging like a dog's, it's oblivious of its fate.

Daniel pulls up to the pumps of an Esso station. A grinning, grease-covered boy who looks about twelve or thirteen puts gas in the car. Daniel asks him if there's somebody here that can disconnect his car alarm.

"Sure," said the boy, "I can do that. No problem."

Daniel looks dubious. "Somebody told me car alarms are kind of complicated."

"It's not complicated. I just need to find the control box. It should be under the dashboard somewhere."

"How long will it take?"

The boy shrugs. "Twenty minutes?"

Daniel drives the car into the garage, and the boy, whose name is Pablo, gets to work. Daniel lights a cigarette and wanders off with his camera, while Roberto goes in the office. A middle-aged man stands at a counter reading a newspaper. Behind him, pretty girls in bathing suits walk up and down a stage on a muted TV, and an oscillating fan stirs up the hot air. He's wearing a gray shirt with the name "Gaspar" embroidered on it in red.

Gaspar looks up from his paper at Roberto. He seems a little astonished, as if Roberto had walked through the door naked, but that's because he has abnormally protruding eyes.

"What can I do for you?" he says.

Roberto explains about the car alarm, and asks him if Pablo really knows how to fix it. Gaspar smiles.

"That boy's a wonder. He came out of his mother's belly knowing everything about cars."

"Is he your son?"

Gaspar beams. "Five daughters and then Pablo. But he was worth the wait."

He speaks the lazy, mellifluent Spanish of the coast, and Roberto asks him if that's where he's from.

"Yes. I shouldn't have ever left, but a young man wants to see things. I still don't know how I wound up in a crappy place like San Lorenzo. Oh, wait, I remember, I met my wife here," and he laughs.

Roberto likes Gaspar. He tells him how the alarm almost got them killed at the checkpoint, and Gaspar laughs so long and hard he has to wipe a tear away from one of his popping eyes.

"There's many different ways to die," he says, "but I've never heard of that one."

"So what's the Army doing outside of town?"

"There's a lot of guerrillas in the area. There have been for many years, they're always trying to stir up trouble with the sugarcane workers. Not that I blame them, the owners treat the workers like shit. But the guerrillas can be very cruel. They killed the son of a friend of mine just last year."

"What happened?"

"Well, it's like this," says Gaspar, and he leans forward with his elbows on the counter and Roberto senses he's about to hear a good story. "The son of my friend was named Juan, but nobody called him that. Everybody called him Panther."

"Why Panther?"

"I don't know, that was just his name. Panther had a friend named Crispulo, they had been best friends ever since they were little kids. But nobody called him Crispulo, they called him Parrot. And they had tattoos on their arms, of a panther and a parrot. But . . . what's your name, my friend?"

"Roberto."

"But Roberto, here's the thing. Panther had the parrot tattoo, and Parrot had the panther tattoo. Some people thought they were homosexuals, but it wasn't like that, they both liked girls. It's just that those two boys loved each other like nothing I've ever seen. They did everything together, they were never apart. They worked construction, and nobody would even think of trying to hire one without the other.

"Panther had a kid brother named Chepe. Chepe was only eighteen, and he was very naïve and easy to talk into things. Panther found out the guerrillas were trying to talk Chepe into joining them. Panther was very angry, and went to the guerrillas and told them to leave his brother alone. Nobody knows exactly what happened, but Panther had a very bad temper and he must have really pissed the guerrillas off because they wound up shooting him. They dumped his body by the side of the road. The police were there when Parrot showed up, he grabbed Panther's body and screamed and cried and the police had to put poor Parrot in handcuffs so they could take the body away."

Suddenly Roberto hears the haunting cries of seagulls. It's the ringtone of Gaspar's cellphone, which makes sense considering where he's from. He picks up the phone and tells someone he'll call them back.

"So what happened to Parrot?" Roberto asks.

Gaspar shakes his head. "Nothing good, I'm sorry to say. Even though they were so close, Panther and Parrot were very different. Panther was very strong and forceful, but Parrot was more the mild, dreamy type. He just couldn't withstand the shock of Panther's death. For a while he went completely crazy. He would babble things that made no sense. He had trouble walking because he thought his feet had become his hands and his hands his feet. Then after a few weeks he seemed to be much better. He even went back to work. Like I said, he worked construction. One day, it was time to have lunch, but Parrot said he wasn't hungry and was going to keep working. When the other guys came back, they found Parrot lying on the floor, dead. They couldn't figure out what had happened at first, but then they saw his head was a little bloody—he'd shot himself with a nail gun. Some people thought it was an accident, but I'm sure it was suicide. I think he just couldn't stand the thought that for the rest of his life he'd be working without Panther at his side."

Gaspar gets Cokes for each of them out of a cooler and because Roberto's a good listener tells him all about his life. Pablo takes only fifteen minutes to disconnect the alarm. Roberto pays Gaspar and says good-bye and then goes out. He looks around for Daniel. He doesn't see him anywhere. He feels a flash of panic and imagines Daniel kidnapped by the guerrillas, then he spots him in a vacant, litter-strewn lot on the other side of the road, talking to some tough-looking young guys drinking beer. They're all laughing at something Daniel has said. He has a way of becoming instant friends with almost anyone he meets. That is, if he doesn't make them so mad they want to kill him. Daniel starts taking pictures of a shaven-headed guy bare to the waist and covered with tattoos. The guy turns around, and Roberto sees he has two eyes tattooed on the back of his head. Daniel takes another picture, and then Roberto calls to him, "Daniel! Let's go!"

Daniel fist-bumps all the guys and then walks back across the road.

"Look," he says, showing Roberto the picture in the LCD screen. "He says the eyes are so nobody can sneak up behind him."

"Maybe that's what we need."

Roberto hears above them, getting louder, a *whup-whup-whup*.

Six Army helicopters pass overhead. They're big American-made Chinooks, olive-green, tandem rotors, made to carry troops and equipment. Daniel points his camera at them. Roberto wonders if they're heading for Tulcán.

* * *

They reach Tarapacá as the sun is going down. It is like a great ulcerous sore growing on the jungle next to the river. Motorcycles and three-wheeled motortaxis buzzing ceaselessly up and down the streets. Trash in the gutters. Skinny dogs trotting along and then waiting like people on corners for the traffic to go by. The broken sidewalks crowded with people moving past the shabby shops and stores. Though Roberto does see one place that seems strangely pristine, glowing with many colors. It sells athletic shoes, Adidas, Nike, whatever you want.

They have a couple of hours to kill before they meet Chano at Juanito's at eight. Daniel parks his Twingo across the street from a park. They get out and walk around. Roberto sees a lot of families strolling together, enjoying the slow cessation of the heat as the day draws to a close. An ice cream vendor's pushing a cart with a tinkling bell. A taxi driver stands on the hood of his taxi and picks a mango from a tree. Mango trees, with their bright round balls of fruit, have always reminded Roberto of Christmas trees.

He pauses at the bird-shit-bespattered statue of some long-dead general, and reads aloud a quote from him on a bronze plaque: "'Everything for the country, and above the country, only God!'" He becomes aware of a sound, a high-pitched chittering that seems to be coming from all over. He looks up and sees small birds with long tails flying around, landing in the treetops. They're coming into the park from all directions, in groups of four or six or eight. Roberto and Daniel watch wonderingly as dozens become hundreds and then thousands. Roberto asks a neatly dressed older gentleman with a gray moustache what's going on. He laughs and says, "Welcome to the Park of the Parakeets. They come in from the jungle to spend the night. Why? I don't know, you should ask them. They begin to arrive precisely at six, you can set your watch to it."

Daniel, trying to take pictures of the parakeets, is cursing the fading light, but Roberto can barely hear him over the tumultuous din they make. They cluster in the branches above them and block out the evening sky, and more and more are coming, zooming in over trees and buildings, it's not as if they're fleeing the jungle but it's like multitudinous bits of the jungle are coming to Tarapacá.

* * *

"I wonder how my fish are doing," Daniel says. "The clown triggerfish still wasn't eating before I left."

"Who's taking care of them?"

"This teenage girl that lives on my floor. She seems responsible, but you never know. How do I know she's not in my apartment right now with some crazy boyfriend? They could be having sex everywhere and doing drugs. Maybe the boyfriend has totally lost his mind, he's pouring vodka into the tank or even peeing in it."

"Relax, that's not happening. Your fish are fine."

Night has fallen. They're sitting in a restaurant at a table with a plastic tablecloth that has a pattern of red and green slices of watermelon. The walls are covered with paintings in a primitive style of jaguars, monkeys, parrots, anacondas, and Indians, including a dusky Virgin Mary and baby Jesus. There's a very weird painting of a pink river dolphin with an enormous penis standing on a riverbank. Mounted above the bar is a monstrous-looking fish about two meters long with a gaping mouth and teeth like a crocodile. According to the waitress, the fish comes from the Gualala River and has a long unpronounceable Indian name and it's what they're having for dinner. It's the best fish Roberto's ever tasted.

"Another beer?" asks the waitress, and Roberto says no and Daniel says yes.

"Take it easy on the drinking," says Roberto.

"Stop talking to me like you're my mother, or I'm going to go home and check on my fish."

"Daniel, you have to stop threatening to go home every time I say something you don't like."

"The only thing I have to do," he says, raising his camera and looking through the viewfinder, "is take her picture."

A stunning mestizo girl of eighteen or so is sitting a few tables away. She walked in with her family not long after Roberto and Daniel arrived. She is tall and leggy and copper-colored and isn't wearing much at all, just little shorts and a sleeveless top.

Daniel is good at taking somebody's picture without them knowing about it. Now he lowers his camera and takes a drink of his beer and gazes at the girl.

"Look how unhappy she is," he says, and he's right: her parents and siblings are laughing and talking around her but she sits sullen and inattentive. "She knows she's far too tall and beautiful to be stuck in a shitty place like this."

It's as if the girl is hearing Daniel somehow. She bares her teeth as she bites into her food, and has the look of an angry animal.

"You're a photographer," Roberto says, "why don't you discover her? Maybe she could become a supermodel, and she'd owe everything to you."

"It's funny you should say that. My agent's been encouraging me to become a fashion photographer. She says the money would be better, and she thinks I'd be really good at it."

"Taking pictures of beautiful women all day and getting paid for it? You should do it."

"Right," Daniel says, forking some fried plantain into his mouth. "I just need to go into the jungle first and takes pictures of piles of dead bodies. Roberto, I'm telling you, if I get skinned alive with a cheese grater, I'll never forgive you."

After they left San Lorenzo, Roberto made the mistake of telling Daniel about the ghastly fate that had befallen Juan Carlos Mejía. Now he can't stop talking about it.

"The odds of that particular thing happening to you or me are very small," says Roberto. "It's probably a thousand times more likely we'd be struck by lightning."

His cellphone rings. He pulls it out of his pocket and looks at it.

"Who is it?" asks Daniel.

"Caroline." He's not planning to pick up, but then suddenly "Don't say anything," he says to Daniel, and then into the phone: "Caroline?"

He hears Caroline say "Roberto," but then her voice begins to break up.

"Caroline, hold on, I'm having trouble hearing you, I'm going to go outside."

He goes out of the restaurant into the humid night.

"Caroline, can you hear me?"

"Yes, Roberto, I can! Are you in Contamana?"

"Yes, I'm here, everything's fine. I was just having something to eat."

"I wasn't expecting to reach you, I was going to leave a message. Because you said cell service is so bad."

"I guess we just got lucky. What are you doing?"

"Cuddling with the cats. Thinking of you."

She says something else but the sound's going in and out.

"Caroline, you're breaking up again."

"Can you hear me now?"

"Yes."

"I just asked you how everything was going so far. Are you getting what you need?"

"Yes, it's been great."

"Oh, I'm glad. Your book's going to be wonderful, I know."

Roberto stands there smelling the stink of gasoline and sewage from the street. The motorcycles and motortaxis are still buzzing back and forth. It was a mistake to pick up, it's killing him to hear her voice.

"Do you know how much I love you?" he says.

He waits for a reply but there is none. The connection has been lost.

* * *

They go to a supermarket and buy several six packs of bottled water for the jungle, along with protein bars and nuts and dried fruit for Roberto and candy bars and packs of cigarettes for Daniel. Then they go to the parking lot where Daniel left his car and put the bags in the trunk, and then they start walking toward Juanito's. They drove by it earlier, it's only a few blocks away.

Roberto just hopes that Chano's there. If something's gone wrong and he's not, there may not be enough time to implement a plan B or C and get into Tulcán. Roberto can't just go blundering into the jungle on his own and hope for the best, he's almost certain to get arrested or worse.

He wonders if the real Chano is going to fit the picture in his head. Lean and sinewy, solid as stone. A swarthy face and a devilish grin. And of course covered with scars, as Javier said.

A cool gust of air blows down the street, scraps of trash tumbling in it. Daniel turns his back to the wind and lights a cigarette. A grimy kid in new-looking orange and blue Nikes appears before him.

"Hey mister," he says, "can I have a cigarette?"

"You're too young to smoke," Daniel says, and then from behind him another grimy kid swoops past, grabbing the camera bag hanging from his shoulder. Roberto lunges at the kid and snags his arm. The first kid kicks Daniel in the shin as the second kid sinks his teeth into Roberto's forearm and Roberto yells and then he sees a knife in the hand of the first kid. He jabs Roberto's arm with it and Roberto yells again and lets go of the second kid, and then the two kids are hauling ass across the street, dodging through the traffic.

"My god, Roberto, are you all right?"

Daniel's staring at him. Roberto's glad to see he's still got his camera bag.

"Shit, I guess so." His heart's bumping against his ribs as he looks at his arm. "I can't believe I just got stabbed."

Now he looks back across the street at the kids. They're running down the sidewalk, laughing. Theft is a game for them. The one that bit Roberto flips him the fuck you sign and the one that stabbed him blows him a kiss.

"You're bleeding," says Daniel. "We should go to a hospital."

There's another gust of wind, followed by the flash and boom of lightning and thunder.

"We don't have time," says Roberto. "Listen, I'm okay, let's go."

They begin to walk quickly down the street, but tropical storms are fast and ferocious, and before they've made it even halfway to the bar, the storm is sweeping across the town. They begin to run, into the whipping wind and sheets of rain, under the exploding sky.

Roberto sees through the rain the neon sign that says Juanito's. He and Daniel stumble through the door, breathing hard and soaked to the skin.

Only a handful of people are there. A female bartender with dark Indian features and platinum-blonde hair. The nice-looking girl she's talking to. A guy wearing glasses sitting a few stools away from the girl and pecking at his cellphone. An elderly black man sitting by himself at a table and staring at his hands, as if he's just strangled somebody with them. At another table, two young guys who look like older versions of the kids that just bit and stabbed Roberto. And coming out of the bathroom, a drunk-looking middle-aged man in a wide straw hat, wiping his mouth off on the sleeve of his shirt. None of them even faintly resemble the picture in Roberto's head of Chano.

Roberto's holding a hand on his forearm so he doesn't bleed all over the floor, though by the looks of the place, it wouldn't be the first time someone has done that.

"I'm going to the bathroom," he says.

Daniel nods, too winded to speak, and sits down at a table.

The concrete floor of the bathroom is painted a sickly green and covered with soggy paper towels. The toilet is splattered with puke, probably belonging to the man in the straw hat. Roberto inspects his right arm in the hard light of an uncovered bulb. The knife has made a small puncture wound that's oozing blood. The bite has formed a red parenthesis of teeth marks; the skin is broken but not actually bleeding.

There's no soap. He rinses his arm off in the stained sink then dries it with paper towels.

Roberto looks at himself in the mirror. His glasses are flecked with rain. He realizes a part of him is hoping Chano doesn't show. He dries his glasses with a paper towel, and holding another paper towel on his arm he goes back out.

Daniel sits at the table, going through the contents of his camera bag.

"Everything all right?" says Roberto as he sits down.

"Yeah, looks like it. The sergeant was right, this town *is* full of criminals," and then he looks around. "No Chano, huh?"

"Not yet." He checks his watch. "It's not even eight yet. He'll be here."

"Man, I hope so. I'd hate to think we made this long drive here for nothing. How's your arm?"

"I'll live."

"Want a beer?"

"Sure."

"Watch my bag."

"Okay."

Daniel goes to the bar. Roberto notices the pretty girl at the bar is looking at him. She's wearing black pants and a pink blouse and has boyishly short dark hair. He smiles at her, but without smiling back she turns away. He wonders why she's by herself. Is she waiting for someone? Or maybe she's a hooker. No. She doesn't have that hooker look.

He notices that somebody else at the bar is looking at him. The drunk guy, smiling musingly at him from under his straw hat. Now he dismounts from his stool and a bit unsteadily heads Roberto's way. It looks like he's about to be hassled for money or a drink. The guy stops in front of him and bows slightly.

"Good evening, my friend, do you mind if I sit down?" and then without waiting for an answer, he sinks down in a chair with an exhausted sigh. He's wearing a white dress shirt and gray trousers, neither of which seems to have seen the inside of a washing machine for a while. On his feet are sandals with black socks. He looks at Roberto's arm; blood's seeping through the paper towel.

"Did you injure yourself?"

"It's just a small cut. Nothing serious."

"I knew a man with a small cut on his foot who ended up losing his entire leg, along with his private parts. It's this revolting climate, it promotes disease and decay. You should have it looked at."

"I'll do that."

Lightning flashes in the window and thunder rumbles through the bar. The man's face takes on a melancholy expression.

"It's an old, old story," he says.

"What is?"

"You. Me. These other people. Lost souls seeking solace in a bottle or a bit of conversation, and outside? The rain, the dreary town, the jungle, and the night," and now he gives Roberto a searching look. "So how are you, my young friend?"

"I'm fine."

The man is striking an oddly familiar tone with Roberto, as if he knows him, and then Roberto's struck with an awful thought. "Are you Chano?"

The guy smiles quizzically. "I'm sorry to disappoint you, but no. Though my name sounds a little like that. Napo. Short for Napoleón. My father named me that. He was a history teacher. He was convinced his son would become a great man," and now Napo grins, revealing yellow rotting teeth. "Obviously he was mistaken."

Daniel returns with two bottles of beer and sits back down.

"That's Napo," Roberto says. "And he's Daniel, and I'm Roberto."

Napo shakes hands with both of them. His hand is very cold, it's like shaking the hand of a dead man.

"I'm very pleased to make your acquaintance."

"Can I buy you a beer, Napo?" asks Daniel.

Napo's face lights up.

"Well, it wouldn't be polite to say no."

"Here, take mine," says Roberto.

"Are you sure?"

Roberto nods. "I didn't really want it."

"Many thanks," he says, taking the bottle from Roberto and then immediately drinking about half of it. Now he sighs with satisfaction.

"I suppose you're wondering what an educated man like myself is doing in a godforsaken backwater like Tarapacá. The answer involves a young lady, as so many sad stories do."

Daniel laughs, and so does Napo. Napo is exactly the kind of character that appeals to Daniel. If left to his own devices, Daniel would doubtless spend the whole night drinking with Napo, and dawn would find them staggering along the banks of the river, singing "Penny Lane" or "Eleanor Rigby."

Napo has a leather bracelet on one wrist, with what appears to be a slender brownish bone dangling from it. Daniel points at it.

"What's that, Napo?"

Napo holds his arm up and taps the bone, making it swing back and forth.

"There was a notorious criminal named Efraín Pineda that used to frequent these parts. They called him the Frog because he was short and squat, that's what he looked like. After his death his bones were taken to a witch who lived deep in the jungle. She did special things to them, and now all his bones are magical and holy like a saint's. This is one of Efraín the Frog's finger bones. It's supposed to protect one from harm. I'm not superstitious, I'm a child of the Enlightenment, but still, I'm half convinced there's something to this. Since obtaining the bone, I've escaped in a nearly miraculous way from several dangerous scrapes."

"Where did you get it?" says Roberto.

"From a man in a bar. For fifty thousand pesos. He assured me of its authenticity," and now he finishes off his beer and belches and stands up. "Thank you for the beer, my friends, I won't bother you any further."

"You don't have to go," says Daniel.

"No, no, you've both been very kind, but it's obvious you're busy men, busy men. Just one more thing. It's a bit embarrassing. I'm expecting a check on Friday, but unfortunately now my pockets are utterly empty. A modest loan to tide me over would be appreciated more than you know."

"Sure, Napo, no problem," Daniel says and then looks at Roberto. Roberto pulls his billfold out, hands Napo two ten thousand pesos bills. The look on his face says it's more than he was expecting.

"Many thanks. I'll pay you back on Friday."

"We won't be here on Friday," says Roberto.

"Then give me your address and I'll mail it to you."

"It's okay, Napo. Don't worry about it."

"Such generosity will not be soon forgotten," Napo says solemnly, doffing his hat and holding it over his heart. "Good-bye, Daniel. And Roberto? I hope you find your Chano."

Napo puts his hat back on, resumes his seat at the end of the bar, and signals to the blonde bartender. She brings him a shot of whiskey, and he hands her one of his ten thousand peso bills. Roberto and Daniel both laugh, and then Daniel looks around.

"Where is Chano anyway?"

Roberto shrugs. He's getting worried. Why didn't Javier give him a way to contact Chano? He has Javier's number, maybe he should call him.

Suddenly the lights go out. The bartender turns on a flashlight and starts lighting candles. She brings one to their table, stuck in a rum bottle.

"Sorry, guys," she says. "This happens every time it rains."

"You think it's like this all over town?" asks Roberto.

"Oh yes, all over."

"How long do you think it will last?"

"Who knows? Maybe five minutes, maybe all night."

The bar is a dump but looks better in the dark, with its overlapping pools of light cast by the candles. Daniel lights a cigarette, and then he says: "Hey, look! The nurses!"

Two young women wearing green medical smocks have hurried in out of the rain, and now they sit down at the bar. Roberto laughs.

"What are their names?" Daniel says.

"Vera and Dolly."

"Well, get ready, Roberto. According to the sergeant, we're about to have a great time."

"I wonder which one's Vera and which one's Dolly."

Roberto's cellphone rings. He looks at the number. He doesn't recognize it.

"Maybe this is Chano," he says, and then into the phone, "Hello?"

"Roberto?" It's a female voice.

"Yes?"

"What's the matter with your arm?"

"Who is this?"

"The girl you smiled at. I'm a friend of Javier's."

Roberto looks toward the bar. The pretty girl is no longer there.

"I was supposed to meet a guy named Chano," says Roberto.

"Exit the bar. Turn right. Walk down the street and you'll see a white Corolla."

The girl ends the call. Roberto pockets the phone and stands up. He looks down at Daniel; smoke's curling around him in the candlelight.

"Who was that?" he says.

"The girl that was at the bar." Roberto throws some money down on the table. "Chano's waiting for us. Just down the street."

They come out of Juanito's into the wet windy night. It's dark except for the lights of the vehicles and their white and red reflections on the pavement. They walk fast down the sidewalk, getting wet all over again, though the rain has slackened as the storm moves away.

"Listen, Roberto," Daniel says, "how do you know this isn't a trap? They could've captured Chano and tortured him, and now they're about to do the same to us."

Roberto doesn't bother to reply. Daniel is coming with him and that's all that matters. He sees a white car parked ahead, water flowing past it along the curb.

"I think that's it."

It's probably at least twenty years old, with a rusting top and a dent in its side. Roberto peers through the passenger window, but it's covered with beads and trickles of rain and he can't see anything. But then the window slides down and the girl is there.

"Get in the back."

He opens the back door and the dome light comes on. As he and Daniel climb inside, Roberto sees the driver of the car looking at them. He's wearing a red baseball cap. A sloping forehead and tight little ears give him an apish look.

"Chano?" says Roberto.

He grins and Roberto sees a gold tooth and the guy shakes his head. "Ernesto."

Daniel pulls the door shut and the dome light goes off and they're back in darkness.

"My name's Lina," says the girl. "So you're Roberto and your friend is . . . ?"

"Daniel," says Daniel.

"Ernesto and I are with the Tulcán Armed Revolutionary Vanguard."

"But where's Chano?" says Roberto.

"He's sick."

"What's the matter with him?"

"It happened suddenly. His appendix burst. He's lucky to be alive."

Roberto tries to get his head around it. No Chano.

"I'm sorry to hear that," he says, "but—"

"Don't worry, Roberto," says Lina. "Chano's absence won't have a negative impact on your assignment. A boat is waiting right now at the river to take you to Tulcán."

* * *

The wipers of the Twingo swipe at the rain, which is coming down very lightly now. Lightning flickers on the horizon, the thunder can barely be heard.

The power is still out in Tarapacá. Daniel follows the taillights of the white Corolla. He'll be leaving his car at a house on the outskirts of town. Meanwhile he is angrily hammering away at Roberto.

"This isn't what I agreed to, Roberto! We were supposed to have this Chano guy as our guide, this legendary jungle fighter. Not some fucking teenage girl!"

"I don't think she's a teenager. She's at least twenty-two or twenty-three. And Ernesto looks pretty tough."

"Ernesto looks like a dumb-ass. They're going to get us killed."

"Look, if they're in the TARV, then they know what they're doing. The Army's scared to death of the TARV."

"As far as I'm concerned, this changes everything. It's the perfect out for us."

"I'm not looking for an out."

"Yes you are, you just don't want to admit it."

"If I didn't want to do this, I wouldn't be here. But if you want out, fine. Just leave me one of your cameras, I'll take the pictures myself."

"I'm not going to leave you one of my cameras. You'll drop it in some swamp. I'll never see it again."

"Well, I guess you're stuck with going with me then."

Daniel curses Roberto under his breath. When working, they're like an old married couple, always bickering about something. Although Daniel's never been quite as difficult as this before.

The road is paved but pocked with potholes, which the car keeps banging into. Now the Corolla turns onto a muddy dirt road, and after a few minutes pulls into the yard of a dilapidated house. The front of the house is festooned with golden strings of old CDs, shining in the head-lights. Daniel parks his car behind the Corolla and they get out.

Three dogs approach, wagging their tails at Lina and Ernesto and barking at Roberto and Daniel. A big-bellied man holding a kerosene lantern comes out on the porch, and is introduced by Lina as Yadier. The man rubs his belly and laughs, as if Lina has made a joke and Yadier is not really his name.

Daniel opens the trunk, and he and Roberto start taking out their stuff. Lina comes over and watches critically.

"Take what you need but not more than you need," she says. "We'll be doing a lot of walking."

"Okay," says Roberto.

"Whatever you're not taking with you, you can leave in the house. It'll be safer there."

"Okay."

"I'd change into some dry clothes if I was you. It will be cold on the river tonight."

"Good idea."

"Wear boots if you have them, you'll be needing them."

"You know, this isn't my first trip to the fucking jungle," Daniel says.

"It's good to hear that," Lina says evenly then walks away.

"Bossy little bitch, isn't she?" says Daniel.

"Cute though."

"She's no beauty queen. But she's okay."

Yadier with his lantern leads them into the house, past his wife and numerous children who are sitting around in the dark and seem to be waiting for the TV to come back on. He takes them into a small bedroom and leaves the lantern with them. They start stripping off their clothes.

"Looks like somebody likes the Happy Boys," says Daniel.

The Happy Boys are a wildly popular singing and dancing group of handsome teenagers. Pictures and posters of them are plastered all over the walls. Now Roberto sees other indications this is the room of a young girl: a hair brush and stuffed animals and a bottle of purple nail polish and a plastic box filled with colorful junk jewelry. Nydia comes into his head. Her shy eyes as she looked up at him. He wonders if she liked the Happy Boys. Has it been only three days since he found her in the out-house? It seems like weeks ago.

He's sitting on the bed pulling on his well-worn waterproof Merrell hiking boots when there's a knock at the door. He opens it and Lina's standing there.

"Are you ready?" she says.

He glances around. Daniel is putting cigarettes and candy bars into his pack.

"Nearly."

She looks at his arm. "You're bleeding. Come on."

Leading the way with a flashlight, she takes him into a bathroom. She turns on the water in the sink, washes his arm with soap.

"You never did tell me what happened," she says.

"Two kids tried to steal Daniel's cameras. One of them bit me and one of them stabbed me with a knife."

"Have you had a tetanus shot?"

"Yes."

She dries his arm with a towel. She opens the medicine cabinet and shines her flashlight in and takes out a bottle of hydrogen peroxide and a tube of antiseptic ointment and a tin box of bandages.

"Is your friend always so pleasant?" she says.

Roberto shrugs. "Daniel's a good guy. Most of the time."

"I don't care if he's a good guy. I just want him to be a good photographer."

"He's one of the best."

Lina is fast and efficient as she puts on the bandages.

"I'm familiar with your work," she says.

"Yeah?"

"Some of it's not too bad."

"Thanks."

The light above the sink comes on. Roberto can hear the children cheering the return of power to the house.

He takes a good look at Lina. She's a small-boned girl of average height or maybe a little less. Smooth dark skin, thick eyebrows over large brown eyes, angular cheeks, a smallish nose and a wide mouth. Her teeth are white and even except for a chipped one at the front. Roberto and Daniel aren't the only ones that have changed clothes. Lina's now wearing boots and khaki cargo pants and a gray T-shirt under an unbuttoned green military-style shirt. As she starts returning things to the medicine cabinet, Roberto detects under the green shirt the gleam of a gun.

"You look different than in the bar," he says.

"That was my 'normal girl' disguise. I can't go marching around town looking like a militant, can I? Tarapacá is full of spies."

He thanks Lina for tending to him then goes back to the bedroom. He decides at the last minute not to take his billfold. There won't be a need for any credit cards where he's going, and if he's unfortunate enough to find himself in a situation where he's being asked for his ID, he'd probably be better off saying a robber took his billfold or he lost it when he fell in a river. He can make up some name and plausible-sounding story about his presence in Tulcán and maybe at least buy himself a little time. He takes the cash out of his billfold and stuffs it in a pocket and puts the billfold in the hidden compartment in his suitcase where he has his passport.

Roberto and Daniel pick up their backpacks and head out of the house. In the living room, the kids are clustered around their resurrected television, watching an American criminal investigation show dubbed into Spanish. Roberto notices one of Yadier's daughters has purple polish on her fingernails.

"Do you like the Happy Boys?" he asks her.

The girl grins. "Yes!"

"Which one's your favorite?"

"Tico!"

* * *

It turns out the Corolla belongs to Yadier. He drives them all down to the river, with Ernesto in the back seat squeezed in between Roberto and Daniel. They pass by the Park of the Parakeets. Not a soul can be seen. Roberto thinks about the thousands of parakeets sleeping in the dark, dripping trees, imagines their clamorous leave-taking tomorrow at dawn as they return to the jungle, the jungle where he'll already be.

Yadier parks above the river. It's not raining at all anymore, though the sky is still cloudy. Roberto and Daniel take their backpacks out of the trunk, and Yadier shakes hands with everyone. "Good luck. And tell Diego to give Princesa a kiss for me."

Lina smiles. "I'll do that."

Roberto and Daniel shoulder their packs, and follow Lina and Ernesto on a path that leads down a muddy slope to the river.

"Who's Diego?" says Roberto.

"We're going to his house," says Lina. "We'll be there tomorrow," and then she adds, "Be careful, it's very slippery."

This is the cue for Daniel's feet to fly out from under him. He lands hard on his butt and his elbows. Roberto hurries to help him. "Hey man, you all right?" he says, but Daniel pushes him away.

"Leave me alone, I'm fine."

They start down the slope again. Roberto's walking behind Daniel, and he can't help but laugh.

"I'm sorry, Daniel, it's just that you're covered with mud."

"Yes, I can see how funny this is."

They reach the river. There are lots of boats there, pulled up on the bank or tied to docks. A bedraggled dog wanders around, looking for someone or something. They walk along the mucky bank to a dock that has a precariously narrow plank walkway leading out to it. On the dock is a young guy with a flashlight. He shines it on the walkway and Ernesto and Lina cross it quickly, even though it's bending under their weight and water sloshes over it. Daniel acts like he's stepping onto a tightrope, but he manages to wobble across it without falling in, and then, pretending he's strolling down a sidewalk in broad daylight, Roberto walks steadily across it to the dock.

"This is Roque," Lina says of the young guy. "Roque, this is Roberto and Daniel."

"How are you?" Roque says, shaking their hands. He's not very tall, but is broad-shouldered and sturdily built. He has a handsome open face and a big smile. A machete in a leather sheath hangs from his belt.

They follow Roque down the dock to a long weathered yellow wooden boat, powered by a small outboard motor. A green plastic roof covers the middle of the boat. Roberto and Daniel climb in, stepping over nets and fishing gear, and sit down under the roof on a bench seat. Lina sits down in front of them. Roque goes to the back of the boat and Ernesto unties the rope, steps into the front, and pushes the boat away from the dock. Roque yanks a cord three times and the motor comes to life, and the boat putters down an inlet and then out upon the broad black river.

Roberto looks back at the lights of Tarapacá, town of criminals and spies. Ahead is a bridge, where the road they drove in on crosses the river and continues on into Tulcán. The bridge is lit up with floodlights, and Roberto can see men who look like soldiers checking vehicles at both ends.

"Is that the Army?" he says.

"No," says Lina, "the National Police."

The National Police wear uniforms and carry weapons that basically make them indistinguishable from the military. They're also like the military in their propensity for violence.

"They're in on it too, huh?"

"Everyone's in on it," says Lina, turning around on her seat to face him. "Everyone's doing their part to crush Tulcán."

"Tell me what's going on there."

"The people are being attacked and they're trying to flee. They're hiding in the forest, or they're coming this way into Chimoyo, or they're heading north and trying to make it to San Miguel." San Miguel is the capital of Tulcán, and at around sixty thousand, the only town of any size. "They've been pouring into Red Cross camps and they have terrible stories to tell. Shootings, rapes, burnings, beheadings."

"Who's doing this? The Army? The paramilitaries?"

"Yes, both. They're working hand in glove."

"Javier told me the Black Jaguars have been involved in a massacre at a ranch called El Encanto."

"That's right. He said that's where you want to go."

"Lina," says Ernesto, "look."

He's pointing at the bridge. A column of Army vehicles has begun to rumble across it, heading north. Roberto can see cargo trucks, armored personnel carriers, Humvees, all painted in camouflage colors, and then two flatbeds carrying tanks. Lina seems excited.

"Do you see, Ernesto? Do you see the tanks?"

Ernesto nods. Daniel has his camera out. He moves up and crouches behind Ernesto and starts taking pictures.

"Be careful, Daniel," Lina says, "don't let them see you," and then to Roberto, "I think those are Leclerc tanks. The Army bought forty of them last year from France. They've never had anything this good."

"Why are they important?"

"Tanks are useless in the jungle. If they're going to Tulcán, that must mean the Army intends to assault San Miguel. They'll find a pretext, they always do. They'll say the terrorists have taken refuge there and they need to root them out. Cleanse the city of them."

Roberto has his notebook out now and is writing all this down. The boat goes under the bridge. Daniel stumbles the length of the boat to the back where Roque is and takes more pictures. Roberto looks at Lina gazing up at the column that continues to pass.

"How does it make you feel?" says Roberto. "To see something like that?"

"How do I feel? Like a terrorist. Because if you take up arms in this country and defend yourself from being murdered, that's what you are."

Roque throttles up the motor, the boat goes round a bend in the river, and the bridge and the town are gone. Roberto knows the Gualala River flows northeast, eventually emptying into the sea. He also knows that at some point, it will meander into Tulcán. But beyond that, he doesn't have the slightest idea where he's going.

"How exactly will we get there?" he says. "To El Encanto."

"We'll go down the river all night," says Lina. "Tomorrow, we'll come to another river called the Maniqui. We'll travel up the Maniqui a couple of hours to Diego's house. From there, we'll walk west into the jungle, until we reach the Otavalo River. That's where El Encanto is. We should reach it before nightfall."

"And there's some people there I'll be able to talk to, right? Who survived the massacre?"

"I hope so. Who knows? The situation's very chaotic."

"Have you been there before? To El Encanto?"

"Several times."

"Javier said it was very special."

Lina smiles, looks out at the river. "It was. It was the kind of place that, when you went there, you wanted to never leave." Now she looks back at Roberto. "Javier said you won't be able to stay long."

"No, I have to be back in Tarapacá by Saturday. On Sunday, I'm catching a plane out of the country."

"You're fleeing too. Like the people in Tulcán."

"Yes. I suppose."

"We're glad you've come, Roberto. I want you to know we'll do anything to help you."

Now she rises, and moves to the front to talk to Ernesto.

Daniel sits down heavily beside Roberto. He checks out some of the pictures he just took on the LCD screen, shakes his head and mutters "Too dark," then puts the camera in the bag. He sighs, and lights a cigarette.

"It's going to be a long fucking night."

"Yeah."

The jungle is a black ragged silhouette on both sides of the river. There's no moon or stars. No lights from other boats. The five of them on the boat seem utterly alone. Moving steadily over the face of some featureless dark immensity.

The river is smooth and slow-flowing. Roberto trails his hand in the warm water.

He takes a flashlight out of his backpack and by its light starts writing in his notebook. He makes notes about what he saw on the bridge, his conversation with Lina, Yadier's house and the Happy Boys posters and the purple nail polish, Napo's sinister good luck charm, Panther and Parrot. When Roque steers the boat a little closer to one bank, a large white bird perched on a stump sticking out of the water is disturbed; it rises slow as a ghost and flaps toward the forest, and Roberto makes a note about that.

* * *

It's silent except for the drone of the outboard motor. Daniel and Lina are both asleep, curled up in the bottom of the boat, but Roberto isn't sleepy. He wishes he was. He's badly in need of sleep. Lack of sleep makes him less efficient, more prone to screw up, and he can't afford to screw up for the next three days. But wishing for sleep only keeps it away.

Ernesto's not asleep either. He sits at the front, keeping an eye out for logs or debris or other boats. He turns on his flashlight if he sees something and communicates to Roque with hand signals, left, right, slower, faster. But once, the boat runs afoul of nets set out by a fisherman, and Roque has to kill the motor and raise the propeller out of the water to get it disentangled.

Lina was right, it's getting cold on the river, with the breeze blowing endlessly in his face. He wonders how she came to be in a fanatical outfit like the TARV. She's certainly an interesting girl, with her intensity and good looks and the gun tucked in her belt. She'll make a great character in his story.

He looks across the water to the jungle and he figures that by now he's probably entered Tulcán. Suddenly fear clenches inside Roberto like a giant fist and he can hardly breathe. What if the dark, savage country he's traveling into has a bit of land that for all eternity has been waiting to welcome his bones, or a turbid river whose task it is to carry his bloated body away?

* * *

The drone of the motor begins to change. It seems to get louder and to relocate itself from the back of the boat to inside Roberto's own head, and then fades away to nearly nothing. Faint voices drift across a black void. Screams come next, but not fearful screams, he seems to be on some kind of amusement park ride, and then his chin jerks up off his chest and his eyes open and he looks around at the river and the jungle.

He climbs over the seat and lies down next to Daniel. He's using his backpack as a pillow and Roberto does the same. Some dirty water's sloshing around in the bottom of the boat, but the wood flooring above it is dry. He squirms around and tries to get comfortable, then seconds later, he's asleep.

It's a long night, as Daniel said it would be. Once Roberto's awakened by rain rattling on the plastic roof. He raises himself up and sees lightning flash and hears thunder, and he wonders if a violent storm is about to catch them on the river, but then the rain stops and he goes back to sleep. He wakes up later to the sound of religious music: some woman is singing with a sob in her voice about how Jesus gave his life to save us from our sins. At first he thinks somebody in the boat must be playing it, but then he realizes it's coming from out on the river. He peers over the side and sees a long barge sliding by, piled high with the trunks of great rain forest trees. The beam of a spotlight probes the dark water. Two guys are standing in the wheelhouse, that's where the music's coming from. A dog walks out of the wheelhouse and sees their boat and barks. Roberto lays his head back down on his pack, and the boat begins to rock as it's hit by swells from the barge. When he awakes again, he's very thirsty and very cold. He takes a bottle of water out of his pack and drinks some. Daniel is snoring softly. Roberto can make out the dim shape of Lina's shoulder where she lies sleeping. And then he looks at Ernesto in the front and Roque in the back and finds something calm and reassuring about their presence. He feels as trusting as a child, they'll stay up all night and make sure nothing bad will happen to him, and then he goes back to sleep and he has a dream.

He's in the jungle. It's green and alive and beautiful and he's not afraid of it, indeed he feels at home. He walks along slowly, looking at things. He hears birds, but doesn't see any. But then a green hummingbird flies through a shaft of sunlight and stops right in front of him, hovering there, its wings a blur. Roberto holds his hand out, and the hummingbird lights on his finger. Its eyes are green too, they're like tiny glittering emeralds as they gaze at him . . .

Three days until the day Roberto is to die

When Roberto awakes, there's a coarse red and black blanket covering him. He sits up, and looks around. In the soft light of dawn, he sees the dark-green jungle, the brownish-green river. He's the last one up. Daniel's up front smoking a cigarette and talking to Ernesto, while Lina is sitting with her back to Roberto, talking on a satellite phone. She's telling someone about the convoy crossing the bridge and the Leclerc tanks. Now as she puts the phone away in her backpack, she sees Roberto's awake, and smiles.

"Good morning."

"Good morning," he says, rubbing his neck. He climbs over the seat and sits down. "Thanks for the blanket."

"Thank Roque, it belongs to him."

Roberto turns back to Roque, holds the blanket up. "Hey, Roque, thanks!"

Roque smiles. "You were . . ." he says, and then he hugs himself and pretends to shiver.

Roberto laughs. "Yeah, I was freezing."

The boat starts rocking a little as Daniel comes back his way. "Hey Roberto, you'll never guess what Ernesto used to do."

"What?"

"He was an artificial inseminator on cattle ranches. He'd get semen from the bulls and put it into the cows."

"So how did the bulls feel about that, Ernesto?" says Roberto.

"It made them sad," says Ernesto. "They'd rather put it into the cows themselves."

Roberto and Daniel laugh, but Lina frowns.

"Cattle ranches. Do you know how destructive they are?"

Daniel yawns and stretches. "I need to piss."

Roque steers the boat to the bank. Everyone gets out to stretch their legs and relieve themselves. The river's low; there's a wide strip of dried mud between it and the edge of the forest. Roberto walks a couple of meters into the trees. As he pees, he sees small dark shapes moving in the treetops.

Roque is near him, peeing too. Roberto points and says, "What kind of monkeys are those?"

Roque smiles. "Squirrel monkeys. They're waking up. They're looking for breakfast."

Roque is wearing a blue baseball cap, a maroon T-shirt, black jeans, and knee-high rubber boots. The cap has the head of a red bull on it, and above that: CHICAGO BULLS. Roberto asks him where he got it.

"From an American. He was a basketball player."

"On the Chicago Bulls?"

"Yes."

They both zip up, then head back to the boat.

"How'd you happen to meet him?" says Roberto.

"I was a guide. At this place in the jungle where tourists would come. He was a black man," and he raises one hand way up. "He was very, very tall. So tall they had to put two beds together for him so he could sleep."

Roberto laughs. "Yeah?"

"He was very nice. Always making jokes with people. He liked me. He said, 'Roque, come to Chicago, I'll buy you a ticket, I'll show you the city, you can come see me play.'"

"Do you think you'll ever go?"

"No. Why? I don't want to leave the jungle."

* * *

The sun rises over the trees and it becomes hot on the river. Roberto rubs sun block on his face and neck and arms. Daniel takes a cap out of his backpack. It's a battered stained green thing, with a cloth attached to the sides and back to cover his neck; it's kind of like what you see the soldiers of the French Foreign Legion wearing in the movies when they're trek-king over the desert. He's always worn this cap when working out in the sun. Roberto thinks it looks a little ridiculous on him, not that Daniel cares. He feels oddly comforted as he watches Daniel put it on; it suggests that for all his moaning and complaining he's ready to do the job, and Roberto feels a sudden surge of affection for him. He knows the only rea-son for Daniel's presence now on this jungle river is his love for Roberto.

He rummages around in his pack for something to eat, and finds the packets of guava-filled cheese he bought at the airport. He holds them out to Daniel.

"Hey Daniel, you want some?"

Daniel smiles. "Oh man, I love those!"

There are seven of them, and Daniel takes four. He opens one and bites into it.

"You're a prince, Roberto. Everyone should fall down at your feet and worship you."

Roberto eats his own guava-filled cheese and looks at the morning. The river is beautiful, flowing through the green forest, sliding placidly toward the sea. There are birds everywhere, and not one of them seems ordinary. Kingfishers dive-bomb the water. A white heron flaps on grace-ful wings from one side of the river to the other. Five great egrets are sitting in a huge tree; they are spaced out evenly, up and down and across the tree, as if they've been placed there as ornaments. Several vultures are hanging out on a sandbar. They're ugly with their naked heads and necks and ungainly as they hop around, but then one of them decides it's time to fly, and in the air it's just as graceful as the white heron. Roberto notices Roque is watching the birds too, through a pair of small, expen-sive-looking binoculars. There are many birds Roberto doesn't know the names of; he'll have to ask Roque about them.

Lina sits down beside Roberto.

"How's your arm?" she says.

He touches the bandages lightly.

"Seems okay. Hasn't been bothering me."

"Good."

The breeze tousles her hair. Roberto wonders if she's ever killed anyone.

"So tell me about Chano," he says. "Have you known him long?"

"Yes. In fact, you could say I wouldn't even be here if it wasn't for him."

"You mean in the TARV?"

"No, I mean physically existing on the planet. Chano grew up in this river town called Aucayo. His father was a white man who got drunk and drowned in the river when Chano was five. His mother was an Indian. When he was a teenager, gold was discovered in the area. People came from all over, they'd dig up the banks of the river and poison the water with mercury and ruin things for the fishermen. And then they'd come into town and get drunk and go after the local girls. Chano got in a fight with one of them and killed him."

"How'd he kill him?"

"With a broken pool cue. He drove it through his throat."

"Wow."

"The police didn't arrest him because they said it was self-defense, but the gold miner's friends came after him, so he had to run away. He went to San Miguel and started working as a laborer. One day he was playing soccer in the park—he was good at soccer, he'd been the best player in Aucayo. He started talking to another player, a young white guy about his age. He was a college student, he was studying sociology. They had absolutely nothing in common but they instantly became great friends. Not long after, Chano's sister came from Aucayo to live with him. Her Indian name was Xochilt. Her white name was María Alejandra. María Alejandra was very beautiful. Chano's new friend met her and they fell in love and got married, and about a year later I came along."

"So Chano's your uncle."

"Yes."

He hears another motor and sees a long skinny boat with three fishermen in it heading their way. The fishermen wave and smile as they go by and everybody waves back. Daniel takes their picture.

"What led Chano to join the TARV?" asks Roberto.

"He didn't really join it; he was one of the people that created it. After eight or nine years in San Miguel, he went back to Aucayo. He saw everything he loved being destroyed by the gold miners, the cattle ranchers, the sugarcane and soybean farmers. He could see the politicians weren't going to be of any help, they were in the pockets of the rich and powerful.

So he decided he needed to take direct action. If that involved shooting people, he didn't mind."

"And how did you get involved in this?"

She thinks about it. "It was a gradual process. I guess really things started to change for me when I was twelve. That's when my mother died."

Roberto's been scribbling all this down in his notebook; now Lina looks at him.

"Roberto? Don't write about me. I don't want to be in your story."

"Why not?"

"Because I'm not important. The victims are important."

"I have no idea what I'll be writing. It depends on what happens over the next couple of days."

The motor splutters and dies, and the boat glides silently through the green water. There are several white plastic containers of gasoline in the back, and now Roque gets one and starts refilling the gas tank.

It's a relief not hearing the motor. Just the cries of birds, the splash of a fish chasing food. Roberto's about to ask Lina another question, but then he hears a new sound. Something mechanical, a throbbing. It's coming from upriver. From behind them. All five of them turn around and look.

About half a kilometer away is a bend in the river. Now helicopters begin to appear, one after another, ten in all, following the river, coming toward them low and fast.

"Daniel, come here!" Roberto yells. Daniel's been at the front of the boat taking pictures, and now he comes stumbling back under the green roof with Roberto and Lina.

Roberto stares at the helicopters as they approach. They're Black Hawks. Sleek machines with three-man crews, armed with two machine guns, capable of carrying eleven soldiers. He's relieved to see they're not slowing down, after all there's no reason they should concern themselves with their little yellow boat, and both Roque and Ernesto smile and wave as they zoom overhead. Roberto watches them continuing down the river, and then Daniel very softly says: "Shit."

The last of the ten Black Hawks is slowing down, is circling around.

"God damn it," says Roberto. "What are they coming back for?"

"Be still," Lina says. "Stay calm."

The Black Hawk stops a little in front of the boat and hovers there, making a great clattering noise and ruffling the river with the wind from its main rotor. Ernesto stands in the front of the boat with his hands on his hips smiling up at the pilots, as if immensely pleased that they've come back to pass the time of day. Roque unhurriedly replaces the cap on the gas tank and then puts away the empty container. Roberto can see the tail of the Black Hawk with its whirring rotor but he can't see the pilot because of the roof, which means they can't see him either. He glances over at Daniel. He wonders if his own face looks so pale with fear. The pilots must clearly see this is just the boat of poor fishermen and at any moment they'll go away. Except the Army after all has come here to sow terror, and at any moment the Black Hawk might open up with its machine guns, shredding the roof, shredding their bodies, turning the boat into a million matchsticks floating on the blood-soaked water.

The wind blows off Ernesto's cap. He laughs and moves to pick it up, which seems to break the spell somehow, as the helicopter turns around and heads back down the river.

Roberto and Daniel look at each other. Daniel shakes his head, reaching in his vest for his cigarettes.

"Motherfuckers," he says.

Lina is doing her best to act as if nothing of any importance has happened.

"Roque," she says, "come on. Let's get going."

It always seems to take Roque exactly three yanks to start the motor, and that's what happens now. The day is getting very hot, and the breeze as the boat picks up speed is welcome. Roberto touches through his shirt the St. Jude medal.

* * *

The yellow boat is not far now from the Maniqui River, which will take them to Diego's house. Roberto sees a boat with a motor with a very long shaft coming toward them. Two teenage boys are in it. The boat's so loaded with watermelons, there's hardly room for the boys. Ernesto waves at them and says to Roque, "Hey, let's get some watermelons!"

Because of the weight of the melons, the sides of the boat are barely above the water, so Roque has to go over to it slowly in order not to swamp it. Ernesto takes two melons after a brief negotiation, and Roberto hands the boys two thousand pesos, which they seem very happy with. They're around fourteen or fifteen. They're wearing nothing except ragged shorts and have thin dark-brown bodies. Roberto assumes they're brothers, but now as he looks from one back to the other he realizes that not only do they look alike, they're mirror images of each other.

"Are you guys twins?" he says.

They smile. "Yes," the one on the right says shyly.

"What are your names?"

"Pepe," says the one on the right.

"Jesús," says the other one.

They both have dark hair falling across their foreheads and they keep brushing it away from their eyes with identical gestures. Daniel of course has his camera out.

"So tell me, guys," he says, "do you ever fool people? Does Pepe pretend to be Jesús and Jesús pretend to be Pepe?"

They look at each other and laugh.

"Sometimes," says Jesús.

Roque motors away from the boat as Ernesto takes a machete and skillfully chops up one of the melons. It's pleasant to be on the river and eat the sweet red meat of the melon and spit out black seeds over the side. Lina sits next to Roberto eating her own red wedge.

"You were telling me about your mother," he says. "How did she die?"

"Cancer. Leukemia."

"How old was she?"

"Thirty-two."

"That must have been hard on you."

She nods. "But it was even harder on my father. The day of the funeral, I remember him falling down on the floor and not being able to move because he was literally paralyzed with grief. In one way, we had opposite reactions to what happened. My mother had been very religious and I'd go to Mass with her, but my father would never go—he wasn't a believer. But he began taking me after she died. He'd listen intently to the priest as he talked about God and Christ and angels and so forth, but I no longer believed a word of it. It all just seemed like a stupid fairy tale.

"Anyway, you asked me how I got into this. I started asking a lot of questions when I was twelve, and I've never really stopped. I realized there's no authority to appeal to, there's no one who can tell you what's right or wrong. You have to figure it out yourself."

"Did you go to college?"

"Yes, to the University of Lima. That's where my father went. I was working on a degree in law and political science, I was planning to become a lawyer, but things started getting so bad here that I felt that I had to come back and try to help somehow. I got a job with the Institute for Agrarian Reform—they build roads and schools and hospitals in rural areas. I loved the work but after about a year, two of my colleagues were abducted and killed. Tortured first of course; the girl was raped."

"Who killed them?"

"Who knows? Does it matter? I just knew I didn't want to be next. So I got in touch with my uncle. Chano. And I've been working with the TARV for the last two years."

"But isn't working with the TARV a lot more dangerous than what you were doing before?"

"No. In a place like this, it's much safer being a combatant than a noncombatant. If you live in some little village, you're at the mercy of whatever armed group happens to come walking out of the jungle. That's why so many poor young men join the Army or the guerrillas or the paramilitaries; they want to be the strong ones for a change and they feel protected by their comrades. It's like they're all the same eighteen-year-old boy, they talk and dress alike and have the same tattoos and listen to the same shitty music. It's not about ideology, which makes it very easy for them to change sides. A guerrilla one day is a guide leading an Army patrol to the guerrillas' hide-out the next day."

Roberto takes a bite of the watermelon and chews on it and looks at her. Thinking about how smart she is. And how pretty. She's getting to him a little.

"You can't help but feel a little sorry for them," Lina says. "They're perpetrators, but they're also victims. Most of them would have led decent, peaceful lives if they'd been born into a different kind of world."

Roberto thinks about Manuel. His own world shrunk to his weights, his dog, his radio, and his rabbit.

A watermelon seed hits Roberto in the face.

He looks toward the front, where Daniel and Ernesto are laughing.

"That's very funny," says Roberto. "Such sophisticated humor."

"Thank you, Roberto," says Daniel. "Hey, Ernesto was just telling me how he gets the semen from the bull, it's fascinating—"

"Lina," Roque says, and now Lina and Roberto look ahead toward where Roque is pointing.

Beyond a curve in the river, black columns of smoke are coming up over the trees.

"That's Jilili," says Ernesto.

"What's Jilili?" says Roberto.

"A little fishing village," says Lina, and now Roberto hears the faint staccato sound of gunfire. Lina tosses what's left of her watermelon into the water and stands up, wiping her hands on her khaki pants.

"Roque," she says, "give me your binoculars."

She takes them and peers through them toward the smoke, and then takes a look at the west side of the river. Hills thick with trees rise up steeply.

"Want to see what's going on?" she says to Roberto.

"Sure."

"Let's go there," she says to Roque, pointing toward a jagged inlet. Roque turns the boat that way. Lina gives him back the binoculars, then pulls back a tarp, revealing two gleaming all-black assault rifles with tubular steel stocks, along with clips of ammunition. The rifles are Galils, the same kind the Army uses. She hands one to Ernesto and keeps the other for herself. Roberto wonders why Roque doesn't have a rifle.

He watches the smoke and listens to the guns. Daniel sits down beside him.

"Here we go, huh?" says Daniel.

"Yeah."

Vultures and turtles are sunning themselves on the bank. The vultures take to the air and the turtles to the river as the boat approaches.

Roque cuts the motor. Ernesto jumps out, splashes through the water, and pulls the boat up on the beach. An expanse of dried, multicolored mud, puddles of water, and twisted pieces of wood leads up to a vine-covered ravine. They all begin walking except for Daniel, who lingers by the boat to take pictures. A yellow butterfly flies up and circles around Roberto and then continues on its way. Daniel catches up with him. Nobody says anything, they're all listening to the gunfire, single shots, *pop, pop, pop,* interspersed with bursts of automatic fire. Roberto pulls a blue bandana out of a pocket and takes his glasses off and cleans them. His heart is beating wildly and he puts his glasses back on and looks up toward the top of the ravine, beyond which lies Jilili.

Roque leads the way up, slashing at the tangle of vines and bushes with his machete. Ernesto and Lina sling their rifles over their backs and follow, and then come Roberto and Daniel. Roque and Ernesto and Lina ascend as steadily as if they're scaling a ladder, but Daniel and Roberto pant and sweat and grope for handholds and slip on the muddy slope. Roberto's glad he's in front, so if Daniel falls, he won't take Roberto with him. Roberto grabs the base of a bush to pull himself up, and it's like a faucet's been turned on but it's not water that comes out but ants, they're big and black and they pour down his arm biting the hell out of him.

"Shit!" he says, slapping at them and trying to brush them off.

Lina looks over her shoulder. "What's the matter?"

"Ants, they're all over me!"

Ernesto laughs. In a couple of minutes Roberto crawls out of the ravine and then reaches down and gives Daniel a hand. A drop of sweat dangles from the end of Daniel's nose, he looks like he's taken a swim in the river. Roberto feels an ant inside his shirt biting him and he slaps at his chest.

About thirty meters up a much gentler slope is the top of a hill. The gunfire is louder now. Added to it is the sound of screams: a long, drawn-out feminine scream, and then the shrill scream of a child, and then a man hoarsely screaming "No!"

Roberto and Daniel exchange a look. Daniel pulls a bottle of water out of one of his vest pockets and takes a drink and hands it to Roberto. Roque and Ernesto are already going up the hill, clearing a way through the undergrowth with their machetes. Lina crouches in front of Roberto, holding her Galil.

"Just stay low and be careful, all right?" she says.

Roberto and Daniel nod. Suddenly Lina whirls and points her rifle at two figures stumbling out of the jungle. It's a young woman holding the hand of a small boy.

"Help us!" the woman says, frantic and weeping. "They're killing us!"

"Who's killing you?" says Lina.

"The soldiers. They came in helicopters. Pedro and I were working in the yucca field, and then we heard them and then they came flying in. We ran to warn the others, but it was too late, helicopters were landing by the river. Pedro and I ran, we were looking for my husband and Carlos, he's my other son, but the soldiers were everywhere and began to shoot people. Pedro and I ran right past them but they didn't see us. God must have covered their eyes so we could escape."

Lina touches the woman's shoulder. "You and Pedro are all right now. Just stay here and hide."

Roque and Ernesto are at the top of the hill. As Roberto and Lina and Daniel approach, Roque and Ernesto look back at them and their faces are grim. When Roberto was eight or nine, he leafed through an old art book at his grandparents' apartment and came upon a medieval painting depicting the tortures of the damned. Hell was a vast cavern lit by leaping flames, and naked men and women were being tormented by demons in every part of it, a man being boiled in a cauldron here, a woman hanging upside down and being stabbed with pitchforks there, here a woman being devoured by rats with human heads and there a man being pursued by a demon with an ax. It was all so deliciously frightening it made Roberto believe in God or at least the Devil for a week or two, and as he peers over the hill he's reminded of that painting.

He has a nice view of the village of Jilili because most of the trees on the hillside have been cut down. He sees around thirty houses built on stilts, with ladders and wood sides and tin roofs; brightly colored clothes hang from lines on the porches of some of them. Many of the houses are on fire and are sending up black smoke. A white sand beach separates the village from the river. Small boats are pulled up on the beach, and extending into the river is a narrow, rickety dock. At the end of the dock a man on his knees is facing a soldier with a rifle. The man's arms are lifted in a supplicatory way. The soldier puts one bullet into the man's forehead. The back of his head is blown off and the man topples into the water.

Other bodies are in the water. Five helicopters are on the beach. Soldiers are everywhere, running along the beach and shooting at people who have taken to the river and are trying to swim away, moving methodically through the village and shooting anything that hasn't been shot already, dogs, pigs, goats, chickens, children, searching each house for anything worth stealing and then setting it on fire. Roberto recognizes the unit the soldiers are with because of their distinctive floppy recon hats and the green and black camouflage paint they've put on their faces. It's the 1st Special Operations Battalion, a so-called counter-terrorist unit that's inevitably described in the media as "elite." It was once led by General of the Armed Forces Horacio Oropeza when he was a mere colonel and it remains his particular baby.

Roberto hears the electronic whirs of Daniel snapping pictures but neither he nor Roberto nor anyone else has uttered a word, indeed it's all Roberto can do to breathe, as he watches the massacre unfold beneath him. Maybe it's becoming boring just to shoot people because the soldiers are finding more creative ways to kill. An elderly couple is soaked with gasoline from a red aluminum can and is set on fire. The man and woman stumble around and scream and then fall against each other and for an awful moment in the middle of the flames they seem to be dancing and the watching soldiers laugh and then they collapse. Half a dozen young men with their hands tied behind their backs are led to three large logs in a rough triangle that seems to serve as a community meeting place. They're forced to kneel and lay their heads on one of the logs. A tall soldier with rippling muscles takes his shirt off, picks up a sledgehammer, and proceeds to smash in the heads of each of the men with a single blow. Other soldiers cheer and clap as if they're watching an amazing feat by the strongman at a circus.

Down on the white sand beach, two soldiers are standing in front of a very pregnant girl, her hands resting protectively on her bulging stomach. One of the soldiers is holding a machete. The other soldier grabs the girl's T-shirt and pulls it off over her head as she struggles with him, and then the first soldier's machete flashes in the sun as he swings it forward and slashes open the girl's belly. Her scream is like an ice pick piercing Roberto's ear, and then the soldier strikes her again making an X and her baby spurts out in a fountain of blood and amniotic fluid and plops at her feet in the white sand.

Roberto hears a sob and thinks it comes from Lina but when he looks sees tears streaming down Ernesto's face. His hands are gripping his rifle tightly.

"Let me kill them, Lina," he says. "Please."

"We can't, Ernesto," Lina says. "There's too many."

"Fucking smoke," Daniel says.

Most of the houses in Jilili are on fire now and smoke's beginning to obscure the view. Daniel scans the slope in front of him.

"I need to get closer," he says, and now he points to a rotting tree trunk thickly covered with vines about a third of the way down the hill. "There. That's perfect."

"No, it's too risky," Lina says, but Daniel ignores her, going into his camera bag for a different lens.

"Daniel," she says, "we have plenty of pictures."

"Forget it," says Roberto. "He's not going to listen to you."

Daniel slings the camera bag over his shoulder. He moves quickly in a crouch down the hill through knee-high grass wearing his absurd cap. Roberto looks at the soldiers in the village but fortunately, none of them casts a glance upwards and Daniel reaches the cover of the tree trunk.

"Your friend's going to get all of us killed," Lina says, but Roberto thinks there's a certain amount of admiration in her eyes as she watches Daniel peer cautiously over the trunk and then resume taking pictures. Roberto hasn't been making notes because he's been unable to tear his eyes away from the phantasmagoric scene. Not that he's likely to ever forget any of it.

Smoke drifts over the top of the hill and stings his eyes. It's becoming quieter down below. Soldiers are walking around with nothing to do, no one to shoot. A large black dog comes running through the burning village in a panic. There's the rattle of a Galil on full automatic, and the dog turns into a tumble of blood and fur, and then it's quiet again.

Roberto's relieved it seems at last to be over. The soldiers will get back on their helicopters and fly away, leaving a village with no inhabitants. Can it really be they've killed everyone in Jilili except for the woman and her son? But now Roberto sees a survivor, a teenage girl, being dragged along by several soldiers. Their painted faces are laughing and smiling. She's struggling and defiant, which only makes them laugh more. She's pretty, with long dark hair. Probably the prettiest girl in the village, which is why she has lived this long. They drag her away from the houses and up the hill. Roberto starts to become alarmed because the soldiers are coming their way, but then they pull her behind a thicket of small trees and shrubs. They're out of sight of the other soldiers but in plain sight of the four on the hill and Daniel behind the tree trunk. She's wearing a shirt and shorts and they start pulling them off and she fights them and gets slapped. They rip off her underwear and she bites one of the soldiers and he punches her in the face. She goes down hard and just lies there, knocked cold, and then after a few seconds she raises herself on one elbow and looks around dazedly. Meanwhile, the guy who hit her is unbuckling and unbuttoning and unzipping, and now he drops his camouflage pants and gets on top of her. The other soldiers await their turn, watching, smoking, commenting on the action.

Roberto looks at Daniel. He's lying on his side, taking pictures around one end of the trunk. He'd hang by his knees from a trapeze to get a shot if that's what it took. Roberto sees that Lina and Ernesto are watching the rape, but Roque is intently gazing up into a tree, as if he's observing a bird or a monkey. Roberto looks up into the tree but doesn't see anything.

The soldier finishes with the girl and stands up, refastening his pants. Another soldier steps forward, but the girl suddenly jumps up and starts to run. She's running up the hill, straight toward the tree trunk behind which Daniel is hiding. The soldier whose turn it was takes off after her, as the other soldiers laugh and urge him on.

Daniel is scrunched down behind the trunk, and Roberto sees he's looking up toward him.

"Shit," Lina says, and she and Ernesto aim their rifles at the soldier.

Roberto watches the girl running naked through the grass. Her long hair makes him think of Teresa telling him about when she was a little girl and she would run and her hair would stream out behind her. The soldier charges up the hill after her, his arms pumping. His hat falls off. His head's been shaved and his scalp's been tattooed and with the green and black paint on his face he looks like some creature that has just come out of a black abyss.

Roberto looks back at Daniel. He's shocked to see what seems to be a gun in his hand.

Roberto's praying the soldier reaches the girl before they get to the tree trunk. He almost catches up with her but stumbles a little and she pulls away, but when she's only about eight or ten meters from Daniel, the soldier grabs her. They go down in the grass together. The soldier hauls her up and she fights him, scratching and kicking. He grabs her by the hair as he pulls a machete out of its sheath, and Roberto hears Lina gasp as the soldier beheads the girl with four whacks.

The girl's body, spouting blood, falls in the grass, and the panting soldier turns around and holds the girl's head up for the other soldiers to see. They curse at him and call him names for spoiling their fun but they're also laughing and the soldier, grinning and blood-bespattered, throws away the head and begins to walk back down the hill.

Roberto looks at Daniel. What the fuck is he doing with a gun?

Roberto takes his glasses off and cleans them. As if the images he's seen might somehow still be clinging to the lenses.

He hears a helicopter.

It's another Black Hawk, coming in low over the river. It swings around then settles down on the white sand beach near the other helicopters. The rotors come to a stop and an officer jumps out. Roberto can tell he's high-ranking because of his entourage, buzzing around him like worker bees around the queen. He's met by another officer, presumably the commander of the unit, who starts talking fast and gesturing in different directions. The high-ranking officer is a burly man wearing camouflage fatigues and a black steel helmet. He looks familiar.

"Roque," says Roberto, "can I borrow your binoculars?"

He looks through them at the officer as he strides away from the beach and toward the village, accompanied by his buzzing bees. Yes, it's General Oropeza, as he thought. In a way he's not surprised to see Oropeza walking past burning houses and bloody corpses. Supposedly he thinks he leads a charmed life and no bullet can harm him, and he's famously beloved by his men for his willingness to expose himself to the same dangers that they face. But in another way, it is a surprise to see him here because tremendous luck is always surprising. Roberto's not sure if Daniel has recognized Oropeza yet but he sees that Daniel's taking pictures of him, and placing the commanding general of the Armed Forces at the site of a massacre that's just been perpetrated by his own soldiers will be the biggest story of Roberto's career, bigger even than the interview with Memo Soto because not only could it bring down Oropeza but it could stop the Sri Lanka option from being carried out in Tulcán.

"It's Oropeza," says Ernesto. "That son of a whore."

He aims his rifle at the general.

"Don't do anything stupid," Lina says.

Ernesto's rifle moves very slowly as it tracks the general's movements.

"Let me, Lina. It would be so easy."

"No. We'd never get out of here."

"I don't care."

"We're not here to kill a general, we're here to help Roberto and Daniel. That's our mission."

Perhaps his life really is charmed, Roberto thinks, as he watches Oropeza through the binoculars.

* * *

After a quick tour of the village, the general rises in his helicopter like a god returning to the sky. The other helicopters follow, the five on the beach and the five that landed in the field where the woman was working with her son. Her name is Conchita. Conchita and Pedro walk down the hill with Roberto and Daniel and Lina and Roque and Ernesto into the hell that was once Jilili. It doesn't take her long to find her husband, lying on his back in a relaxed attitude except his chest has been ripped open by gunfire. She finds Carlos, her other son, on the outskirts of the village, hanging from a tree with three other children. He looks about five or six. He's wearing a blue, red, and yellow Superman T-shirt. Ernesto and Roque cut the ropes with knives and lay the children down side by side.

Other people have begun to come out of the forest where they were hiding to look for their loved ones or to see if they can find anything worth saving in the smoking ruins of their houses. Daniel is taking pictures and so is Lina, with her cellphone. Roberto wanders with them down toward the river. They see two vultures feeding on a body and they chase them away. They walk toward an area on the white sand where it looks like buckets of blood have been dumped. The girl who had her baby cut out of her is lying there. Before she died, she managed somehow to grab the baby and is holding it against her. The baby is dead too. It's the most terrible thing Roberto's ever seen. Daniel raises his camera, but then changes his mind. He turns away and lights a cigarette. But Lina takes a picture with her cellphone.

"We have to document everything," she says, "it's important."

Roberto hears the growl of a motor and looks out at the river. A boat is coming into view. In it are the twins, Jesús and Pepe, and their green load of watermelons. They must be from Jilili. Roberto's hoping at least some of their family members are still alive.

He hears a helicopter. It's not an unknown tactic for the Army to return to the scene of an operation in hopes of catching survivors by surprise. Roberto, Daniel, and Lina begin to run. The sand sucks at their boots then they splash through a little stream that cuts through the beach and then they run into the shade of some trees. Roberto crouches down, breathing hard, and looks out at the river.

He can see the helicopter now. A Black Hawk. Hovering above the water not far from the boat. The twins look up at the helicopter as the wind from its rotor beats down on them. Suddenly its machine guns open up.

The melons begin exploding, geysers of water are shooting up all around the boat, Roberto sees the head of either Jesús or Pepe explode like one of the melons. In ten seconds it's all over. The Black Hawk flies away. What's left of the melons, the boat, and the boys drifts slowly towards the sea.

* * *

The yellow boat sticks close to the bank after they leave Jilili. Maybe if another helicopter happens by, they'll have time to get in the jungle before they're spotted.

It might as well be a boatload of mutes for all the conversation that's going on. Daniel smokes. Lina writes in a notebook. Roque steers the boat. Ernesto looks at the river. And Roberto watches a hawk gliding against a background of billowy white clouds. He tries to imagine that he is it. A feathery, bony, ferocious thing, gazing down on its domain of river and trees. He'll never leave this place, he is this place, the atoms of the jungle endlessly forming and reforming themselves into this or that, a monkey or a plant or a fish or a hawk. It doesn't matter much what he is at any particular time, he's been everything and will continue to be everything. And he dreamily floats over the river.

Pain pulls him out of the sky and back to the boat. He looks at his right arm. It's covered with red swollen bites. It's had a tough time of it. The kids in Tarapacá last night, the ants today.

Lina sits down beside Roberto, and takes a look at his arm too.

"Wow, they really bit you."

"Yeah."

"The best treatment for ant bites is wild honey. When we get to Diego's, we'll put some on."

"So who is this Diego guy?"

"He lives in the jungle. It's very remote. No other people around except Indians who still live like Indians; they wear loincloths and hunt with blowguns and bows and arrows. It's wonderful there. The forest is full of animals, the trees have never been cut. He used to make money from tourists, they would come there and stay, it would be a real jungle adventure for them. We were trying to develop an ecotourism industry, lots of rich Europeans and Americans and Australians would come here, but the fighting has ended all that."

"Yeah, Roque was telling me he used to be a tourist guide."

Lina glances back at him.

"Poor Roque. Now he guides people like us. People with guns."

"How come Roque doesn't have a gun?"

"He's not really one of us. He's not a member of the TARV. He's too gentle. Too kind." She sighs. "I love Roque. He's like my little brother. I wish I could get him away from this."

"He told me he doesn't want to leave."

"I know. He'll die here. Like the rest of us."

* * *

In about an hour, they reach the confluence of the Gualala and the Maniqui. Roque swings the boat around, and they head up the murky brown-green river. It's much smaller than the Gualala. On either side, the jungle is near at hand.

A large brown and white bird flies over the river. It reminds Roberto of a seagull the way its wings cut through the air. It plunges into the water, and comes up with a wiggling fish in its talons.

"Roque," says Roberto, "what kind of bird is that?"

Roque watches it fly into a tree.

"An osprey." Now he holds out his binoculars to Roberto. "Here."

Roque slows the boat as Roberto observes the osprey through the binoculars. It holds the fish down with its talons and tears chunks out of it with its curved beak.

"Fishermen watch the osprey," Roque says. "They go where it goes. That's where the fish are."

Roberto looks at Roque's fancy Leica binoculars. He wonders how Roque could possibly afford them. "These are nice," he says.

"Two Australians gave them to me."

"Yeah?"

Roque nods. "They were very old. Over sixty. One of them wrote books and the other was a movie director. I showed them the jungle for two weeks. I didn't have binoculars then. Before they came my boat turned over, and I lost my old pair in the river. And then about two months after they left, a package came for me in the mail. It was from Australia. I opened it and it was the binoculars. I couldn't believe it. I was so happy."

"They must have thought you were a very good guide."

He shrugs. "I don't know. But they spent a lot of money and came a long way. They wanted to see the jungle and learn about it, and I did my best to help them."

"Did they speak Spanish?"

"No. I speak English."

"Really? How did you learn?"

"From the people I guided. Even the ones from Europe, most of them spoke English."

"How many languages do you speak?"

"Three. Spanish. English. O'wa."

"You're an O'wa?"

"Yes."

They're quiet for a moment. Roque's calm face under his Chicago Bulls baseball cap looks at the river.

"Back there?" Roberto says. "At the village?"

"Yes?"

"You kept looking up into a tree, but I couldn't see anything. What were you looking at?"

Roque is silent.

"Roque? Don't you want to tell me?"

"Sometimes I tell people things and they don't believe me. They laugh."

"I won't laugh."

"I was looking at a spirit."

"What kind of spirit?"

"I don't know. But I've seen her before. Many times. Always up in the trees."

"Her?"

"Yes."

"When was the first time you saw her?"

"When I was a little boy. The river changed course and our village was washed away. Many people were drowned. I was lost in the jungle all night. I saw her up in a tree and she said, 'Roque, don't be afraid, everything will be all right.' And the next morning my uncle found me."

"What does she look like? Like a girl?"

"No. She's like . . . flashes of light on water. Except she's up in the trees."

"Did she speak to you today?"

He nods. "She said, 'Roque, look at me. Don't look down at the village. Just keep looking at me.'" And then he smiles and points. "An agami heron!"

Roberto sits with Roque and he gives names to all the birds Roberto sees and Roberto studies them with the binoculars: a snowy egret, a black-collared hawk, a white-throated toucan, a solitary eagle, a ringed kingfisher, a capped heron, a great black hawk.

"Those are *caciques*," Roque says of a noisy flock of black birds with yellow tails. "People make a soup out of their brains and give them to their babies when they're a year old. It makes the babies smarter."

"So did you have the soup when you were a year old?"

He grins. "Yes. But I'm still not very smart. Maybe I should have had another bowl."

The birds help blot out the images of Jilili. The river narrows and the trees seem taller. Turtles topple off logs and plop in the water at the passing of the yellow boat. Roberto sees flashes of pink, it's a dolphin chasing fish. Roque warns him to never make eye contact with a dolphin or he'll have nightmares the rest of his life. A snake swims sinuously in the shallows, and monkeys perform acrobatic tricks in the treetops. A dozen blue and red and yellow macaws fly down the river and disappear around a bend.

"Roberto," Daniel says, "look at those monsters!"

A pair of black caimans are lying torpidly on the bank. They're huge, three and a half, maybe four meters long. Roque takes the boat closer, and Daniel snaps pictures until the caimans, annoyed at having their siesta disturbed, slither off into the water.

The sun begins to sink in the western sky, and the jungle's shadow covers the river. The river becomes shallower, and they encounter islands covered with grass of an almost supernatural greenness, it's as if it's lit from within. Spindly-legged birds walk around in the grass, eying them warily as they go by. The boat's passing through a narrow channel between two islands when the propeller begins to churn and the boat grinds into the bottom. Roque shuts the motor off and everyone has to get out and push. The boat moves along a meter or two and then won't budge.

"Okay," Lina says, "one, two, *three*!" and everyone gives it their all, grunting and gasping. Roberto slips and falls in the water and feels weak and clumsy until Ernesto does the same. Finally the boat begins to slide and then glides free and they all climb back in.

Chest heaving, Daniel unscrews the cap from a bottle of water, but then stops and stares at nothing.

"You okay, Daniel?" asks Roberto, and Daniel nods and then leans out and vomits into the river.

Roque takes the boat slowly through a labyrinth of little islands. The Maniqui's starting to seem more like a swamp than a river. Wherever Diego lives, it's not easy to get to. Roberto's heart gives a lurch when he sees a giant caiman right next to the boat but then it turns into a gnarly floating log. And then he sees a long blue boat with a tin roof pulled up on a muddy bank, and Roque cuts the motor and they're there.

Roberto and Daniel grab their backpacks and get out of the boat. On top of a hill is a large house of unpainted gray wood surrounded by palm trees. Two men are walking down a path. Lina introduces them to Roberto and Daniel. One is Diego and the other is named Quique.

Diego is wearing a white shirt, blue pants, and no shoes. He has a long brown face with handsome sharp features. He grins as he pumps Roberto's hand and couldn't seem happier to meet him. As Roberto shakes Quique's hand, he's thinking this is how he thought Chano would look. Tattooed jaguar whiskers extend from under his nose across his cheeks. It appears someone has taken a machete to his neck, judging by the long scar on one side of it. His belt buckle is made of five rifle rounds. He looks Roberto over with a mixture of skepticism and contempt.

"We were getting worried," says Diego. "Did you have any trouble?"

"Yes," says Lina, "in Jilili. The Army attacked it and killed nearly everyone."

"Shit," says Diego.

"It's too late to leave for El Encanto. We'll stay here tonight. We'll leave at first light."

"Okay, Lina, I'll have Alquimedes make us a big dinner," and then Diego shouts up the hill, "My son, get your ass down here! Hurry!"

A teenage boy is walking down the path, taking his time. Diego shakes his head. "That kid's so lazy. All he cares about is music. He wants to be one of the Happy Boys, what are the chances of that, huh?"

"Oh, let him dream, Diego," Lina says. "He's got plenty of time to get his head on straight."

He's certainly cute enough to be a Happy Boy, Roberto thinks, as the boy ambles up. He has big eyes under thick dark eyebrows and full red lips. He's dressed somewhat flamboyantly for the jungle in a backward orange baseball cap, a matching sky-blue T-shirt and shorts, orange leggings, and orange athletic shoes. Roberto's first thought is he's gay, but then he sees how he looks at Lina, ignoring everyone else.

"Hi, Lina," he says.

"How are you, Marco?"

"Okay. Great."

"My son, take their packs and put them in the guesthouse," Diego says, gesturing toward Daniel and Roberto. They both protest they can carry their own packs but Diego says, "No, let him do some work for a change. It won't kill him."

Led by Diego, they all head up the path. A bony, brown and black dog with long shaggy hair comes to greet them, tail wagging, barking excitedly.

"Shut up, Duque!" Diego yells. He kicks at the dog but it dodges away.

Roberto feels a sense of relief as they go up the hill. He's glad he won't be slogging through the jungle to El Encanto until tomorrow. How pleasant it will be to eat a dinner prepared by a cook named Alquimedes and then to have a good night's sleep in the guesthouse because he can't remember a time when he was this tired.

* * *

The sun is close to setting and sends soft light slanting across the top of the hill. Roberto and Daniel are being shown around by Diego, who is proud of his place. The guesthouse is a large round hut with a thatched roof. It has six hammocks, each of a different color, red, blue, green, purple, yellow, and orange, all with matching mosquito nets.

"The colored hammocks was Marco's idea. I wasn't convinced but I gave it a try and guess what? The guests loved it. Because we all have a favorite color, right?"

Now Diego leads them to a wooden building near the guesthouse.

"Here's the bathroom. It has a toilet that flushes and a sink and a shower. It's not easy building a bathroom like this in the jungle, but I had to make my guests comfortable if I expected them to come back," and he smiles sadly. "But now they'll never come back."

"You never know," says Roberto. "Things change."

"Well, if they do come back, I'll be here. I was born here; my mother buried my umbilical cord under that tree there for good luck. My grandparents, my parents, and my wife are buried here, but it ends with me. Marco wants to go to the big city to dance all night in discos with flashing lights and beautiful girls. The jungle has always wanted to take the hill back, and someday it will."

As they're walking beneath a tree, something drops from its branches and lands on Roberto's back and grabs his hair. He lets out a shout as Diego and Daniel nearly bust their sides laughing.

"It's Chico," Diego says. "He just wants to introduce himself."

Chico's a large chorongo monkey with dark-brown woolly fur and a black face and black hands. He perches on Roberto's shoulder, leans down, gazes at his beard as if he's never seen one before, and gently tugs at it.

Daniel raises his camera. "Smile, Chico!"

Suddenly Chico snatches Roberto's glasses. "Hey!" he says and grabs for the glasses, but Chico springs back up into the tree. He scrambles out of reach and then hangs by his tail from a branch so he can examine the glasses at his leisure. Roberto looks up at the blur of the monkey in the blur of the tree. He brought an extra pair, but that doesn't stop him from feeling anxious. He really can't see without his glasses, and what if something were to happen to both pairs of them?

"Hey, Chico," says Roberto, "give me my fucking glasses! This isn't funny, Chico!"

"You're wrong, Roberto," Daniel says, snapping pictures, "this is very funny."

Diego spreads his arms out. "Come on down, Chico, let's go, baby! Chico!"

Chico leaps out of the tree and lands in Diego's arms. Diego takes the glasses and hands them back to Roberto. Chico's left them dirty and smeared and Roberto cleans them with his bandana.

"Let's go meet Princesa," says Diego.

They head toward a wooden structure that is evidently the abode of Princesa, whatever she is. Chico jumps to the ground and walks along with them, but then all at once Duque comes charging up. Chico lets out a shriek and runs toward a tree as Diego swings his leg at Duque, this time connecting solidly. Duque yelps and runs off but then circles back to the tree where Chico has taken refuge and barks up at him as Chico screams indignantly down at Duque. Diego laughs.

"Duque and Chico don't like each other. Duque chases Chico, and Chico sneaks up on Duque when he's sleeping and pulls his tail."

The structure's constructed of heavy planks, as if whatever's inside is large and powerful. Diego opens the door. "Welcome to Princesa's palace," he says, and ushers them in.

There's no roof overhead, just chicken wire. The floor is covered with grass and plants. A long shallow hole is filled with water. Roberto looks around uneasily for Princesa, then sees in one corner the knot-like coils and twists of a gigantic snake.

"Princesa," Diego says, "wake up. You have visitors."

Diego picks up Princesa and puts her on his shoulders. She's a dull brown-gold color with a pattern of black spots. She's around four meters long, not that big as anacondas go. Diego carries her outside.

"When I first caught her she was very wild," he says. "I think she wanted to kill me. One time she got wrapped around my neck and started to squeeze, I thought it was all over for me, but thank god Alquimedes was able to pull her off. Then a shaman told me I should rub her body all over with tobacco and aguardiente for three days in a row, and it worked. See how sweet and loving she is now?" and he caresses her body as it curls around him. "Here, Roberto, you take her."

He has an aversion to snakes like most people, and he takes a step back as Diego approaches with Princesa.

"Thanks, Diego, but I'd rather not."

"Oh, go ahead," Daniel says, enjoying every second of this. "You don't want to hurt her feelings."

"She won't hurt you, I promise," says Diego.

It feels awkward to keeping saying no, so Roberto lets Diego drape Princesa over his shoulders. He staggers a little under her weight. One expects living things to be warm, but her skin is cold. Like Napo's hand in Tarapacá. Her head with its lightless eyes glides down Roberto's chest, he can feel her tremendous strength rippling through her body.

Daniel's taking pictures. "What does she eat?" he says.

"Mostly fish," says Diego. "Sometimes frogs, turtles, chickens. It's been over a year since she ate a person."

He and Daniel laugh. Princesa's head is now moving down Roberto's leg.

"I think she wants down," he says, and he bends over and Diego lifts her off and puts her down on the grass.

Lina walks up. She surveys the scene with obvious disapproval.

"Why don't you guys leave her alone? She's not some kind of toy."

"She doesn't mind," says Diego. "She likes people. She likes her life here."

Princesa is slithering away through the grass.

"If she likes it so much," says Lina, "how come every time you put her on the ground she heads straight for the jungle?"

Diego walks after Princesa and picks her up. "Lina doesn't understand you like I do," he says to her.

Roberto watches him returning Princesa to her prison.

"The only reason he got her to begin with was to make money off her," Lina says. "She was just an attraction for the tourists."

Lina's hair's wet. She looks refreshed and smells of soap.

"Did you take a shower?" Roberto asks.

She smiles, showing her chipped front tooth.

"Yes, it was wonderful."

* * *

It's wonderful. He doesn't even mind that the water's not hot. Roberto washes the grime of the journey on the river off his body, he lathers up his hair, he scrunches his eyes shut as he rinses off the soap. He peels the bandages off his arm and gently cleans the knife wound and the boy bite and the ant bites, hoping that nothing gets infected. Napo was right about infections acquired in the jungle: Roberto's seen them before and they're not pretty. He turns off the water. The soldier holding the head of the girl by the hair in Jilili comes into his mind and he expels him and rubs a towel over himself. He has just the one pair of pants so he's forced to put them back on, but he did bring a couple of extra shirts along with a pair of flip-flops so he doesn't have to clomp around in his muddy boots. Lina's given him a jar of wild honey and two bandages. He dabs the ant bites with the honey and puts on the bandages and rubs insect repellent on his face and neck and arms and feet and then, feeling half human again, he goes to the guesthouse.

Daniel's preceded him in the shower, and now he's sitting at a small wooden table, wearing only his baggy underwear. His cameras are on the table and he's looking at the photos he took today. Roberto sits down at the table with him.

"How long have you been carrying a gun?" says Roberto.

He shrugs. "I don't know. A year? It was after I got mugged. I thought that motherfucker was going to kill me. So I got it for protection."

"Journalists don't carry guns."

"I'm not a journalist." He lights a cigarette and returns to his camera. "These are amazing pictures, man. Here, look at this one," and he shows Roberto an image on the LCD screen. "Here's Oropeza standing right next to the guys that got their heads hammered in. And you see the soldier standing next to him? That's the guy that did the hammering. We've got a bunch of pictures like this. Showing him right in the fucking middle of the massacre. We've nailed that bastard."

"No, *you* nailed him. You took the pictures."

"No I didn't."

"What do you mean?"

"This has gone way beyond taking pictures for a story, now it's documenting war crimes. How long do you think I'd last once these pictures come out? I don't want to leave the country like you. For the first time, I'm starting to like my life a little."

"But who would I say took the pictures?"

"I don't know. Make up somebody, or say you took them. I don't care. Just leave me out of it."

"People will guess."

"Well, they better not guess or I'm fucked." He exhales some smoke and looks at Roberto. "You didn't tell anyone else I was coming with you, did you?"

"No."

But Roberto must not have sounded very convincing.

"Okay, Roberto. Who'd you tell?"

"Nobody. It's just that I told Andrés I was planning to ask you to come. But I didn't talk to him after that, so he doesn't know what happened."

"When we get back, you need to call Andrés. Say I was too drunk, say I was an asshole, whatever. Just tell him I didn't go with you. Okay?"

"Okay. But it's a shame. You could win the Bolívar Prize for this."

"I'm not a news photographer anymore. I photograph food and furniture and girls. The only thing winning the Bolívar Prize would do for me is get me killed."

"Whatever you say. But all I know is, you did a hell of a job today."

Chico walks through the door. He glances at Roberto, bares his teeth in an affable grin-like way, then climbs into the yellow hammock.

"Don't get too comfortable, pal," says Daniel. "Yellow's my favorite color."

"Think I'll join him," says Roberto. He gets up and goes to the blue hammock and lies down on it. He closes his eyes. Sleep immediately begins to envelop him like a rolling black cloud.

"Roberto?" says Daniel.

Roberto forces his eyes open.

"Yeah?"

"I've been thinking."

"Yeah?"

"Does it really make any sense to go on to this El Encanto place tomorrow?"

Roberto's puzzled. "Why are you asking?"

"We've already got what we came for. *More* than what we came for. What happened today is one of the biggest stories in years. But what's the story in El Encanto? We'll be covering the aftermath of a massacre. We've done that plenty of times. I say in the morning we get back in the boat. Get the hell out of Tulcán before we get killed."

Lina comes in. They both look at her.

"Excuse me," she says, "did I interrupt something?"

Reluctantly, Roberto sits up in his hammock. "Daniel thinks we shouldn't risk going to El Encanto since the big story is what happened in Jilili. He thinks we should head back to Tarapacá tomorrow."

Before Lina can respond, Chico jumps out of his hammock and runs over to her and jumps up in her arms and grabs a handful of her hair.

"Ow!" says Lina. "Stop it, Chico!" She walks to the door and tosses him outside. "Go play with Duque, all right?" Now she comes back and smiles apologetically. "Sorry."

"So what do you think?" Daniel says. "About El Encanto?"

Lina seems hesitant. "I'm here to help you guys. Whatever you decide to do is fine with me."

"But what's your opinion?" says Roberto.

"I can see Daniel's point. I'm sorry the people in Jilili had to die, but I'm happy we were there to witness it. It's very important to get their story out to the world."

"But what happened in El Encanto's important too. There's no reason we can't do both stories."

"We can't do either story if we're dead," Daniel says.

"So how dangerous do you think it is?" Roberto asks Lina.

"Going there, we should be okay. Neither the Army nor the paramilitaries like to operate in the jungle if they can help it."

"But what about poisonous snakes?" says Daniel. "They like to operate in the jungle."

Lina smiles. "That's true. You just have to be careful where you step. But once we get to El Encanto, who knows what we'll encounter? There's been a lot of hostile activity along the Otavalo River."

Daniel and Lina both look at Roberto. It's up to him.

If he regards the matter pragmatically, Daniel's probably right. Why take a chance of blundering into a bad situation and being killed when he's already succeeded beyond his wildest imaginings? But what Javier told him about El Encanto has been haunting him. The fairy tale castle on the jungle river, the sweet little man who makes up stories about his chess pieces, the peacocks and the hedge maze and the evil that came there . . . it's a story he wants to tell . . . he *has* to tell.

"Look, Daniel," he says. "You and I have always been lucky. We just need to be lucky for a couple of more days."

* * *

Cicadas buzz in the dusk. A single star shines. There's something very pure and simple about it. Lina and Roberto are walking toward the house.

"I spoke to my superiors," she says. "I told them about the massacre. They couldn't believe we've got pictures of Oropeza. They wanted me to thank you and Daniel for the work you're doing."

"We're not doing this to help the TARV. We're just trying to get the story."

"I understand."

A bat flickers overhead, feasting on the mosquitoes that are swarming out as the night comes on.

"So they must be happy with you," says Roberto. "Your superiors."

"I hope so. This is the most responsibility I've ever been given. I'm just trying not to screw it up."

They reach the house. He smells diesel fumes. A rickety generator's running and the windows are filled with light. Beneath the house, a rooster and some chickens are settling in for the night. Duque comes down the steps to greet them, panting and grinning.

They go in the dining room and sit down at a long table with Daniel, Ernesto, Roque, Marco, Quique, and Diego. A squawking blue and yellow parrot sits on a perch, which it's attached to by a cord tied around one leg. Alquimedes, a bony old man who has no eyeball in his right eye socket, and Amparo, a teenage girl with a long black braid falling down her back, bring in food from the kitchen: fried fish, fried yucca, and a dish of beans, potatoes, onions, and chiles.

Roberto hasn't eaten all day except for the guava-filled cheese from the airport and he's famished. The fish is even better than what he had in Tarapacá. It's *pirarucu*, a large river fish that Diego's raising in a pond covered with green scum. Alquimedes and Amparo finish their serving duties and sit down at the end of the table with plates of their own. Roberto compliments Alquimedes on his cooking.

"Thank you, sir," he says with a smile. His mouth is nearly toothless, and he has a necklace of blue, red, and green feathers around his stringy neck. "It's taken me most of my life to find something I'm good at. I thank God and Diego for that."

"In that order?" says Diego.

"I thank Diego and God," says Alquimedes and everyone laughs.

Roberto's curious about that empty eye socket but thinks it might seem rude to ask about it.

"I can see you're wondering about my eyeball," says Alquimedes.

Quique groans. "Oh no. He's going to tell us his life story again."

"I was only going to tell him about my eyeball."

"Yes, and it'll take you an hour to do it."

"Alquimedes loves to tell people about how he lost his eyeball," says Diego. "If he can't find anybody to listen to him, he'll go out in the jungle and find a snake or a monkey and tell them about it."

"Don't listen to them, Alquimedes," says Lina. "Tell Roberto about your eye."

"Yes," Roberto says, "I'd love to hear about it."

"Me too," says Daniel.

"Very well. Since you're asking. I lost my eyeball in the House of Rabbits. The neighbors called it that because the people that lived there raised and sold rabbits. I was a young man, but I don't know what my exact age was. My whole life, I've never known how old I was. My earliest memory—"

"Okay, here we go," says Quique, and Ernesto laughs.

"If they're going to understand how I came to be in the House of Rabbits in the first place," says Alquimedes patiently, "they need to have a little background. My earliest memory, I was probably seven or eight years old, and I was walking, walking, walking. I didn't know where I came from or where I was going. I was in a terrible land, a land of death. Cow skulls on fence posts. Dogs hanging from trees. Empty houses, no people anywhere. Finally I came to a river, and I sat down and waited. Pretty soon a boat came along. An old man was in the boat. He was smoking a pipe. He looked at me and said, 'Just stay happy and take it all in stride. Nothing is as bad as it seems.'

"Well, I got in the boat with him. He asked me my name. I said I didn't know, so he called me Alquimedes. He sold, you know, this and that, little things: amulets, medicines, candles, perfumes, pictures of the saints. He had a tiny black dog with huge ears, he called him Negrito. So I went up and down the river with the old man and his dog for years. Eventually Negrito got old and died, and we buried him on the riverbank, and then one day, I buried the old man on the riverbank, too. Before he died, the old man told me I could have his boat, so I just kept going up and down the river selling candles and perfumes and so forth. I liked the life, and I'd probably still be doing that, but God had another plan. A big storm caught me on the river, and the boat sunk, along with all the potions and perfumes and amulets, and I was lucky to make it to the bank without drowning. I walked until I reached a town called Peribuela. I figured Peribuela was as good a place as any to start a new life. I got a job in a grocery store. I slept in a shed out back until I made enough money to rent a spare room in the House of Rabbits.

"A girl would come into the store from time to time; her name was Emma. She wasn't pretty exactly, but there was something about her that caught a man's eye. I know it's hard to believe but I was a handsome devil then, and pretty soon Emma and I were seeing each other secretly. It had to be in secret because of her father. His name was Bartolomé Lúrquin, but everybody called him the Turk because his grandparents were Lebanese. He was the richest man in town, he had a finger in every pie. Emma didn't think he would approve of me.

"Well that, my friends, was an understatement," and Alquimedes laughs. "One night, I was in my room in the House of Rabbits, and the door opened. Two men came in. One of them said, 'This is a message from the Turk,' and they beat me in the head with iron bars. My eyeball fell out of my face and onto the floor. They carried me out in the jungle and threw me in a ravine. They thought I was dead, but after a while I woke up. I heard barking. I looked up, and I saw Negrito with his big ears at the top of the ravine barking down at me. You can say it was a dream or a hallucination, but that's what I saw. I didn't know what else to do except crawl out of the ravine and start walking again. And so that's how I lost my eyeball."

They've all been supplied with bottles of beer, and now Daniel grins and lifts his. "Here's to your lost eyeball, Alquimedes."

"That's not a bad story, even if I have heard it before," says Ernesto.

The talk turns to Jilili.

"How do you explain it?" Diego says, shaking his head in bewilderment. "How can God allow it?"

"It's easy to allow something when you don't actually exist," says Daniel.

"Tell God he doesn't exist when you see him on the Day of Judgment."

Daniel laughs. "Okay, I'll do that."

"Killing you have to expect," says Quique. "It's what war's all about. But setting old people on fire and hanging children from trees? That's just crazy."

"But it's not crazy at all," says Lina. "Once you understand that violent repression in this country is not a deviation from the norm but is the norm itself, then things start to make sense. The perpetrators of violence aren't crazy and out of control, they're acting according to the dictates of logic and reason. Their actions flow naturally from the premises they start with."

"So what are the premises?" says Roberto.

"Study economics at any university, and they'll teach them to you. The Army and the oligarchy take our land, use it up, destroy it, to make products to put on the global market. This is happening everywhere. In the name of the market, they're chewing through the earth like locusts; soon there will be nothing left except an endless wasteland. And if you resist you're called a terrorist. The war on Communism, the war on drugs, the war on terror . . . it's the same war every time, a war on the poor and the powerless, a war on animals and birds and fish and plants."

"I love you, Lina," Diego says, "but sometimes you talk like a book. I don't always understand what you're saying."

"Well, I understand," says Quique. "In this country, it's all about those on the top staying there, and those on the bottom staying there, too."

"Amparo," says Lina, "you look like you want to say something."

Everyone looks at Amparo. A delicate silver cross hangs at her neck. She looks shyly down at her plate, and shakes her head.

"No."

"Oh, go on, girl," says Alquimedes. "I've always found you worth listening to."

"Well," Amparo says, slowly looking up. "I was just thinking . . . how strange life is."

"In what way?" says Lina.

"The people in the village didn't wake up this morning knowing they were going to die. It must have seemed like just a normal day to them. It just seems like when something so important is going to happen, you ought to know about it."

Lina gives her an encouraging smile. It's clear she's taken an interest in her. The parrot is shouting "Hello!" and "Lucho!" again and again. Lucho is its name, and those seem to be the only two words it knows.

"All I know is," Quique says, "the Army had its day, and we'll have ours."

"Are you coming with us tomorrow, Quique?" asks Roberto.

"Of course. Why else do you think I'm here? It's to babysit your ass!" and Quique looks around the table and laughs.

Roberto's not offended. In fact, he laughs too. He couldn't be any happier that Quique is going to accompany them to El Encanto, and then hopefully back.

* * *

After dinner, everyone goes out on the porch to have a beer and talk, but

Roberto walks back to the guesthouse. It's night now, and the croaking of what seems like thousands of frogs floats out of the jungle. He gets his toiletry kit out of his pack and goes to the bathroom. As he switches on the light, a scorpion scuttles across the floor, its wicked-looking tail curled over its back, and disappears behind the toilet. Roberto stands at the sink and brushes his teeth. His arm is red and throbbing and sticky with honey. Suddenly the bare light bulb hanging from the ceiling goes out. He feels uneasy about sharing the darkness with the scorpion, his flip-flops leave plenty of skin on his feet exposed to that poisonous tail, so he hurriedly washes his mouth out and leaves.

Roberto finds Amparo in the guesthouse, leaning over a hurricane lamp on the table, lighting the candle in it.

"What happened to the power?" he says.

"Diego only runs the generator for two hours every night."

The silver cross on its thin chain dangles and shines.

"Where'd you get that? The cross."

"My father gave it to me."

"It's very pretty."

"Thank you."

"Where is your father?"

"He died. When I was ten."

"What happened to him?"

She's silent. Staring down at the candle.

"It's all right," says Roberto. "If you don't want to talk about it."

She looks up at him. He can see the gleam of the candle deep in her dark eyes.

"No. I don't mind. My father was a traveling dentist. He carried all his equipment on a mule. I went everywhere with him."

"Where was your mother?"

"I don't know. He never talked about her. Usually we traveled along the river, but one day, we were going to a village, and some men told us about a short cut through the forest. So we took it, and pretty soon we saw the men again. They beat my father and robbed him and took the mule and all the dental equipment and left. My father was unconscious. I kept waiting for him to wake up, but in the middle of the night, he stopped breathing. When the sun came up, I tried to find my way out of the forest, but I got lost. I was lost for three days, but then I was found by wild

Indians. They were hardly wearing any clothes, and they had feathers and bones in their noses and ears and paint on their faces, and they carried spears and blowguns. I'd always heard Indians were cannibals, and I was scared they'd stick me with their spears and eat me. But they gave me food and took care of me. I stayed with them for a few weeks, and then they brought me here. Diego knows their language and he's friends with them."

"Do you like it here?"

"Yes. Everyone's nice. Especially Alquimedes. But I want to leave."

"Why?"

"I'd like to go to school. Learn about the world. See things. Travel. Lina says she'll help me."

Amparo leaves, and Roberto sits down at the table in the glow of the lamp with his notebook. The first thing he writes down is everything Amparo just told him, trying to remember her exact words as much as possible. Then he goes to the other end of the day. He and Roque peeing together in the morning coolness and watching the squirrel monkeys in the treetops. The twins and the watermelons. The ten helicopters, and the one that was so frighteningly curious about them, and Ernesto, hands on hips, grinning up at it. But he is stopped cold when he gets to Jilili. He takes his glasses off and rubs his eyes. A mosquito whines in his ear and he brushes it away. He cannot write about Jilili, but it seems to exist in a ghostly swirling all around him. He continues to rub his eyes, it feels comforting to do so. The frogs grow louder and louder, it's like their noise will swallow him like a fly. The birds on the river. The way Roque smiled, looking at the monkeys. The murdered girl with her murdered baby. He cannot understand life, he cannot understand this day. The beautiful and terrible all entangled.

* * *

"Roberto? Roberto?"

He awakes to Roque gently shaking his shoulder. He lifts his head off the table. It feels like it weighs fifty kilos.

"I'm sorry, Roberto. But it's Daniel."

"What's the matter with him?" His tongue's so thick with sleep he can hardly form the words.

"He's very drunk."

"Shit."

Roberto gets up and puts his notebook away in his backpack.

"What's he drinking? Beer?"

"No, Diego brought out a bottle of rum, and Daniel's drunk about half of it."

"Great. Rum. Just what Daniel needs."

Roberto and Roque walk toward the house. He can hear music and Daniel talking loudly.

"Is he pissing people off?" he asks.

"Maybe. A little." Roque laughs. "But he's also very funny."

They go up the steps. The soft light of a lamp spills out of a window onto the porch. A CD player plays an insipid pop song, and Marco laughs as Amparo tries to teach Chico the monkey how to dance. Further down the porch, Lina, Ernesto, Diego, and Quique are sitting in chairs around a table, while Daniel stands, leaning against the railing. Lucho the parrot is tethered to the railing and greets Roberto with a happy "Hello!"

"Hey, Roberto!" says Daniel. "Just in time! Join the party!"

He's smiling broadly at Roberto, a cup of rum in one hand and a cigarette in the other.

"It's getting late," says Roberto. "Let's go to bed."

"Late, are you crazy?" and he looks at his watch. "It's not even nine o'clock."

"We have to get up early—"

"Alquimedes!" yells Daniel, and the old man's gaunt face appears in a window. "Bring a cup out for Roberto, this man wants a drink!"

"No thanks, Alquimedes," says Roberto. "I'm fine."

"Whatever you say, boss," says Alquimedes.

"We're having a very interesting conversation with your friend," Quique says, as he hand-rolls a cigarette. "He's explaining to us his philosophy of life."

"I'd love to hear all about it," says Roberto, "but—"

"It's simple," says Daniel. "The world's a meaningless shithole and we're stuck here until we die. Therefore, we should try to have as much fun as possible in the meantime. Everything else is a waste of time."

"That's very uplifting," says Roberto.

"So you mean we should all be like Marco?" says Diego, and now he shouts, "My son! Turn the music down!"

"Sure," Daniel says, moving unsteadily toward the table, "we should all be like Marco."

He picks up the bottle of rum and peers critically at it.

"Shit. We're nearly out. We better have another bottle, or somebody's going to have to go to the liquor store," and he giggles and refills his cup.

Roberto watches him nervously. When he gets like this, anything can happen. He might climb up on the table and start to sing or take a swing at Quique or grab Lina's boob. Roberto really doesn't want to alienate these people who are risking their lives for Daniel and him.

"I like to have fun as much as anyone else," says Ernesto. "But there's things worth fighting for too."

Daniel gives a scornful snort. "Like what? Your crummy little piece of jungle? Everybody should just clear out and leave the jungle to the monkeys and birds. At least they belong here."

"But we belong here too," says Ernesto.

"Like hell we do. We're just an invasive species, we're these killer apes that came out of Africa and now we've spread over the whole fucking world."

"I agree with you that we're animals," says Lina, "but we're not only animals. We also have a spiritual aspect."

"Spiritual aspect my ass. You saw the same thing I saw today."

"I saw evil. I saw something that needs to be fought."

"Fighting's pointless. In the long run, the bad guys will always win because they're ruthless. They'll do anything. But the good guys have scruples and so they lose."

Quique smiles, his jaguar whiskers lifting. "You think we have scruples?"

"You think you're the good guys?"

Roberto takes Daniel's arm. "Come on. That's enough. Let's go."

But Daniel jerks his arm away.

"Get your fucking hands off me!" Now he talks to the people sitting at the table and points at Roberto. "This guy makes me sick. You know why? Because he's such a good guy. He makes me feel like a worm all the time. He makes me want to puke."

"Why do you hate yourself so much?" says Lina.

"Why are you such a self-righteous little cunt?"

Quique stands up from the table and looks at Roberto.

"If you need any help taking your friend to bed, I'd be glad to give it to you."

Roberto firmly grabs a handful of Daniel's vest. Quique exhales some cigarette smoke as he watches Roberto take Daniel away.

"No, Roberto," Daniel says. "Just one more little drinkie-winkie, please?"

"Shut up."

Daniel stumbles along as Roberto pulls him across the top of the hill. Now he points dramatically at the sky. "Look at the stars, Roberto! My god! There's so many of them!" And then he starts singing in English: *"Lucy in the sky with diamonds, Lucy in the sky with diamonds!"*

Roberto gets him in the guesthouse, sits him down in the yellow hammock, helps him swing his legs up and lie back.

"Are you mad at me, Roberto?"

"No."

"Do you love me, Roberto?"

"Yes."

"Good. I love you too."

He closes his eyes, and immediately starts to breathe heavily. Roberto lowers the shroud of the mosquito net.

* * *

Daniel was right: there's so many of them.

Roberto's sitting on the grass in an open space on top of the hill, looking up at the night sky. These jungle stars put the city stars to shame. He feels immersed in eternity. He thinks about what Daniel said about humans being just a kind of ape, but they're apes that sometimes look with wonder and awe up at the stars so there must be something good about them.

Everyone seems to have gone to bed but him. He could hardly stay awake all evening until he climbed into his hammock and lay there listening to the snores and sighs and farts and mutterings of the five others in the guesthouse, and after a few minutes, he pulled up the mosquito net and came out here.

He hears the whirr and chirr of insects, the groaning of toads and frogs. Every now and then, a harsh squawking noise that sounds like a chicken being throttled comes out of the darkness. Hungry mosquitoes hum around him but he doesn't think he's been bit a single time yet. His insect repellent is excellent.

Lina comes into his mind. Roberto can't remember the last time he met someone that impressed him so much. This is a macho country, men here don't generally like taking orders from women, particularly one as young as Lina, but she has a quiet charisma about her and has no problem getting what she wants. And now, as if doing his telepathic bidding, Lina emerges from the guesthouse and walks his way.

"So you couldn't sleep either," she says.

Roberto shakes his head. She's wearing shorts and a T-shirt and is barefoot. She sits down in the grass beside him.

"I'm sorry about Daniel," says Roberto. "About what he said to you."

She shrugs. "Don't worry. My feelings weren't hurt."

"He's really a good guy."

"You keep saying that."

"I think you were right about one thing. He does seem to hate himself."

"Has he always been like that?"

"No."

He tells her about college, about him and Daniel and Andrés and Franz, and Monica, the Communist girl. He tells her how Daniel was arrested and held by the Army for three weeks and tortured until he convinced them he wasn't a subversive and they let him go. He tells her that Daniel always refused to talk about what was done to him until a few days ago when he told Roberto the story of how they took him to his mother's house and threatened to kidnap and torture her unless he cooperated.

"He said that was the worst moment," says Roberto. "Watching one of those guys talking to his mother and knowing he couldn't protect her."

"And he was released not long after that?" says Lina.

"Yeah, about a week."

"You know what that tells me?"

"What?"

"That he agreed to cooperate."

"I asked him about that. I said he was already cooperating with them because he had nothing to hide since he wasn't a Communist. So what more did they want?"

"And what did he say?"

"Nothing. He wouldn't talk about it anymore."

"So what do you think happened?"

Roberto's quiet for a moment. Thinking things through.

"He must have given them names," he says. "People he met when he was seeing that girl. Maybe some of them were arrested and tortured, maybe they were even disappeared. And he feels guilty about it; he can't forgive himself."

"Of course he gave names, everybody does. Why do you think we're instructed to put a bullet in our head if we're about to be captured? Because no one can withstand torture. But it wouldn't have taken two weeks for him to start spilling names. They must have wanted something else from him."

"Like what?"

"Maybe they wanted him to work for them. Be an informant."

Roberto gives an incredulous laugh. "Daniel? A spy for the Army? Come on."

"Think about it. You're a leftist journalist, and he's gone all over the country with you. A good way to find out about things."

"That's ridiculous, Lina. Anyway, he's a commercial photographer now, we haven't been working together for two years. He just came this time as a favor to me."

"When you worked together, did anybody ever get arrested or killed after talking to you? Anybody whose identity you thought you'd protected?"

"Yes, of course, but that's just the way it goes. I often talk to people whose lives are already under threat."

"But you don't know for sure. He could have been passing along information."

"Daniel's like a brother to me. He would never use me like that."

"Is his mother still alive?"

"Yes."

"He may have felt like he had no choice except to go along with them. To protect his mother."

Roberto feels his face getting hot; he's shocked at what Lina's suggesting.

"Was he acting like an Army spy today at Jilili? He risked his life getting those pictures!"

Lina puts her hand lightly on his knee.

"I'm sorry, Roberto, I didn't mean to upset you. I have to be suspicious. Of everybody. But you're right, Daniel was wonderful today."

Roberto nods. Lina takes her hand away. She hugs her knees and looks at the sky. Half of a moon is easing up over the trees and taking a peek down at the clearing.

"It's nice tonight, isn't it?" she says. "There's been a lot of rain lately. This is the first clear night we've had in a while."

"It is nice."

"Last night? When I told you I thought some of your work wasn't too bad?"

"Yeah?"

"I don't know why I said that."

"You mean you don't like any of it?"

She laughs. "No, I mean I like *all* of it. I think you're an amazing journalist. But I guess I felt too shy to tell you that. To me, it was like meeting a celebrity."

"Oh, come on."

"I'm serious. I've read everything you've written for years. When I was at the University of Lima, I would always look for your stuff online. You were the one writer I felt I could trust about what was really going on here."

He adjusts his glasses on his nose a little. A gesture he makes when pleased.

"Thanks. That means a lot."

"I'm so sorry you have to leave."

"Yeah. Me too."

"Javier said you were going to Saint Lucia."

"That's right."

"Why there?"

"My girlfriend's there. Caroline. She's staying with her parents."

"What are they like?"

"Her father's retired—he was an executive at Coca-Cola. He's a great guy, he loves to have fun. He always says that when you're lying on your deathbed, the only sin you should concern yourself with is not having danced enough."

Lina laughs. "And her mother?"

"She's English. More reserved. But nice. Unfortunately she has cancer; she's very sick now. That's why Caroline's there."

"And Caroline? Tell me about her."

"She's tall. Very attractive. Has green eyes, like her mother. Likes to dance, like her father. She has a master's degree in art history. She's thinking about getting her PhD, but hasn't really decided yet."

"How did you meet?"

"It was at a play, three years ago. I was there with my friend Andrés. The play was so bad that during intermission we were thinking about leaving, but then I saw her standing in the lobby. So I went over and started talking to her."

Lina smiles. "That was bold. So what did you say?"

"I said something about it being a nice crowd tonight. And she looked around and said, 'Yes, I suppose.' And then I said, 'Do you like the play?' And she said, 'No, not really. I think it's pretty bad, don't you?' And I looked devastated, and I said, 'I'm sorry. I should have told you that I'm the playwright.'" Lina starts to laugh. "And you should have seen her face! She said, 'Oh no! I'm so sorry, I didn't really mean that, I—' And then I just started to laugh. I told her I was kidding, and my only connection to the play was that one of the actors was a friend of a friend of mine."

"And what was her reaction?"

"She was mad. She told me I was awful."

"But she didn't really think you were awful."

"Guess not. So do you have a boyfriend?"

Lina shakes her head. "No."

"Any reason?

"Because it would be a bad idea in the position I'm in. Who would my boyfriend be except someone in the TARV? And how am I supposed to lead or to be led by someone I'm sleeping with?"

"But I'll bet it happens all the time."

"You're right, I've seen it happen. And I've seen it really mess things up. Jealousy, possessiveness, hurt feelings . . . what we're doing is too important to have all that crap enter into it."

"So you plan to be some kind of warrior nun until the end of this?"

She shrugs. "I don't really plan things. I just do my best, and whatever happens, happens. Anyway," and now she glances up at the sky, "I feel like *they're* on my side."

"The stars?"

"Destiny, fate, whatever you want to call it. I guess it sounds silly but . . .
ever since I was a little girl, I've felt like I was meant to do something in my
life. Something important," and now she gives Roberto a rueful smile. "I
don't know why I'm telling you all this. I've never talked about it to anyone."

"I'm glad you trust me."

The mysterious chicken-being-throttled sound floats up from the
trees again.

"What is that?" says Roberto.

"I don't know. Some kind of bird?"

"Lina, I'm disappointed in you. I would have thought a jungle girl like
you would have had an instant answer to that question."

"Sorry. I haven't been a jungle girl for long."

"I'll ask Roque."

"Good idea."

He's on this little hill in the jungle, surrounded by danger and death,
and yet for the moment he feels only like a guy hanging out with a pretty
girl. This is the most he's seen of her. Her bare arms and legs. The shape of
her breasts through her shirt.

"You know," he says, "I was thinking Javier might be your boyfriend."

She looks amused. "I love Javier; no one can make me laugh like him.
But Javier as a boyfriend? No."

Roberto seems to have run out of words, and so has Lina. The frogs
and toads and insects fill the silence, they're so loud it's like he could hear
them on the moon. Roberto and Lina regard the stars. Then she looks
over at him.

"We should go to sleep," she says, and now she gets up off the grass.
"We have a long walk tomorrow."

But he stays where he is, and sighs. "I think I'm too tired to move."

"Get up, let's go," she says with a smile as she reaches down. He grabs
her hand and she pulls him up. He finds himself standing face to face
with her and very close.

He looks down into her starlit eyes. He knows when a girl likes him,
and Lina likes him. He knows when a girl wants to be held and kissed,
and that's what Lina wants.

He brushes some hair away from her forehead, and she leans into
his hand.

"I'll worry about you," he says. "After I've left."

"Don't worry. I'll be okay."

And now she takes his hand and pulls it away and squeezes it slightly and lets it go.

"We should go inside, Roberto."

He nods. He walks with Lina into the guesthouse.

* * *

Roberto lies in the dark in the blue hammock under the blue mosquito net. He hates mosquito nets; they make him feel like he's suffocating and mosquitoes seldom bite him anyway but he always uses them just in case. He's careful that way. He doesn't take unnecessary risks.

Daniel and Ernesto seem to be having a contest to see who can snore louder, but it won't be enough to keep Roberto awake. In his last seconds of consciousness, his mind drifts back across the day. From the first light on the river to the moon above the jungle.

His trip so far has gone well. He's getting what he came for. Tulcán—gracious, generous, accommodating—has opened its dark heart to him.

Two days until the day
Roberto is to die

While it's still dark, they eat a breakfast of fried eggs, yucca rolls, sliced bananas sprinkled with brown sugar, and juice and coffee. Alquimedes seems to be in a good mood as he serves them, he keeps singing and humming a line from a song: *"Life is a lottery, lottery, lottery!"* Lucho is likewise in a good mood, cheerfully shouting out "Lucho!" and "Hello!" But nobody else has much to say. Daniel is obviously hung over, though not as much as one might think; he's always had an amazing capacity to bounce back quickly from his drinking bouts.

Marco slouches in when everyone else is almost finished. He's wearing only his sky-blue shorts, and shows a lean, ripped body. He yawns and scratches his stomach and sits down at the table.

"I'm glad you decided to join us, my son," says Diego. "I thought you were going to sleep all day."

"Come on, Dad. The sun's not even up yet."

Marco grabs a yucca roll and takes a bite.

"Dad? Could I get a tattoo?"

"No."

"Why not?"

"Because I said no."

"I'm seventeen. I should be able to decide if I want a tattoo or not."

"What kind of tattoo do you want, Marco?" Lina says.

"He wants to have the name 'Lina' tattooed inside a heart," says

Ernesto, and he and Quique laugh. Marco looks sheepish and shuts up. Everybody takes a last bite of something and one more gulp of coffee and goes out. The eastern sky has begun to brighten. The chickens are coming out from under the house. The rooster gathers himself and flaps his wings and then lets loose with a mighty crow, as though officially announcing the commencement of the day.

Those going get their backpacks and then say good-bye to those staying. Roberto shakes hands with Diego, who's holding Chico in his arms.

"Thanks for everything, Diego."

Diego smiles. "I'll see you soon, Roberto. Go with God."

"Bye, Chico."

Chico extends his black little hand as if he's going to shake hands too but instead he makes a grab for Roberto's glasses. Roberto jerks his head back as Diego laughs.

Amparo shyly hands Lina a folded-up piece of paper. "This is something I wrote. Last night."

Lina smiles and slides the paper into a pocket.

"Thanks, Amparo. I look forward to reading it."

They walk off across the hill, past the guesthouse and Princesa's palace and a little graveyard with eight crosses in it.

"What did Amparo give you?" Roberto asks Lina.

"Probably a poem or a little story. She loves to write, and she's actually quite good at it."

"She told me about her father. How he was robbed and murdered."

"I'm sure she didn't tell you she was raped. They slashed her vagina with a knife so they could fit inside her. She nearly bled to death. It's a miracle she got out of the jungle alive."

Duque, as if it's his duty, accompanies them down the hill then turns around and trots back up. They enter the jungle. They are six. Roque, as usual, takes the lead. Behind him, Lina, Ernesto, and Quique carry assault rifles along with their packs. Roberto and Daniel bring up the rear.

Daniel winces and rubs his temple under his French Foreign Legion-looking cap.

"Head hurt?" says Roberto.

"Yeah."

"I have no sympathy for you."

"What happened last night? Did I do anything stupid?"

"What do you think?"

"Stupider than usual?"

"No, not really. But I'd be careful around Quique."

Daniel casts a worried glance up ahead at Quique.

"Shit. I don't want to get on that guy's bad side."

They walk through the forest in the dim light of the dawn. The ground is swampy; leaden pools and puddles of water are gleaming everywhere. They follow Roque across narrow planks and slippery log bridges, provided perhaps by Diego for his tourists. The trees are taller than any Roberto's ever seen, and their interwoven tops block out the sun. There's very little undergrowth. Roberto slips off a log and goes knee-deep into black muck. He thinks about old jungle movies and people disappearing into quicksand. Soon after, Daniel slips and goes cursing into the swamp too. Roque and Ernesto take their machetes and swiftly chop down and strip two saplings for Daniel and Roberto to use as staffs.

In about half an hour the logs and planks come to an end and they're on firm ground. The sun must be up now, because the humid twilight has brightened a bit. The ground is covered with dead leaves and the crumbling detritus of plants, and Roberto breaths in a rich organic smell of rot. It's surprisingly quiet. No bird or insect sounds except for the occasional whine of a mosquito in his ear. The forest is a green inscrutable mass to him. They say the Eskimos have a thousand words for snow, but Roberto sees around him a thousand things and cannot muster up one word for any of them.

He knows there must be animals around, but they have chosen not to show themselves. He'd love to see a jaguar. He's never seen one in the wild before. They definitely represent a danger—if you go walking alone in the jungle it's quite possible a jaguar could decide to make you its next meal but it's not going to attack you if you're in a group. What makes Roberto really nervous are snakes. Lots of poisonous snakes in the jungle. If you put a hand or a foot in the wrong place, you might soon find yourself flopping about on the ground, eyes rolled up in your head, bleeding from every orifice.

A brilliantly blue gigantic butterfly floats past.

"Hey, look!" Roberto says. "A blue morpho!"

He's seen them in other jungles. Its wings become brown with eyespots like a peacock when it lands on a branch and folds them over its back. Daniel raises his camera and moves up close. Robert goes over to it too.

Lina has paused and is looking back.

"What's up?" she says.

"A blue morpho!" says Roberto, happy to actually know the name of something.

She comes walking back to take a look.

"I have a friend who raises them," she says. "She makes quite a bit of money at it."

"Why do people want them?"

"They release them at weddings and parties and peace marches and so forth."

The blue morpho's wings become blue again as it launches itself into the air. Daniel keeps snapping pictures. Roberto watches Lina watching the butterfly dancing off through the trees.

He thinks about last night, when he and Lina nearly kissed. Meeting a girl like her was the last thing he expected on this trip.

They're moving ahead again. A determined column of ants troop over a fallen tree trunk, and Robert steps over it too. Ernesto and Quique are talking about something, and they laugh. It sounds very loud in the hush of the forest, like laughter in an empty cathedral.

Roberto's always been faithful to his girlfriends, except for one time with Teresa (she found out about it and was so distraught he can hardly bear to think about it). But last night, he came very close to being unfaithful to Caroline. Much closer than with Clara. Infidelity with Clara had an alarming crime-against-nature quality to it, but there's none of that with Lina. The world he's in is so intense as to render other worlds unreal. Can there actually be a beautiful island in a peaceful sea where a girl named Caroline awaits him? What is she doing right now? Petting one of her plump cats? No, it's hard to believe in the existence of Caroline and her cats. The one true world is the jungle, and these people, and a place called El Encanto.

He looks at Lina ahead of him, in her green army shirt and her jungle boots, with her backpack and her assault rifle. The very picture of a girl guerrilla. And if the girl guerrilla and the young journalist were to fall at some point into each other's arms, it would seem in this place like a natural thing, like a leaf dropping from a tree or a hawk flying over the river. Roberto doubts he'd ever feel much guilt about it, because from the perspective of the future him, it is this world that will be unreal, these days in the jungle will seem like a feverish fantasy, a wild green dream.

But why didn't it happen last night? It was Lina who made it not happen. It was as if she wanted it to but changed her mind, removing his hand from her face and walking away. She strikes him as the kind of girl who doesn't give herself easily to another, but once she decides to do so, her giving knows no bounds. She knew that in a few days he'd be flying off in a plane never to return, and she probably did not want to be left in the jungle with a heart full of love for him.

* * *

Roberto walks up front with Roque for a while; he wants Roque to show and tell him things.

"You smell that?" says Roque.

Roberto sniffs the air and wrinkles his nose.

"Yeah, what is that?"

"A howler monkey has taken a big shit. He does it to mark his territory."

He points out to Roberto a little toad the color of the dead leaves it hops across. A giant red cricket. A rainbow-colored caterpillar.

"You hear that?" says Roque.

Roberto nods. It's coming from up in the forest canopy.

"It sounds kind of like dripping water."

"It's a bird. An *oropendola*," and now Roque makes the exact same sound. In a moment, the oropendola seems to answer.

"What's he saying?" asks Roberto.

"He says he's lonely. He's looking for a girlfriend."

Roque shows him the wedge-shaped hoof prints of a wild pig, and then he points at something else.

"See, Roberto? A jaguar's following him."

Hands on knees, Roberto gazes in awe upon the paw print of the jaguar.

"Wow. So are these fresh tracks?"

"Very fresh."

Lina and the others are moving past.

"Come on, guys, let's go," says Lina. "This isn't a nature hike."

They start walking again.

"So you think we'll see him?" says Roberto. "The jaguar?"

Roque shrugs. "You only see a jaguar when he wants you to see him."

"Have you seen many?"

"Yes," he says, and then he smiles a little.

"What?"

"When you see a jaguar, it's not always a jaguar."

"What is it?"

"Sometimes it's a shaman."

"So if I see a jaguar that's really a shaman, should I be scared? Is it going to eat me?"

"Maybe, maybe not. Both live shamans and dead shamans can turn themselves into jaguars, but dead shamans are always evil. Live shamans can be either good or evil."

"How can you tell a regular jaguar from a shaman that's turned himself into a jaguar?"

"If a jaguar is a shaman, they say it has the balls of a man. But you have to get pretty close to see that."

Roberto laughs.

"So how does a shaman learn to turn himself into a jaguar?"

"He takes ayahuasca, and then he travels to the place of the dead. He learns many things there. All about plants and how to heal people, and he can also learn bad things."

"Like what?"

"My cousin liked a girl, and a very bad man liked her too. He paid a shaman to put the soil of the dead in my cousin's coffee, and it killed him."

"What's the soil of the dead?"

"Soil from a cemetery."

"Have you ever taken ayahuasca?"

"Many times."

"How old were you when you first took it?"

"Fourteen. See that tree?"

Roberto and Roque walk over to a stupendously large tree. Roberto leans his head back and gazes at a trunk that goes up and up and only when it's soared past the other trees does it spread itself out majestically into limbs, branches, and leaves. He rubs one of the twisted roots that rise to the level of his head. It's a tree he recognizes.

"This is a ceiba tree, right?"

"Yes, but we call it the mother tree. Because the spirit of the mother of the jungle lives inside it. It makes a very loud noise when you hit it, so if you're ever lost and you want someone to find you?"

"Yes?"

"Hit it like this," and Roque begins striking the tree with the blunt side of his machete. The sound resonates through the forest.

* * *

The invisible sun begins to make it very hot under the green canopy. Sweat pours off Roberto. His glasses are steaming up, and he takes his bandana out and cleans them. He looks at his watch. It's nearly ten. Lina said they should reach El Encanto by midday. A black bee lights on his arm next to the watch, and then he's set upon by dozens of bees, a black swirling swarm of them. He flails his arms and cries out.

He hears laughter and sees Quique and his grinning jaguar whiskers.

"What are you hollering about? They can't hurt you, they don't have any stingers!"

"They like sweat," says Lina. "They're drinking your sweat."

"Go drink somebody else's sweat!" Roberto yells at the bees. Even if they don't have stingers, he doesn't like having them crawling all over him. Trying not to be too frantic about it, he brushes them off his face and arms, and now they regroup and fly away.

Daniel is holding his camera and checking out the LCD screen.

"I got some great pictures, Roberto. You're going to have to pay me a lot of money to keep them off the Internet."

The trek resumes.

"You got any water?" says Daniel. "I'm out."

"In my pack."

He pulls a bottle of water out of Roberto's pack and takes a drink. His face is red, he's sweating twice as much as Roberto.

"You don't look too good," says Roberto. "You doing okay?"

"Sure. Just sweating out the booze."

They walk in silence for a bit, and then Daniel shakes his head.

"You know, I'm really worried about the boyfriend."

"What boyfriend?"

"The crazy boyfriend of the girl that's taking care of my fish."

"There is no crazy boyfriend. He's a figment of your imagination."

"You sure?"

"Yeah."

"Maybe this whole thing's a figment of my imagination. I hope so."

Roberto hasn't been able to get out of his mind what Lina said last night about Daniel. He doesn't think Daniel's been a spy for the Army of course, that's ridiculous, but her belief that he must have cooperated in some way with his interrogators is almost certainly true. It would explain a lot if he blames himself for the arrests and torture and perhaps deaths of others. Roberto wishes he would just level with him, tell him what happened.

"Hey, Daniel. Whatever happened to Monica?"

"The Communist cunt?"

"Yeah."

"I still see her around sometimes. She's not a Communist anymore. She designs jewelry and purses." He takes a drink of his water. "Why'd you ask?"

"I don't know. I was just thinking about what you told me the other night."

"Well, stop thinking about it. It's a waste of time."

"I don't think it's a waste of time."

"Why are you so interested in it after all these years?"

"Maybe because it's been all these years. You know, you can really tell me anything, and I'll understand."

"I doubt it."

"It's true. Listen. There's something I'd like to do."

"What?"

"I'd like to talk to my father about it. He knows everybody. There are experts who deal with victims of trauma; I'm sure he can set you up with the best person in the country."

"First of all, I'm not a fucking victim. Second of all, are you seriously suggesting I go see a shrink?"

"Yeah."

"I'm just trying to get out of this fucking jungle alive," Daniel says, his voice rising, "and you're making me listen to this *bullshit*?"

His red face is getting even redder. Both Lina and Ernesto glance back to see what's going on.

"Okay," says Roberto, "don't get so mad, I'll shut up."

The character of the jungle begins to change. The trees are closer together and not as tall. The undergrowth thickens. Roque and Ernesto and Quique slash away with their machetes at bushes and saplings and creepers and vines. Spanish moss brushes Roberto's face, spider webs with fat spiders in them stretch across their path. It seems to be getting hotter by the minute. He's starting to feel a little dizzy and nauseous. The ground is cut with gullies that he stumbles into and out of, they wade through streams made as dark as coffee by decaying vegetable matter. Monkeys hoot and jabber at them from the treetops. Daniel lets out a yell as he bumps into a tree with sharp spines sticking out of it. Roberto feels the fecundity of the forest, the buzz and hum and heat and throb of it, the flourishings and the perishings as tens of thousands of species play the great game of life. Roque stops and points into a tree. A bright-green snake about a meter long is lying on a low branch.

"Be careful," says Roque. "It's very poisonous. It likes to jump down on people and bite them in the neck."

"Great," Daniel says, gasping for air. "That's just fucking great."

Quique chops it in two with his machete. The pieces of the snake drop to the ground. Everybody takes a wide berth as they walk past it. The two halves of the snake are wriggling in the rotting leaves, not quite ready to give up the ghost. Roberto sees the first ant running up to it. Maybe the last thing it will ever see is Roberto bending over it and studying it. It's a beautiful shade of green, it seems to glow with its own light.

They reach a clearing. It's planted with corn and manioc. Roque says it belongs to Indians. He says they were here recently, maybe two or three hours ago. Roberto asks him how he knows, and he points at the ground.

"Because of the tracks. See?"

Roberto does see, sort of. Or maybe not. They take their packs off and sit down in the shade at the edge of the clearing. Lina brings out some *arepas* stuffed with spicy chicken that Alquimedes sent along. Roberto's not hungry, but he forces himself to take a few bites of one. He asks Roque if he thinks these Indians are the same ones that found Amparo and took her to Diego's.

He nods. "They're the same."

"Do you know them?"

"Yes. Their language is different from O'wa, but I can understand them."

"Are these some of the Indians that Javier lived with?" Roberto asks Lina.

"No, when Javier tried to contact them, they shot arrows at him, and he had to run for his life. They hate white people, for obvious reasons. They kill them whenever they get the chance."

"How come they didn't kill Amparo?"

"Because she was pretty and they felt sorry for her."

Roberto takes out his notebook. Sweat drips on the page and makes it hard to write. He wonders if the Indians are out there watching them. Waiting for their chance. After a few minutes, they all pick up their packs and press on. They come to a stream with a fallen tree athwart it. It would make a perfect bridge except an anaconda twice the size of Princesa has gotten there first. It seems to be taking a nap. Midway down its glistening, mottled body is a big bulge.

"What do you think that is, Roque?" says Roberto.

"Probably a pig," he says, and then proceeds to tell him an anaconda story. When he was a kid, he was playing with some other kids at the edge of the river at dusk, and a little girl named Penhana went wading into the water. Her mother called to her to come back, and she turned around and looked back at her mother and laughed, and then an anaconda as big as the one on the tree leapt out of the water and wrapped itself around Penhana and dragged her under and she was never seen again.

The water's to Roberto's waist as they wade across the stream. The anaconda ignores them. He hopes its brother or cousin's not lurking about. Daniel takes some pictures. Roberto steps in a hole and goes in up to his chest and then flounders his way out onto the other bank. He's worried about the contents of his backpack but everything's still dry. He squishes along in his boots and soaking clothes. The wetness doesn't make things any cooler. He feels just a little bit like he might faint. Surely El Encanto can't be far. He hears a rumble of thunder, and a breeze cuts through the trees. Rain rattles above them on the leaves. They come to an open area covered in elephant grass higher than their heads. Roiling black clouds fill up the sky. A lightning bolt cleaves the clouds and thunder crashes. The tall grass tosses in a hard wind. Ernesto's cap is blown off like when he was on the boat and he scrambles to pick it up. Now he and Roque and Quique begin to hack a path through the grass. Lina and Roberto and Daniel follow, drenched by the rain. It's coming down with such intensity it seems like a weight on his shoulders that is pushing him toward the ground. About halfway across the elephant grass there's a blinding white flash and a deafening crack of thunder as lightning strikes the top of a tree seventy or eighty meters away.

"Jesus!" says Daniel.

They come to the end of the grass and reenter the forest. The trees are like a giant umbrella shielding them from the rain. Under the tree that was hit by lightning they find a large branch that was sheared off, along with the scorched, still-smoking bodies of half a dozen monkeys. They have soft brown fur; they're chorongo monkeys, they all look like Chico. It's a shocking sight to Roberto, and the others seem to feel the same as they stand there and stare down at them.

"It's bad," Roque says.

"What do you mean?" says Lina.

"Six monkeys. Six of us."

* * *

They follow a dirt track through the forest. The trees are widely spaced and are shot through with sunlight. Lina takes Ernesto's machete and whacks a tree. White sap trickles down the trunk, it's like white blood.

"This is a rubber tree," Lina says. "Before El Encanto was anything else, it was a rubber station."

"We've reached El Encanto?" says Roberto.

Lina smiles. "Nearly."

In a few minutes, they emerge from the forest, and Roberto looks out upon a green sea of sugarcane. They head down a narrow dirt road that runs as straight as a ruler across the field. The plants are much taller, greener, and more robust than the sickly-looking ones he saw on the way to Tarapacá. The sun is at its highest point and beats down on them. Roberto's been rationing his water and now drinks the last of it. It's quiet except for the indolent buzz of insects. A green grasshopper leaps onto the road then flies off in a blur of wings. A hawk circles overhead, keeping an eye out for lunch.

As they're leaving the sugarcane, a breeze brings them a whiff of death. The rutty road goes across a pasture. Scattered across it are the carcasses of several dozen dairy cows. They've been pretty well picked over by vultures and other scavengers, so there's not much left beyond bones and maggoty hides. The pasture, however, does contain one living creature: a blue roan horse, standing in the shade of a tree. As they walk toward it, it moves its head and seems to be looking their way, but as they get closer Roberto sees that couldn't possibly be the case.

Quique gives a disgusted snort.

"The bastards put its eyes out," he says.

There's a crust of dried blood beneath its eyes. Flies crawl over its face, and its eye sockets are squirming with maggots.

The horse shuffles nervously as Lina walks up to it.

"Shh, it's okay," she says, and she gently rubs its neck. It pushes into her hand, and makes a noise deep in its throat.

"Poor thing. I'm sorry."

Lina steps back and pulls her gun out from under her shirt, racks a round into the chamber, and shoots the horse between its blind eyes. It crumples to the ground. The flies zoom around erratically in the shade, then settle back down on the still body.

They go through a stand of trees, then come out on a little lake. Water lilies float upon it, tall birds walk in the shallows. On the far bank, a walkway with handrails extends into the lake and ends at a round, pavilion-like structure. Beyond the lake, rising above more trees, Roberto sees a stone tower.

They walk around the lake. Roberto watches a white egret gliding over it, perfectly mirrored in the water. He notices Quique and Ernesto and Lina have unslung their weapons. He doesn't know what to expect. Bodies everywhere? Maybe the Black Jaguars have come back.

What they're walking through is beautiful: lush grass and flowers, carefully sculpted bushes, all kinds of fruit trees, mango, papaya, lulo, guanabana, mangostino, dragon fruit. The trees are filled with capuchin monkeys, chattering excitedly among themselves and leaping from tree to tree as they follow Roberto and the rest.

"Juan Carlos loved the monkeys," says Lina. "He'd bring them bananas, that's their favorite food and they'd just go nuts," and Lina smiles. They'd jump all over him, he'd be covered head to toe in monkeys. You could hardly see him anymore but you could hear him laughing."

They're approaching the house from the rear. Roberto can see it now: it's two stories and made of reddish stone. As they move toward it, they come to another structure made of the same material. Lina says it's the guesthouse. Roberto peers through a window, sees a bed with a blue bedspread and a blue mosquito net. They go by a playground with a swing and a slide and a seesaw and a jungle gym and then a tennis court with a forlorn yellow tennis ball lying on it and now Roberto gets a better view of the house. It's not large but it's utterly lovely. It does seem, as Javier said, a bit like a castle out of a fairy tale, though the satellite dish near the spired tower does ruin the effect somewhat.

Behind the house is a flagstone patio surrounded by a stone balustrade. A bronze statue of a praying angel rises out of a small fishpond. In one corner is a wrought-iron table with wrought-iron chairs and a green umbrella over it; taking advantage of the shade are three vultures, two sitting on the table and one in a chair. They couldn't seem more at home, they hardly bother to glance at them as they walk onto the patio.

"Hello!" shouts Quique toward the house. "Is anyone here?"

It's quiet except for the sounds of birds. A few of the monkeys have followed them to the patio and are looking around as if they're wondering whatever became of the man with the bananas. Daniel walks over toward the vultures and starts taking pictures.

Roberto's worried about his story. He needs the witnesses: the cook's helper and the kid who climbed the tree and the mother and daughter who hid in the forest.

"Where do you think they are?" he says.

"The workers' houses aren't far from here," says Lina. "Hopefully they're there."

"Hey!" says Ernesto. "Come here!"

He's standing by the fishpond, staring down into it. Everyone goes over and takes a look. Several dead fish and a rotting human head are floating in the water. You can tell the head belongs to an adult male because it has a moustache.

Nobody says a word. They leave the patio and walk around the house toward the front. A glorious efflorescence of bougainvillea climbs up the wall and nearly reaches the roof; Roberto hears the murmurous hum of hundreds of bees sucking up the nectar. He sees the hedge maze Javier talked of. The thought of wandering in it and of what horrible thing he might find at this or that turning gives him a shiver. Suddenly a series of screeches split the air, they're like: *"Eeeee! Eeeee! Eeeee! Eeeee!"*

They're heart-stoppingly close. Ernesto points his Galil at something that's stepping out from behind a bush. He laughs and lowers the rifle when he sees it's a peacock.

"Hello," says Lina. "Where are all your friends?"

The peacock responds by unfurling his magnificent, many-eyed, blue and green tail. They move on to the front of the house and there discover his friends, sadly all dead, shot to pieces, their beautiful feathers scattered across the lawn. The house is set on a rise, with the Otavalo River in the distance gleaming through the trees. In the middle of the wide lawn, a smiling, life-size bronze elephant stands on its hind legs; it's supposed to be spouting water out of its trunk, but the fountain is bone-dry. A cluster of vultures sits under a shade tree, killing time until something else dies. The heavy oak door of the house is standing open. They go up some steps and pass through the door.

They're in the great hall. They take off their packs and drop them on the floor and look around. Despite the looting and the smashing and the broken windows and the overturned furniture, you can still make out what the house used to be. Lina tells Roberto it took Juan Carlos years to build it. It was constructed from red sandstone quarried in Arran, an island off the coast of Scotland. Juan Carlos made trips to Italy and France and personally picked out each chair and table and sofa and bed and bathroom fixture and chandelier. He went to the Middle East and got rugs in Iran and ancient statues of cats in Cairo and he journeyed to Japan to find the perfect wallpaper for his bedroom. Everything had to be taken by boat down the river into the jungle. He hired only the most skilled workers and craftsmen to help him create El Encanto. He paid them well and tried to make them happy. On Sundays they would compete in tennis, badminton, and croquet tournaments. A famous American pop singer was helicoptered in for a concert under the stars. A sculptress from Mexico City and a carpenter from Caracas fell in love, and Juan Carlos paid for their lavish wedding and gave the bride away. The province of Tulcán had never seen such a party as was thrown when the house was completed, and many workers wept when they had to board the boat that would take them back to "civilization."

Roberto steps over a toppled grandfather's clock as Lina tells him about the artwork. Many famous painters (including Pombo!) had their work hung in the radiant rooms of El Encanto, and a Swedish painter lay on his back like Michelangelo for two years painting scenes from Greek, Norse, and Chinese mythology on all the ceilings. And there were sculptures, vases, music boxes, primitive masks, plates of beaten gold, crystal figurines of mermaids, unicorns, centaurs, and dragons, antique toys, and old movie posters that Juan Carlos had collected from every corner of the earth.

"It's all gone now," Lina says, indicating an empty wall. "They took everything."

Roberto realizes Javier was wrong in thinking some kind of perverse cruelty had played a role in the Black Jaguars making an awful example out of the gentle soul that Juan Carlos was. Obviously it was greed, pure greed, that had sent their muddy boots clomping across the polished stone floors of this magic house.

In the billiard room, a blue lizard with a yellow streak down its back is enjoying the sun on a windowsill. Somebody took a dump on the billiard table. The seven ball sits atop the dried-up mound of shit like a cherry on a sundae.

The paramilitaries seem to have spent a lot of time in an entertainment room, where there are video games, a ping-pong table, and a wide-screen TV. Roberto sees empty wine and liquor bottles and beer cans and cigarette butts and food covered with flies and ants. But they don't seem to have been interested in reading, because the library with its thousands of volumes is undisturbed.

"They were idiots," Lina says. "Juan Carlos collected rare books. The contents of this room are worth a fortune."

Roberto goes in the kitchen, where Juan Carlos Mejía met his horrific end. A sturdy wooden worktable is stained with dried blood, and there are black pools of it on the floor. He looks around the room, and then goes to the sink. He calls Daniel over. Daniel stares down into the sink, looking sick.

"The famous cheese grater," he says, and then takes a picture.

They mount a marble staircase to the second story. That's where all the bedrooms are. Roberto goes in Juan Carlos's, looks at the Japanese wallpaper. Water lilies and dragonflies. In the high ceiling among the Swedish painter's satyrs and nymphs is a skylight made of stained glass.

Lina walks beneath it. The sun's directly overhead, and a column of colored light envelops her. She stands there gazing up, her rifle slung over her shoulder, her mouth open a little. Roberto catches Daniel's eye and nods at Lina, and he raises his camera and captures the moment. Then he walks over to a door and peers in.

"Thank god," he says. "A toilet!"

He goes in the bathroom and shuts the door. Lina moves out of the polychromatic light.

"Would you like to see the tower?" she asks.

A pair of capuchin monkeys scamper ahead of Roberto and Lina as they walk down the hallway. Now Lina opens a heavy metal door, and Roberto sees a spiral staircase. Lina leads the way up. It's dark and he stumbles on a step, but it gets brighter as they near the top. They emerge into the tower. It's not very big; it's bare of furnishings except for a small round table and two chairs. There are two diamond-paned windows, one looking out on the jungle and one on the river.

"Juan Carlos would play chess up here," says Lina.

"Yeah, Javier said he used to play with him. He said he had an antique chess set and the pieces were made of gold and silver."

Lina sighs. "God knows where those pieces are now."

She moves to the window that gives on the river, and Roberto joins her. The Otavalo's sluggish, broad, and brown. A small boat heads up the river—a guy in the back with the motor and a woman sitting in front of him under a purple parasol.

"Don't you wonder where they're going?" Lina says, a bit wistfully. "Who they are?"

"Their names are Juan and Anita. They've been married for twelve years. They've been visiting friends, and now they're on their way home."

"Very impressive. And how do you know this?"

"I'm a reporter. It's my job to know."

"You like being a reporter, don't you?"

"Very much. It's like having a seat on the front row of life."

"I'm sorry you have to leave, Roberto. I know you don't want to."

They're quiet for a moment, watching the boat on the river. Now it passes out of sight behind some trees.

"We're in opposite situations," Lina says. "You don't want to leave, but you have to. And I don't want to stay, but I have to."

"But you're free, Lina. You're not a prisoner. You can do anything you want."

She shrugs. "You've seen what's going on here. My people need me."

"When you do leave . . . what do you want to do?"

"I'd like to just be a regular girl again. Go back to school."

"In Lima?"

"Mm-hm. I liked it there. I made a lot of friends," and now she smiles a little. "I had a dog when I lived there. Cruz, he was an Irish setter. I was taking Cruz for a walk one day in the park. Two people were lying on their stomachs on a blanket. There was nothing special about them, they weren't well-dressed, he wasn't handsome, she wasn't pretty. Just two people. She was reading a book, and he was eating something with a spoon out of a container. He held the spoon to her mouth, and she took a bite of whatever it was, and I saw how perfectly happy they were, how at ease with each other, and I realized something about life and love: it's the small moments that are important. I know that sounds trite, but . . ."

"No, I understand. It's true."

He wants to grab her up in his arms, to carry her out of this tower, to take her away from this benighted, brutal land. But take her to where? Saint Lucia?

"We need to find the witnesses," he says.

* * *

They walk through the trees along a path that parallels the river for five minutes or so, then they come to the workers' houses. There are fourteen of them, built on stilts, with wooden sides and tin roofs. They're well constructed, with sturdy steps instead of the usual ladders, and painted in bright shades of green, purple, yellow, and blue. The only signs of life are some black chickens, pecking in the dirt, and two barking dogs.

"Fercho!" Lina shouts. "Jota! Manuela! We're friends! Come out! Everything's all right!"

Three people drift out of the forest: Fercho, a skinny, shoeless, shirtless man in his thirties, Manuela, a worn-looking woman who could be anywhere from thirty to fifty, and a little girl who seems to have been in a fire and bears the most hideous scars Roberto has ever seen.

"Where's Jota?" asks Lina.

"He went down to the river to catch some fish," says Fercho.

"Roque, go find Jota," says Lina. Roque heads toward the river, as Lina explains to the three who Roberto and Daniel are and why they've come. Then it's up to Roberto to say something. Though he can hardly bear to look into their eyes at the anguish there.

"I'm so sorry for what's happened to your family and your friends. I can't imagine the pain you must be feeling. But I do hope you'll talk to me and tell me what happened. I want to tell your story so that others will know."

Fercho rubs his hand over the top of his head, scrunches up his face and looks toward the sky.

"Okay," he says finally. "Sure."

"Manuela?" Lina says softly. "What about you? Will you talk to Roberto?"

Manuela nods. They walk up the steps of Fercho's lime-green house. Fercho goes inside and brings some plastic chairs out on the porch, then goes back in and returns with warm bottles of Coke for everyone. Quique and Ernesto take their Cokes and amble off on their own, while Roberto and Lina sit down with Fercho and Manuela. The little girl, whose name is Yineth, sits on the steps. Daniel takes some pictures.

Roberto turns his digital voice recorder on. He looks at Yineth. She has a doll with blonde hair and a missing leg, and is fussing with its clothes. It's like the lower half of Yineth's face has melted onto her shoulders. She has no neck, just a thick trunk of scar tissue. Her mouth's pulled permanently open, showing her tongue and teeth. Roberto asks her mother what happened to her.

She says Yineth was with her grandmother in the house when the kerosene cook stove exploded. Her grandmother was killed and Yineth was expected to die too but Mr. Mejía got her to a hospital and Manuela prayed on her knees for days and Yineth survived. Mr. Mejía was planning to send her to a hospital in San Miguel for a series of operations, but of course now that will never happen. It is only herself and Yineth now, because her husband and her five other children were killed by the paramilitaries. She said when she found out they were all dead she took Yineth down to the river and held her hand and walked out into the water, she was going to drown herself and Yineth but instead she just stood there, she doesn't know for how long. She wanted to go to heaven with Yineth and be with her husband and children, but killing yourself is a sin, and she was afraid God might not let her into heaven, so she and Yineth left the river and came back here. She knows it's not safe here anymore, that the bad men might come back, but she can't bring herself to leave the graves of her husband and children. Also, the people here were kind to Yineth and accepted her, and she's afraid if they went somewhere else, Yineth would be laughed at and made fun of.

Roberto asks her how she and Yineth managed to escape the fate of the others. She says Yineth has always loved to wander in the jungle and be with the animals and birds, she's always worrying Yineth will be eaten by a jaguar or bitten by a snake but Yineth insists that all the creatures of the jungle know her and would never hurt her. She says Yineth came running to her and said she had seen this beautiful bird and she wanted to show it to her. She went out in the jungle with Yineth and she saw the bird, it was pure white and had golden eyes and she had never seen another bird like it and then they heard the gunfire and the screaming and they hid in the jungle till the Black Jaguars were gone. Manuela thinks the bird wasn't a bird at all but an angel sent by God to save Yineth from the bad men.

Roberto asks Fercho to tell him about the arrival of the Black Jaguars. He said they showed up a couple of hours before the sun went down. He said the timing was unlucky because if they'd come sooner the children would have still been in school in Santa Rosa del Opón a few kilometers down the river, but just a few minutes after the children got off the boat that took them back and forth, the boats carrying the Black Jaguars appeared.

"How many men were in the boats?" asks Roberto.

"I don't know," says Fercho. "Many. One hundred? Two hundred?"

"Did you know right away who they were?"

"No, but we knew it wasn't good. Everybody was scared."

Roberto asks him how they were dressed. Fercho says they wore camouflage uniforms and black berets and patches depicting black jaguars on their right sleeves. He said at first they didn't hurt anyone, they acted friendly, but when they started yelling at everyone to gather in one place behind the house Fercho feared the worst and ran into the pantry. He hid behind cardboard boxes of canned goods and packages of rice and pasta. After a while he heard guns being fired. At one point the door to the pantry opened and he heard boots walking on the floor and saw through a crack between the boxes the green and brown colors of a uniform, and he thought his smell might give away his hiding place because he dirtied his pants he was so afraid. But the paramilitary went away and it was quiet for a while and then he heard Mr. Mejía out in the kitchen. He was begging for his life and Fercho heard the voices and laughter of other men, and then he heard Mr. Mejía's inhuman howls. He squeezed his eyes shut and put his hands over his ears and sat there in his own shit until the howling finally stopped.

It became dark in the pantry. He could hear music and loud talking and knew the Black Jaguars hadn't left. He sat there all night unmoving behind the boxes, a mouse would have made more noise than he did. He didn't sleep for a second, he was afraid they might hear him snoring, his wife was always complaining about it. At last the daylight came. He could hear people moving around, and then it became quiet again. But still he sat there, hour after hour, until finally he worked up the courage to creep out of the pantry. The Black Jaguars were gone. He found the red, flayed form of Mr. Mejía outside, under a bush. He also found the bodies of all the other people who had lived at El Encanto, including his wife and son and daughter, and now Fercho lowers his head and pinches the bridge of his nose to try to stop the crying.

"They were killed while I was hiding like a coward in the pantry. Maybe I could have saved them."

"Don't blame yourself, Fercho," Lina murmurs. "There was nothing you could have done."

Fercho says that people from Santa Rosa del Opón arrived that afternoon. The bodies were already beginning to go bad in the tropical heat, so graves were dug and prayers were said. Two days later, the Army came on a humanitarian mission to evacuate the people of Santa Rosa del Opón, who after all they'd seen in El Encanto were more than ready to leave. They were taken by boat to a refugee camp, but Fercho stayed behind with Manuela and Yineth and Jota, the boy who climbed the tree.

And now Jota arrives with Roque. He's a scrawny kid of eleven or twelve. He's carrying nine plump *pirañas* strung on a stick. Despite their ferocious reputation, they've very pretty fish, silvery with bright-orange bellies. Jota grins and holds up the pirañas as Daniel takes his picture. Now Lina tells him who Roberto and Daniel are.

"You want to talk to me?" says Jota. "Great, I'll talk all day. Yineth, get me a Coke!"

Yineth hurries inside the house. Manuela takes the fish from Jota and he sits down in her chair.

"Is it okay if I record you?" asks Roberto.

"Sure," says Jota, looking delighted. "I've never been recorded before." He picks up the recorder and looks it over. "How much does one of these cost?"

"Well, this one's a pretty good one. Maybe two hundred thousand pesos?"

He nods, and puts it back down. Yineth comes back with his Coke. She seems very happy to serve him.

"Thanks, honey." He takes a swig and looks at Roberto. "So what do you want to know?"

This is definitely not the traumatized child he was expecting. Jota's wearing shorts and an old gray T-shirt with the number 1991 on it in a variety of styles, sizes, and colors.

"What does your shirt mean?" says Roberto. "Did something happen in 1991?"

Jota pulls the shirt away from his body, takes an upside-down look at it. "Shit, I don't know. This gringo missionary gave it to me. His name was Brother Jim. His church had a band and they let me play the trumpet. Everybody would sing and clap and then Brother Jim would preach a sermon. It was always the same thing, the fucking world was about to end but it didn't really matter, because we were all going to heaven because we believed in the fucking Lord. I stayed there with a bunch of other homeless kids. Brother Jim and his wife, Sister Donna, they were real nice and we got plenty to eat and all, but after a couple of years I took off. I just got tired of hearing about the Lord all the time."

"How'd you end up here?"

"Well, the cops were chasing me in this town called El Banco one night—"

"Why were they chasing you?"

Jota smiles slyly. "I don't know. They must've got me mixed up with some other kid. Anyway, I ran down to the river and I hid on a boat under a tarp. It seemed like a pretty good place to spend the night, so I went to sleep. The next morning I crawled out, and the boat was headed down the river. The guys on the boat said they were going to tie me to a rope and throw me in the water and use me as crocodile bait, but they were just kidding, they were nice guys. I asked them where they were going, and they said they were taking supplies to this place called El Encanto. When we got here, I figured I should make myself useful because I thought I could stay with them for a while, so I helped them unload the boat. I saw this little bald guy watching me; after a while, he came up and said I seemed awful small to be carrying such big boxes. I usually lie in situations like that, but I decided to tell the truth for a change and I told him about the cops and everything. He said I could live here if I wanted to, but I'd have to not do anything that would make the cops chase me and I'd have to go to school every day. I told him he had a deal."

"That was Mr. Mejía?"

"Yeah. He said I could live with the foreman and his wife. He said they already had so many kids he bet he could slip in one more and they'd never know the difference," and Jota laughed. "Mr. Mejía was a funny dude, he always had everybody laughing."

"How long have you been here, Jota?"

"About a year."

"Have you been happy?"

"Sure. I'm always happy. When the cops were chasing me, I was happy, I thought it was fun."

"Tell me about the day the Black Jaguars came."

"Well, I went to school, and then I came back, and then I heard somebody yelling that guys with guns were coming from the river. I ran and took a look. I'd seen guys like that before and I knew what they were up to and I turned back around and ran again. I was going to hide in the jungle, but then I saw some more of these dudes, they were coming up from behind the house, they were all over the fucking place, so I climbed up in a tree. I've always liked climbing trees, I like to hide and watch people, I'm good at hiding, people can look right at me and not see me. There were a lot of monkeys up in the tree with me, the monkeys and me were pals. Sometimes people would come to visit, and Mr. Mejía would give them bananas to feed the monkeys, so the monkeys were watching these guys and hoping they'd get some bananas. A lot of people had tried to hide or run off, and it took them awhile to get everybody rounded up. They brought Mr. Mejía out of the house, and then they started killing everybody."

"How did they kill them?"

"They shot most of them, but then they got a chainsaw and started cutting people up. By this time the monkeys had figured out they weren't going to get any bananas and they took off. They were jumping from tree to tree and pretty soon there wasn't a monkey in sight. It felt kind of lonely without the monkeys. I was wishing I could jump through the trees like that and get away."

"So how did you feel? Seeing what was happening?"

"I felt bad," Jota says matter-of-factly. "But I was glad I was up in the tree and not down there." He's quiet for a moment. "I felt bad about the Arredondos. That was the family I was staying with. They were real nice to me. But they were all shot, so that was good. I mean it was a lot better than being cut up in pieces by a chainsaw."

"What happened to Mr. Mejía?"

"After everybody was dead, they took him back inside. Then I heard somebody screaming, that went on for quite a while. Then somebody came out of the house, he was all red and bloody, he'd had his skin cut off. It didn't look like Mr. Mejía, but I knew it was him."

"What did he do?"

"Just walked around, real slow. He was holding his arms out real stiff," and Jota demonstrates. "He seemed to be looking at things. Then he walked under the tree I was in, and he looked up and saw me."

Roberto's surprised. "He saw you?"

"Yeah, he looked right at me. I don't know how he knew I was up there. I was afraid somebody would see him looking at me, but nobody was paying any attention. And then he kept on walking, and pretty soon he laid down on the ground. He didn't move after that. I guess he was dead. The sun went down and it got dark. I was hoping they'd leave but they didn't. It was like they were having a big party, everybody got real drunk. This fat dude walked over and started pissing on the tree. He was standing right under me, I could've pissed on *him* if I'd wanted to— in fact I did want to, I needed to piss bad, that would've been funny if I'd pissed on him. Finally it got quiet, they all went to sleep. I climbed down out of the tree. Most of them were in the house, but some of them were sitting in chairs or laying on the ground, snoring their ugly fucking heads off. I walked right past them. I can be real quiet when I want to be. And then I didn't see any of them anymore, and I started to run. I've never run that fast before, not even when the cops were chasing me. I ran in the jungle and hid. Usually I'm afraid of jaguars but that night I didn't give a fuck about them. The jungle seemed like the safest place in the world."

* * *

"How do you like them?" asks Roque.

"A little bony," says Roberto. "But not bad."

"I love pirañas," says Quique. "They make my pecker hard."

"I would rather eat pirañas," Daniel says, "than have pirañas eating me."

Everyone's sitting in the shade eating Jota's pirañas and drinking warm beer provided by Fercho. Manuela fried the fish whole; they still have their eyeballs and their gaping mouths show rows of sharp teeth. Roberto's looks like it's ready to jump up off his plate and chomp down on his nose.

He feels good about the interviews. Maybe the big story is Jilili but this is going to be a hell of a story too. Roberto remembers Lieutenant Matallana smiling at him in the parking lot downtown as he called out, "I think we're going to get those bastards!" He was talking about the Committee to Protect the Nation, and exposing the atrocities committed by their paramilitary arm at El Encanto will provide payback against them for what they did to Uriel the juggler and Manuel and his mother and Nydia and finally Lieutenant Matallana himself. Maybe Roberto and Matallana actually will get them after all.

"What do you know about the Black Jaguars?" he asks Lina, Quique, and Ernesto. "Have you ever come up against them?"

"All I've ever seen of them is their fat asses," says Quique. "Because they turn around and run when they see us coming."

Ernesto's gold tooth flashes as he laughs. "But they have nice uniforms, you've got to admit that. I think I'd look great in one of those black berets."

"I've got bad news for you, Ernesto," says Quique. "Nothing could ever make you look great. You're stuck with the face God gave you."

Ernesto laughs again, fishing a piraña bone out of his mouth.

"They're not a real fighting force," says Lina. "They're a collection of criminals, perverts, psychopaths, and drunks. Their job is to terrorize helpless civilians, and they're very good at that."

"What about their leader, Hernán 40?" says Roberto. "What do you know about him?"

"Nothing really," says Lina. "He's created a mythology around himself. Who knows what's true or not?"

"So what's the mythology?"

"Well, supposedly he executes his own men if they're not cruel enough. And he likes killing people with a *champeta*. That's a knife used by fishermen on the coast for gutting and descaling fish."

"I heard he always wears mirror sunglasses," says Quique. "That way when he's cutting somebody up, they can see it in his sunglasses, they can see themselves dying."

Jota's been listening and now he pipes up. "Hey, I saw a guy that had sunglasses like that. He seemed to be giving the orders too."

"What did he look like?" says Roberto.

"Kind of tall and skinny. He had a beard. I didn't see him killing anybody with a knife though."

"They say he was born without a soul," Ernesto says. "They say his mother mated with a demon in the form of a dog."

"And you believe that bullshit?" says Quique.

"I didn't say I believe it. I just said I heard it."

"Well, if I ever get my hands on him," says Quique, "I'll put his sunglasses on and he can watch me rip his head off and shove it up his faggot ass," and Quique laughs.

* * *

Fercho and Manuela lead them to the graves. They're in a clearing a few minutes' walk from the houses. Roberto counts them, there are twenty-three, although many of them contain more than one body. The gravediggers from Santa Rosa del Opón tried to put families together as much as possible. Lina attempts to compile a list of the names of all the dead but doesn't get very far; neither Fercho nor Manuela can handle talking about it. Fercho falls apart completely, collapsing on the dark dirt where his family's buried. "My wife and children are angels now," he sobs. "Nobody evil can ever hurt them again!" Even Quique's eyes get wet as he watches this. Daniel kneels and takes a picture.

Roberto walks up to Lina, who's looking over her notes.

"How many do you think?" he says.

"I'd guess somewhere between sixty and seventy."

He starts making some notes of his own. Daniel's showing Jota how his camera works; now he lets him take a few pictures. Daniel asks Yineth if she'd like to give it a try. She shakes her head, but Daniel persists, and in short order, Yineth is taking pictures too. Jota clowns for the camera, then they all take a look at the results in the LCD screen. Jota and Yineth laugh.

Lina's watching with a half smile.

"Daniel's good with kids," she says.

"Yeah, he loves kids," says Roberto. "And animals. He doesn't like adult human beings very much."

"Is he married? Does he have kids of his own?"

"No. He's good with kids but bad with women. He insists he'll never get married and I believe him." He closes his notebook and puts his pen away. "So do you still think he's an Army spy?"

She shrugs. "I wasn't accusing him of anything. All I was saying was, you have to keep your eyes open."

"I think I do that."

"Have you gotten everything you need here?"

"Yes, I think so."

"Then we should leave soon. If we want to get you back to Tarapacá tomorrow."

Roberto looks at the sky. The sun's not far from setting.

"So we'll be going through the jungle at night," he says.

"Yes."

"Isn't that dangerous?"

"Somewhat. But it would be more dangerous to spend the night here. You never know what might come in off the river."

Lina tells the four survivors she'd be glad to take them all to Tarapacá, but none are ready to leave. They make their good-byes to Fercho and Manuela and Yineth, but Jota decides to tag along to the house with them.

They walk back down the path that runs near the river. Roberto can see a shine of water through the trees. Suddenly Daniel groans and scuttles toward the trees holding his stomach.

"What's the matter?" says Roberto.

"I got the shits, what the hell do you think's the matter?"

He disappears behind some bushes. They all stand around and wait.

Roberto hears the buzz of a boat out on the river, but he can't see anything. It gets louder, and then it fades away. It seems like Daniel is taking a long time.

"Hey, Daniel," Roberto calls, "are you still alive?"

"Yeah!" he calls back. "Go on ahead, I'll catch up!"

"But we can't leave you!" Ernesto says and he winks at Quique. "A jaguar might eat you!"

"Good," says Daniel, "I hope one does!"

Ernesto and Quique laugh. Soon after, Daniel appears, walking slowly, his face pale and sweaty. Lina looks at him with concern.

"Drink," she says, handing him a bottle of water. "You don't want to get dehydrated."

Daniel nods, and dutifully drinks most of the water.

"And I've got some Lomotil in my pack," Lina adds, referring to the country's most popular diarrhea remedy.

They come out of the trees and see Juan Carlos Mejía's house. They walk across the lawn, big and green as the fairway of a golf course. They go by the waterless happy elephant fountain. Jota picks up a long tail feather from one of the dead peacocks, swishes it around like a sword. The same group of vultures that eyed them as they left eye them as they return.

A small bird is fluttering around near the ceiling of the great hall. Lina takes her medical kit out of her backpack and gets a bottle of Lomotil for Daniel. Roberto opens his pack, puts away his notebook, and puts his voice recorder in the ziplock plastic bag that already contains his cellphone. Now Lina addresses everyone.

"Okay, listen! We're going to rest for half an hour, and then we're heading back to Diego's. From there we'll be going to Tarapacá. It's going to be a long night, so try to get a little sleep if you can."

"Can we turn on the generator and watch some TV?" says Ernesto. "I haven't watched TV in weeks."

"No. I want you to sleep."

"Lina, you never let us have any fun," says Quique.

"We'll have fun tomorrow in Tarapacá, I promise. We'll have a big party at Yadier's house, and we'll all get blasted."

"You too, Lina?" says Roque.

"Me especially."

"And are you going to dance?" says Quique.

"Of course," says Lina. "I'm going to dance all night."

"You should see her, Roberto," Ernesto says, "she's a great dancer. She could win a contest, she's so good."

Lina laughs. "Go on, get some rest. The clock's ticking."

Everybody looks for some place comfortable to sit or lie down. Lina moves over to Roberto.

"You too, Roberto. You should rest."

"You know what? I'm not really tired. I'm feeling okay, for some reason."

"In that case, is there anything else you want to see before we leave? It's your last chance."

He thinks a moment.

"Could we take another look at the lake? It was so beautiful. I would imagine Juan Carlos spent a lot of time there."

"He did," says Lina, and then she calls out to her guys. "Roberto and I are going to the lake, we'll be back in twenty minutes."

Quique hauls himself up from the plush depths of a satin armchair, picks up his rifle. "I'll go with you."

"No, stay here."

"Are you sure?"

"Yes, we'll be fine."

Quique looks happy to sit back down. Roberto goes over to a couch where Daniel is lying sprawled on his back, his eyes closed, one arm and leg hanging off, his French Foreign Legion cap sitting on his stomach.

"How do you feel?"

"Ready to get out of the fucking jungle," he says, without opening his eyes.

"Do you think the malaria medicine is making you sick?"

"No, probably just the filthy food and water. I always get sick when I go to the jungle."

"We'll be out of here before you know it."

"I hope so."

Roberto and Lina walk down a hallway toward the back of the house. Suddenly Lina stops, and takes the rifle off her shoulder.

"What's wrong?" says Roberto.

"Shh. When we left, that door was closed."

She's talking about the door to the library. They move forward quietly.

Now she motions for him to stop. She goes to the door and peers through it, then lowers her rifle and looks back at him and smiles.

He joins Lina in the doorway. Jota's curled up in a big leather armchair, reading a book.

"Hey, Jota," says Roberto, as he and Lina walk in. "What are you reading?"

Jota holds the book up; the tattered jacket shows a man in tails and a top hat riding in the gondola of a red and white balloon.

"*Around the World in Eighty Days*," he says.

"I read that when I was a kid. Jules Verne was one of my favorite writers. Have you ever read *Journey to the Center of the Earth*? *Twenty Thousand Leagues Under the Sea*?"

"No, are they good?"

"I loved them."

"Great. I saw them on the shelf, I'll read them next."

"So you like to read?" says Lina.

"Yes. Sister Donna taught me. She told me I learned it faster than anybody else she'd ever seen. And then Mr. Mejía caught me in here one day looking at his books. I thought he'd be mad, but he didn't mind at all. He said I could read any book I wanted as long as I didn't take it out of the library and when I finished I put it back in the same place I found it."

"Jota," says Lina, "are you sure you don't want to come with us? We'll help you find a place to live."

"No thanks. I need to take care of Fercho and Yineth and her mother. They wouldn't know what to do if I wasn't around."

Roberto and Lina leave the library and walk down the hall.

"That kid's amazing," says Lina.

"Someday Jota will either be the biggest criminal in the country, or else the president."

"What's the difference?"

He laughs. They exit the house onto the patio. The three vultures have vacated the wrought-iron table in the corner. Three capuchin monkeys sit on the balustrade, still hoping perhaps for bananas. Roberto looks at the statue of the praying angel in the fishpond and remembers something unpleasant. So does Lina.

"Shit," she says. "I forgot about the head. We'll bury it when we come back."

They step off the patio onto the grass. "*Eeeee! Eeeee! Eeeee!*" Roberto hears, and he sees the peacock walking around near the tennis court. Lonely, the last of its kind, at least at El Encanto. He was truthful with Lina, he's not tired at all. He's feeling the surge of excitement that comes with the knowledge that a job is nearly done. Maybe he'll get a last detail or two at the lake that will make it into his story, and then he can leave El Encanto with the knowledge he's done everything he set out to do and more. Even now the story is forming itself in his brain, it feels in some sense already written. He knows the journey across the jungle and then up the river to Tarapacá will have its dangers, but the situation is different now because he won't be putting himself and Daniel in harm's way to gather information like he did in Jilili. His only purpose will be to avoid trouble till he and Daniel can jump in his Twingo and head for Robledo.

Roberto walks with the girl guerrilla, her Galil slung over her shoulder. They're among the fruit trees and the monkeys now. Maybe it's not so much that he wanted to see the lake as that he wanted to be alone with Lina; this will probably be the last time.

"El Encanto," says Roberto. The Enchantment. "That's a great name for this place."

"It used to have another name," says Lina.

"What?"

"Las Matanzas." The Massacres.

"Why was it called that?"

"It all had to do with rubber. Lots of rubber trees grew around here. The Indians called it the weeping tree, which turned out to be prophetic. In the late nineteenth century, rubber became very valuable. The automobile was invented, and they needed rubber for tires. Instead of a gold rush, it was a rubber rush. One day a man called Aquileo Vendaño showed up here. He'd tried and failed at many different trades, including selling hats. He'd scraped together a little money, and he established a rubber station. At first, he brought in workers from outside, but they would die of disease or run away because of the horrible working conditions and anyway Vendaño had to pay them. He decided a better business plan would be to enslave the local Indians. If they resisted, they were massacred. There were many massacres. Vendaño and his men treated the Indians with unspeakable cruelty. They would flog them, decapitate them, burn them alive. They turned little girls into whores, they had contests to see who could shoot the genitals off little boys, they chopped up babies and fed them to their dogs. All up and down the river people would see Indians with terrible scars, and the scars became known as 'the mark of Vendaño.' Vendaño became very rich; he was one of the most important men in Tulcán. There was one last massacre in 1913—the Indians rose up and killed Vendaño and all the other whites, and that was the end of Las Matanzas. It would have been finished anyway because the rubber boom was ending. All the business was moving to rubber plantations in the Far East."

"So now it's not rubber anymore," says Roberto. "It's coltan."

"Exactly. Nothing's changed. Thousands of greedy bastards like Vendaño will be coming down the river to rip the jungle apart."

They reach the lake. The sun is going down and it's mostly covered in shadow. A breeze is coming in off the river, ruffling the green water. They walk along the edge of the lake toward the pavilion. A heron lets them know they're getting too close, and flaps away on wide white wings. Dragonflies are flying over the water lilies, it's like the wallpaper in Juan Carlos's bedroom come to life. Roberto tries to fix all this in his mind, like a photograph. Roberto and Lina by the lake at El Encanto.

They step onto the walkway that leads out to the pavilion. A lizard skitters out of their way. Lina walks ahead. Roberto's boots are covered with mud, but he notices there's hardly a speck of it on hers.

The pavilion's covered with a thatched roof and open on the sides. Around its circumference are a railing and seven brightly painted wooden statues: a jaguar, an anaconda, a parrot, a monkey, a great egret, a bare-breasted mermaid, and a pink dolphin with a huge erect phallus jutting out from it.

"So what's the deal with all these dolphins with dicks?" says Roberto. "I saw a painting of one in Tarapacá."

"Supposedly dolphins can transform themselves into handsome young men. They come out of the river at night and seduce the prettiest girl in the village. Nine months later she'll give birth to a baby that's part dolphin."

"So can female dolphins transform themselves into beautiful girls and seduce the best-looking guy in the village?"

"No, I've never heard that. But travelers have been known to see beautiful wild laughing girls on the other side of the river who call out to them, and then they try to swim across the river to the girls and drown."

"Hm. Sounds like sex can be dangerous around here."

Lina laughs. "People have such funny ideas about sex. When I was a little girl, I thought that falling in love with a boy would make you pregnant, so I was always afraid of liking a boy too much. My mother became very worried about me because she thought I wasn't interested in boys. She would pray to Saint Antonio for a husband for me."

"Have you ever come close to getting married?"

"No, not really. How about you? Are you and Caroline getting married?"

"Yes. As soon as I get to Saint Lucia."

She nods. Roberto goes to the railing, leans his arms on it, and looks out at the lake. Lina joins him. As the fierce heat of the day subsides, the pace of life quickens. Birds are everywhere, he needs Roque here to name them, he's never seen such vivid colors, it's like the changing patterns of a kaleidoscope or something you might see on ayahuasca. There are sudden splashes all across the lake as fish begin to feed, and monkeys jump and scream in the trees. Turtles stick their heads out from among the water lilies. On the other side of the lake, the two dogs he saw at the workers' houses are trotting along briskly to some obviously important destination.

"I'll never forget this," Lina says. "Not any of it."

"I won't either, Lina."

She looks at her watch.

"We should go."

"We've got a few minutes."

"And what's going to happen in the next few minutes?"

"I don't know." They're both silent, and then he says, "I'm half in love with you. Do you know that?"

"Yes."

"What are we going to do?"

"We're going to go back to Tarapacá, and then we're going to say good-bye."

"And I'll never see you again?"

"Probably not. Look, I don't like it either; I care about you too. But it's life. You deal with it. You don't ask why."

"I can't stand the thought of leaving you here. You're going to get yourself killed, and it will all be for nothing. You can't save Tulcán. The world wants it, and it will get it, and it will do whatever it wants to with it. And people who try to stand in the way, they'll just be stepped on, like bugs."

"If you really believed that, you wouldn't be here now. Things are going to look very different in a couple of days. You're going to be where you're supposed to be, and you're going to have a happy life with Caroline. And I'm going to live through this, and I'm going to have a happy life too. And the years will go by, and maybe from time to time we'll think of each other, and we'll smile a little."

Now she holds her hand out to him.

"Come on, Roberto. Let's go."

He takes her hand, but stays where he is.

"I've got an idea."

"What?"

"Are you really a good dancer?"

"Why?"

"Well, since Daniel and I are going to miss out on the party tomorrow night, I thought we could dance now."

"But we don't have any music."

"We'll imagine music. Something beautiful."

She gives him a musing smile. "Okay. But only for a minute."

She slips the rifle off her shoulder, leans it against the railing. She comes into his arms. Roberto dances slowly with Lina over the hardwood floor of the pavilion. Her head's on his shoulder; he feels her warmth and softness. The statues of the jaguar and the parrot and the monkey and the rest all seem to be watching, as if this is a solemn performance put on just for them.

He closes his eyes. He hears her sigh. He feels not half in love with her but fully. For the first time since he entered the jungle he's in no hurry to leave it. Or maybe he's already left it, it's like he's dancing with Lina in no particular place or else every place at once as space and time become mere words and fade away. He was supposed to dance for just a minute but thank god there is no such thing as a minute.

"Roberto—"

Lina's pulling away from him, looking in the direction of the walkway.

Roberto sees uniformed men with guns coming out of the trees. They're wearing black berets.

Lina makes a lunge for her rifle.

"Lina, no!" says Roberto.

She grabs the rifle but he wrenches it from her grasp and throws it in the water. He looks back toward the bank and sees twenty-five or thirty men with their guns pointed at them, and then he sees Lina pulling the pistol from under her shirt. Expecting bullets at any instant to start tearing through them, he grabs her arm and struggles with her.

"No, Roberto, let me!"

The gun fires with a startling bang and then he gets it away from her and throws it in the water too.

"They would've killed us, Lina!"

"Of course, that's what I wanted!"

They stand ranged along the edge of the lake, the men in the black berets, the Black Jaguars. Roberto sticks his hands in the air. He notices Lina slipping her cellphone out of a pocket and tossing it in the water, and then she raises her hands too. Four Black Jaguars are moving quickly down the walkway. The one in the lead is screaming and motioning with the barrel of his assault rifle for them to lie down on their stomachs, and Roberto and Lina comply.

They lie side by side. Roberto hears the clomping of their boots getting louder. Lina whispers, "We just met today. My name is Carmen. That's all you know about me."

He sees boots and the barrels of guns and then his arms are roughly twisted up behind him. His hands are secured with zip tie plastic cuffs and then he's dragged to his feet. Lina's received the same treatment. They both are searched. The thick hands of a man with a moustache go all over Roberto. He finds the wad of cash in his pants pocket and pulls it out. A young grinning guy is searching Lina. His hands slide over her breasts and squeeze her buttocks.

"That's enough of that, Chávez," someone says.

Another Black Jaguar comes strolling onto the pavilion. He's tall and fair, with very light eyes, more gray than blue. He seems like a slightly older version of Franz. He looks Roberto and Lina over in a not unpleasant way.

"So what do we have here, sergeant?"

"No ID on either of them," says the guy who searched Roberto. "I saw the girl throw something in the water, probably her cellphone. I found this in his pocket."

The sergeant hands Roberto's money to the man with the light eyes. He looks through it quickly.

"It's wet," he says to Roberto. "Why?"

"I was wading across a stream, and I stepped in a hole and fell in."

The man hands the money back to the sergeant, and then barks out, "Chávez! Go in the lake and get the cellphone, the rifle, and the handgun."

Chávez makes a face. "Why me, colonel? How come I always get the crummy jobs?"

The colonel gives Chávez a wintry smile.

"Because you're a crummy soldier, Chávez, and that's the only kind of job I can trust you with."

Chávez starts taking off his boots. "There better not be any fucking piraña in there."

The colonel turns back to Roberto, lifting his eyebrows a little and giving a slight shake of his head as if to say: See what I have to put up with?

"What's your name?" he says.

"Antonio Rios."

"And yours?" he says to Lina.

"Carmen Higuera."

"Are there others with you?"

"No," says Roberto. "Just us."

"What are you doing in El Encanto?"

Roberto's glad Lina answers first.

"I was trying to get a boat for *him*," she says, with a nod toward Roberto. "I found him wandering in the jungle this morning. He'd gotten in some trouble."

The colonel looks at Roberto with polite interest. "What sort of trouble?"

"I'm an anthropologist. I came to Tulcán a few days ago, I'm studying the Indians in this region."

"Are you an academic?"

"Yes."

"Where do you teach?"

"The University of Lima."

"I'm an academic myself. On sabbatical, you might say."

"What field are you in?" Roberto asks. Hoping the answer is not anthropology.

"I'm a law professor."

Roberto nods. He repeats to himself: Be calm, be calm, be calm.

"You know," says the colonel, "there's no reason to be afraid. As long as you're telling the truth."

"Yes, I know. It's just that I've never been in a situation like this," and Roberto glances back at his bound hands.

The colonel shrugs. "It's war. It turns everything topsy-turvy. So you were telling me how you got into trouble."

"I was trying to find a particular group of Indians, no anthropologist has ever contacted them before."

"What tribe?"

"O'wa."

"Continue."

"I hired two brothers in Tarapacá as guides. They were half O'wa, they spoke the language and said they actually knew the group I was looking for. But my guess is it was all a ruse from the beginning. Once we got into the jungle, they robbed me at gunpoint, they took everything I had, billfold, credit cards, camera, cellphone—"

"How come they didn't take your money?"

"They didn't know it was there. There was also money in my billfold."

"Continue."

"They also took my compass, which meant I couldn't find my way out. I wandered around lost for three days with no food and hardly any sleep. Thank god Carmen found me or I'm sure I'd still be out there."

The colonel turns to Lina. "What was a heavily armed girl doing in the jungle? Hunting?"

"As a matter of fact, yes. I was hunting for my lost dog."

Lina looks the way she always looks. But Roberto knows she must be as scared as he is.

"How was your dog lost?" asks the colonel.

"I live on a cattle ranch about ten kilometers from here with my father and three brothers. A jaguar's been killing our cattle, so my brothers went out looking for it. They took Rufo with them because he's a great tracker.

They promised to bring back the skin of the jaguar, but they came back yesterday with no jaguar skin and no Rufo. They said he'd run away. Rufo is really my dog, I've raised him from a puppy, and I was very angry with my brothers for leaving him. So I went out this morning to look for him, and I found Antonio instead."

"You went out alone?"

"Yes. This is my home, I've lived here all my life. I'm not afraid of the jungle."

"Colonel!"

It's Chávez. He's wearing only soggy clinging green underwear, and is dripping water as he approaches proudly with Lina's rifle in one hand and her pistol in the other.

"I found them!" he says, and he hands them to the colonel.

"And the cellphone?"

"I couldn't find it."

"Back in the water, Chávez. With the piraña."

Not looking too happy, Chávez walks to the railing and vaults over it. He splashes water on one of the other men, who curses Chávez. The colonel's looking over Lina's weapons.

"Do you always go armed like Rambo when you go looking for a lost dog?"

"I said I wasn't afraid of the jungle, I didn't say I was a fool. The jungle's full of predators, both animal and human. I believe in being prepared."

"This is an Israeli rifle. A Galil. It's what the Army uses. Where did you get it?"

Lina shrugs. "My father bought it, I have no idea where. It's no problem buying any gun in this country if you have the money. I'm sure you know that."

"Maybe you got the rifle off a dead soldier."

"No. Of course not."

The colonel hands the rifle and the pistol to the sergeant.

"We use the Kalashnikov," he says. "Perhaps it's not as 'sexy' as some of the newer weapons, but it's proved itself in combat all over the world," and then he smiles at Roberto.

"You work fast, Antonio!"

"I'm sorry," says Roberto. "What do you mean?"

"Well, you just met this girl this morning, and then five minutes ago, you had her in your arms. Are you sure you haven't known her longer than a few hours?"

"Colonel, I promise you, we just met."

"Like I said. You work fast," and now he looks at Lina. "You immediately went for your weapon when you saw us. If Antonio hadn't stopped you, there would have been a very bad outcome for both of you. Why did you do that?"

"I saw strange men coming out of the jungle with guns. I was afraid for my life. I was afraid of being raped."

"Why did you throw your cellphone in the water?"

"I have private information stored on my phone. Would you want strangers looking through *your* phone?"

"Perhaps the private information has to do with other members of the TARV. Their names, their phone numbers, maybe their photographs—"

Lina gives an incredulous laugh. "You think I'm with the TARV? I hate them even more than—"

She stops herself.

"Than you hate us?" the colonel says. "Do you know who we are?"

Lina's eyes flicker toward the black jaguar patch on the colonel's sleeve.

"I have an idea."

"I suggest you have *no* idea who we are. It's the terrorists that have turned Tulcán into an inferno, not us. Why do you hate the TARV?"

"They're always coming by our ranch, stealing our cattle—or 'requisitioning supplies for the revolution,' as they call it. They try to get my brothers to join them, they make veiled threats, 'if you're not with us you're against us,' that kind of thing. My family produces high-quality beef, it goes to fine restaurants all over this country, people serve it in their houses. What we're doing is important and we shouldn't be hounded by the TARV or by you. We just want to be left alone. My father's a powerful man, he has connections. You have no right to detain us! I demand that you let us go!"

The colonel's silent. He cocks his head a little to one side, studying Lina.

Amid the cries of birds and the chatter of monkeys, Roberto hears a sound that doesn't fit: a phone ringing.

"Colonel Luna!"

One of his men is coming toward him, holding up a satellite phone. "It's him!" he says.

Colonel Luna takes the phone and moves onto the walkway out of earshot.

Roberto wonders who "he" is. Hernán 40? Now he and Lina look at each other. It feels terrible not to be able to talk.

Roberto looks at the stone tower rising above the trees. Are they still in the house? It's obvious Colonel Luna doesn't know they're there. It's also obvious there aren't other Black Jaguars trying to capture them because they'd never allow themselves to be taken alive and Roberto would have heard the noise of a hell of a firefight. Maybe they heard the shot Lina fired, maybe that's why she fired it. He scans the trees. They could be out there right now watching him and Lina, and making plans to effect a rescue.

The zip ties are cutting into his wrists; he tries to move his hands and get some circulation going. He looks at Luna; he's looking at Roberto and Lina as he talks on the sat phone, probably discussing them with "him." Several of his men are wandering around the pavilion looking at the statues. One guy caresses the breasts of the mermaid as his buddy takes his picture with a cellphone. The dolphin with the huge dick elicits much joking and laughter.

The paramilitaries are young and fit-looking, and don't really seem like the ragtag bunch of losers described by Lina. There's one exception though: a fat guy who looks a decade older than the others and has a pale moonlike head under his black beret. Roberto wonders if he's the fat Black Jaguar that peed against the tree Jota was hiding in. He's standing next to a guy who's much taller than everybody else, and has a remarkably ugly face, with a heavy caveman brow, thick lips, and a jutting jaw. They're smoking cigarettes and appear to be discussing Lina. Now the tall ugly one walks over to her, and pulls a pack of cigarettes out of his pocket.

"Hey, angel," he says. "Would you like a smoke?"

Lina gives him the briefest of glances.

"No thanks."

"Maybe a drink of water?" he says, reaching for his canteen.

"I'm not thirsty."

"Okay. Suit yourself."

He takes a slow drag on his cigarette, doing his best to be suave about it.

"Did you know you're really beautiful?"

Lina doesn't deign to answer.

"You look like a girl I used to fuck."

Now Lina looks at him curiously.

"That's surprising."

"What?"

"That any girl would actually want to fuck you."

This causes his fat friend to explode into laughter. "Hey, she got you, Vladimiro! She completely destroyed you!"

Vladimiro turns away from Lina with a bitter smile. Now he and the fat guy see the colonel has finished his call and is headed their way, and they drift over to the railing, next to the parrot statue.

"Just a few more questions," says Colonel Luna, but now Chávez comes climbing out of the lake and over the railing.

"Colonel, I found it!" he says, waving Lina's cellphone in the air. He hands it to Luna, who holds it up and watches water draining out.

"Probably ruined," he says.

"They say you can pack a wet cellphone in dry rice for three days," says Chávez, "and it will come back to life."

"Like Jesus?" Now the colonel looks at Lina. "Why didn't you just take Antonio back to your ranch when you found him, if he was really in such dire straits? Why bring him to El Encanto?"

"We were actually closer to El Encanto than the ranch," says Lina. "And this is where he wanted to come anyway, so he could get a boat to leave Tulcán. But when we got here, everyone was gone. We were just about to go to Santa Rosa del Opón when you arrived. So do you know what happened to everyone? Where's Juan Carlos Mejía?"

"So you knew Mejía?"

"Yes, we've been neighbors for many years."

"If you're such good neighbors, why don't you know what happened here last week?"

"Being neighbors in the jungle isn't the same as being neighbors in the city. You can't just drop by for a cup of coffee. And what did happen here? Is Juan Carlos all right?"

"He's dead, along with everyone else in El Encanto. And if you'd gone to Santo Rosa del Opón, you would have found it a ghost town. Its residents have been evacuated by the Army for their own protection."

"But what happened?" says Roberto.

"That's what I'm here to find out. But the massacre is believed to have been carried out by the TARV," and he looks at Lina. "Apparently they were making the same sort of threats against Mejía as they've been making against your family. I'd like to take a formal statement from you as part of my investigation."

"I'll help in any way I can, of course," says Lina. "Poor Juan Carlos. I can't believe he's dead."

There's a silence. Colonel Luna has a sort of benignly blank look on his face.

"Now maybe you can take *these* off?" says Lina, referring to the plastic cuffs.

"I have just another question or two for Antonio," says Luna, and now he turns his cool blue-gray eyes on Roberto. "So there was a travel ban issued a few days ago. No one is allowed to enter Tulcán unless authorized by the Army. Did you obtain that authorization?"

"No, Colonel, I didn't. To be honest, I did hear something about it in Tarapacá when I was making the final preparations for my trip, but I decided to go ahead. What I'm doing has nothing to do with politics, I couldn't care less about any of that. I didn't expect to see anyone except the O'wa."

"By your presence here, you're in violation of the law."

"I understand. I made a mistake. I'm prepared to leave immediately. Actually, I can't get out of here fast enough."

Luna chuckles. "Sergeant? Release this man."

The sergeant pulls a knife from its sheath, steps behind Roberto, and cuts the cuffs. Roberto feels a wave of relief wash over him, he can't believe he and Lina have talked themselves out of this. He looks at Lina as he rubs his wrists. She gives him a tentative smile.

"It's been interesting meeting you, Antonio," the colonel says, and extends his hand. Roberto takes it. The colonel shakes his hand with a very firm grip.

"Just one more question."

"Yes?"

"What is the name of the god of the O'wa?"

Roberto's heart skips a beat, or maybe adds an extra one. His mouth opens a little, but no word comes out. Luna's eyes are boring into his. He slides his hand down to Roberto's wrist, and squeezes it hard, as with his other hand he grasps Roberto's little finger. He begins to bend it back. Roberto gasps, and sinks to his knees. With a quick movement the colonel snaps the bone, and it's like lightning flashes in front of Roberto's eyes and it's the loudest scream he's ever screamed. He feels dizzy and his face is hot and suddenly he leans over and vomits.

Colonel Luna looks down at him dispassionately.

"That's just one little bone. The body's full of bones. We'll break them all and take our time doing it if you don't start telling us the truth."

Roberto looks up at him. "What do you want to know?"

"Your real name and what you're doing here."

"I'm Antonio Alvarado. I'm with an NGO called the South American Center for Human Rights. I came to investigate reports of a massacre in El Encanto. But everything else I told you is true. I really was robbed by my guides and left in the jungle. Carmen found me this morning, and agreed to bring me here. She's done nothing wrong, please let her return to her family."

"Nobody's returning anywhere at the moment. Get up."

Roberto gets to his feet. He still feels dizzy and pain throbs through his hand. He glances at Lina and he feels ashamed about the vomit and the screaming and he glimpses the fear in her face. The sergeant pulls his arms behind his back and puts on a new pair of plastic cuffs. He jostles Roberto's broken finger and he stifles a cry.

Colonel Luna stands in front of Roberto in a self-consciously powerful pose, hands on hips, his gleaming boots set wide apart. The law professor pretending to be the determined jungle warrior.

"There are three possibilities. You are both telling the truth. You are both lying. One is telling the truth, and one is lying. In any case, it will take some time to sort this out. Our commander will be here tomorrow. He wishes to interview each of you personally."

Now Luna turns and starts to walk away.

"Colonel?" says Roberto. The colonel pauses and looks back. "Do *you* know?"

"Know what?"

"The O'wa word for God."

The colonel smiles slightly.

"Tamoi. I suggest you pray to him. Or to some other god of your choosing."

* * *

The day is ending. The birds and monkeys are going quiet. Fireflies decorate the dusk. Roberto and Lina walk with bound hands under the fruit trees with the Black Jaguars.

Roberto's ahead of Lina and still can't talk to her. They're moving toward the house. He sees the tower silhouetted against the fading sky. And Daniel, Quique, Roque, Ernesto . . . where are they? They have to know by now what's happened. They're somewhere out there hiding, deciding what to do. Calculating the odds. Four of them and about thirty paramilitaries. But Roque's armed only with a machete and Daniel with his silly little pistol so it's really thirty against two. No matter how formidable Quique and Ernesto are and what poor excuses for fighters the Black Jaguars may be, the odds are still long, virtually suicidal. But Roberto knows there's not a chance in the world they won't be coming for Lina and him.

He assumes they're being taken to the house, but as they're passing the guesthouse, everybody stops. He sees Colonel Luna talking to the sergeant. They both glance his and Lina's way. Now the sergeant leaves the colonel.

"Ramirez, Mojica, Chávez, Chino, Falconi," says the sergeant, "come with me! And bring the prisoners!"

Colonel Luna and the rest of his men continue toward the house, as the sergeant and his guys take Roberto and Lina into the guesthouse. The air's hot and stuffy. What light there is comes in through the windows. Roberto sees the same sort of French and Italian furnishings that he saw in the main house. The guys take off their packs. One of them is the fat Black Jaguar, and he plops down in an armchair with a sigh.

"I could get used to this," he says. "Somebody turn on the TV."

"Yeah, let's get the power on," says a guy with a snake tattoo winding around his neck. "I don't want to sit here in the fucking dark all night."

"We're on an operation," says the sergeant, "not on vacation at a resort. The colonel says if the prisoners try to escape, shoot them. Otherwise, leave them alone. Especially the girl. Are you listening to me, Chino?"

"Hey, don't worry, she's not my type," Chino says. He's doubtless called Chino—Chinaman—because of his slightly slanted eyes. "I like tall girls with big tits."

"You like anything with a pussy in it," the sergeant says.

"Everybody else is going to be having a big party," Chávez whines, "and we'll be stuck out here."

"At least bring us something decent to eat," says Chino. "I'm tired of eating slop."

"I'll see what I can do," says the sergeant, heading toward the door.

"Hey, sergeant," says the guy with the snake tattoo, "what are we supposed to do with them?" Indicating Roberto and Lina. "Put them in a closet or something?"

"I don't give a shit where you put them. As long as they're still here in the morning."

As the sergeant opens the front door, Roberto hears the peacock shrieking in the distance. The sergeant closes the door behind him. Everybody's looking at Lina and Roberto.

"Please don't put us in a closet," says Roberto. "We won't give you any trouble. We promise."

The guy with the snake tattoo grabs Roberto's arm and pulls him over to a chair and pushes him down. "Sit your ass down here and don't move." Now he takes Lina's arm and, treating her more gently, brings her to a couch and has her sit down at one end.

"You comfortable, sweetheart?"

"Yes," says Lina. "Thank you."

"Hey, boys," says Chino, reaching in his pack, "fuck everybody else. We're going to have our own party."

He holds up a bottle of premium scotch. Glasses are procured from the kitchen, and all five Black Jaguars begin to drink. None of them are paying any attention to Roberto and Lina. He looks at her across the darkening room. She manages a smile, and he smiles back. He'd like to tell her how wonderful she was back at the lake. So cool under pressure, so fast with her answers. He wonders what she's thinking. He wonders if they both will live to see the morning.

The lights come on. The Black Jaguars clap. The first thing they do is turn on the TV, and then they start arguing about what to watch. They finally settle on a telenovela about a handsome young *vallenato* singer from the coast who comes to the capital city to seek his fame and fortune. He achieves great success but handles it badly, all the money and women and false friends and drugs send him down a path that may lead to his destruction. His sweet, pretty girlfriend from back home arrives in the big city to try to save him.

* * *

They go through the scotch pretty fast, and then a bottle of aguardiente appears. Roberto attaches names to all five of them: besides Chino and Chávez, there's Oscar, the fat one, Alfonso, the one with the snake tattoo, and Joaco, a short silent guy with dark Indian features. Roberto's pleased they're drinking so much, pleased they seem to have forgotten that he and Lina are even here, pleased they're out in the guesthouse away from the main group of paramilitaries. He thinks the odds of rescue are improving by the minute.

It's clear now Luna was toying with them at the lake. He had no intention of letting Roberto or Lina go before he'd checked their stories out. It's lucky there's no Internet out here and nobody can google "antonio alvarado south american center for human rights." It's also lucky that the law professor/colonel turned out to be such an inept interrogator; because he didn't question Roberto and Lina separately, they could create a story together. So they've been able to buy some time, at least until the "commander" (Hernán 40?) arrives.

A large green moth bumps against a light shade, throws its fluttering shadow against the wall. Roberto sees Lina watching it, and now she looks at him. It's like a silent communication: you and I are watching the moth together. What wouldn't Roberto give if he could go back to yesterday when he and Lina and Daniel were in Diego's guesthouse debating whether to continue to El Encanto or go back to Tarapacá? If he'd just listened to them, they'd all probably be in Tarapacá right now, maybe partying at Yadier's house. He thinks of the six dead monkeys and what Roque said; it's Roberto's fault if any of the six of them die.

Emergency Room is on the TV now. It's based on an American show and is about a handsome young doctor who saves a dozen patients a night and makes all the nurses fall in love with him. Roberto wonders where Daniel is at this moment. He imagines the jungle surrounding Daniel, the strange sounds and the mosquitoes and the shadows and the fear. He's probably cursing Roberto incessantly in his mind at the same time he's getting ready to risk his life for him.

Alfonso's talking about a rich businessman he used to work for as a bodyguard. "He took his girlfriend to Miami and bought her some fucking purse made out of African crocodile skin. Do you know how much it cost? Fifty-one thousand American dollars!"

Chino gives a contemptuous snort. "I used to wipe my ass on fifty-one thousand dollars."

Oscar takes a puff of his cigarette and looks at Chino skeptically. "Have you ever told the truth about anything, Chino?"

"Not very often. But I'm telling the truth now."

"So how'd you get so rich?"

"Moving drugs, of course. But I was forced out by the three letters." That's drug slang for the American Drug Enforcement Agency. "They had me by the balls. They said they were going to arrest me and extradite me to America if I didn't become an informer. Do you know what they do to informers if they're caught? You don't want to know, it would make you throw up. So I took off, I left my wife and kids behind, I changed my name. It was the best thing I ever did. The drug business is too dangerous, everybody's always killing everybody. Money's no good to a dead man. And the wife and kids were a pain in the ass, I'm glad to be rid of them."

Alfonso laughs. "And you spent all your fucking money, huh? What an idiot."

"Who says I spent all my money? My brother and me are buying a ranch in Spain, you think that comes cheap? Some of the best fighting bulls in the country are raised on that ranch."

"I've always wanted to go to Spain," says Oscar, and then he looks at Lina. "Have you ever been to Spain, Carmen?"

"Yes. Once."

"How did you like it?"

Lina shrugs. "I was only five or six years old, I hardly even remember it."

"But you must remember something."

Lina thinks a moment. "I remember being on the beach with my parents. Playing in the sand. And chasing a seagull."

Roberto was in Spain last year with Caroline. They were driving from Madrid to Galicia, and decided to stop off in Segovia. It's a romantic oasis of a city, with an old Moorish castle called the Alcázar rising before you as you approach. Roberto and Caroline toured the Alcázar, then had great seafood and wine at a dimly lit restaurant in the shadow of the castle. As evening fell, so did snow, with the snowflakes gently turning the dusk into a dream.

Chávez is sitting on the other end of the couch from Lina. Now he replenishes his glass with aguardiente and stands up and heads her way.

"You look like you could use a drink."

"No thanks," says Lina.

He sits down beside her. "It'll make you feel better, I promise."

He tries to put the glass to her lips but she turns her head away.

"No! I don't want any!"

Chávez laughs and grabs her hair. "Yes, you do, you bitch! Open wide!"

Chávez tries to keep her head still as he forces the glass between her lips. Aguardiente dribbles down her chin.

"Stop it!" says Roberto. "She doesn't want it!"

"Oh, she wants it all right—"

Joaco, the quiet Indian guy, comes up behind Chávez, locks a forearm across his throat, drags him away from Lina, and drops him on the floor. Chávez coughs and rubs his throat and looks up at Joaco in astonishment.

"What the fuck you do that for?"

"The sergeant said to leave her alone."

Chávez gets to his feet.

"Well, I don't see the sergeant anywhere, do you?" and now he starts jabbing his forefinger at Joaco. "And if you ever touch me again, I'll fucking kill you!"

Joaco pulls his knife out of its sheath.

"Kill me now."

The other three Black Jaguars are watching with big grins—this is more entertaining than *Emergency Room*.

Chávez glances at the knife, obviously losing his nerve.

"Not today, you Indian piece of shit. But it's coming, just you wait!"

Joaco smirks and resheathes his knife. Chávez sees Roberto looking at him.

"And I'll kill you too, you motherfucker! Don't you ever tell me what to do!"

Oscar laughs. "You're going to kill everyone, Chávez. There won't be anyone left in the world but you."

Roberto looks at Lina. Her shirt's splotched with the spilled liquor. They're totally at the mercy of these drunken killers. Roberto looks at the front door. He imagines it bursting open, Quique and Ernesto coming through, spraying the room with their Galils, taking out the lot of them.

* * *

It seems appropriate that the opening credits of a reality show about cooking have just begun when some food arrives: spaghetti with tomato sauce and slices of fresh fruit, brought by the sergeant and two other men. Roberto and Lina's plastic cuffs are removed and they're both given plates of food and glasses of water. Roberto balances the plate on his knees and forces himself to eat. His broken finger hurts bad and looks like a fat purplish sausage stuck on his hand. He twines some spaghetti strands around his fork, reflecting that if this were an action movie and he its hero, he could lunge at the nearest Black Jaguar and stab the fork into his throat and grab his weapon and kill everybody and then he and Lina could escape into the night.

The sergeant says he wants a man standing guard outside the guesthouse and orders Chávez to take the first shift, and then he and the two others leave. Chávez gets some more spaghetti and takes his plate outside, all the while bitching bitterly. Roberto and Lina finish their food. Their plates and forks are taken away and then they're allowed to go to the bathroom, Lina first. Oscar escorts her. As she moves past Roberto, her eyes meet his, and though it lasts only a moment there's something about the look that makes him feel as if an electric shock is going through him. She's telling him: *Be ready.*

He watches Lina and Oscar disappearing down a hallway, his rifle pointing in a general way at her. With his soft face and big stomach and ambling way of walking, he could not look less like a soldier. Roberto thinks: *She's going to try to get his gun.* This is her chance with the handcuffs off. It's the kind of thing she's been trained to do. Roberto never asked her if she'd ever killed anyone, but one has to assume the answer's yes. She's Chano's niece, after all.

Roberto's heart starts pounding. Be ready, okay. But be ready to do what? He looks around, locates everyone. Joaco is walking into the kitchen, taking his Kalashnikov with him. Chino is sitting on the couch, Alfonso in a nearby armchair. They're drinking and loudly talking to each other; their weapons are leaning against the furniture they're sitting on. Chávez is outside. What does Roberto do when the shooting starts, when the hallway thunders with gunfire and flashes with light? He can't just sit here like some spectator at a sporting event and watch Lina take on five armed men by herself. He hasn't even been in a fistfight since he was a kid but he has to do something, hurl himself at someone, divert their attention long enough to allow Lina to shoot them.

Roberto tries to stay calm. He sits and waits. Each second seems to extend longer than he can stand it.

Joaco comes out of the kitchen. He clasps Roberto's forearm, lifts it up, and takes a look at his watch. It's an inexpensive Swatch he's had since college. Now Joaco pulls it off Roberto's wrist and puts it on his own wrist and walks away.

Alfonso's talking to Chino about his girlfriend. "She took off her fucking shoes and threw them at me, then she ran across the street, and she was nearly hit by a bus!" and he laughs. "She's Brazilian-Italian, so beautiful and yet so crazy, it's in her blood."

On the cooking show, a crestfallen contestant who's just made a disastrous Beef Stroganov has his apron taken away by the judges.

And then Lina appears, followed by Oscar. She glances at Roberto and gives the slightest of shrugs. Oscar zip-ties her hands again and sits her back down on the couch, then looks at Roberto.

"Your turn."

Roberto walks down the hallway with Oscar behind him. Oscar's maintaining a careful distance from Roberto. He must not have given Lina a good opportunity to disarm him. Well, he doesn't have anything to worry about with Roberto.

Roberto goes in the bathroom and takes his stance in front of the toilet. As he unzips and pees, Oscar leans in the doorway, smoking a cigarette and humming to himself. He's not paying Roberto any particular attention, as though attempting to provide him with a bit of privacy.

"You're not like the others," says Roberto.

Oscar looks at him and smiles. "You're right. I'm not."

"What's your story?"

"Well, that's the rub, isn't it? I seem to have no story. My father's a man of considerable influence—maybe that's my story. He thought serving a stretch in the Black Jaguars would be good for me, make me a man and so forth. That remains to be seen."

Roberto shakes out the last drops, then zips up and flushes. He turns to Oscar.

"What will happen tomorrow?"

Oscar looks at him with a certain amount of sympathy.

"I don't know. Honestly."

Roberto nods. "Can I wash my hands?"

"Sure."

Roberto goes to the sink and turns on the water. He washes his hands then takes off his glasses and splashes water on his face. He takes a towel and dries his face and hands and then cleans his glasses, which are filthy. Now he puts them back on, and regards himself in the mirror.

He seems to be looking not at a mirror but through a window at somebody else. For a moment it feels ineffably strange to be him, he has no idea what he is or what life is. Is he a man called Roberto, or just some phantom the mind of the jungle has dreamed up?

* * *

Oscar's snoring. He's sprawled across one end of the couch, his boots off, his black beret askew. Joaco, Chino, and Alfonso are drinking and watching the replay of a soccer game. Lina's eyes are closed, but Roberto doesn't get the sense that she's asleep. Maybe she's meditating, or she's trying to figure a way out of this fix, or she's lost herself in the beauty and bliss of some time in her past. Roberto knows so little about her really, he has no idea how her mind works.

A few minutes ago, he heard bursts of automatic weapon fire and people shouting and he expected Lina's comrades to come through the door, but it turned out it was just a couple of drunken Black Jaguars who claimed they had spotted an actual jaguar slinking through the trees. They're probably waiting to make their move till everyone falls into a stuporous sleep, though there's another possibility. Presumably they have Lina's satellite phone, so maybe they've made contact with other members of the TARV who are in the area and are even now hurrying their way.

This time it could be the Black Jaguars that get massacred at El Encanto, at Las Matanzas.

Roberto hears voices outside the front door and it opens and Chávez comes in with two other guys. One looks no older than seventeen or eighteen and has such a cute, sweet face he looks more like a Happy Boy than a paramilitary. The other is Vladimiro, the tall ugly guy who was doing his best to charm Lina at the lake. They're welcomed warmly since they've brought a nearly full bottle of El Dorado rum. Chávez announces his shift outside is over, and Alfonso, who seems to be in charge as much as anybody, sends Joaco out to stand guard.

The bottle's passed around. Chino fills his glass to the brim.

"Hey, you pig," says Chávez, grabbing the bottle away, "leave some for the rest of us."

Roberto looks at Lina. Her eyes are open now, and she's warily watching Vladimiro.

The young guy is extremely drunk. He stands swaying a little, staring at the TV with glazed eyes and a silly grin.

"Who's winning?" he says.

"Nobody," says Alfonso.

"How can nobody be winning?"

"Because it's tied, you idiot. See? It's right up there on the screen."

"So how are our prisoners?" says Vladimiro. "Have they been behaving themselves?"

"Not her," says Chávez, jerking his chin toward Lina. "She's been a bitch."

"Yeah?"

"Yeah. She thinks she's too good to drink with us."

"Is that right, beautiful? Are you too good to drink with us?"

"I don't drink," says Lina.

"Too bad," says Vladimiro. "You're missing out on a lot of fun."

He wanders over to Roberto.

"What about you," he says, "do you drink?"

"Yes."

"Go ahead."

He puts the glass to Roberto's lips, and the sweet rum runs down his throat.

"More?"

Roberto nods, and Vladimiro tilts the glass again, as if he's a sympathetic nurse and Roberto's his feeble bedridden patient. Roberto's hoping the rum numbs the agony of this night just a little.

"How's your finger?" says Vladimiro.

"It hurts."

"You'll be hurting a lot more tomorrow," says Chino, "when Hernán 40 gets finished with you," and he laughs. Roberto and Lina look at each other.

One of Vladimiro's big hands reaches toward Roberto's throat. He thinks for a moment Vladimiro's about to strangle him, but then he slips a finger under the thin silver chain around Roberto's neck and lifts out of his shirt the medal Diana Langenberg gave him.

"What's this?" says Vladimiro.

"It's a St. Jude Thaddeus medal."

"Who's he?"

"The patron saint of desperate cases. It's supposed to protect you from danger."

Vladimiro gazes at the golden bearded image of St. Jude, then he gives the medal a sharp pull and pops the chain. He pockets the medal, then goes over to the couch and sits down between Oscar and Lina. Oscar's still asleep, and he gives his shoulder a shove.

"Wake up, asshole!"

Oscar looks around dazedly, smacking his dry lips, then smiles at Vladimiro.

"Vladimiro! Good to see you. Where have you been keeping yourself?"

"You know what I've been thinking about all night?" His big head slowly swivels from Oscar to Lina. "Her. I've been thinking about her."

Oscar reaches for his cigarettes. "Not too surprising. Studies reveal that most men spend most of their time thinking about sexual intercourse."

"Did you hear how she talked to me?"

Alfonso laughs. "Sure, we all did. It was hilarious."

"I've never had a woman talk to me like that before."

"Well," Oscar says, "maybe she'll apologize."

"I'm sorry," says Lina. "I didn't mean it."

"Okay," says Oscar, "now we're all friends."

Vladimiro is silent, still staring at Lina. Now he reaches out and slides the back of a finger over her cheek. Lina moves her head away and looks at Roberto.

"What are you looking at your boyfriend for?" says Vladimiro. "He can't help you."

"See," says Chávez, "I told you she was a bitch."

"I'm not leaving here without fucking her."

"Colonel Luna gave you direct orders to leave her alone," says Roberto.

"Shut the fuck up," says Vladimiro.

"I'm afraid Antonio's right," says Oscar. "No matter how tempting the young lady is, we have our orders."

"But it's like I was saying before," says Chávez, "it don't matter what the sergeant says or the colonel says. They're not here; they're not gonna know."

"*They'll* know," says Alfonso, indicating Lina and Roberto.

"But they won't say anything," says Chino. "Not if they want to keep living."

The room becomes quiet except for the soccer game on TV. The hungry eyes of Chino, Chávez, and Vladimiro are fixed on Lina. For hours, Roberto's tried to keep at bay the horror of the situation, but now it's like a black suffocating wave breaking over him. *Lina's about to be raped.*

"I won't stay quiet," says Lina. "I'll tell everybody, and then when I get out of here, I'll tell my father and my brothers. They'll hunt you down, they'll kill you!"

Vladimiro laughs, and puts his hand on her thigh and squeezes.

"You're making my dick hard, girl."

"Alfonso," says Oscar, "tell them not to do this."

But Alfonso shakes his head and looks resolutely at the TV. "I'm staying out of this."

Vladimiro stands up and pulls Lina to her feet.

"Let's go."

"No!" says Lina, struggling to break free, but Vladimiro slaps her across the face and knocks her back down on the couch. Roberto rises up off his chair and charges at him but he's made it only a couple of steps when Chino swings his fist into his stomach. The air's blown out of his lungs and he drops to his knees and his glasses go clattering to the floor. He looks up, Vladimiro and Lina are blurs.

"Don't beat her up!" says Chino. "Don't leave any marks!"

"Fuck you," says Vladimiro, "I'll do whatever I want."

And then he and Lina are gone, headed to the bedroom. Oscar comes over to Roberto and helps him up. Roberto can't talk, he can only whisper.

"Do something."

"I can't," says Oscar. He reseats Roberto on his chair, then picks up his glasses and puts them back on his face.

"How come he gets to go first?" says Chávez.

"I don't know, Chávez," says Chino. "Why don't you go in there and tell him you're taking over?" He laughs, as does the Happy Boy-looking guy.

"Hey, Enrique," says Chino, "you want a piece of her too?"

"Sure," says Enrique. "Why not?"

"I'll bet Enrique's never even fucked a girl," says Chávez. "He probably doesn't know how."

"I've fucked plenty of girls."

"Sisters don't count."

"He's probably too drunk to get it up," says Chino.

"I'll get it up, don't worry," says Enrique, and then he gets a sudden sick look on his face and runs for the bathroom. A moment later Roberto hears loud puking noises, and Chino and Chávez laugh. Soon Enrique comes tottering back, pale as a ghost. He collapses on the couch and passes out.

Roberto sits there, head hanging, eyes closed, seeing Vladimiro taking Lina away, again and again he takes her away, like a hideous ogre dragging a girl off to its lair. Roberto remembers seeing the blue bed through the window this afternoon. What's going on there right now, what's he doing to her? Roberto starts repeating to himself: *God, get Lina and me out of this. God, get Lina and me out of this. God—*

A bone-chilling female scream rips through the night. Roberto's eyes open and his head jerks up. A second scream starts, and then abruptly stops.

Alfonso mutes the TV. Everyone listens. It's so quiet Roberto can hear the soft thud of the moth as it hits the light shade.

"What the hell was that?" says Alfonso.

Chávez grins. "Sounds like a whore that's having a good time."

"Somebody should go in there!" says Roberto. "Stop him!"

"If Vladimiro really hurts her," says Oscar, "we're all in trouble."

"He's not gonna hurt her," says Chino. "He's not that stupid."

"Oh, but he is," says Oscar. "Remember the girl in Miscamayo? The mayor's niece? Hernán 40 was furious. The mayor was on our side."

"A lot of shit goes down in the jungle," says Chino. "Vladimiro's not the only one."

Alfonso unmutes the TV. The announcer's yelling hoarsely as a goalie makes a great save.

"Just relax," Alfonso says. "He'll be done soon. Everything'll be fine."

Enrique on the couch groans in his sleep, then farts.

God, get Lina and me out of this.

Time seems mired in an endless present of pain and fear. The universe is this room and nothing else. How will his heart be able to beat and not simply burst as one criminal after another goes in the bedroom to rape Lina?

Vladimiro walks in. His face is flushed and he's dripping with sweat.

"How was it?" says Chávez.

Vladimiro gives a weak laugh. "Not bad."

He grabs the bottle of rum, takes a drink. Chino stands up.

"Where you going?" says Chávez.

"Where do you think?"

"Why should you be next?"

"Because I am. That's why."

"We should at least flip a coin or something."

"Fuck that."

Vladimiro laughs again. "Well, whoever it is, you better hurry up. Before she gets cold."

Everyone stares at Vladimiro.

"My god," says Oscar. "You killed her?"

"She kneed me in the balls. I got mad. The bitch."

"Are you sure she's dead?" says Alfonso.

"Go in there and look if you don't believe me."

Vladimiro sits down on the couch, rubs his hands over his bony brow, his thick lips.

"I didn't mean to. I don't know what happened."

Chávez is smiling strangely. "How did you do it?"

Vladimiro moves his hands away from his face and looks at them as if surprised to see them there.

"With these."

Roberto can hardly hear their voices because there is a roaring everywhere, like a train in a tunnel or a hurricane or like all the atoms of the earth are shuddering and shaking and are about to crumble into a pile of nothing.

"You fucked up, Vladimiro," says Alfonso. "You fucked up bad."

"It wasn't just me, it was all of us. We were all going to do it. I was just the unlucky one."

"Don't try to drag me into this," says Alfonso.

"Or me," says Oscar. "We're not taking the fall for this. You're on your own."

"What were we supposed to do with some piece of shit girl," says Vladimiro, "put a ring on her finger and marry her?"

Roberto stands up. He starts walking toward Vladimiro, his legs moving stiffly, as though they're made of wood. Oscar intercepts him. He guides Roberto back to his chair. His eyes seem ashamed.

"Sit down, Antonio. Please."

"There's an easy way out of this," says Chino.

"What?" says Chávez.

"You all heard the sergeant say to shoot the prisoners if they try to escape. Well, that's what happened. We took the cuffs off so they could go to the bathroom and then they made a grab for our guns. We had no choice."

Vladimiro bares his gappy teeth in a grin. "That's perfect!"

"So let's go get the girl and put some holes in her," says Chino.

"And then we'll take care of *him*," says Chávez, nodding at Roberto.

So, Roberto thinks. It ends here. Just like that.

"Alfonso?" says Oscar. "What are you going to do?"

"Nothing," says Alfonso. "I'm going to sit here and do nothing."

Oscar goes over to the couch and pulls on his boots, and then looks at Roberto.

"I'm sorry, Antonio."

Now he starts walking toward the front door.

"Oscar!" says Chino. "Where are you going?"

"I'm washing my hands of this," Oscar says, and opens the door. The doorway is filled with flashes of light and bullets slap into Oscar's fat stomach. He lands on the floor on his back as Quique appears, with

Ernesto right behind, their Galils raking the room. The Black Jaguars hardly have time even to reach for their weapons before their uniforms begin spouting blood, before their flesh and bone get blown from their bodies. Roberto sees Alfonso falling, the top of Chino's head disintegrating just above his Chinese eyes, Vladimiro rising from the couch then sitting back down with a dozen bullets in his chest, and then he sees the improbable sight of Daniel in his Foreign Legion cap, his camera bag swinging from his shoulder, his mouth agape and his eyes huge as he wildly fires his pistol. He actually hits somebody, a chunk of Chávez's cheek goes flying and then a burst from Ernesto's rifle knocks him back against a wall; he slides down it, leaving a smear of blood. Enrique is the last to die, and the only one to say anything. He sits up dazedly on the couch and looks at Quique's ferocious face, his jaguar whiskers. He pitifully lifts up both hands to protect himself and cries out "No!" and then his palms are punctured and his fingers severed and his face is turned into something that is no longer cute or sweet.

Killing them all has taken mere seconds. Roberto's been the still center of a whirlwind of violence; now he shakily comes to his feet. Ernesto pulls out his knife and cuts his cuffs.

"Where's Lina?" says Quique.

"In the bedroom."

"Anyone with her?"

"No."

Roberto and Quique and Daniel run toward the bedroom as Ernesto moves back toward the front door. Roberto's thinking she may still be alive, Vladimiro was a cretin who was too drunk to know what he'd actually done. They pass the bathroom and reach the closed door of the bedroom.

Quique opens it, and they go in. A bedside lamp casts a mellow light. Through the diaphanous blue folds of the mosquito net, Roberto can see Lina lying on the bed. Quique lifts the net.

She's on her back, naked from the waist down. Her hands are still bound behind her. There are red marks on her neck. Her eyes are startling. They're wide-open, and seem to be looking toward the ceiling. Because of the burst blood vessels caused by her strangulation, their whites are red.

"Shit," says Daniel.

Roberto leans over her and touches her hair. He says, "Lina."

Quique grabs his arm.

"Let's go! Come on!"

"Let's go, Roberto!" says Daniel.

And then Roberto finds himself running down the hallway again and into the living room. Ernesto has turned the light off and is standing at the front door, peering toward the house.

"They're coming!" he says.

Roberto stumbles over a body in the dark.

"Lina?" says Ernesto.

"Dead," Quique says.

"Where's Roque?" says Roberto.

"He's waiting for us by the lake," says Quique. "We just need to get to the jungle and we'll be okay. Now get ready to run like hell."

They step outside. Roberto sees Joaco lying on the ground. A black pool of blood has formed at his throat where it's been slit. Roberto hears voices in the distance, and looks back at the house. The dark tower looms against the starry sky, with the half moon floating just above it. Some lights are on in the house, and he can see the shapes of people moving around outside. The beams of flashlights slash through the night. The four of them begin to run. An automatic rifle opens up. Roberto hears a bullet snap past his ear. His legs are weak and clumsy from all the sitting and he trips over something and falls. Quique grabs his arm and pulls him up.

"Go!" says Quique.

Roberto stumbles away. Quique fires a quick burst at the muzzle flashes of the Kalashnikov. As he turns to run again, a bullet hits him in the back of the head and he drops to the ground like the blind horse Lina shot.

Roberto stops and looks back at Quique.

"Let's go, let's go!" Ernesto screams.

"Run, Roberto!" Daniel gasps.

Roberto runs. Other rifles are firing now. A flashlight traps him briefly in its beam but then they're among the fruit trees. After the trees will be the lake, the pasture, the sugarcane field, and then the jungle. Roberto swerves among the trunks and he's running faster now and he won't fall again. Daniel is to his left, he's running with the pistol in one hand and the other hand holding the camera bag so it won't bang against his body, but where's Ernesto? Roberto looks back and sees him walking unsteadily with one hand clasped to his side.

"Daniel!" Roberto says.

He and Daniel hurry back to Ernesto.

"Ernesto, are you hit?" says Daniel.

Ernesto pulls up his blood-soaked shirt. There's a hole in his back and a hole in his belly. He laughs. "It went right through." And then he sits down heavily at the foot of a tree. "You guys better get going."

"But we can't leave you," says Roberto.

"We all die. It's my turn today," and then he laughs again. "Don't worry, I won't let them take me. And I'll send some of those bastards to hell first."

There's the sound of shooting but it's at a distance, they're not shooting at them. His breathing labored, Ernesto takes a position behind the tree, waits with his rifle. Roberto and Daniel look at each other.

Now Roberto hears voices, sees a flashlight in the trees. He leans down and grasps Ernesto's shoulder.

"Thank you, Ernesto."

"Good-bye, Ernesto," says Daniel.

Ernesto looks back at them and smiles.

"Good luck. And find Roque, he'll take you home."

Roberto and Daniel continue through the trees. Just as they reach the lake, they hear the sound of gunfire behind them. Many guns. Ernesto's engaging the enemy.

The lake lies still and beautiful under the stars and the half moon. They pause, trying to catch their breath.

"Where's Roque?" says Roberto.

Daniel points down the bank toward the pavilion. "We left him there. With all our packs."

Roberto squints toward the pavilion. For a moment, he thinks his eyes are playing tricks, but no, they're definitely there: several dark shapes moving on the pavilion, another one on the walkway.

"Daniel, there's people down there!"

"Fuck!"

They duck back into the trees.

"You think they have Roque?" Daniel says.

"I don't know."

"What do we do, Roberto?"

He sounds terrified. Roberto's terrified too. With Roque missing, they're all alone. Gunfire's still erupting. Ernesto can't hold them off for long.

"We have to make it to the jungle, Daniel. We can't stop running till we're there. Okay?"

Daniel nods. Now they begin to run, skirting the edge of the lake, keeping low and in the trees. The noise of the firefight reaches a crescendo, and then there's an explosion, maybe a grenade, and then sporadic shooting and finally silence. They've doubtless killed Ernesto, and they'll be coming.

Daniel and Roberto are past the lake and into the stand of trees, and then they emerge into the pasture. The rutted dirt road crosses it diagonally and then disappears into the sugarcane field. On the far side of the field is the dark mass of the jungle.

They run through the pasture. Around them the dead cows are scattered over the grass. Roberto sees the single tree with the dead horse lying beneath it; some small animal that's been feeding on it scampers away. Now Daniel stops and bends over with his elbows on his knees and his chest heaving.

"I can't breathe," he says.

"Come on," says Roberto, grabbing a handful of Daniel's shirt and giving it a pull. "We're almost there."

Daniel stumbles on. They get to the dirt road and start running down it. A falling star streaks across the sky above the sugarcane field. They pass the last dead cow. They're about fifteen meters from the field when Roberto hears an automatic weapon firing. He looks back and sees men swarming out of the trees and into the pasture. He sees the flashes from their rifles and bullets are flying past him and into the sugarcane. He and Daniel reach the field and run up the road, if the frantic flailing of their exhausted limbs can still be called running. Their pursuers can't see them now. At the end of the perfectly straight road is the jungle, into which the Black Jaguars supposedly are too cowardly to follow them. They groan and sob as they run, and curse God and call on him to save them. The sugarcane arises darkly on both sides above their heads, and now a wind springs up and the plants lean and sway and make shushing sounds as if telling them to calm down, quit struggling, accept their fate.

They're about three quarters of the way across the field when their long shadows appear on the road as a flashlight hits them in the back, and then bullets start kicking up the dirt around their feet. Roberto shoves Daniel into the sugarcane and dives in after him. The field's planted in closely packed rows and they go off down one of them. They disturb some rats, which squeak and scatter. Now they stop and listen. They hear voices, getting louder, moving up the road.

"Let's go that way," Roberto whispers, pointing in the direction of the jungle. "We're nearly there. Maybe a hundred meters."

Daniel nods. They push through the stalks of sugarcane into the next row, then into the next. Roberto hears shooting, then shouts, then more shooting—they must be randomly firing into the field or else at the ghosts of the people they slaughtered last week. It won't be easy for them to find him and Daniel in a sugarcane field at night. They keep cutting across the rows, there's only so many of them, soon there won't be any, and the jungle will begin.

Something black hurtles past Roberto, and then something actually runs into his legs, knocking him off his feet. It snorts and squeals, it's a wild pig. The pigs make their escape through the sugarcane as a Kalashnikov opens up. Daniel joins Roberto on the ground and they both lie flat and listen to the bullets passing above them.

"Over here!" they hear someone yell. "We've found them!"

Other weapons start to fire. The stalks of sugarcane jerk and tremble as the bullets slice through them; one falls almost on top of Roberto.

"Cease fire," yells someone, "cease fire!

The fusillade stops. Roberto's not sure what to do: get up and run or stay put and hide? But then he sees a flashlight probing the field not far from them and realizes it's too late to run.

"Roberto," Daniel whispers.

Roberto can barely see him in the darkness. Just the glistening of his eyes and of the pistol in his hand.

"Listen," he says. "I won't let them take me prisoner. I won't let myself be tortured again. Do you understand?"

After a moment's pause, Roberto whispers, "Yes."

"But don't worry, Roberto, I'll shoot you first."

"What? No! Are you crazy?"

"Trust me, it's the right thing—"

"You're not shooting anybody yet. We're getting out of this."

"You're the one who's crazy."

The flashlight's getting closer.

"Shut up," Roberto whispers.

He can see him now, or at least glimpses of him through the sugarcane. He's moving down the row next to them, in one hand the flashlight and in the other a pistol. And now Roberto sees at least two more Black Jaguars are behind him. Their movements are slow and stealthy, the movements of hunters, hunters of men. The flashlight slides to the left and the right.

They're only meters away. The sweat's pouring off Roberto, a drop stings his eye. Some many-legged something is crawling across his arm. His heart's thudding against the ground and he's shivering as if cold. He doesn't dare look at Daniel but knows he's clutching the pistol and is about to shoot somebody: whether Roberto, himself, or a Black Jaguar, he has no idea.

An assault rifle rattles in the dark, and then Roberto hears voices: "We've got them! They're here! This way! Hurry!"

"Let's go!" says the guy with the flashlight, and he and his two comrades crash off through the sugarcane. Roberto hears more shooting, probably at the pigs. He grabs Daniel's arm and pulls him up.

"Come on, Daniel, here's our chance!"

He and Daniel run, stumble, stagger, fall, tumble, and crawl through row after row of sugarcane. They're not trying to be quiet anymore, all they want is to reach the jungle.

They stop where the sugarcane stops. Beyond an open area of about twenty-five meters, they see the trees. Roberto cautiously sticks out his head and looks both ways. No one's in sight. Behind them the shooting continues as the Black Jaguars close in on the pigs. They start running again. They splash through a shallow drainage ditch filled with slime-covered water, and then the jungle takes them.

* * *

Daniel has a flashlight, but they don't use it at first. They're afraid the paramilitaries are pursuing and might see it. But the trees keep crowding closer together and blocking out whatever light comes from the stars and moon. Finally they come to a stop and just stand there, looking around at a smothering blackness.

"Turn your flashlight on," says Roberto.

It's small, hardly bigger than a big cigar. Daniel moves around its thin, weak beam. Roberto sees the trunks of trees, dangling vines. He doesn't hear shooting anymore. Just frogs, and the buzz of mosquitoes in his ear. The air's warm and damp and still and rotten-smelling. The enormity of their situation hits him. They're utterly alone in the jungle at night. When day comes, merciless men will enter the jungle and try to kill them.

Daniel is obviously thinking along the same lines.

"Jesus Christ," he says in an awestruck whisper. "What are we going to do?"

"Keep moving. Get as far away from El Encanto as we can. Head for Diego's."

"We'll never make it by ourselves."

"We have to."

"We need Roque."

"We don't know where he is. We don't even know if he's still alive."

"Maybe he's close. Maybe he's trying to find us."

"We can't just stand here and wait for him."

"Okay, Roberto. So which way is Diego?"

Roberto takes the flashlight from Daniel and shines it around, as if he might discover a sign in the shape of an arrow that says, "Diego."

"This way," he says, pointing in the direction he thinks is away from the river.

They start walking again. Soon the ground under its covering of dead leaves and twigs begins to get mushy, and puddles of water appear.

"Shit," Daniel says, "are we walking into a swamp?"

Within a dozen steps their boots are sinking into the muck.

"I'm not going any further, Roberto! If we get lost in a swamp we'll never get out."

Roberto directs the dim beam of the flashlight to the left and the right.

"Maybe we can go around it."

"I think we should go back the way we came."

"Toward El Encanto? Right into the arms of the Black Jaguars?"

"Maybe we can sneak down to the river. Steal a boat."

"The river's crawling with soldiers and paramilitaries. We'll never get out that way."

"And we'll never get out trying to cross the jungle! It's crazy to think we can! There's a hundred different ways for us to die here! Maybe we'll run into those Indians that kill white people on sight, they'll chase us down and spear us like pigs!"

Roberto swings the flashlight to the left. "I think it looks a little better that way."

The mud pulls at his boots as he walks.

"I'm not going with you!" says Daniel.

"Fine. Stay here."

"Then leave me my flashlight!"

But Roberto just keeps walking. Daniel curses at him and hurries to catch up. They haven't gone far when Roberto hears splashing noises off to their right. He moves the flashlight and sees a black expanse of water with trees sticking out of it. Seven or eight pairs of luminous eyes are looking back at him. Two of the eyes are gliding along slowly and he can see they're affixed to a long dark body.

"Jesus," says Daniel.

Suddenly one of the caimans lunges at something, sending up a sheet of water. Both Roberto and Daniel take a startled step back.

"This is fucked up!" says Daniel.

"Yeah."

They stand there and stare into the swamp.

"You have any water?" says Roberto.

Daniel nods. He takes a plastic bottle out of one of his vest pockets, drinks from it, then passes it to Roberto. He drinks the rest of it.

"Is this it?"

"Yes."

Roberto tosses the empty bottle on the ground. Something about the eyes of the monstrous creatures in the dark water makes him fear this is the end. Daniel is right; it's crazy to think they can traverse the jungle to Diego's by themselves.

He moves the light around, trying to determine where to go, and there it is: the gigantic trunk of a tree with tall, twisted roots. It's not ten meters away. He walks over to it, cranes his neck and points the flashlight up. The tree disappears into the darkness; it could reach the sky, for all he can see.

"Daniel, do you remember Roque hitting a tree with his machete? It was a ceiba tree. Like this one."

"Yeah? What about it?"

"Do you remember how loud the sound was? Roque said if you're ever lost in the jungle and you want someone to find you, you should hit this tree!"

Daniel comes over to the tree. Puts his hand on the trunk, and rubs it. There's a glimmer of hope in his eyes.

"Okay," he says. "So let's bang the shit out of this motherfucker!"

They don't have a machete or anything else to hit it with, so they look around for something. Lots of limbs and branches are lying on the ground, but things rot fast in the jungle and they'd probably shatter with the first blow.

"What about this?" says Daniel.

He's holding up a sturdy-looking piece of wood about a meter and a half long. Roberto takes it from him, and hefts it. It seems like it might do the trick.

"Let's try it," he says, and hands the flashlight to Daniel.

"So what if someone shows up," Daniel says, "and it's not Roque?"

"I guess you better make sure your gun's loaded."

Roberto swings the wood and strikes the trunk. The sound produced is nowhere near as loud as what Roque made.

"Harder, Roberto," says Daniel. "You have to hit it harder."

He swings again, as hard as he can, and the results are better this time. And now he gets in a rhythm, swinging every couple of seconds. Soon he's dripping with sweat and gasping for air. Daniel asks him if he wants him to take over but Roberto shakes his head, it feels impossible to stop until Roque shows up or he drops dead from exhaustion. But after a while he forgets all about Roque, it's just him in the jungle with his piece of wood, it's like he's summoning some spirit or primeval being that's been living here since the beginning, and who knows what it will want to do with him when it arrives?

"Roberto!" he hears Daniel say, but he keeps hitting the ceiba tree. "Roberto! Stop!"

He looks over at Daniel. Standing next to him is Roque. He's a matter-of-fact presence in his Chicago Bulls baseball cap, holding his machete and a flashlight.

"Where are the others?" he says.

"They're dead, Roque," says Roberto.

Roque looks stunned.

"Dead?"

"I'm sorry, Roque," Daniel says, putting his hand on Roque's shoulder. He nods vaguely.

"We should go," he says. "They're nearby."

But there's something Roberto needs to do first. He drops the piece of wood and takes Daniel's flashlight. He shines it around till it picks up the dull gleam of the empty water bottle. He walks over to it and picks it up. Lina would not have wanted him to leave it as trash in the forest.

One day until the day
Roberto is to die

Pale moths float by, like ghosts that need to be gone before the sunrise. He hears dripping water, then realizes it's an oropendola. Other birds, bestirred by the dawn, begin to sing their songs and utter their cries.

Roque walks ahead of him with his machete, while Daniel is dragging along behind him. They have not stopped walking all night. Hardly a word's been said. The closest thing to a conversation was when Roberto heard a growling in the darkness and asked Roque if it was a jaguar, and he replied no, it was a monkey pretending to be a jaguar to keep the jaguars away.

They go down a slope into a hollow filled with thick white mist. Their legs below their knees disappear as they walk through it. Roberto looks at Roque eerily drifting over the mist and wonders if his spirit girl that lives in the trees helped him out last night.

Roberto's passed into some state beyond exhaustion. It's like he's lost the last shred of himself and has become an automaton programmed to go forward, only forward. As the night fades from the jungle, he feels no pleasure that it's gone, just a dull wonder that he's still alive.

In a small clearing on a little hill, Roque calls a halt, and they all sit down. Roque has water and food in his pack. Roberto and Daniel tear open cellophane packages of raisins and nuts, while Roque eats a tin of sardines.

"How much longer to Diego's?" asks Daniel.

Roque shrugs. "Two hours?"

Roberto knows Roque has a slippery sense of time, and things usually take "two hours" with him.

"What happened to your finger?" he says to Roberto.

Roberto tells him about Colonel Luna, and he nods.

"He was tall and had very light skin, yes?"

Roberto's surprised. "You saw him?"

And now Roque tells him what happened after Roberto and Lina left the house at El Encanto.

He, Daniel, Quique, and Ernesto rested. After about twenty minutes, he heard what he was certain was a gunshot. The others were dozing and didn't hear it, but everyone trusted Roque's ears. They all jumped up and grabbed their packs and also Roberto's and Lina's and took off for the lake. Halfway there they ran into Jota. After Jota's encounter with Roberto and Lina in the library, for the fun of it he'd followed them to the lake. He was spying on them from the trees as Roberto danced with Lina on the pavilion, and then he saw the arrival of the Black Jaguars and Roberto struggling with Lina over her gun and the gun going off. At that point, he turned and ran back toward the house to warn the others. They got to the lake just in time to see Roberto and Lina being led away as prisoners. They followed at a distance and saw them entering the guesthouse along with their five guards.

Quique called his superiors in the TARV on Lina's sat phone. He was hoping they could send help, but he was told they were on their own, and they were ordered to attempt a rescue under cover of darkness. When night fell, Jota sneaked up to the guesthouse and looked through a window and saw Roberto sitting in a chair and Lina on the couch.

"Wait a second," says Roberto. "Jota was looking at us through a *window*?"

Daniel laughs. "Yeah, does that kid have balls or what? He said all your guards were sitting around drinking and watching television."

"I'm surprised they let you come," Roberto says to Daniel.

Daniel pops some peanuts into his mouth. "Well, they didn't want to."

"Daniel told them to fuck themselves, he was coming," Roque says.

"We were going toward the guesthouse," Daniel says, "and we heard a scream and we thought it was Lina. There was a guard outside. Quique killed him with a knife. But we were too late for Lina."

"What happened to Lina?" says Roque.

Roberto tells him.

"And what happened to Ernesto and Quique?"

Roberto tells him that too. His eyes well up, and he is silent. Roberto asks him what happened at the lake.

He says shortly after Daniel and Ernesto and Quique left, he heard voices and saw a flashlight. He managed to carry all the packs into the trees and hide there, and then five or six Black Jaguars walked up. They were drunk and talking loud and laughing. They went out on the pavilion, and then Roque heard gunfire. It got louder and Roque could see the flashes of it through the trees. He kept expecting Ernesto, Quique, and Daniel to return with Roberto and Lina, but no one came. The gunfire passed the lake and moved toward the pasture, and Roque followed in the darkness. He crossed the pasture and then heard gunfire coming from the sugarcane field. He saw the Black Jaguars were searching the field. He was hoping that at least some of the five others had been able to escape into the jungle. He entered the sugarcane and came out the other side. He went into the jungle and tried to find them or at least some trace of them but there was nothing and he was afraid they were all dead, and then he heard the banging on the ceiba tree. He hoped to find all of them there, but he was glad the mother tree had saved at least Daniel and Roberto.

Daniel lights a cigarette. Monkeys move in the treetops. Daniel takes one of his cameras out of the bag, aims it upwards.

"Thank god we still have this," says Roberto, indicating the camera.

Daniel lowers the camera and looks at it. "That's right, Roberto. We still have what we came for."

"But I've lost my notebook. And my voice recorder. I got some great interviews yesterday, and now they're gone."

"So how bad is it you don't have them?"

Roberto shrugs. "I can still write my story. It just won't be as good."

Roque goes into his pack, pulls out Roberto's blue spiral notebook and the ziplock bag containing both his cellphone and his voice recorder. He hands them to Roberto.

Roberto looks at them. He fights the urge to burst into tears. Three people have died for this.

"Thank you, Roque," is all he says.

* * *

They're walking through the swampy area near Diego's house. Roque points out some vertical grooves on the trunk of a tree.

"A jaguar was sharpening his claws," he says.

"Was it recent?" asks Roberto.

He touches the grooves. "Yes. The scratch marks haven't dried out yet."

Roberto looks around. He hasn't given up hope of seeing a jaguar. He wonders if it's watching him now with its savage golden eyes.

"Do you smell that?" asks Roque.

"What?" says Daniel.

"Smoke."

Neither Daniel nor Roberto does. They continue through the forest, under the great, still trees, past the gleaming pools of water, across the planks and the slippery logs. And now Roberto smells it too.

They reach the hill Diego's house is built on. Roberto can see the smoke now, wisping through the treetops. As they climb the hill, he hears, very close at hand, "Hello! Hello!" and then "Lucho! Lucho! Hello!" He looks up and sees Lucho, Diego's blue and yellow parrot, sitting in a tree.

"How come Lucho's loose?" says Roque.

Daniel takes his pistol out of a pocket. Now Roberto sees Duque, Diego's shaggy, brown and black dog, at the top of the hill, barking down at them. A moment later, Amparo appears behind him. She smiles when she sees them, and then calls over her shoulder, "They're here! They're back!" She hurries down the hill to meet them, but her smile fades as she sees only three.

"Where are the rest?"

"Amparo," says Roberto. "We have terrible news."

Her eyes widen. "What?"

"They were killed last night. By the Black Jaguars. In El Encanto."

"Lina? She's dead?"

"Yes."

"No!" Amparo wails. "No!"

Roque puts his arms around Amparo, and she sobs against his shoulder.

"It can't be! It can't be!"

"Amparo, I'm sorry," says Roberto, "but is everything okay here? Why is there smoke?"

"They burned it," she says. "The house. But they're gone now."

And now the four of them go up the hill. Alquimedes, shirtless and bathed in sweat, stands in the little graveyard among the eight white crosses, shoveling dirt into a new grave. He regards them with his single eye as they approach.

"Why's she crying?" he asks.

"Lina, Ernesto, and Quique," says Roque. "They're all dead. They were killed by the paramilitaries."

Alquimedes seems unsurprised. He leans on his shovel and gazes down into the grave.

"It's a day for death."

The grave is half filled in with dirt.

"Who's in there?" Daniel says. "Diego?"

Alquimedes shakes his head. "Marco."

Roberto looks off across the hill, sees among the scorched palm trees the charred and still-smoking ruins of the house.

"What happened?" he says.

"We'd just finished breakfast, and then Duque started barking. Then we heard helicopters. We looked out the window and saw two Army helicopters landing right there." He points toward the open space where Roberto and Lina sat together beneath the stars. "Diego kept an automatic rifle hidden in the wall behind a board, and he ran and got it. He yelled at us to run and hide in the jungle and he'd hold them off. Amparo and I started to run out, but Marco was hanging back. He said, 'Dad, I can't leave you here!' Diego said, 'Go, my son, please!' and then he looked at me and he said, 'Alquimedes!' I grabbed Marco and pulled him out of the house. We ran down the hill toward the jungle. Marco had tears streaming down his face. We heard guns beginning to fire. Marco said, 'I have to go back, I have to help Dad!' Amparo and I tried to stop him, but he was young and strong, and he broke away from us and ran back up the hill. Amparo and I ran into the jungle, we ran for a long time. And then we stopped, and we waited for a long time."

Alquimedes' fingers pluck absently at the necklace of bright feathers. A fly lands on his cheek. Roberto thinks it's about to crawl into his empty eye socket, but then it flies away.

"Maybe it wasn't my bravest moment, I don't know. But at least I can tell myself I was protecting Amparo. Finally we came back here. The helicopters had left, and the soldiers were gone. The house was burning. We found Marco lying on his back in front of the house. He'd been shot several times. But not in the face. His beautiful face was like it always was. You could still see the tears on his eyelashes."

"And what about Diego?" asks Daniel.

"Diego was nowhere to be found. The soldiers must have taken him with them. Why, I don't know."

"Did you get a look at the soldiers?" says Roberto.

"Yes. Just a glimpse."

"What kind of uniforms were they wearing?"

"I just remember they were wearing hats, and their faces were painted black and green like wild Indians."

They were almost certainly with the 1st Special Operations Battalion, the unit that conducted the massacre at Jilili. Alquimedes resumes filling the grave with dirt.

"Let me help you with that," says Roque.

"No thanks."

"What are you going to do, Alquimedes?" asks Roberto. "You can't stay here."

"No, no. We can't stay here."

"You're welcome to come with us to Tarapacá," says Daniel.

"There's nothing for me in Tarapacá. No, I was thinking about going down the river the other way, to a town called Cenizo. When I was going up and down the river, I was always falling in love with girls in these little towns, and I fell in love with a girl in Cenizo. She married someone else, but I've always remembered it as a happy place. But maybe Amparo would like to go with you. Amparo, do you want to go with them to Tarapacá?"

Amparo's staring at nothing, her arms hanging limply at her sides, her long black braid gleaming in the morning sunlight.

"Amparo?" says Alquimedes. "Did you hear me?"

"I don't want to do anything," Amparo says. "I don't want to go anywhere."

"Well, you can't just stand there like a statue the rest of your life. The birds will build a nest in your hair, and then what?"

"Amparo," says Roberto, "why don't you come with us? Daniel and I won't just leave you in Tarapacá."

"That's right," says Daniel. "We'll do whatever we can to help you."

But Amparo doesn't answer. She just walks slowly off toward the pirarucu pond.

"Ah, she'll be okay," says Alquimedes as he throws more dirt in the grave. "There's nothing like being young. What I wouldn't give to be her age again."

Roberto looks around the hilltop for the monkey.

"Where's Chico?"

"I haven't seen him since the shooting started," Alquimedes says. "I guess he ran and hid in the jungle like me."

* * *

Roberto walks toward the river with Roque and Daniel. He's afraid the soldiers might have destroyed the boats, leaving them stranded, so he's relieved when he looks down the hill and sees the boats pulled up on the bank, just as they left them. They need gasoline for the return trip, and Roque leads them to a storage shed where Diego keeps a supply. The door has a padlock on it. Roque whacks the lock a few times with the blunt side of his machete and pops it open, and then they carry red metal containers of gas down the hill. Roque and Daniel stay with the boat as Roberto goes back to find Alquimedes and Amparo.

He walks past the guesthouse and peers in at the brightly colored hammocks. Everything he sees is making him think of Lina. How can she not exist anymore? It seems not possible.

He stops at the wooden shed where the anaconda's kept. Remembering that Lina was standing right *there* in the grass. Her hair was wet. She smelled of soap. He never got a chance to ask her how she chipped her tooth.

He opens the door of Princesa's palace. She's coiled in one dim corner. Grunting with the effort, he picks up her cold, twisting body and carries her out. He lays her down, and immediately she starts gliding through the grass toward the jungle.

"Hello!" he hears. "Lucho!"

Alquimedes is approaching with Lucho perched on his shoulder. The parrot and his empty eye socket and his bare dirty feet and his drooping bedraggled pants make him look like a shipwrecked pirate. He shows what few teeth he has in a delighted grin.

"I called his name like a dog and he came flying out of the jungle! Soaring like an eagle! It was a thrilling sight to see!"

"We're leaving," says Roberto. "So what about Amparo?"

He shrugs. "She still won't talk to me. She's being difficult, like a typical woman. Maybe you should give it a try."

She's sitting by the pirarucu pond.

"Amparo?" says Roberto.

She doesn't even glance at him. He sits down beside her.

"We're about to go now. You need to make a decision about what you want to do."

"Just leave me alone," she says in almost a whisper. "Please."

"I know how heartbroken you are, but you can't just stay here. Remember after your father was killed and you were lost in the jungle? You were just a little girl, but somehow you found the strength to survive. You have to do that again."

"I wish I'd died in the jungle. I wish the Indians had never found me."

"Lina thought very highly of you, Amparo. She cared about you very much. You know that, don't you?"

Amparo looks at Roberto, and nods.

"You told me how much you wanted to leave here and see the world, and you said Lina was going to help you. She's gone now, but she can still help you. Just ask yourself what she would want you to do now."

Amparo's silent. There's a splash and a swirling in the green scum on the pond as a pirarucu breaks the surface. Now Amparo stands up, and so does Roberto.

"Are you coming with us?"

She shakes her head. "I've loved four people. My father, Lina, Marco, and Alquimedes. I think I should go with Alquimedes."

Alquimedes calls for Duque and he comes running, and then Roberto walks with the old man, the teenage girl, the dog, and the parrot down the hill and along the path that leads to the river. He sees below him Roque and Daniel, waiting by the boats. Daniel's smoking a cigarette. No doubt he'll be as glad as Roberto to get back on the boat that will take them to Tarapacá.

Alquimedes climbs into Diego's long blue boat, then moves beneath the tin roof toward the motor in the back. Roque is helping Amparo into the boat when Roberto hears a series of shrill piercing cries, and Duque begins to bark. They all look around and see the chorongo monkey, hysterical at the prospect of being left behind, running at breakneck speed down the hill.

"Chico!" says Amparo. She holds out her arms, and Chico launches himself into the air.

* * *

The yellow boat and the blue boat motor at a steady pace down the Maniqui River. Roberto sees all the birds that Roque's given names to and turtles and monkeys and a cute family of capybaras, a kind of giant rodent, at play along the riverbank. He sees a swarm of black and red dragonflies, and the head and back of a pink dolphin emerging from the murky water and glistening briefly in the sunlight, and then a beautiful mermaid comes swimming up to the boat. Her long black hair streams around her shoulders and swirls over her breasts, and the lower half of her is covered with sparkling emerald scales. She looks like the sculpture of the mermaid at the lake at El Encanto. She smiles up at Roberto and says some words in a language he can't understand or maybe it's not even a language but is like the cry of a bird or the rain falling on leaves, and then he sees the black caimans. Half a dozen of them are lying on the bank, and now they slide into the water. They're swimming toward the mermaid, and Roberto looks around and sees that caimans are on every side of the boat, the river is filled with them. He knows he's going to have to pull the mermaid into the boat to save her. He makes a lunge and grabs her but she's slippery and frightened and she fights him, and then he loses his grip and starts to fall into the water and his head lifts up and he opens his eyes. He hears the drone of the monotonous motor. He sees Daniel lying asleep in the bottom of the boat. Did he look the dolphin in the eye, is that why he had the nightmare? Or did he dream the dolphin too?

As the sun reaches its zenith, the two boats come to the end of the Maniqui and enter the Gualala. Alquimedes raises a bony arm in farewell as he points the blue boat down the river toward Cenizo where fifty years ago he met a girl. Amparo waves good-bye forlornly. This morning they had a place in life and they woke up in their own beds and now those beds have been turned to ash and they possess nothing except the clothes they're wearing and a parrot that says hello and a dog and a monkey that hate each other. But Roberto guesses that's better than being buried in grave number nine or carried away in a helicopter by sadistic soldiers. The yellow boat heads up the Gualala toward Tarapacá. After a while Roberto looks back over his shoulder for the blue boat, but it's already lost in the shine and glitter of the river.

Daniel's lying in the bottom of the boat like a man that's been hit in the head by a board. Roberto hopes he's okay. All last night as they walked through the jungle Daniel would periodically groan and drop his pants and squat and leave behind smelly dumps like a howler monkey. He needs some Lomotil. Roberto's sleepy too but he knows Jilili isn't far, and he wants to see it as they pass. He's still a reporter, after all.

He glances back at Roque. His face under his baseball cap is blank, impassive. He must be in a state of shock. He's such a gentle soul to have been plunged into such horror. Perhaps Roberto ought to go back and talk to him, but what is he supposed to say? Sorry your friends were killed. Thanks for saving our lives. Can't you make this boat go a little faster because Daniel and I really want to get the fuck out of here.

* * *

Roberto cleans his glasses with his blue bandana and puts them back on and looks at Jilili. It seems deserted, except for some vultures on the white beach. He sees a dark area on the sand where the young woman and her unborn child were killed, but he doesn't see any bodies anywhere. All the fishing boats are gone too.

Roque slows the boat and takes it closer to the village. Roberto looks through Roque's binoculars at the burned-down houses in the shade of the trees. Again, no bodies, and no living people either. What's happened to Conchita and her son Pedro and the other survivors? Did they leave in the boats? Are they hiding in the jungle? Or did the Army come on a humanitarian mission as they did in Santa Rosa del Opón and take them away?

A small brown dog comes out on the beach and barks at the boat. Perhaps the last inhabitant of Jilili. Roberto hands Roque back his binoculars.

"Thanks, Roque."

"You're welcome."

Roque speeds the boat back up.

"How are you?" says Roberto.

"Okay. Sad."

"Me too."

"Don't worry, Roberto. You and Daniel will be home soon."

Roberto goes back to his seat. Above him, a loose piece of the green plastic roof is flapping in the wind. He knows the way home remains fraught with danger, they might encounter a boatload of paramilitaries around the next bend or a helicopter could come along and shoot them to pieces, but still he feels they're going to make it. Not like in the sugarcane field, not like in the swamp. He looks down at Daniel in the bottom of the boat and wonders if Daniel really would have shot him.

Roberto lies down in the bottom of the boat too. He curls up on his side, with one arm as a pillow under his head. He wiggles around, trying to get comfortable, expecting to fall asleep quickly, and yet the state he enters is less sleep than delirium. The boat seems to be moving, not on a river, but on a sea of suffering, an ocean of agony. The earth churns with life but to what end? So that its beautiful creatures might die and pass into oblivion. He sees the snake Quique cut into two equal pieces twisting on the forest floor, and the green light fading from its flesh as it becomes food for ants. The guesthouse turned into a slaughterhouse by Quique and Ernesto, and the body on the bed, the red stare of death. The *danse macabre* of the old people burning up in Jilili, and Willie Hernandez on Mount Cabanacande admiring Memo Soto's watch. Not long before Willie took it off Soto's bullet-riddled body, Soto had heard the thunder of the approaching helicopters and called his daughter Lucero on his cellphone to tell her he loved her and to say good-bye. If even a monster like Memo Soto is capable of tenderness and love, how much more love and tenderness is there in the good people? But it's all for nothing, it dissipates like smoke, it's like grains of sand dragged back into the ocean by a receding wave. Teresa will lie in bed waiting for Roberto but he will never come. Lina will never be a college girl again and take her dog for a walk in the park. His father will drop dead of a heart attack on the tennis court, and Clara's beauty will wither, she'll become old and dry, and no one will come to her dinner parties anymore. And nothing Roberto writes will matter, none of it will change things, all the beautiful creatures of the earth will continue to perish, to gasp out their last breaths, to be thrown away like trash—

Roberto moans and sits up, clutching his belly. He seems to have what Daniel has. He tells Roque to hurry to the bank, or else he'll have to hang his butt over the side of the boat and befoul the river. The boat grounds on a sandbar, and Roberto hops out and runs across it and then splashes through some shallow water and clambers up the bank and then he's back in the jungle. It's like moving into a different element, earth to air or air to water, the green humid light, the ancient silence. He fumbles at his pants and jerks them down and squats and the shit flows out of him like warm mud. There are three separate spasms of it, and then he grabs a handful of leaves. He wipes himself, hoping the leaves aren't coated with some virulent poison, and then he sees the jaguar. Just a few meters away.

He's lying on one side, calm, at ease, watching Roberto. As if to prove he's not some trick of light and shade, he lifts one paw and licks it a few times, then lowers it and looks back at Roberto. Roberto basks in the golden light of the jaguar's eyes. He can't see his balls, but he knows somehow he's a real jaguar and not a shaman. Roberto's not afraid. Even if the jaguar were to leap at him and devour him, he doesn't think he'd be afraid. After all, isn't this why he came to the jungle? To rendezvous with him? The jaguar knows him better than he knows himself, loves him with the profoundest love.

The jaguar's eyes rise as Roberto rises. His eyes never stop looking into Roberto's. And then Roberto zips up and buckles his belt and walks out of the jungle. He walks through the water and then onto the sandbar. He sees an orange butterfly, and then a yellow one, and then suddenly he's in the middle of a fantastical swirl of orange and yellow butterflies. He lifts up his arms and begins to slowly turn around as if he wants to become a part of their swirl. Orange and yellow, yellow and orange, orange and orange, yellow and yellow. They seem to be flying faster—

"Roberto!"

"Roberto, are you all right?"

"Roberto!"

He opens his eyes. He's lying on his back on the sandbar. The worried faces of Daniel and Roque are hovering over him. He sits up slowly.

"I'm okay," he murmurs.

"What happened?" says Daniel.

"I just passed out, I guess. I'm okay now. Really."

They help Roberto stand up, and then they help him get back into the boat.

* * *

The river's broad and peaceful and the wind hits Roberto in the face and he drinks some water and feels better. Roque says there's a town up ahead where they can get some Lomotil for him and Daniel.

A few minutes later, Roque ties the boat up at a floating dock, and the three of them walk into the town. It's called Occo. Roberto didn't see it on the trip down the river three days ago because they passed it during the night. It's dirty and wretched and seems hopeless in the heat. They walk by a tiny post office with the national flag that courageous Colonel Cordoba gave his life to protect drooping from a slightly crooked pole. A shabby schoolhouse is deserted because it's Saturday. Dogs wander around panting with their tongues out or lie sprawled and dead-looking in the shade. The only sign of energy or enterprise is a man mixing concrete in a wheelbarrow but even he seems to be at the point of toppling over like Roberto at the sandbar.

"Shit," says Daniel under his breath. "What the hell are they doing here?"

Four soldiers are sitting in orange plastic chairs at a blue plastic table in front of a green restaurant drinking beer. Their rifles lean against the table.

"Just keep walking," says Roberto.

"They're looking at us," says Roque.

Roque is right. Roberto's suddenly aware of how filthy and mud-bespattered he and Daniel are. Nothing to do but bluff their way through this.

"Good afternoon," says Roberto to the soldiers with a smile.

The soldiers smile and say good afternoons of their own. Three of them could be teenagers, the fourth is a little older.

"Where have you guys been?" the older one says. He seems more curious than suspicious. They don't really have any choice except to approach the table. If the soldiers ask for their IDs they're fucked.

"We were hunting wild pigs," says Roberto, "but we didn't have much luck."

"Well, that's an understatement," Daniel says ruefully, and now he points at Roque. "They told us in Tarapacá *this* little motherfucker was the best guide in town, but he'd get lost trying to cross the street."

Roque looks sheepish as the soldiers laugh.

"But I always knew where we were," says Roque. "We were never lost."

"Is that why we spent eight hours walking in circles?" says Roberto.

"But we weren't walking in circles," says Roque, "we were tracking the pigs."

Daniel rolls his eyes. "Is that what you call being lost? 'Tracking the pigs'?"

The soldiers laugh again. Roberto notices under the table a little monkey tied by a cord to one of the table legs.

"Wild pigs are mean," says one of the soldiers.

"I heard a pack of wild pigs chased a man down and ate him," says another of the soldiers.

"On top of everything else, my friend here has the shits," Daniel says, jerking a thumb at Roberto. "Do you know any place we could get some Lomotil?"

"There's a store that way," the older soldier says, pointing up the street. "They probably have some."

They thank the soldiers and move on. Daniel and Roberto discreetly exchange that familiar look of relief at having gotten out of a tight spot. They do find Lomotil in the store, and also buy a six-pack of water and a six-pack of the apple-flavored soft drink that Willie Rivera likes so much and three cans of sausages and a package of cookies and a bag of Cheetos. The exhausted-looking woman behind the counter has a small baby in her arms, which is sucking from a bottle filled with coffee.

They walk back down the street past the soldiers.

"Did they have Lomotil?" the older soldier calls out.

"Yes," Roberto calls back, "thanks a lot!"

The soldier smiles and waves. Under the table the monkey stares out at them, sitting in its own shit like Fercho in the pantry.

They go out on the floating dock and climb back in the boat.

"How much longer till we get out of Tulcán?" asks Roberto.

"We're not in Tulcán anymore," says Roque. "We're in Chimoyo."

* * *

Roberto doesn't usually like sugary drinks, but he downs a bottle of the pink apple drink pretty fast; he feels his system could use a jolt of sugar. He eats several cookies, then pulls soft pink sausages out of their can with his fingers; god knows what they're made of but they're very tasty. Meanwhile, Daniel has turned his fingers orange emptying the bag of Cheetos.

"I'll see my fish soon," he says, licking his fingers. Now he looks out at the river and says in English, *"Dark brown is the river, golden is the sand. It flows along forever, with trees on either hand."*

"You must be feeling good," says Roberto, "if you're reciting poetry."

Daniel smiles. "I am, Roberto. I never thought we'd make it out of there."

Roberto didn't either. He knows that until the wheels of his plane lift off the runway at Robledo he's not completely safe, but at least he's not in Tulcán. As he leaves the jungle, the pull of the life he's led before is like the gravitational field of a planet. He's returning to not the real world, but another world, his world. Memories of the jungle are being supplanted by thoughts of his friends, his family, the future. Is it really possible that he'll be at the airport at Saint Lucia tomorrow night, that Caroline will come running into his arms?

Daniel discovers one of the watermelons they bought from the twins still lying in the bottom of the boat.

"It seems a shame to let it go to waste," he says.

"You're right," says Roberto. "Let's eat it."

Daniel borrows Roque's machete. He puts the watermelon on one of the wooden seats and prepares to whack it open.

"Try not to cut any fingers off," says Roberto. "I prefer my watermelon without blood on it."

"I'll do my best."

Whack. The green melon parts to reveal the crisp red meat. Roberto takes two wedges to the back of the boat. He hands one to Roque, and sits down and eats with him. The pink juice runs down their chins. He thinks about the twins and is drawn back into the past.

Roque waves at someone. Roberto looks and sees a man poling along a raft in the shallow water near the bank. The raft's made of inner tubes tied together with wooden planking on top. It's carrying an old bicycle, some wooden crates and burlap bags, and a wire cage with a couple of chickens in it. Roberto waves at the man too, and he waves back.

"How long till we get to Tarapacá?" says Roberto.

Roque shrugs. "Two hours?"

If Roberto wants to say anything to Roque, now's the time.

"I don't know what to say, Roque. Except I'm so sorry about Lina and Quique and Ernesto. We owe you guys our lives, we owe you everything.

We're hoping the story I'm going to write and the photographs Daniel took are going to make things better in Tulcán. Maybe they'll help to stop the violence."

"I hope so, Roberto. That would be nice."

"You were very close to Lina, weren't you?"

"Yes. She was like my sister. She always worried about me. She always worried about everyone, but never about herself."

"Lina thought of you as her little brother. She told me that."

Roque is silent. A tear eases out of an eye and slides down his face.

"Where are you going after this?" says Roberto.

"Home. To my village."

"Do you have family there?"

Roque smiles. "I have a wife. And a daughter. Her name's Ana."

"Really! How old's Ana?"

"She's only a baby. A few months."

"So on her first birthday, are you going to give her that soup that makes her smarter? It's made out of bird brains, what's the name of the bird?"

"Caciques. Of course."

"Thanks for teaching me about the jungle."

"When I would tell you things, and you would write them down in your notebook? That always made me feel good. It made me feel that what I was telling you was important."

"It was important. Very important."

"Do you have a wife, Roberto?"

"Not yet, but I will soon. My fiancée lives on an island in the Caribbean called Saint Lucia. I'm flying there tomorrow. I plan to live there for a while. Saint Lucia's very beautiful. You should come visit me there."

"'Saint Lucia.' It sounds nice. Yes, I'd like to come."

Roberto looks at him skeptically. "So you're really coming to visit me, Roque?"

"Yes," said Roque, and then he adds, with a sly smile, "Maybe on my way to Chicago."

Roberto laughs. The boat drones on up the river. Near sunset, they reach Tarapacá.

It's just routine civilian traffic on the bridge today. No convoys. Roque leaves the main channel of the river and enters the little inlet, which is crowded with boats coming back from the day's fishing. The boat putters along till it reaches a dock, on which Yadier is standing. Roque has called him on his cellphone and already broken the terrible news. Tears are streaming down Yadier's face, and he hugs each of them as they climb on the dock, pressing them against his fat belly.

"I can't believe they're gone, but it's God's will," he says. "They'll be happy in heaven forever now."

Roberto can perhaps imagine Lina and Ernesto in heaven, but it's hard to picture Quique with his jaguar whiskers there. Roque is going back to Yadier's house with them. They trudge up the hill to Yadier's white Corolla, and Roberto and Daniel get into the back. The radio's tuned to a salsa station. Despite the lively music, Yadier sighs and sniffles and blows his nose as he drives into town. Motorcycles and motortaxis are buzzing and zipping all around, street urchins dash through the traffic, a woman with a grotesque purple growth coming out of the side of her head begs for money from passersby. They've returned to civilization.

Yadier's car goes by the Park of the Parakeets. Bright fruit hangs in the mango trees. It must be about six, because thousands of parakeets are flying out of the jungle and over the town and converging on the park. Roberto gazes out the window at them, thinking the last time he saw them he didn't know it yet but he was just about to meet Lina.

"Hey, Roberto," Daniel says with a grin, "look who's here!"

He's pointing toward a man in a straw hat sitting on a bench.

"Napo!" says Roberto.

Napo seems to be in the same clothes he was wearing at the bar. He's perusing a newspaper, his legs crossed in a relaxed way.

"You know, he was supposed to have gotten that check yesterday," says Daniel. "If you wanted to stop, I'm sure he'd be glad to pay you back the twenty thousand pesos you loaned him."

Roberto laughs. "I'd probably just end up giving him another twenty thousand."

It's dusk by the time they arrive at Yadier's house. There's Daniel's yellow Twingo sitting under a tree. Yadier's dogs bark at them, his numerous children stand around and stare. His wife asks if she can make Roberto and Daniel dinner, but they just want to change their clothes and hit the road. They go in the Happy Boys bedroom. Roberto opens his suitcase, is reassured to find his billfold and his passport still in the hidden compartment. As the Happy Boys watch from all the walls, Roberto and Daniel take off their muddy boots and clothes. They put on clean clothes and put the dirty ones in plastic garbage bags provided by Yadier's wife. Roberto goes in the bathroom and washes his face and neck and hands and arms, and then he and Daniel go out to Daniel's car and load their stuff in the trunk. Roberto thanks Yadier, who gives Roberto another hearty, tearful hug, and then Roque approaches and hugs him in a curiously shy way, barely making contact.

"Be safe, Roberto," Roque says.

"You be safe too, Roque. I won't forget you."

Roque nods. Roberto and Daniel get in the car, and Daniel starts it up and turns on the headlights. He drives away down the dirt road. It's dark now and he can't see that Roberto's crying. Soon Daniel reaches the main road, turns right, and heads for Robledo.

* * *

"You're going to asphyxiate me with your cigarette," says Roberto.

"Sorry," says Daniel. He lowers his window. They've been on the road about an hour. There's very little traffic. The jungle's been left behind, and they're traveling through dark fields planted in soybeans and cotton.

They should pull up at the old hotel that was once the hacienda of the Saldamandos around one or two in the morning. Since Roberto's plane doesn't leave till the early afternoon, he'll have plenty of time to sleep late, to take a long hot shower, to have a leisurely breakfast with Daniel, to walk around the enchanting town, to look at the oak trees and the bright blue sky.

Roberto takes out his cellphone. He wants to check his messages to see if Caroline has left him any, but he discovers his phone is dead. He'd really love to hear Caroline's voice. He considers borrowing Daniel's cellphone and calling her now, but then he decides it would be a bad idea. He intends to maintain the fiction that he's been in Contamana researching his book until he gets to Saint Lucia at which point he'll tell Caroline everything (minus a few things about Lina, of course). But he's so wiped out physically and emotionally that if he were to get on the phone with her now he doesn't trust himself not to burst into tears and blurt out the truth. Better to get a good night's sleep and call her tomorrow from Robledo.

It's nice to be back in the Twingo. It's a return to normal life. He looks over at Daniel, smoking his cigarette, staring at the road, and then he thinks about last night at El Encanto. Daniel coming through the door of the guesthouse with his eyes so big and panicky as he waved his gun around. There would have been something almost comical about it if the circumstances hadn't been so dire. Roberto doesn't think anyone else he knows except his father or his grandmother would have been willing to do something like that for him. He's not sure if he would have had the guts to do it if the circumstances were reversed. And this was just one moment of a trip on which Daniel's life was in danger all the time. He wants to find the words to thank him, but just like with Caroline, he's afraid he'd fall apart if he tried to do it now. Tomorrow over breakfast in Robledo.

The radio is on and an announcer is giving a news update, and now Roberto hears President Dávila talking today about Tulcán. "In Tulcán, the greatest evil known to humankind, namely terrorism, is being dealt with in an exemplary fashion." The president's voice is so resonant and smooth he could be a radio announcer himself. "The Army, under the able leadership of General Oropeza, is conducting counterterrorism operations in such a way as to minimize civilian casualties. Even one innocent life lost is one life too many. Unfortunately, our enemy has no such compunctions."

"Excuse me, Roberto," says Daniel. "I need to stick my head out the window while I puke."

"You know, I think I prefer Landazábal to Dávila. At least Landazábal doesn't pretend to be anything except what he is, an unrepentant old fascist. He's not some phony 'technocrat' that acts like he's on the side of the people."

"I wonder what he's going to say about Oropeza's leadership when he sees the pictures of him at Jilili," and now Daniel yawns. "Shit. Can't wait to get into a real bed."

"You want me to drive for a while?"

"No, I'm okay for now."

Roberto settles into his seat, closes his eyes. He imagines sitting on a plane ten thousand meters over the earth, listening to the muted powerful roar of its engines as it takes him to Saint Lucia. "What would you like to drink?" a flight attendant asks him.

"Whiskey," he replies. "A double whiskey. On the rocks."

Next thing he knows, he's waking up. Daniel's parking the car in front of a restaurant.

"Where are we?" asks Roberto.

"That shithole town we stopped at to get my car alarm fixed. I need food and coffee. Especially coffee."

They go inside and sit down at a table. The place is almost empty. A waitress wearing huge gold hoop earrings and red stretch pants comes over, not looking happy that they're here.

"All we got left in the kitchen's tripe soup and beef with beans," she says. "But if you want any you'll have to eat it fast because we're about to close."

"Will you agree to eat fast, Roberto?" Daniel says.

"Sure."

"Me too."

The waitress gives a weary sigh. "Tripe soup or beef with beans?"

"I'll have both. Roberto?"

"I'll have both too."

"We'll both have both," Daniel says to the waitress. "And bring us coffee. Lots of coffee."

The waitress nods, and walks away.

"She's charming," says Daniel. "I think I'm in love."

Roberto laughs. He gets up and goes in the bathroom. He's been taking the Lomotil, but it hasn't quite done the job yet. The toilet's filthy. It was actually more pleasant shitting in the jungle than here.

When Roberto comes back, the food and coffee are already on the table. He sits down across from Daniel.

"That was fast," says Roberto.

Daniel nods. He drinks some coffee, looks out the window at an eighteen-wheeler rumbling by on the road. His mood seems to have changed in just the few minutes Roberto was gone.

"Everything okay?" says Roberto.

"I was just thinking about Diego."

"Yeah. Poor guy."

"That's not what I meant. What if he told them about us?"

"The soldiers?"

"Yeah."

"What's he going to tell them? He doesn't even know our last names."

"How hard will it be to figure out? How many reporter-photographer teams are there with the names Roberto and Daniel? I mean, you're leaving the country tomorrow, but what about me? How long before they come for me?"

"Calm down, they're not coming for you."

"You don't know that."

"We're not even sure what happened to Diego. He could have been seriously wounded, he could have died already."

"Or else he's still alive and he's being interrogated. Tortured. Who knows what he's told them? They could be looking for us right now."

"I think you're overreacting. Like with your fish and the crazy boyfriend."

"Come on, Roberto. This is nothing like that."

Roberto takes a sip of his coffee, and thinks about it. He sees the waitress glaring at them. Waiting for them to begin eating.

"Look," says Roberto, "the Army didn't know we were in Tulcán, so they'd have no reason to ask Diego about us. And I don't think he'd volunteer any information. But if it's something you're really concerned about, maybe you should think about leaving the country too. At least for a while, till this all blows over."

Daniel looks gloomy.

"Shit. I knew this was going to bite me in the ass."

* * *

When they come out of the restaurant, Roberto takes the wheel of the Twingo and drives it out of San Lorenzo. Beside him, Daniel crosses his arms and turns away and is quickly filling the car with snores. Roberto thinks about Diego. Despite what he said to Daniel, he doesn't think it's unreasonable to be concerned about what Diego may have told Army interrogators. Diego knows not only that they were going to El Encanto but that they were present at the massacre in Jilili. If by some chance the Army's already looking for them, there's no way they could know where they are. If Roberto's luck holds, he should be able to slip out of the country tomorrow, but what about Daniel? And even if Diego dies without telling the Army anything about them, what happens when Roberto's story comes out? It's possible that the photographic evidence the Army massacred the people of Jilili and the fact General Oropeza was there when it happened will be more important than his story itself. Won't the government want to know who took the pictures? Roberto and Daniel can deny all they want that it was Daniel, but he'll still be an object of suspicion. And in this country, suspicion is often all it takes to get you killed.

Roberto sees the half moon rising over the sugarcane fields. He's starting to get drowsy. He turns up the music on the radio and lowers the window and the wind rushes in. It won't be long till they get to Robledo if he can just stay awake. But his eyelids keep drooping, and his chin keeps dropping toward his chest, and then he snaps his head up and gives it a little shake. He'd rather be in a soft bed with fluffy pillows by himself than have the most beautiful girl in the world with him because all he wants to do is sleep. The bed begins to bump and jump and then he opens his eyes. They're no longer on the road but are headed into a ditch. Daniel wakes up cursing. Roberto twists the steering wheel and returns the car to the road.

"Roberto," Daniel says, "what the fuck?"

"Sorry. I fell asleep."

"We need to stop someplace. We can't go through all this and then get killed in a car wreck. Like those German tourists."

"I agree, let's stop. At the next motel."

"You know, we're not far from Ramiro Navia's house. We should stay there instead of some fleabag motel."

"Fine with me."

Daniel gets his cellphone out, punches in a number.

"You said Ramiro's not there, right?" says Roberto.

"No, but the caretakers are always there," and now he says into the phone: "Gabriel! It's Daniel. What's happening, man? I didn't wake you up, did I? Listen, I'm in the area with a friend, we were wondering if we could stop off and spend the night. Great. No, we already ate, all we need's a couple of beds. Okay, we'll see you soon. Bye." He puts his phone away. "Do you think you can stay awake till we get there? Or do you want me to drive?"

"No, I think I'm okay."

"Maybe we should think of something that will keep you awake."

"Like what?"

"I could recite some Swinburne to you. There are parts of 'Tristram of Lyonesse' that are really amazing."

"If you promise not to recite Swinburne to me, I'll promise not to go to sleep."

Daniel laughs, and lights a cigarette.

* * *

The road begins to rise into the mountains. Rain splatters the windshield. Roberto turns on the wipers, peers through them at the twisting road. It rains hard, but soon the splatters turn into speckles and then cease altogether. Just a passing shower. The wet pavement gleams in the headlights as he takes the Twingo up and up, and then Daniel says, "Slow down. It's just around the next curve."

Roberto turns left onto the eroded dirt road. It goes straight up the hill, and is dauntingly steep. Immediately the car starts sliding around.

"Gun it, Roberto!" says Daniel.

Roberto pushes the gas pedal, and the tires begin spinning and the car goes nowhere. The rain seems to have lasted just long enough to thwart their ascent.

"Get out," says Daniel. "I'll drive."

Roberto shrugs. "Okay."

He stops the car and they both get out. Roberto starts to walk around to the passenger side but Daniel says, "No, you walk up. We need to make the car lighter."

Roberto stands by the car as Daniel gets behind the wheel.

"So you really think you can do better?" says Roberto.

"I can take this car up Mount Everest."

The car moves forward, and Daniel skillfully slithers his way up the side of the hill in it. He stops at the top and waits for Roberto to walk up. He slips a couple of times in the mud and nearly falls as he did so many times in the jungle, and then he climbs back in the Twingo. Daniel regards him with a smirk.

"Don't feel bad. You're good at some things, just not at driving."

"Shut up. Let's go."

Daniel laughs. He drives a minute or two along the road and then turns down another road, at the end of which a tall white wall and a wooden gate are lit up by the headlights. The gate is open, and a young man is standing there, along with two yellow Labrador retrievers. Daniel drives up to the gate, and the young man comes around to the driver's side. His nose is covered with a white bandage.

"Hey, Gabriel," says Daniel, "what happened to your nose?"

"I was clearing brush, and my machete hit something hard and bounced back and—" Gabriel shrugs and smiles. "I don't know what I did, but I did it."

"Sounds like me. Gabriel, this is my friend, Roberto."

Gabriel and Roberto exchange greetings, then Daniel drives through the gate. He takes the car down a sloping brick drive and parks in front of the house. They get out and Daniel opens the trunk as Gabriel and the dogs come down the drive. The dogs jump up on Daniel as he pets and rubs them.

"Hey, Tantar, hey, Ramón, how are you guys?" and then he says to Gabriel: "Ramón's gotten big."

"Yes, he's not a puppy anymore. But he's still crazy."

The house is white stucco with a red tile roof, with small palm trees and plants in pots all around. Gabriel grabs Roberto's suitcase and Daniel's backpack, and they follow him inside. They're met by his wife, María, who's slim and pretty and has a warm, welcoming smile.

"Are you hungry?" she says. "Let me make you something. Or let me get you something to drink."

But they both want only to go to bed. Gabriel conducts them down a hallway. He opens a bedroom door and takes in Daniel's pack. Daniel turns to Roberto.

"Well—see you in the morning, Roberto."

Roberto nods. He and Daniel look at each other with one of those looks that convey more than millions of words, and then they hug. Then Daniel goes into his room and shuts the door and Gabriel takes Roberto down the hallway to his room. Gabriel puts the suitcase down on a carved wooden chest at the foot of the bed.

"If you need anything," he says, "just let us know."

Roberto thanks him and he leaves. The rough plaster walls are painted a soft green. There are lace curtains on the windows, and a very skinny and elongated Christ is nailed to a cross above the bed. It's a little warm so Roberto turns on the ceiling fan. He goes in the bathroom and pees. The bathtub and shower look very inviting; he'll enjoy them in the morning.

He'd like to brush his teeth, but he realizes he doesn't have a toothbrush or toothpaste; he left them in his backpack in El Encanto. There's a glass by the sink and he fills it with water and takes it in the bedroom.

The bed's been turned down. A bath towel folded in the shape of a swan and tied with a ribbon has been placed between the pillows. He puts the water on the bedside table and takes off his clothes and turns off the light and crawls into bed. The window's open. It's very quiet outside except for a cicada or two. No hooting jungle birds or growling beasts. The ceiling fan is loose in its fastenings, causing it to move back and forth and make a noise that sounds like tapping.

The day Roberto is to die

When he wakes up, the room is filled with light. He doesn't know what time it is, since his watch was stolen, and his cellphone is still dead because he forgot to charge it last night, and there's no clock in the room. It doesn't feel late, but the last thing he wants to do is miss his flight out of Robledo. He gets out of bed and pulls on his jeans. He walks over to the window. It's lovely outside: so green, so many flowers. At the bottom of a long slope is a blue swimming pool and an arbor with a table and chairs beneath it. In the far distance, he sees bluish mountains with clouds floating around their tops.

He finishes dressing, puts his cellphone in its charger, turns off the ceiling fan, and goes out. He walks down the hallway toward the sound of voices. He passes through an arched doorway, and then another arched doorway. When he came in last night he was too tired to notice how beautiful everything is. Tile floors of a rich red color and Persian rugs, yellow and blue and red plaster walls, vaulted ceilings with wood beams, crystal chandeliers, candles in bronze sconces, dreamy landscapes in gilded frames, furniture in an engaging hodgepodge of styles, Spanish Colonial, Victorian, Mediterranean. He hears Daniel laughing, and comes out into an expansive dining room and kitchen. Daniel's sitting at an old mahogany table, drinking coffee. With him is a cute little girl with a long brown braid hanging from each side of her head. She's holding a cat in her arms.

"Good morning," says Roberto.

"Good morning!" calls María from the kitchen, where she's cooking breakfast. "Would you like coffee?"

"I'd love some."

The little girl looks at Roberto as he walks up to the table.

"Sofía," says Daniel, "this is Roberto."

"Hi, Sofía," Roberto says.

Sofía smiles, adorably revealing two missing front teeth; Roberto's reminded of Abril, Franz's daughter.

María comes over with Roberto's coffee. He thanks her, and sits down at the table. He adds some cream to the coffee, and looks at the cat.

"Who's this?"

"Doki," Sofía says shyly.

Doki's a skinny white cat with a little yellow in his ears and faint tiger stripes on his tail.

"Doki's got great eyes," Daniel says, as he rubs a finger under Doki's chin. "He's cross-eyed, see?"

His eyes are great. Piercing blue and slightly crossed.

"Sofía, take Doki outside!" María calls from the kitchen; some kind of meat is sizzling and popping in a pan. "I don't want him in the house, he scratches the furniture!"

Daniel looks at Sofía and shrugs, and Sofía shrugs too.

"Come on, Doki," she says as she walks toward the door, holding her cat. "We'll play."

Roberto drinks his coffee and looks out the windows at the lush greenness, at the mountains and clouds.

"Don't you love this place?" says Daniel.

"Yeah. Wish we could stay longer. What time is it?"

Daniel checks his watch. "A little after eight."

"We should go soon."

"We've got plenty of time. Anyway, we're not leaving till we take a swim in the pool. That pool's fucking paradise."

María brings in eggs and arepas and sliced mangos and gold-en-brown chorizos and tangerine juice. It's delicious, Roberto can't eat it fast enough, he's like a man who's escaped from prison and has been wandering without food for days. Daniel's eating in the same way, and when María comes over with a pitcher of juice to refill their glasses, she laughs at the speed with which they've cleaned their plates.

"Would you like some more?" she asks.

They both nod eagerly, and María laughs again and goes back to the kitchen. Roberto wipes his mouth with his napkin.

"I think you should come with me," he says.

"To the airport?" Daniel says. He's eating his last chorizo with his fingers. "Of course I'm coming, I'll keep you company. We can have a few beers."

"No. I mean come with me to Saint Lucia."

Daniel stares at Roberto. "Are you serious?"

"I've been thinking about it a lot. I think you're right: Diego's something we need to be concerned about. But even if it turns out he didn't tell them anything, I think you should still be out of the country when our story comes out. There's no way it's not going to be huge, and some people are going to put two and two together and think you took the pictures."

"Damn it, Roberto! I told you this was a bad idea."

"I'm sorry."

Daniel's quiet for a moment, and then he sighs. "Look, even if I wanted to go with you, I can't now, I don't have my passport with me. And I can't just walk away from my life. What about my apartment, what about my fish?"

"Take me to Robledo. Drive back to your apartment and get your passport. Go to the airport and catch a plane out of the country. To anywhere, you can worry about getting to Saint Lucia later. And as far as your apartment goes, do what I did. I'm renting it out furnished. You have a great place, you won't have any trouble finding a tenant. And you can even put it in the lease they have to take care of your fish. And then you can go back there when the heat dies down, and you and your fish can live happily ever after."

Daniel lights a cigarette, exhales some smoke. He looks amused.

"What?" says Roberto.

"I was just imagining how Caroline would react if I showed up at her doorstep in Saint Lucia."

"She'd be fine with it. Especially after I tell her everything that's happened," and then Roberto leans toward Daniel across the table. "Listen. I got you into this fix, so just let me help get you out of it. Just think about it. It all makes sense."

* * *

Roberto returns to his bedroom with a toothbrush and toothpaste and a pair of swim trunks with a pattern of blue and white checks. It feels great to brush his teeth, and even better to step into the shower. He handles his right arm gingerly as he soaps himself up. It carries a physical record of encounters he had on his journey: the kids in Tarapacá, the ants in the jungle outside Jilili, Colonel Luna on the pavilion in El Encanto. The bites, both ant and human, look okay, but the knife wound is red and swollen and could be infected, and the broken finger is still fat, purple, and painful. As Roberto washes around his neck and shoulders, he misses the St. Jude medal being there. There were times over the last few days he felt like it might actually be protecting him, though having possession of it didn't do Vladimiro much good.

He takes the ribbon off the towel shaped like a swan and dries himself, then he puts on the swim trunks and goes outside. It's warm and humid, but not like the jungle. Winding stone steps lead down the hill to the swimming pool. Daniel's already in it. The dogs are running around like they want to come in too. Daniel splashes water at them, and they jump back and bark. As Roberto goes down the steps, he sees Gabriel pushing a wheelbarrow piled high with dirt. Gabriel waves and smiles and the white bandage on his nose is bright in a beam of sunlight.

Ramón, the younger dog, sees Roberto coming and runs up the hill to meet him. He jumps all over Roberto then races back to the pool barking joyfully as if announcing his arrival.

"Come on, Roberto," yells Daniel, "jump in! Make a big splash!"

But he eases into the water till it's up to his waist, then launches himself forward and swims around slowly. Trying not to get his glasses wet. Looking at the trees, the flowers, the sky. Daniel is right, this is like paradise.

Neither of them says much. The contrast between here and where they've been is too obvious to point out. Roberto finds himself wondering, why did the ceiba tree appear before his eyes in the swamp as it did? He and Daniel almost certainly never would have gotten out of the jungle alive if it hadn't. It seems like there must be some kind of meaning to it, like it couldn't have been mere chance. But if Roberto and Daniel were favored by fortune that night, then how come Lina and Ernesto and Quique weren't? The two of them are floating in a swimming pool at the same time as the bodies of the others are decaying in the tropical heat, where's the meaning in that?

After a few minutes, María comes down the steps. She's carrying a tray with two bottles of beer and two glasses on it. She puts the beer and the glasses down on the ornately tiled table under the arbor, then goes back up the hill. Roberto and Daniel climb out of the pool, water sluicing over them. Daniel's big stomach hangs over his swim trunks, which are red with white stripes down the sides. They sit down at the table and pour their beer into the glasses.

"*Salud*," says Roberto.

"Salud."

They bump glasses and drink. Daniel smacks his lips and says "Ahhh," and then he holds the glass up and looks at it. "You know, if you'd never seen a glass of beer before, you'd be amazed at how beautiful it was. The white foam, the golden beer. The way the bubbles sparkle as they stream up."

"So have you decided what you're going to do?"

Daniel reaches for his cigarettes.

"Maybe you're right, maybe I should leave. But that doesn't mean I have to go to Saint Lucia. I can go anywhere. Antarctica, for example. I can take pictures of penguins."

"That's true. But why not Saint Lucia? It's a cool place and you've never been there. And I need somebody to hang out with."

Daniel lights his cigarette, then shrugs.

"Okay. Why not?"

"Great."

They sit in silence for a while. Drinking their beers, listening to the birds. And then Daniel says, "Did you know Ernesto had two sons?"

Roberto shakes his head.

"He said they were very different. 'As different as the night is from the day,' he said. One was kind of loud and happy, like him. The other was very shy and had deep thoughts. He was crazy about them," and now Daniel shakes his head. "They were good people. They didn't deserve to die."

"No."

"Did you love her?"

Roberto looks at Daniel. "What do you mean?"

"Come on, Roberto. I know you. You're a romantic. You fall in love at the drop of a hat."

Roberto drinks some beer, looks at the pool. "I don't know how I felt. Suddenly I met her, and then suddenly she was dead."

"I hope you don't blame yourself."

"I do. I do blame myself."

"It was the war that killed them. They knew what they were getting into."

The peaceful morning erupts with snarls and yelps. Tantar and Ramón are fighting beside the pool. Ramón quickly capitulates, lying on his back with Tantar's teeth clamped around his throat.

"Tantar!" yells Daniel. "Let him go! Now! Tantar!"

Tantar releases his grip, and Ramón jumps up and runs away. Tantar is panting and looking pleased with himself.

"Tantar's getting old," says Daniel, "and he likes to be left alone, but Ramón's always pestering him. So every so often he has to show Ramón his balls are still bigger than his." Now he finishes his beer and stands up. "I guess we should get going."

"I'll be up in a minute."

Daniel heads up the hill. Tantar joins him, with Ramón circling around them at a respectful distance.

There will come a day when Roberto will think about Lina and what she meant and he will hold his head in his hands and moan in grief and horror at what happened, but that day is not today. Today is for feeling the warmth of the air on his skin, for being happy to be here on this earth. It will be a long hectic day of travel, he'll be changing planes in Caracas and his connection time there is short, and so he savors a few moments of calm and solitude. A rowdy band of parakeets chitter in the trees. A bee nuzzles a flower. A woodpecker hammers. A speck of a spider descends from the top of the arbor via an invisible strand of silk. The arbor has a blue railing, and black ants are running along it, going and coming, seemingly in a huge hurry.

Time to go. Roberto walks past the pool and up the stone steps toward the house. A wind rustles the trees. He's reminded it's Sunday as he hears a church bell tolling in the distance. I call the living. I mourn the dead.

He goes in the bedroom, takes off his swim trunks, and puts on his clothes. He takes his phone out of its charger. He packs up his suitcase, tries to straighten up the bed a bit. Now he goes to the window and takes a last look.

A green hummingbird flies up. It hovers in front of the window, gazing in at him, and then it zips away.

Roberto rolls his suitcase down the hall to Daniel's room. The door is closed. He's about to knock, but then he hears Daniel's voice inside. He must be on his cellphone. Roberto can't make out the words, but he sounds angry, upset. And now Roberto goes ahead and knocks.

Daniel opens the door. He's still in his red and white swim trunks. He's holding his cellphone.

"Is everything all right?" says Roberto.

"Yeah, everything's fine. I'm talking to my agent. She booked me for some bullshit job I never wanted in the first place, and now that I've done it they don't want to pay me. And it's a lot of money."

"Sorry."

Daniel smiles ruefully. "That's the way it goes. Just give me a couple of minutes. I'll meet you by the car. And don't worry, you won't miss your plane."

Roberto nods. Daniel shuts the door. Roberto stands there a moment. He doesn't hear Daniel's voice again. Now he walks on down the hallway. The wheels on his suitcase make noise on the tile, are silent when they hit a rug.

He goes out the front door and walks to Daniel's car. He's disturbed by what just happened. It seems like a strange time to be talking to your agent. He's pretty sure Daniel was lying. He hopes Daniel's not in some kind of trouble.

He rolls his suitcase to the trunk end of the Twingo, and looks around. He's surprised by how much property the tall white walls enclose. He walks off slowly through the trees. He sees Doki sitting under a bush, observing him with his blue, crossed eyes. He thinks about Caroline. She would love to have a place like this. Of course she would probably spend months, if not years, and untold tens of millions of pesos, remodeling it. He thinks about the desk she bought him, waiting for him in front of the window, where he's to write his book. *A Town Called Contamana.* He already has the first line: "Between the mountains and the sea lies a town called Contamana."

Roberto sees some old weathered boards nailed to a tree trunk, and up in the tree a tree house. He would have loved to have something like that when he was a kid. He remembers falling out of the eucalyptus tree at Andrés's house and breaking his arm. In the emergency room with his parents, he was manfully trying not to cry. It's funny, his mother seemed to take it all in stride, but his father, a doctor, seemed very shaken. How gray and anxious his face was as he looked at his son.

And now Roberto sees through the trees a small, curious-looking structure. He walks toward it. It rises to about the height of his nose. It has a green tile roof, and little windows with lace curtains in them. He bends down and peers through a window. He sees a round table with four chairs, an armchair, a pink wooden stool. All of it scaled for little kids or dwarfs.

There's a rubber Donald Duck welcome mat in front of the door. Roberto pushes the door open, and crouches low to enter. Now he squats in the middle of the playhouse and looks around.

The walls are painted orange-pink. On the table are teacups and saucers, a silver tea service, two blue glass goblets. There's a glass cabinet with a few books in it, and glass figurines of animals and insects.

Roberto doesn't know anything about Ramiro Navia's children, but he would guess they're a mixture: the tree house is for his boy or boys, the playhouse is for his girl or girls. He moves over to the cabinet, being careful not to bump his head on the ceiling, and then he squats down again. He leans his head to the right, trying to read the titles on the spines of the books. He hears something behind him, and sees Daniel reflected in the glass door of the cabinet as he comes in.

"Hey Daniel, isn't this—?" *Cool*, he's about to say, but he sees in the glass Daniel raising his arm and pointing his gun at the back of Roberto's head. Roberto jerks his head to one side as the gun fires, making a tremendous sound in the confined space. The glass breaks in the cabinet and he feels a searing pain in his neck and he turns and lunges toward Daniel. He grabs his right arm and grapples for the gun, Daniel's still wearing his swim trunks, his naked flesh seems gross against Roberto, his contorted terrible face is just inches away.

"*Daniel*," screams Roberto, "*what are you doing?*"

Daniel's much bigger than Roberto and they crash and thrash around in the tiny house, and Daniel becomes red and slippery with blood from the wound on the side of Roberto's neck. Roberto's head bangs against the ceiling and then he falls back on the table with Daniel on top of him and the table turns over and the teacups and saucers shatter on the floor and his glasses fall off and he yells, "*Stop it! Stop it, Daniel! Stop it!*"

They're both on the floor now and Roberto struggles to get up and then Daniel grabs a leg of the little pink stool and hits Roberto in the head with it. He falls back against the orange-pink wall. He sits there, dazed. Daniel's looming over him, he's just a blur. He's pointing the gun at him. Roberto can hear him panting. Roberto's breathing hard too. He's holding a hand over the wound in his neck.

"Daniel," he gasps. "What's going on? Have you gone crazy?"

"They're coming for us, Roberto! They'll torture you before they kill you, I can't let them do that!"

"Who's coming?"

"The Army. They know about us. Diego told them."

"But . . . how do you know?"

"They called me. I had to tell them where we are, they said they'd kill my mother if I didn't!"

Roberto gazes up at the pinkish blur of Daniel's face, the gleam of his gun.

"You've been working for them, haven't you? Like Lina said."

"I had to, they would have killed my mother, they would have killed me!"

Roberto can tell Daniel is crying now. His gun arm has dropped a little, but now he raises it again.

"I love you, Roberto."

Roberto lifts his arms in an imploring way, like the man at the end of the dock in Jilili.

"Daniel, don't do this! It's not too late! We can run! Let's go! We can get away, we've always gotten away! Daniel—"

Roberto's smitten in the forehead with a flash of white light. A moment of wild confusion follows, a babble of voices, and then silence. He sees a street. It's after a rain, and the sun has come out. He sees bright drops of rain dripping out of the trees. But what happens beyond that, he cannot report.

About the Author

Author photo © Carlos Gaviria

Tom Epperson is a native of Malvern, Arkansas. He received a B.A. in English from the University of Arkansas at Little Rock and an M.A. in English from the University of Arkansas at Fayetteville, then headed west with his boyhood friend Billy Bob Thornton to pursue a career in show business. Epperson's co-written the scripts for *One False Move*, *A Family Thing*, *The Gift*, *A Gun, a Car, a Blonde*, and *Jayne Mansfield's Car*. His book *The Kind One* was nominated in 2009 for both the Edgar Award and the Barry Award for Best First Novel. His second novel, *Sailor*, was published in 2012. He lives in Los Angeles with his wife, Stefani, three pampered cats, and a frisky dog.

www.tomepperson.com